SAPPHIRE

SAPPHIRE

THE LAST PSION BOOK 3

Maxwell Farmer

Podium

To Rachel,

Your unfailing love and support have always lifted me up. Thank you.

You've made me more than I could've ever become.

Cover design by Richard Sashigane

ISBN: 978-1-0394-5521-4

Published in 2025 by Podium Publishing
www.podiumentertainment.com

Recap of Events

When last we met Kiru and Pandemonium, they were in the orc nation of Imakandi in hopes of finding Kiru's father's next artifact and leave before anyone from the Kingdom of Blades or elsewhere realized their true identities. Their plans to avoid getting embroiled in a big mess unfortunately didn't go as planned.

They learned that Mutt's father, the leader of Imakandi, had passed away. Kiru also discovered that Imakandi doesn't have a classic succession based on heritage. Instead, their pantheon, the Beast Gods, ordained that the tribes undergo a sacred ritual to choose their next leader. It wouldn't have been so bad had not S'Vol, leader of the cruel and murderous jormun cult, been working his way for the throne. The jormuns worshipped Jormungandr, the serpent Beast God forcibly imprisoned in the Beast Gods' realm, for his cruelty and refusal to join the other gods in leaving Alterra as their power was too great for the realm to handle.

The party saved a small leokin, one of a sacred line of beasts that serve as head shamans for the Beast Gods, from the jormuns. They realized they needed to help and go to Dissé, the orc capital, to offer aid to Mutt's sister and the queen regent, M'Baku Myev. In order to stop a murderous cult from taking over the nation, they found that they would need to gather more allies. There they were able to convince Myev of Kiru's true identity as a psion and garner enough trust to be permitted to help. Myev informed the party that to be able to contend for the throne, she would need the support of three of the ten founding tribes. Myev had two of her own, the M'Baku, and the Tau, but she lacked the third. All others were forced to either back S'Vol or the brutal warlord Grimtusk. There was only one exception, the L'Khan, ogres that lived in the Wastelands.

So, Pandemonium was assigned to join with an envoy of Myev to go to the Wastelands on the queen-regent's behalf. The week before they left, they trained. Brunhilda was able to place her goddess's pedestal in the capital's Vasir temple, putting Hlin one step closer to becoming a major god. Zhaden worked to use heat to help with his stealth. Mutt learned more about his techniques with the aid of the leokin cub they saved, and Kiru made slow progress in creating a fourth technique.

After the week was over, the envoy and Pandemonium made their way to the Wastelands. There, they saved a L'Khan scouting party from an ambush in a bloody battle. They weren't without loss, but it was still a victory and they got to meet their leader, Chief Snout. The chief explained the truth as to why the ogres were in the Wastelands. A tragedy had befallen and weakened the beast god they worshipped, and the deity needed help. Snout also went on to explain that the tribe was in the midst of a civil war as the chief's exiled brother had acquired an army of sacred beasts, gnolls, as well as some traitorous ogres to try and take control of the clan.

As a member of the royal M'Baku clan, Mutt was able to make an official promise to Snout that the clan would help them and their deity in the future as well as take care of their in-fighting in exchange for their backing of Myev. Snout agreed, and Pandemonium with the surviving members of the envoy, went to sneak-attack the rebellion leader, the Exile. The party defeated the coup leader but lost all but one scout from the original envoy. Though they had their losses, Pandemonium was able to reap immediate benefits from the battle. After helping the former captive, a leokin prisoner helped Brunhilda acquire her fourth technique and thus was able to ascend to Ruby.

While the Myev had been making plans however, the jormuns had too. The cult had infiltrated the capital with their spies and learned of Myev's plan to enlist the L'Khan's aid. So, they sent assassins to kill Pandemonium and the L'Khans and staged a coup in the capital itself. Due to Zhaden's overall caution and paranoia, Kiru was fortunately saved and they were able to eliminate the jormun assassins and rush to the capital to help Myev with the L'Khan's aid.

Unfortunately, while she did survive, Myev ended up losing an arm and getting envenomated by a shaman spy who had used a specific venom laced with toxins from Jormungandr himself. Myev was an Emerald, so she would recover, but not in time to compete in the ritual for choosing the nation's new leader. There had only ever been one time that Jormungandr's venom was truly cured in the legends of Imakandi, and since Mutt was still a royal, he ordered the shamans to let Kiru scan through their sacred history with his perfect memory and recall in order to find it. Thankfully, Kiru was able to find it, and to his surprise, the cure required a psion, meaning Kiru was the only one who could do it. After taking some time to understand the cure, Kiru was able to remove the venom from Myev's body, nearly succumbing to its effects himself.

While it was hard, both Kiru and Myev came out of it for the better. Myev was cured and Kiru gained a greater understanding and manipulation of mana. That understanding helped Kiru finally create his fourth technique, Brainstorm.

With that new technique, he was able to undergo a ritual to ascend to Ruby himself. Myev had been granted an artificial arm as a gift from the ogres, and with the three tribes' backing and accompaniment from Pandemonium and others in her envoy, she made her way to the first temple, the sight where the ritual to choose their nation's next leader would take place.

The first temple was the home of the leokin who would help conduct the ritual. Projections of the Beast Gods, even the bound Jormungandr appeared before all present to preside over the ritual. It was there, after all three contestants had arrived, that S'Vol and the jormuns enacted their final plan. Using suicide attackers, the cult was able to temporarily sever the link between all Beast Gods except Jormungandr and the temple. They also had an army hidden that began to storm the temple in attempts to kill all non-jormuns and to destroy the runes on the temple's central pyramid that help keep their god bound to another realm.

It was then that Jormungandr revealed to all that he was not just a serpent, he was a dragon and a follower of Nidhogg. He empowered all of his followers to take on draconic aspects and his forces began slaughtering their way toward the temple. Myev and Grimtusk fought S'Vol while their followers and the members of Pandemonium fought back against the amassed army. The party was able to discover a way to weaken the invading army's power by destroying Jormungandr's statue. Kiru was able to do so, evening the playing field. S'Vol still had one trick left up his sleeve. The cult leader swallowed a scale of Jormungandr, corrupting his form to match that of his god's, and morphed into a true dragon.

Realizing that the fight wasn't going Myev's way, Kiru communicated with the Emerald orc via Telepathy to relay one final, desperate plan. Kiru knew that since he was a psion, that he was the natural enemy of dragons. As such, his power was specifically suited to helping kill S'Vol. He managed to stab S'Vol in a previously injured spot and served as a living lightning rod for Myev's power. Using the ability to manipulate mana and his Brainstorm technique, Kiru transformed the Thunder Rooster's Call technique Myev struck him with into an overpowered Brainstorm. The Emerald-level power killed the dragon that S'Vol had become but nearly killed Kiru in the process.

With Jormungandr's follower dead and his plan foiled, the other Beast Gods ended the draconic deity once and for all, and Myev was proclaimed to be queen of Imakandi. Their plan did not come without cost, however. Many orcs died, and Kiru's mental mana core was damaged and nearly destroyed, only stabilized by William's intervention. He was gifted dragon bone armor made from S'Vol's remnants by the leokin for his aid, but the psion had acquired a serious handicap as well. He could no longer summon William since the imp was the only thing keeping his core intact, nor could he risk using the volatile Brainstorm technique anymore.

Kiru would recover over time, but he knew that time was a luxury he didn't have with his goal of stopping the upcoming war. So, after their business was concluded at the temple, Pandemonium continued south to find Ruken's second artifact. It was on their way that they learned that their exploits in the orc nation had not gone unnoticed. The Kingdom of Blades had gotten word of their actions and had sent their elite killing force, the Inquisition, to either capture or eliminate Kiru and his friends. The party was ambushed but managed to drive off the Inquisition and their manic dwarf second-in-command at the cost of one of their ally's lives. An orc scout named Ebysso whom Zhaden had grown close to had died from her wounds in protecting Pandemonium.

Not having the time for a proper burial, the party burned her corpse and continued deeper into Imakandi. There, they eventually found a forest and lake inside a large crater. At the lake's center was a small temple with Kiru's father's second item, the Mask of Fenrir. After answering some riddles and acquiring the second item, Kiru was greeted with another projection of Ruken, only this temporary image was more than just a recording. It was able to interact *with* Kiru for a limited time. Seizing that chance, Kiru asked Ruken how to fix his core. Ruken said that aside from drinking the blood of a mental mana cultivator, Kiru needed to drink liquid mental mana. As for where to find that, Kiru had two options: the human kingdom of Rowe at the very north of the continent or the Torn Empire. The Torn Empire comprised the very southern tip of the continent as well as the ocean and islands dotting it beneath the tip.

The party had originally planned on going north, but Kiru's mask picked up the scent of the inquisitors in that direction. They were tracking the party and looking for another fight. Seeing as that option was not viable, and that they weren't far from the Torn Empire's border, Pandemonium turned south to get outside of the Great Alliance's domain.

SAPPHIRE

"You become what you think about."
Earl Nightingale

CHAPTER ONE

Xiomara

A what?!" Xiomara van Blaine shouted as she read the message the courier had delivered to her.

The young man kept his head low in deference to the queen, but that didn't spare him as her aura forced him flat to the ground, and before he could even process what had happened to him, she gripped his throat and raised him up in the air.

"Who else has read this message?" she growled, giving the man a savage glare.

The servant choked, his eyes bulging in obvious surprise. "No one, Your . . . gah . . . Majesty . . . The Messengers' Guild ensures that no one but the intended reads their message," he barely got out.

"Lies," she spat angrily. Her nails bit into the flesh of his neck. Dark veins of necrosis started traveling through his skin.

"It's true," the courier desperately wheezed out.

"Swear it!" the queen shouted and slammed the nearby table with her free hand, which was balled into a fist. The force from her strike shattered the thick wood into splinters.

"I swear! I swear on my core that no one has read it," he gasped out desperately as she just barely lightened her grip on his throat. Both noble and courier felt the resonance of the oath within their cores, and when the courier didn't drop dead from any false promise, Xiomara released him. The young man, likely not even in his twenties, fell to the stone of the castle floor and gave a pained inhale, which soon devolved into a coughing fit. His face was beet-red from having been nearly suffocated.

After he got his breathing under control, he suddenly seemed to realize that his neck itched terribly. The courier rubbed at it with a desperate intensity while still lying on the ground. When he saw the sharp-toed boot step right by his head, he immediately halted and tried to get up, hand still gripped at his neck. "I'm sorry for any offense, Your Majesty," he groaned, just managing to get to one knee, keeping his head low all the while.

"Tut, tut, tut. No, it is I who is sorry," the queen replied, her mood seeming to instantly shift to a kindly facade.

The courier blushed at her actually apologizing to him. "No need for apologies, ma'am," he said, before he felt one of her long painted black nails right under his chin.

Xiomara raised the young courier's head up to look her directly in the eyes. The woman was an undeniable beauty and had carefully crafted an image of both power and mystery. She was an Onyx, one of the highest ranks of cultivation, but none besides her husband knew of that. With her high ascension, her body had reformed so while she looked to be in her mid-thirties, none knew her actual age. Her eyes were bright green, a striking contrast against her flawless dark-olive skin. Her hair was jet-black, which matched the color of her nails. Her bright-pink lips were a sharp contrast, currently puckered as she looked at the courier apologetically.

"Tell me, what is your name, young man?" she asked, making sure her voice was now sultry with all traces of her previous rage gone. She knew that her beauty was a weapon in and of itself and the boy was easy prey.

". . . Andor, Jakobi Andor, Your Highness," the courier answered, his face aflush, completely taken by the beauty and attention of the woman before him.

"Jakobi Andor," she trailed off while rubbing her finger over his lips, then abruptly pulling her hand away. "Come, allow me to explain my . . . response," the queen said and turned away from the young courier, motioning him to follow.

Jakobi had been walking for about five minutes on shaky legs, both desiring to make the queen happy and terrified of displeasing her. He had glanced at the table she had smashed with her fist. Not only had it been shattered by pure force, but a large portion of it had somehow turned into ashes. Jakobi gulped and put a hand to his throat.

Xiomara looked back and smiled wryly to the young courier but quickly turned away and continued walking along the dark, stone hallway. "Your cultivation— you are Tier-Three Silver?" she asked.

Jakobi held his head up high at the question. He wasn't like the monsters who had qualified to be at the Royal Academy at a young age, but the Andor family hadn't had someone reach a rank as high as his at his age for many generations. "Yes, Your Majesty. That's what has allowed me to advance to such a height within the Messengers' Guild."

"Ah, well done," she said. The young man felt himself beam at the praise. The dark, windowless hallway, dimly illuminated by torches, came to a dead end.

The queen turned back, smiling at Jakobi and handing him the letter that had angered her so. "Please, read."

Jakobi's heart thumped nervously. Whatever was in that letter had almost led to his death. He thought about refusing, but he didn't dare deny her. With shaky hands, he took it.

> *Missing students found in Imakandi.*
> *All alive and heading south.*
> *Half-elf is a psion.*
> *In pursuit.*

Jakobi furrowed his brow. "Um, I'm afraid I don't know what this means, Your Majesty," he said, wincing in fear.

"I suspected not," she said before pressing her hand against one of the stones on the wall, revealing a hidden door. The queen then slid it open to reveal a hidden spiraling staircase that descended into pure darkness. She grabbed a nearby torch and beckoned Jakobi to follow.

The courier was terrified. The hallway was already creepy, but the stairway looked even worse. Still, he trusted his queen would keep him safe—and, also, the idea of denying her scared him more. So, he followed.

"Do you know what's south of Imakandi, Jakobi?" she asked as they walked down the stone steps.

"Ma'am?" he asked.

"The territory south of the orcs' homeland? Do you know of it?" she elaborated.

"Oh, yes, Your Majesty. It's called the Torn Empire. It's a very dangerous, wild area made up of a desert coastline and numerous islands," the courier answered.

"What else do you know of it?" the queen pressed.

"I know that it's filled with pirates and savages. It's so dangerous that if someone requires that our guild use that route to reach the other side of the continent rather than by river, land travel, or even contracting flying-sacred-beast riders, we demand an exorbitant fee for our troubles. I know we have to pay any sailor a large sum to even consider that journey."

"Savages, hm?" Queen Xiomara asked.

"Yes, ma'am. I mean, that's what I've been told. My tasks have been focused on ensuring letters get delivered within the capital here," Jakobi nervously explained.

The queen didn't say anything. She just continued leading him down. After a few minutes of awkward silence in the poorly lit stairwell, Xiomara finally guided Jakobi to the bottom.

Jakobi couldn't see anything, just more darkness and a stone floor illuminated by the dim torchlight that matched everything else he'd seen. The young man felt himself reflexively quiver in fear, and he couldn't help but slow his steps, uneasily. He quickly noticed that the queen hadn't stopped walking and he hurriedly ran up to get close to her as he didn't want to be left behind in the dark.

It wasn't long until they made it to the end of the chamber, and she stopped before an obsidian pedestal nearly as tall as the queen herself. A large bowl made of the same material was on top. Wicked-looking spikes were lined all along its edge. On the other side of the pedestal, Jakobi could see that the wall was a giant mirror.

The queen turned her head slightly to look back at the young courier. "Did you know I'm from the Torn Empire?"

Terror gripped his heart at those words. "Oh my gods," he gasped under his breath. "Forgive me please, Your Majesty! I meant no offense!" Jakobi fell to his knees, putting his hands up pleadingly, palms out.

The beautiful woman just smirked. "There's nothing to forgive, Jakobi."

The young man closed his eyes as he sighed in relief. That relief was short-lived, however, because as soon as he opened his eyes, he saw the queen's alluring face was now warped by a wicked, sharp-toothed smile. Her mouth looked too big for her face. Xiomara raised her right hand up and clenched her fist.

Suddenly, Jakobi's ears were full of the sickening squelch of flesh bursting. His neck and chest were suddenly wet, the stench of rotten meat filling his nostrils, and a terrible corrosive pain coursed through his body. The courier's eyes widened as he put a hand to his neck. Where her nails had touched his flesh earlier—the same spots where his neck had itched terribly—were wounds now spurting gouts of black blood and necrotic flesh. Jakobi shook as a cold sweat covered his body, and he looked up to the queen in abject horror.

Xiomara van Blaine just smirked and walked toward the dying courier. She gave an evil smile, her pink lips now cracked and black, and she picked him up by his curly, dirty blonde hair. He struggled futilely, still desperately pressing both of his hands to his neck, which was rotting away by the second. "There's nothing to forgive, young man," the queen said.

The monstrous royal then turned back and walked to the bowl, continuing to carry Jakobi aloft.

"P-please," he managed to squeeze out, blood now dripping from his mouth too.

Xiomara just shook her head. "Shhh, shhh, you'll be serving a greater purpose here." She lowered him down to eye level. "See, I'll let you in on a little secret. While I was born in the Torn Empire, I wasn't raised there. I was rescued from that place by my father's minions."

"Father?" Jakobi managed to ask, his vision starting to go hazy. His blood spattered against Xiomara's face, but she didn't pay it any mind.

"Yes, why don't you say hello?" she said, then slammed his rotting neck against the spikes along the bowl, impaling him. Jakobi coughed in a mix of pain and fear as his fetid blood pooled in the bowl. The obsidian pedestal glowed red and his blood was immediately drained through the bottom of the bowl and into the pedestal itself. A primal part of the courier's brain forced him to try and free himself from the spikes, but he was now too weak from blood loss. He was too dazed and disoriented to even fully realize that his head was now barely connected to his body at all.

The last thing the young courier saw before death took him was the mirror. Their reflections were now gone. Instead, it displayed a massive reptilian eye. "N—" he started to utter, but his life escaped him before he could finish.

The queen suppressed a grin when the boy's head completely disconnected from his body and plopped into the pool of blood in the bowl. His pathetic fear had entertained her, and now his body would let her power the enchanted communication device to reach her father.

"Daughter," the massive creature said. His voice was deep, ancient, and sinister.

"Father," Xiomara replied, quickly taking a knee and bowing her head.

"Report," he ordered.

"Our plan is well underway. Soon—in less than a decade, by my calculations— the tower's power will fail. There has, however, been a complication."

"Complication?" he asked, a hint of anger evident.

Xiomara gulped and nodded. "I've recently discovered that a child escaped our purge of the psions twenty years ago."

"*What?*" the creature bellowed with such force that it shook the chamber Xiomara was in. "Explain."

"There was a boy who participated in the yearly tournament here. He won but disappeared after a section of the prize room collapsed. When investigating the collapse, we discovered the corpse of an elf who'd made himself an abomination by grafting the heads of deceased psions onto himself. He was dead when we found him, so we couldn't question him." She quickly added the last part to not anger her father more.

The massive eyes narrowed, and he growled, indicating he wanted her to continue.

Xiomara happily obliged. "Naturally, I was suspicious. So, I sent the lackeys I'd created to scour the alliance to find the boy and his team, dead or alive."

"Inquisition," he said.

"Yes, I created the slaves by warping their minds, Father. They know not my true intentions, but they are loyal to me above all else. They couldn't resist even if they wanted to." She cleared her throat and continued. "My Inquisition found him in Imakandi. They are in pursuit, but the boy is headed south towards the Torn Empire."

"Mmm, Imakandi . . . Jormungandr . . ." The creature trailed off in thought. After half a minute of silence, the yellow, slitted eye constricted. "Dead? Dead! Jormungandr is dead!" he shouted, shaking the castle once more.

"Are you sure?" she asked in disbelief. *The World Serpent is one of Father's most powerful allies, and a god no less! It would take a lot to kill him.*

The eye refocused on the queen.

She could see the brimming rage in it, but before her father could say anything, she hurriedly continued. "It's just . . . It's just hard to process."

"No, it is not hard to process, Daughter," the great being snarled. "*That* is the power of a psion. *That* is why the wretched boy must die."

Xiomara was stunned. *The boy had killed a* god? Last time she'd seen him, he had just been a Gold.

"I want him dead, yet my forces cannot safely enter the Torn Empire to deal with him. He poses a threat to all of my plans. I am displeased, Daughter," he growled.

Xiomara furrowed her brow and looked down to keep her frustration from being seen. She feared her father's wrath, but she feared disappointing him even more so. She looked back up to the massive reptilian eye staring down at her. "It will be done, Father. No matter what, New Draconia will make its return. You, Nidhogg, will rule all."

"As I should. See it done, Daughter." And with that, the screen changed back into a mirror, and the red runes faded away.

Xiomara stood up and wiped the blood off of her face. Then, she used her unique version of death mana to disintegrate the remains of the headless courier within seconds, leaving no trace behind. The queen quickly turned away and began walking back up the winding staircase. She had work to do.

The Torn Empire was too volatile a place to send in all of the Inquisition or any of the kingdom's forces. She would trust her slaves close behind the boy to continue their pursuit, though. Still, even though she knew all-too-well how dangerous the Torn Empire was, that didn't mean she would be able to handle it. *If, for some miraculous reason, this Kiru manages to get out, my forces will be waiting.* Her Inquisition would be in every territory in the Great Alliance, lying in wait. If the Torn Empire didn't kill him, Xiomara would make sure her forces did.

An evil smile reappeared on her face as she thought about what else she could do. In the meantime, she would press any connections to the boy's friends she could find. Any such connection was a weakness, and for Nidhogg, she would find them all.

CHAPTER TWO

No Going Back

G rah!" Kiru heard the cackling dwarf inquisitor gleefully shout as his stone dagger slammed against Brunhilda's shield. The mad, beardless dwarf had regrouped with more of his allies and had been relentlessly pursuing Kiru and the other members of Pandemonium. He'd been so excited to kill the psion and Brunhilda in particular that he'd rushed a quarter mile ahead of his counterparts, using some sort of tunneling technique to surge underground right in front of the paladin and attacked without waiting for his allies. Just like every member of the Inquisition, he had four blades seared around his head like a makeshift crown.

It was unfortunate timing for Pandemonium, too, as he had appeared right in between them and the stone bridge that crossed over a large gorge separating the team of cultivators from their destination, The Torn Empire. Mutt went to pounce on the inquisitor, but the dwarf did a backflip to avoid the orc's claws. "Hehehe! Too slow, orc! I don't care about you, anyway. I just want the psion and dwarf's heads."

"Did they burn out yer brains when they seared those blades to yer skull? Ye be mad. Is it because ye got no beard?" Brunhilda asked.

The inquisitor scowled. "I don't need a beard!" he shouted, then threw a pair of stone daggers. While they were still in flight, he slammed his palms together. "Pebblestorm!" The stone blades immediately exploded into hundreds of sharp fragments hurtling toward the party.

"Watch out!" Kiru shouted as both he and Mutt rolled and got behind Brunhilda's twin shields.

Brunhilda then expertly blocked the storm of rocks.

The bladehead—as inquisitors' victims derogatorily called them—had already crafted two more daggers from stone in the meantime. He made a move to begin a charge at the trio when he glanced to his right. Then he kicked up some dirt in that direction, revealing the silhouette of a tall, lanky drakonid. "I could feel your footsteps vibrating the ground," he said.

The drakonid's form fully materialized as he dismissed Invisibility and lunged, blades aimed at the dwarf's neck.

The inquisitor immediately dropped back into the ground, reminding Kiru of a mole, other than the fact that the ground hadn't been visibly undisturbed—there was no evidence of the dwarf in sight.

"Too slow," he said as his crowned head emerged from the dirt behind Zhaden. He then slashed the drakonid's right calf with one of the blades on his head before disappearing back into the ground.

Despite Zhaden's speed, he still wasn't able to keep up with the dwarf popping in and out of the earth. It would've been almost comical, had the party not been in a life-and-death situation.

Kiru could track the inquisitor with his eyes, but just barely. The psion wanted to use his Brainstorm technique on the dwarf—given the technique was electrical in nature, a set of metal blades grafted to his head was a potential weakness for the dwarf.

With the damage Kiru had recently sustained to his core though, he couldn't risk it.

The crazed dwarf was continuing to cut Zhaden over and over again, jumping in and out of the ground in rapid succession, too fast for the drakonid to counter. His scaled legs had now received multiple lacerations. Thankfully, none of the injuries were too serious yet.

"Mutt, catch me," Kiru said, then shut off Telekinesis on himself. His body went limp, and the orc caught him with ease. Kiru kept focusing on the blade-head attacking his friend, tracking him, and once he saw the dwarf pop up once more, he activated Telekinesis on him. A sharp pain lanced through Kiru's brain, threatening to break his focus, but he managed to hold his concentration. The inquisitor tried to sink back down into the ground, but Kiru's technique froze him in place. The dwarf shook a little in resistance, but it wasn't enough.

That moment of forced hesitation was all Zhaden needed.

The drakonid spun and struck the inquisitor square in the chest with a swing of his tail. Kiru dismissed his technique right on contact, and the now-bug-eyed dwarf was sent flying until his back struck the side of the stone bridge. The dwarf gasped, the breath was knocked out of him, before gravity took effect, and he fell deep into the gorge, screaming.

Kiru wanted to lean over and watch the mad inquisitor's descent, but there was a sudden and more pressing concern: the bridge itself. There was a loud snap from the thin stone structure, and the party looked up to see a large crack across its middle where the dwarf had slammed into it. The crack was also growing.

"Run!" Kiru shouted, and the four members of Pandemonium then took off toward the bridge. Mutt grabbed the psion with one of his scarred, muscular arms and heaved Kiru over his shoulder. Normally, Kiru would've protested, but with the pressing urgency of their situation, he decided not to.

They all sprinted desperately to get across the bridge. More loud snaps echoed out as a growing number of cracks spread across the structure. The entire bridge shook, beginning to shift and collapse. Zhaden zoomed safely across to the other side, but Brunhilda tripped and fell to her knees as the bridge continued to vibrate. She was about halfway across while Mutt and Kiru had only twenty feet left.

Hearing what had happened to the paladin, the blind orc took Kiru off his shoulder and grabbed him by the collar of his armor. "Sorry, Boss," Mutt said before spinning and throwing Kiru like a discus.

Kiru let out a cry of surprise as he flew forward and crashed into a small sand dune before he could react. He shook his head free from the sand, grateful this time that he couldn't feel pain in most of his body, and he looked back to the bridge. He saw that Mutt had gone down on all fours and run back to Brunhilda. The dwarf paladin had just gotten back to her feet when the section of bridge underneath her collapsed. Luckily, she managed to grab the edge of the bridge in front of her. That section began to crack immediately, however, and despair gripped her heart.

Fortunately for her, Mutt ran and slid toward her just in time. Right as the section of bridge she clung onto gave way, he stuck out his legs and caught her by bracing his feet under her armpits. In a feat of impressive athleticism, he threw Brunhilda up in the air and toward their friends. Mutt then spun back on all fours and activated his Fenrir's Claws technique. His fingernails elongated into sharp claws that gave him a better grip and helped increase his speed.

Mutt raced down the bridge with the swiftness of an alpha predator. Kiru saw Brunhilda had just reached her apex in the air and was now falling in an arc. Mutt was able to perfectly time himself to be in just the right spot for Brunhilda; she landed right in the middle of his back, letting out a squeak and wrapping both her arms and legs tight around him.

Kiru heard Zhaden hiss; he turned his head to see the gold drakonid looking on intently at the others. The young psion could tell his friend's heart was likely racing as fast as his own as the rest of the bridge under their friends began to collapse.

Mutt and Brunhilda were just fifty feet away when it gave way entirely. Both Kiru and Zhaden shouted in fear for their safety. Though their concern was well-founded, Mutt was up to the task. With animalistic agility and grace, the orc jumped, hopped, clawed, and crawled from section to section of falling stone fragments. In a matter of seconds, he had managed to traverse the stone pieces to make it across the large gorge safely.

Mutt landed on all fours, then rose back up. He gave both Zhaden and Kiru a wry grin. "Whoa. Let's do that again! That's even more fun than croc-hopping."

Both Kiru and Zhaden just chuckled and shook their heads. *Man, he's almost never bothered by anything,* Kiru thought.

"No, let's *not* do that again, ya idgit," Brunhilda said and smacked the orc on the back of his head before hopping off of him. She was breathing heavily, and her face was flushed purple.

"Oh, I'm sorry, Brunhilda. Are you hurt?" he asked as he leaned down and put a hand on her arm.

This time, her face turned an even darker hue. They had only just become an official item, and it was obvious to Kiru that Brunhilda was easily embarrassed by open displays of affection. "No, I be okay," she answered, looking away from the orc. "Are ye alright, Mutt?"

"Oh, yeah, Brunhilda. Never better." He smiled.

"Good," she said and quickly stood on her tiptoes and kissed the orc's forehead. "Thank ye. I just don't want to lose ye," she said.

It was Mutt's turn to blush this time. Zhaden loudly cleared his throat. Both Brunhilda and Mutt's eyes widened when they were reminded that they weren't the only ones present. They both turned to their friends and smiled sheepishly. The gold drakonid had been digging Kiru out of the sand and was now helping him sit upright.

"*Ugh, gross.*" Kiru heard inside his head. It was the voice of his familiar.

Because William was inside his core, he had to deal with his thoughts nearly every waking moment.

"*I wouldn't call it gross, but yeah, I don't want to watch them make out either,*" Kiru sent back, wincing slightly at using Telepathy.

"*Yeah, cuz it's gross. Duh . . .*" William replied.

Kiru rolled his eyes at the imp's comment. "Mutt, would you mind carrying me? I need to cultivate."

"Sure, Boss," the orc replied and lifted Kiru onto him, piggyback-style.

The party all then took a moment to look into the gorge. It was so deep that none of them could tell how far down it went.

"Do ye suppose he survived that fall?" Brunhilda asked.

"I do not know what lies below, but the odds are . . . unlikely." Zhaden answered.

The party all then turned away from the large ravine and faced south. They were now in the Torn Empire, which consisted of the southern tip of the continent and the various islands to the south of it. The landscape they now faced was very different from where they had just come from. Just across the large gorge, that section of Imakandi was a windswept, rolling grassland filled with numerous lakes and ponds that appeared to have formed from small craters.

What they faced now was desert. Massive rolling dunes were visible as far as the eye could see. Kiru hadn't realized it at first as they ran for their lives across the bridge, but the breeze was now completely gone too. The extremely strong winds from the southern section of Imakandi were completely absent. It was as if the gorge were a barrier, preventing it from coming over. Without that breeze, the heat became instantly oppressive.

While they had been in a desert in a different section of Imakandi, the feel of this one was . . . different. The sun's rays beat down more strongly, and it was eerily silent. It made Kiru feel on edge. The sand also wasn't a light brown but mostly stark white with some gray flecked in.

"So, this is the Torn Empire," Zhaden said.

"Aye," Brunhilda responded. Her uncle Jayson was a merchant and one of the few within the Great Alliance that had traversed the waters of the Torn Empire before, so she had some knowledge about it. Even so, she was not a fan of going this way. She'd made her displeasure about their destination known when they'd discussed it several days prior, but she'd been outvoted. "So Kiru, we be here now. Where do we need to go?"

"We're just at the edge of this territory. My father said we need to get to the very center of the Torn Empire," Kiru answered. Not long after Pandemonium had successfully aided Mutt's sister to claim leadership of Imakandi, they had found the second item Kiru's father had left for him. Just as with his enchanted circlet and psyslime, the young psion got to see a mental mana projection of his father, the late King Ruken.

Unlike the other times, the temporary projection was self-aware and even allowed Kiru to ask questions of it before it faded. That was where Kiru learned how to fix his damaged mental mana core more quickly. It would mend on its own over time, but time wasn't a luxury Kiru had. So, Ruken had told him that he would need to drink either the blood of a mental mana cultivator—which clearly wasn't a viable option as Kiru knew of only psions being able to be able to cultivate mental mana, and he was the last of his kind—or imbibe pure liquid mental mana. Ruken had informed him that the only two places where he could find that was at the human kingdom of Rowe to the north or the very center of the Torn Empire to the south. After learning that they were being pursued by the Kingdom of Blades' Inquisition, the Torn Empire had become the only viable choice for Pandemonium.

"Then I suggest we move with haste. Mutt did tell us earlier that he smelled the inquisitor's compatriots, so they're likely not far behind," Zhaden hissed.

Reminded that they were not clear of the immediate threat, they all began jogging across the desert sands.

There was no going back now, Kiru thought as they moved south.

CHAPTER THREE

Tier Two

For the next three days and nights, the party moved south across the desert. To the psion's surprise, they hadn't seen a single living creature, not even a cactus, on their entire journey so far. *I thought this place was supposed to be dangerous. Maybe whatever makes it so risky is the reason there's nothing living here?* he thought.

Kiru was also taken aback by the drastic temperature differences the place exhibited depending on the time of day. During the daylight hours, it was terribly hot and dry. Much of Kiru and Brunhilda's exposed skin was sunburnt from the constant exposure. Zhaden, on the other hand, thrived in the oppressive heat. The cold-blooded drakonid's golden scales soaked up the sun readily, seeming to energize him. As such, he served as their scout, regularly moving ahead to scan for possible danger.

Night in the desert, however, was the complete opposite, temperature-wise. When the sun set and the twin moons rose up in the sky, it got dramatically colder. The cultivators would all huddle together in one tent to stay warm, making sure to keep Kiru in the middle since he couldn't truly feel most of his body and was thus more susceptible to hypothermia than the rest.

Mutt's Dweller Bear's Fur technique was a tremendous boon to the psion during that time.

And while Zhaden did the best during the day, he undoubtedly suffered the worst of them during the night. He would shake dreadfully, his sharp teeth chattering loudly.

On the third night, not long after everyone had fallen asleep, Zhaden accidentally woke everyone up with a growl of frustration.

Mutt yawned loudly. "What's going on, Stabby?"

"I . . . am . . . angry . . . because . . . I . . . am . . . cold!" Zhaden hissed in between shaky breaths. "Unlike . . . some . . . other . . . drakonids . . . gold drakonids . . . don't . . . like . . . cold!"

Kiru and Brunhilda blinked their eyes open. Kiru had only just gone to bed recently because he'd been cultivating the mental mana coming off of his friends' dreaming minds. So, unlike Mutt and Brunhilda, he was still fully conscious. "So there are drakonid types that don't mind cold?"

Zhaden shook his head side-to-side and clutched his jacket tight against his body. Back at the Royal Academy in the Kingdom of Blades, they had all been gifted with jackets—each with a large, bedazzled flower on the back—by Kiru's sponsor, the elf Niajar J'sarko. While they were admittedly an eyesore to look at, they were undeniably useful. They had been enchanted with temperature-regulation abilities. Kiru's had unfortunately been destroyed while they were in Imakandi, but the others still had theirs.

Mutt's jacket was sleeveless, but he evidently didn't need it, thanks to the thick hair his technique provided him with. "Here ya go, Stabby," he said to Zhaden as he threw him his sleeveless blue jacket.

The gold drakonid hastily snapped it out of the air and put it around his legs. He audibly sighed in relief just seconds afterward.

Once the rogue was more comfortable, he finally answered Kiru's earlier question. "As I've stated before, we gold drakonids typically favor fire mana. With our cold-blooded natures, most drakonids are fonder of warm environments. There are exceptions, however," he said. "My ancestors passed down stories about certain chromatic brethren that either favored or were immune to cold: white and gray drakonids."

Zhaden then shivered again, "Though I do hope that when I reach Tier Two in Ruby as you have, Mutt, I will be stronger in resisting this c-cold," he stuttered.

"I mean, you might, Stabby, but I wouldn't get your hopes up. Reaching Tier Two may make your body more durable, but it's not going to be as significant a difference as you're thinking," Mutt explained.

Kiru's heart skipped a beat at the reminder of Mutt's cultivation rank. Every single one of the party members other than Mutt were at Tier One Ruby. Back at the ancient Beast God temple, the blind orc had been gifted with a "blessing" by the leokin. It was their own way of advancing from Tier One to Two in Ruby, and it only worked for those who cultivated beast mana, as Zengaz—one of the leokin who served Nom, the leokin who had helped Mutt with his ascension—had explained to Kiru when he'd asked. Kiru wanted the details, hoping to possibly be able to use them to extrapolate so the rest of his party could reach Tier Two.

Unfortunately, however, Zengaz wasn't allowed to tell Kiru how *exactly* they helped. All Kiru knew was what he could glean from observing Mutt. From what he could see, after Mutt had spent days cultivating, the leokin cub Nom and five other leokin had bitten down hard on Mutt's flesh, drawing blood from the wounds. Somehow, Mutt had grown in power through the process. To Kiru's surprise, after the time was up, Mutt had emerged as Tier Two. It was obvious that Nom and the others had given Mutt their own mana to help him, but Kiru didn't know the details. Zengaz did, however, say that the psion could ask Mutt, as that wouldn't break the leokins' rules about disclosing information.

Kiru had been so busy with their recent attempt to get his father's second item and escape the Inquisition, however, that he had completely forgotten to ask Mutt about the process. "Hey Mutt, would you mind telling us how exactly the leokin helped you reach Tier Two?"

The blind orc yawned before answering. "Yeah, sure Boss, but can it wait until morning? I wanna get some sleep."

"I'll let you sleep late tomorrow morning if you want, but I think Zhaden, Brunhilda, and I need this information as soon as possible. Also, remember that I took some info about how to help a beast mana cultivator reach Sapphire too," Kiru mentioned. While in the orc capital, Dissé, Kiru had spent some time in a repository of knowledge under the Beast God temple. He'd only been shown the area and permitted there because he was desperately working to help Myev heal from having been poisoned. He had found some text carved in the stone there detailing how to help a beast mana cultivator ascend from Ruby to Sapphire.

At Kiru's words, all of his friends perked up.

"Oh! Good point, Boss! Now, let's see . . ." Mutt trailed off, stroking his wild goatee. "So, it was kinda weird. From what I learned, I just had to flood my entire body with mana." The orc gave another yawn before continuing. "Since the temple was so full of beast mana, I was able to do so in a matter of days versus the weeks it could've been otherwise. I had to draw in so much mana that it was literally oozing out of my meridians and spreading throughout my body."

"So, you're saying that the way to get to Tier Two is to just entirely fill our bodies with mana?" Zhaden asked. "I mean no offense, Mutt, but that seems entirely too easy."

"Aye, that sounds just like how I got to Gold from Silver. That be how many ascend to that rank, actually. All ye need to do is cultivate in a place with an abundance of yer mana type—enough to force yer meridians open. Are ye saying we need to do that *again*, Mutt?" Brunhilda asked.

"Not exactly. Oh . . . Now that you mention it, Brunhilda, Zengaz did mention something about it being similar to people reaching Gold." Mutt grimaced. "Unfortunately, he also said that if you already used that method to get to Gold, then the way I got to Tier Two Ruby won't work for you. Sorry."

Brunhilda looked disappointed, but it didn't last long. She turned to Zhaden and Kiru. "Did either of ye two use that method to get to Gold?"

Zhaden shook his head. "No. As I've mentioned previously, Clan Ironclaw's mana type is an abnormality amongst my gold drakonid brethren. Most of my kin use fire mana. Dream mana is rare, so I had to use a different method to reach Gold."

Kiru then saw their gazes focus on him. "I didn't use that method, either. Instead, I gathered enough mana inside my core to force open my main meridians and form extra meridians manually, one at a time."

"Whoa, Boss. That sounds . . . slow," Mutt said.

"It was," Kiru answered, not elaborating further.

"So, from what I understand, there be a way ye two—" she said, nodding to Zhaden and Kiru, "—could use information from Mutt's ascension to also ascend, aye?"

"Seems so," Kiru said. "What else can you remember about how you reached Tier Two, Mutt?"

"Ehh, not much more, Boss," the blind orc replied as he cleaned his left ear with a finger. "The only other thing was at the end. I was having trouble taking in any more mana. It felt like I was about to burst. I *knew* I was right at the edge of ascending, you know? It was like that for a couple days or so, and then that little sacred beast guy—"

"Nom," Brunhilda interjected, making sure Mutt called him by his name.

"Yeah, Nom. Anyway, that's when he and a few more of his friends bit me. They can bite hard, by the way. It hurt at first, but then it felt good, like *really* good," Mutt said.

There was an awkward silence as his friends waited for him to elaborate, but he never did. After about fifteen seconds, Brunhilda spoke up. "Mutt, dearie, would ye be so kind as to explain *why* it felt good?" the paladin delicately asked.

Mutt didn't appear perturbed in the slightest at her question. "Yeah, Brunhilda. The little guy and his followers were somehow doing some weird leokin thing and put their beast mana directly into my blood. My meridians felt like they were about to burst, but after a few seconds, the pressure was gone, and I felt great. In a matter of moments, I realized it was because I'd reached Tier Two."

Zhaden spun the tip of his tail in a subtle circle, a gesture Kiru had just recently realized meant the gold drakonid was curious, "And what of the mana?" Zhaden asked.

"What of it?" Mutt said, clearly confused at the question.

Now Zhaden's tail went stiff in frustration. "What happened to the mana after the leokin gave you more? *How* exactly did it strengthen you enough to reach Tier Two?"

"Oh, well, I don't know exactly. I'd been afraid my meridians were in danger of popping, but then all the pressure on them vanished. Then I felt the mana spread out and sink into my whole body."

The orc then flexed his hands. "I can't explain how, but I can *feel* the mana in my skin and muscles now."

Kiru sighed. That wasn't much to go on. "Okay. Well, is there anything about your body or meridians that is noticeably different?" he asked, hoping that his open-ended question would help to give him something more to work on.

"Hmm, let me check," Mutt said. For the next couple of minutes, the blind orc began using all of his other senses on himself. At first it was a little funny seeing him smell one of his armpits, but then it got flat-out weird when he started licking himself to check for any subtle differences.

"Uh, well, what about yer *meridians*, dearie?" Brunhilda quickly interjected in hopes of interrupting Mutt's self-examination.

"Hm? Well, now that you mention it, yeah," Mutt said.

Everyone leaned forward eagerly.

"Go on," the dwarf encouraged.

"Nah, I don't see a . . . wait. Oh, that's weird. My meridians," he said and rubbed his shoulder. "The little guy made a new meridian for me! I didn't realize until now, but yeah, that's what he did." He chuckled.

"That must've been what happened when you said his mana touched your meridians." Kiru smiled. *Normally, I would be suspicious of someone seeming so dense as to not notice new meridians in their body, but Mutt is . . . well, at least he's consistent*, he thought. Still, Kiru couldn't ask for a better ally and friend.

"Haha! Oh, yeah, Boss. Now it's all coming together!"

Now that they were getting somewhere, Kiru wanted Mutt to keep going. After fifteen more minutes of targeted questions, they were able to parse more fully what happened. The little leokin leader had somehow used his own mana to create a new meridian for Mutt. That was surprising. Kiru had been taught that, once you reached Gold, you could no longer form any meridians . . . meaning you were stuck with what you had. He didn't know exactly *how* the leokins had performed the impossible, but Kiru presumed it had to do with Mutt not creating new meridians *for himself* and instead others doing it for him.

The party learned that the new meridian was connected to one of the six main meridians. They also presumed that new head shaman of the leokin, Nom, had been the one who was directly responsible for connecting to one of the six main meridians. The newly made meridian, unlike any of Mutt's other meridians, reached all the way to the surface of his skin. That was definitely strange, as far as Kiru knew.

Meridians weren't known to extend to the outside of one's body. If they had, mana might have unintentionally leaked out. Mutt didn't seem to have that problem, though. With that objective data, Kiru thought back on what he knew of all the cultivation stages. The perfect recall he had thanks to William being inside his core was utterly astonishing during times like this where he's trying to piece together a mystery.

Kiru knew Ruby was the stage where you ascended to gain insight with your physical body. Kiru knew very little about Sapphire, only that it was called the

Shroud Rank. Kiru deduced from the name that it was when a cultivator actually formed the shroud of mana that many high-ranking ones had.

Knowing all those things and that Mutt said he could somehow "feel" the mana in his muscles and skin, Kiru grinned. He believed he had come up with a plausible objective way to reach Ruby Tier Two. "It has to be something like permeating our bodies with mana so that every inch of us is exuding it," he said.

"I suppose, Kiru, but if that be the case, it'll be a bloody hard thing to accomplish," Brunhilda said.

"While your idea does sound viable, my friend, I must concur with Brunhilda. To do this, you would not only need a location that was abundantly full of your specific mana type, but you would need an exorbitant amount of time to lace every single part of you inside and out without using *any* mana at all so as not to lose your saturation. Using any would delay your progress," Zhaden added.

Kiru shrugged. "Maybe, but this idea is the best I can come up with."

"It not be without merit, Kiru," Brunhilda conceded.

Zhaden nodded. "I concur."

"Well, if you come up with anything better, let me know. Two heads are better than one, and three beats two when trying to solve problems," Kiru said. "In the meantime, let's do our best to be conservative with our mana usage. Maybe we'll find some information as to how to reach the next tier out here. My father said that a potential cure to my issue lies in the Torn Empire. Who knows what other things of value may be here? If we do happen to learn the true hurdle we need to get over, and if overall quantity of mana is important, we'll already be prepared."

They all nodded in agreement.

Kiru thought it was a bit silly for him to even say that out loud. They were wanted fugitives in hostile foreign territory. Of course they were going to conserve their mana in case of a sudden attack or emergency. Still, he wasn't wrong for saying that.

They all laid down to go back to sleep, Mutt only doing so because Kiru promised to start going over what he'd learned about how to get the beast mana cultivator to Sapphire after they made camp tomorrow. Kiru did give Mutt a pair of Sapphire beast mana cores they'd acquired previously from an ogre they'd fought back in Imakandi that night too, the only reason he hadn't before then was him honestly just forgetting about them. Kiru had some difficulty nodding off after that conversation, however. He was a bit frustrated with his own plan of mana conservation because he, unlike his allies, was currently at a point where it was near-impossible to conserve almost any mana due to the damage to his core. Still, he took comfort in the fact that, if his friends could get stronger, they *all* had a better chance of surviving. With thoughts of power floating through his mind, he finally fell asleep.

CHAPTER FOUR

Two Heads Are Better Than One

It was on the next day when things finally began to change. Mutt had been kind enough to carry Kiru most of the time so as to allow the psion to cultivate more mana. Kiru was appreciative of the gesture, which helped him store more mana plus avoid more of the sharp headaches that came when he activated a technique. Kiru noticed as they continued further south that the gray and white dunes had started to change in color, eventually turning to pure white. Pillars of burnt-orange-colored stone varying from fifty to 150 feet tall, by the psion's estimation, started to become visible. All of the pillars were mottled and pock-marked as if they were giant melted wax candles or an insect hive. Kiru was grateful for the change of scenery because just seeing nothing but sand dunes for days on end had grown rather dull.

None of those differences were what Kiru was *most* grateful for, however. That honor went to the wind. For the first time since arriving in the Torn Empire, they had *finally* felt a breeze. With the brutal heat from the sun and no cloud shelter, it had been hard for them to find relief. Now, though, Kiru and his friends were fortunately getting some reprieve.

Mutt raised his head and took a big inhale through his nostrils. "Ahhh," he sighed happily, a big grin on his face. "The air here is nice. Salty, too."

"Salty?" Kiru asked.

"Yeah, Boss. The desert air here has always been a little off. I got a hint of death from it. This air, though—" He paused as he took in another big inhale. "—It's full of life. I can smell birds and even water! We gotta be close, guys!" he exclaimed.

"*We've been walking through a wasteland of death?!*" William asked, an edge to his voice. "*I feel such mixed emotions. On the one hand, walking through death sounds awesome. On the other, I don't want to be breathing poison.*"

"*First off, you can't breathe anything when you're inside my core. Second, Mutt's sense of smell would've warned him if there was something actually toxic in the air,*" Kiru sent back, wincing only slightly as he used his mana for Telepathy.

The psion could rival Mutt's sense of smell when he wore his enchanted Mask of Fenrir, but he was a bit wary of the item. It was the second of his father's that he'd collected; it enhanced Kiru's senses to that of an alpha dire wolf, but when he'd put it on, animalistic urges threatened to take over his mind. The mask also seemed to have at least a partial will of its own. Kiru had overcome it before, but he still only wanted to use it as needed.

"*Well that's good, but do we have to keep going this way? I hate the water,*" William grumbled inside Kiru's mind. Ever since a persistent and rather large koi fish had tried to eat William, the imp had grown a rather strong disdain for any and all bodies of water. Kiru had even caught him growling at some large cups full of liquid the last time he'd been out of Kiru's core.

"*We don't have a choice, William. My father said the liquid mental mana—the cure for my injury—is in the very center of the Torn Empire.*" Kiru grimaced as they continued walking up a rather large dune. When they finally crested the top, they got their first view over the ocean. They all paused and smiled. Well, all except for William. The ocean was bright blue, reflecting the sun on a cloudless day. *Looks like we're above sea level and are going to have to find a way down to the water's edge once we get closer,* the psion thought.

"*That doesn't mean I can't hate the water.*" William sent back to Kiru's earlier telepathic reply.

"*How about this, William—as soon as my core is healed, I'll summon you out and I'll get a big juicy fish for you to eat as revenge,*" Kiru offered.

"*Showing those stupid fish that I am the one to be feared, plus getting a yummy meal? Mmmph. That is . . . acceptable,*" the imp agreed, acting magnanimous.

Kiru smiled at this successful negotiation, then he thought about their next steps for their journey. He had no clue *where* that was exactly, but Ruken had said that the psion would be able to sense it when he got closer. Seeing as that had happened when he'd gotten closer to his father's two previous items, Kiru had faith in Ruken's words. Now that they were nearing the coast and still no sign that the liquid mana was near, the psion had come to the unfortunate conclusion that they were going to have to traverse the dangerous ocean waters.

Kiru hadn't formed much of a plan for that eventuality, to his embarrassment. He'd been so preoccupied with cultivating, pondering his core, and trying to prevent heat stroke that he hadn't given that potential scenario much thought. At best, he had a rough idea. *Find a local settlement—preferably pirates over those mad islanders Brunhilda said were called "The Crazed." Once we find a settlement, we'll have to steal a small vessel in the middle of the night,* he thought as Brunhilda had made it apparent that she knew of no friendly forces within the Empire.

I remember Zhaden mentioning that he had some sailing experience one time back at the academy, so he'll have to take point while we assist as best we can. If things get too complicated, we'll just have to force a couple of low-ranked pirates to sail for us. Man, I sound like William. Kiru shuddered at the realization. Still, it was the best idea he could come up with for the time being. He had never sailed before but reasoned that, with a few competent people backing them up, it shouldn't be too hard.

After a few minutes walking across the final stretch of sand and stone, Kiru heard a strangled sound of rattling wood. He looked down to his belt to see that the Mask of Fenrir was vibrating. Kiru's heart sank. It had only ever done that once before, and that was right before an attack.

At the same time, Mutt abruptly halted his steps and held out a hand for the others to stop as well. The hair on the orc's body stood on end. "So, I'm all down for a good hunt, but I like to be the one who's hunting. Based off of what my feet are feeling, I'm pretty sure something is hunting us," Mutt said.

Kiru activated Telekinesis, wincing at the sharp pain that came with it, but bore it and hopped off Mutt's back. Fortunately, it only lasted for a few moments before turning into a dull throb.

The blind orc dug his bare feet into the sand. "It's coming, and it's big."

Everyone drew their weapons and began scanning their surroundings for this unseen foe. For half a minute, they all stood on edge. Not wanting this enemy to get the jump on them, Kiru decided it was time to don his mask once again. *If it makes me go feral, I trust my friends to subdue me,* he thought. Kiru swiftly strapped on the dark-red wooden mask, carved in the shape of a wolf's mouth, covering the lower half of his face from his nose down. As soon as it was in place, small hair-like needles jutted out from it and embedded themselves into Kiru's flesh. Tendrils of beast mana shot out from the needles, winding around the covered areas of his face and weaving a complex web of mana under the psion's skin.

Instantly, Kiru's body began to morph into that of an alpha dire wolf. His eyes turned yellow and now could see farther with absolute clarity. He could also smell gull excrement along the coastline up ahead. His ears twitched as they picked up on the subtle noise of sand shifting, growing louder by the second. The psion let out a reflexive growl as his mouth salivated, craving the lifeblood of his enemies. He could see Mutt's body tensing too, the orc's senses no doubt picking up the noise as well.

Kiru tensed and staggered as he regained control of his senses. The mask tried to take advantage of his fight-or-flight response in an attempt to assert dominance. The psion almost succumbed, but his will overcame that of the mask. Still, that momentary lapse did cause his focus on his environment to falter for a split second, and before he could fully regain his wits, a giant monstrous creature surged through one of the white sand dunes. Luckily, Mutt tackled him out of the way, saving him from being crushed.

Kiru rolled, and the members of Pandemonium all lowered their weapons as they got their first good look at the creature that had been pursuing them. The monster had dry, dark-grey, leathery skin. It was about ten feet tall and looked like a cross between an earthworm and a mole. It had a long, tubular body with two thin arms ending in massive claws, with webbing between each of its eight fingers. Its serpentine neck ended in a head that looked too small for its body, possessing no eyes and a pink fleshy nose with a bunch of appendages hanging off of it.

"Wow, that is the grossest thing I've ever seen, and I've seen a lot," William sent in disgust.

The creature growled and clicked as it faced the group. No one made a sound. Kiru couldn't even hear anyone's breath. Whether that was due to him being completely focused on the monster or not, he wasn't sure. The tension was almost palpable. The creature just continued to click and scan its head back and forth, in seeming confusion. It didn't strike, but it didn't leave, either.

Now in full control, Kiru used his enhanced bestial senses to examine the creature. He couldn't see its eyes, but that didn't mean it didn't have any. It continued to click louder now. His eyes picked up that the creature's arms and body were slowly tensing. It was about to strike.

"Is it doing what I think it's doing?" Mutt asked, but before any of them could respond, the creature let out a shriek and turned its head in the orc's direction. Its large, mole-like nose split open vertically down the middle, revealing a set of sharp jaws that spread and connected with its other mouth below it. Then, like Kiru had predicted, it struck. The creature launched itself at Mutt like a crossbow bolt, its mouth open wide to bite him in half.

The psion wasn't caught unaware this time, though. Kiru concentrated more of his mental mana into his legs and surged forward. Using his Monarch's Razor form, he decapitated the creature in one quick motion. Its body fell limp beside them, quickly followed by its head. Dark-red blood splotched the sand, leaking from its stump.

"Thanks, Boss," Mutt said in between heavy breaths.

"No problem," Kiru replied, adrenaline still surging through him.

"What do ye suppose it be?" Brunhilda asked, as she looked down at the strange creature.

"I'm unsure. I've never read about any creature with this kind of physiology," Kiru said.

"Bleh! Whatever it was, it was ugly," William scoffed inside the psion's mind.

Mutt leaned down and sniffed the corpse before dipping a finger in its blood and tasting it. "Weird. It smells like a hydra, but it's way smaller than any hydra I've ever hunted. Also, its blood . . . The blood tastes . . . off."

"What be a hydra, Mutt?" Brunhilda asked.

Before the orc could answer her, the creature's body doubled in size and, in a matter of seconds, two new heads grew out of the bleeding stump, which immediately struck out at Brunhilda—but she managed to raise her shields and stop the sets of jaws from biting down on her just in time. With some effort, she pushed off and shield-bashed one of the heads, freeing herself from it.

"Wait!" Mutt called out, though Kiru only barely heard the warning.

In a flash, both Kiru and Zhaden were on the other head, which was still clamped on Brunhilda's right shield. The assassin jumped and stabbed the head with a pair of daggers, and Kiru followed right behind, decapitating it once more. The one remaining head cried out in pain, and the creature hastily backed away.

The psion, drakonid, and dwarf all glared and were ready to charge at it when Mutt ran up in front of them, "Waaiiit!" the orc shouted.

The others stopped and looked at him in bemusement.

"You can't kill it like that. It's definitely some sort of hydra. Each time you cut off a head—"

The creature let out a pained squelch, which interrupted Mutt's words, and each member of the party let out a small gasp as two *more* heads grew out from its new stump. The hydra's body swelled, too, getting both taller and more muscular yet again.

"—two more grow in each's place," Mutt finished.

The now three-headed and thirty-foot-tall monster raised its heads up in the air and roared in fury.

"*Run, bitch, run!*" William shouted inside Kiru's mind.

Kiru didn't need any encouragement—he did just that. The others hurried after him and began desperately running across the sand in the direction of the water. Kiru was hoping it would provide them some sort of refuge. Mutt grabbed Brunhilda and threw her on his back before running on all fours. The armor-laden dwarf was both the heaviest and slowest of the group, so now they all were sprinting away from the monster pursuing them at the same speed.

The hydra was faster than Kiru expected, its lower half moving in a serpentine pattern across the sand while its two arms were pressed against its side, seeming to help make it more aerodynamic.

"Mutt, you know what this thing is. How do we beat i—oh *shit!!*" Kiru shouted the last bit just as the hydra leapt at him. In a panic, he used Telekinesis to fling himself both forward and up. Kiru looked like a puppet being held up by a single string as he levitated and flew forward.

The hydra's jaws snapped and only caught air. The moment after it missed Kiru, it dove down into the white sand, burying its body within moments. That didn't mean it stopped its pursuit, however. A large mound of visibly distorted sand still kept moving forward, indicating its location.

"Unless you have some sort of explosive, we have to crush it, Boss! You know? Like bludgeon it!" Mutt shouted back as he continued running. Immediately, the hydra turned and moved toward Mutt directly.

"Master, it uses both vibrations and sound to track its prey! It's blind, just like the orc!" William advised.

Kiru noticed that, too, his perfect memory helping him to recall that Mutt used his senses in a similar way. Every single time someone spoke aloud, the creature went after them. It made sense with it having no eyes. Now Kiru just needed to formulate a plan to exploit it. *How in the world are we going to be able to crush a thirty-foot-tall monster?* he thought as he continued to fly forward. It was a good thing he'd been able to cultivate more mana than normal these past few days too, because he was using the magical energy prodigiously at the moment.

Then, his enhanced sense of smell picked up on something new—something musty. The distinct scent of damp, which was particularly perplexing in the middle of a desert. Kiru raised himself higher in the air to get a better vantage point. He quickly found the source. One of the stone pillars not far ahead had a large hole at its bottom. *A cave!* he thought. Kiru couldn't tell how deep it was, but it was promising, nonetheless. A few hundred feet away from it was another pillar, notably flimsier than the other and riddled with significant pockmarks.

He wanted everyone to run to the cave, but there would be no way to get there without the hydra catching up to them. He needed a distraction. A piece of the flimsy pillar fell off the top and crashed into the sand below it. The whole thing looked ready to collapse. Kiru smiled. They needed something big to crush this hydra, and something big had just presented itself. He sent a telepathic message to his allies: *"Everyone, follow me and listen up. I have a plan."*

CHAPTER FIVE

Corsairs

G*et readyyy! And, now!"* Kiru sent, putting his plan into action. The psion lowered himself back to the ground and began running across the white sand again. He was a few feet ahead of his friends, who all made a sharp right turn toward one of the nearby pillars, which was nearly parallel with the crumbling one a few hundred feet or so farther away. Kiru started shouting and making noise to attract the hydra's attention—which it did, immediately.

The monster was about twenty feet away from Kiru, now fully focused on the psion. Meanwhile, his friends continued to move in a diagonal line to where they would pass right by the cave mouth. Just as they neared it, Kiru sent the mental command for the next step. While still running forward, Mutt cocked his head back and used his Bounder's Howl technique.

A menacing roar shot out from his mouth back toward the hydra. It immediately stopped in its tracks, all three of its heads breaking the sand's surface. They screeched and writhed, momentarily stunned.

In a feat of athletic grace, Zhaden leapt to his right, rolling into the cave. Brunhilda, however, didn't possess the drakonid's grace, so Kiru flung her into the cave right after Zhaden with his Telekinesis. She crashed into Zhaden, and they landed in a heap farther into the cave.

Just as the heads regained their senses, Kiru hopped on top of Mutt's back, pointed his psyslime Fu Tao at the monster and shouted once again.

The heads snapped towards him, and they all snarled at once, enraged that they had been startled—and seemingly forgetting about the dwarf and drakonid altogether. The hydra let out a chorus of shrill screams, and it surged forward once again. Mutt and Kiru promptly started running away from both the monster and the cave where their friends were hiding. They were unable to make enough distance from their foe, because the enraged blind hydra started using its arms to propel it forward even faster.

Mutt was dashing at a dead sprint, carrying Kiru on his back. In a matter of seconds, they would run straight into the crumbling pillar before them, but Kiru knew Mutt was ready.

"Jump now!" Kiru shouted. Mutt immediately complied and leapt toward the pillar. In midair, he activated two techniques: Fenrir's Claws and Harpy Eagle's Talons. His fingernails extended into thick, sharp claws while his feet changed into yellow, three-toed talons. Without skipping a beat, Mutt immediately began climbing up the stone, Kiru still clinging onto his back with his legs.

The hydra wasn't so lucky. The multi-headed creature was charging so recklessly that it crashed straight into the stone, releasing a cacophony of pained screams and afterwards appearing disoriented as it reared back. A large crack now ran through the pillar, but it was still intact for the time being. Kiru nearly jumped off of Mutt to show the hydra who the real predator was, but he quickly regained his senses, realizing the mask was trying to influence him. Before the hydra could lose track of them, Kiru forced his psyslime blade into the shape of a whip.

"Hey, ugly!" he shouted, then snapped his whip down at the monster, striking one of its heads and earning its ire once again.

The hydra's three heads hissed as it began clawing its way up and continuing to follow them up the pillar. Kiru gave a slight grin under his wolf mask. They had successfully lured it up, as planned.

Now was the final step.

"Gnash and Grind!" Brunhilda shouted from outside the cave mouth in the other pillar.

A large, spectral goat head surged out from each of her shields. It was the paladin's one and only purely offensive technique. The heads flew forward, opening their toothy maws wide. Each of them reached the cracked pillar and bit a pair of massive chunks out of it before dissipating.

CRA-KOOM!

Just as Kiru had hoped, the base of the pillar gave way. The large crack deepened and violently extended all the way across the stone, sending out a cloud of gray dust.

The pillar immediately started leaning forward as it began to fall. Mutt tensed, and his claws bit deep into the stone to hang on. The monster kept climbing, though, so Mutt had no choice but to do the same. He had climbed three-fourths of the way to the top, but it was clear from what Kiru saw that the two of them weren't going to make it to the top. The shadow from the falling stone they were clinging to had now completely obscured the light from the sun, and wind began to rush against their backs from their descent. In just seconds they, along with the hydra, would be crushed by the stone.

Kiru had miscalculated how quickly Mutt would be able to crawl up. His original plan was for them to reach up there, then jump off right as the pillar made impact with the sand below. He had a contingency plan, though, and that was why he was there with Mutt. "Don't resist, Mutt," Kiru shouted right before he extended the use of his Telekinesis on the orc as well, forcing himself to ignore the pain that came with the exertion. Their bodies were flung completely sideways as if fired from a slingshot, and they narrowly avoided being crushed. The last thing that Kiru saw of the hydra before they crashed into the sand was one of its heads reaching out before the massive stone squashed it into the ground with a boom.

Kiru's vision went black as he impacted the sand. A sharp ringing assaulted his ears, dazing and disorienting the psion. He didn't know how long he laid there, but eventually his vision started to clear, and he began to shake off the ringing along with the sand from his thick black hair. He was grateful for the protective enchantment on his headband, which had clearly protected his skull from being cracked. Some loud albeit muffled noises started coming in. As different colors started to come into focus, Kiru saw Mutt kneeling down over him.

"Boss! Boss! Are you okay?" The orc's long, wild hair was absolutely covered in sand.

"Y-Yeah," Kiru groaned. "It looks like we made it. You got yourself a little dirty there, Mutt," he said, each word sounding more confident as both his focus and clarity returned.

"Eh—" Mutt uttered as he pointed to himself, slack-jawed. Then, he began to laugh long and hard.

"*Impudent fool!*" William bristled. "*Master, you should slap him across the face for his audacity. No one should ever laugh at you but me!*"

"*Wait, who said* **you** *could laugh at me?*" Kiru asked.

"*I did. I saved your life after all. I'm owed.*"

"*No. I've saved your life way too many times to be indebted,*" Kiru countered.

"*Oh, come on! Just once?*"

Kiru sighed. "*Fine, you can make fun of me just once.*"

"*Awww, yeah! I win! Take that!*"

Despite the pain, Kiru couldn't help but chuckle at that, which then brought his focus back to what was happening outside of his head. Mutt had finally finished laughing and was now wiping a tear away from one eye. "Phew! That was a good one, Boss."

Kiru was confused. "Why?" he asked, still not getting the punchline.

"Oh! You don't realize yet, do you?" Kiru was about to shout at Mutt to spit it out, but then the orc said, "Look down, Boss."

The psion did just that. The first thing he noticed was that his mask seemed to have popped off his face from the impact. The second thing was just . . . sand. He was entirely submerged from the neck down! Since he could never feel his body and hadn't been paying full attention before, he had had no clue. *No wonder Mutt was laughing earlier!* Kiru let out a reflexive gasp of surprise, then couldn't help but shake his head and smile. "I seem to be pretty dirty too."

"Haha! Yep," Mutt said before digging the psion free.

Once extracted from the sandy prison, Kiru tied his mask back to his waist, then they began walking back over to the cave. Kiru had used most of his accumulated extra mana for the fight against the hydra, but he didn't feel like being carried again now. So, he trudged in the sand alongside Mutt. As they got closer to the cave, however, Kiru noticed that Brunhilda and Zhaden weren't standing outside waiting for them.

He was concerned at their absence, and that soon blossomed into full-blown fear when two bodies were flung out of the cave mouth with a set of pained cries. Kiru and Mutt ran over and quickly ascertained that those were not their friends. They both looked like elves with their pointed ears and tall but skinny bodies. It was clear that each had been killed in an entirely different way.

The upper half of one of the corpse's skulls was caved in, but Kiru could see dull gray skin and a set of crooked but sharpened yellow teeth. Its head was covered in wild, solid black hair. The other dead body had a gaping stab wound in his neck and was swimming in a pool of black blood that looked more like tar underneath him. His eyes were open, revealing tiny black pupils while the whites of the eyes were bloodshot. Mutt sniffed one of them tentatively, then recoiled as the foul scent of their blood hit his sensitive nostrils.

Kiru's heart raced. These looked more like monsters than people. He and Mutt quickly turned to run into the cave, but then their friends walked out, followed closely by about twelve more of those strange, grey-skinned people. The psion's heart sank—around Brunhilda and Zhaden's necks and wrists were collars and cuffs made of trollstone.

Trollstone was a rare substance that somehow inhibited both the flow and control of mana of anyone it touched. As such, it was the ideal material for restraining powerful cultivators, as it prevented the use of their supernatural abilities. Behind both Zhaden and Brunhilda, a pair of the hostiles stood, holding daggers against the cultivators' throats as well. *Looks like the cave we chose was inhabited.* Kiru thought. He figured Zhaden and Brunhilda must've been too distracted by the pillar crashing to realize they hadn't been alone in there.

The captors fanned out in a semicircle, revealing more body types aside from the two corpses by the psion.

Mutt's entire body tensed as he crouched and looked ready to pounce, but Kiru sent a mental message to his friend: *"Not yet."*

All their enemies had the same manic eyes, dull gray skin, and crooked teeth, but that was where most of their similarities ended. There were more wiry-looking elves, but there were other races there was well, including bulky orcs with bulbous bellies, humans with prominent black veins, a couple of gnomes with mouths

too wide for their faces, and one bald dwarf with a long white mustache and goatee that was braided and adorned with bones.

"What is wrong with these guys?" William asked.

Kiru didn't respond but wondered the same. *Are they sick? Are these the Crazed
who Brunhilda warned me about?* They certainly looked crazed to him. *No, she
said they were savage islanders. We're still on the mainland, and these people are
wearing a mix of cotton and rough-spun clothing.* Kiru noticed that some even had
leather vests and boots, not matching the description of loincloth-wearing primitive people that Brunhilda had described. All of the gray-skinned ones wielded a
sword of some form, most of them brandishing a rusty cutlass. Kiru had never
met a pirate in person before, but they *definitely* fit the definition.

Mutt growled loudly and summoned his claws once more. Kiru kept his hands
on his weapons' hilts and took a few steps forward. "I don't know who you are,
but if you don't release my friends at once—"He slowly and deliberately began to
unsheathe his blades. "—things will become . . . unpleasant for you."

Mutt let out a subtle snarl for emphasis.

Most of the pirates tensed at that display, the ones holding blades to the rogue
and paladin's throats pressing in a little harder to draw thin lines of blood. The
dwarf pirate, however, just grinned wide. "Ahoy there, lads. I'm afraid yer not fully
graspin' yer situation. When it be coming to negotiations, ye got to have leverage,
see? Now, while it may be true that some of us would die a gruesome death to yer
blades, it wouldn't be 'fore my men here sliced yer friends' throats wide open. Ye
don't look like the kinda man who'd take that risk . . . or am I wrong?"

"Oh no he didn't!" William shouted. *"Master, show these fools their folly.
Decapitate this guy for threatening our friends."*

Kiru grimaced but held his blades back for now. This strange dwarf was right.
Kiru wouldn't risk his friends dying. Maybe he'd have been more willing to take
a risk if Brunhilda hadn't had a trollstone collar on, but he knew they wouldn't
be able to heal any serious injuries without her direct aid. "Who are you, and what
do you want?" Kiru asked.

The dwarf looked mockingly affronted at the question. "Why, sir! That be
awfully rude of ye. Yer friends and ye intrude in our territory, destroy me second-
favorite pillar in this desert, and kill two of me men. Now, ye got a pair on ye to
demand answers from me! Pfft! He clearly doesn't know who we be, boys!" The
dwarf laughed, and his men joined in, flashing the psion a sea of cruel smiles.

Kiru took a quick disliking to the dwarf.

The dwarf turned his head back to Kiru, his smile now replaced with a scowl.
"Lemme speak plainly, boy. Ye have nothing we need, and we got ye by the balls,
along with yer pals over there. So, surrender and put on these collars," he said,
raising a pair of trollstone collars just like the ones on Brunhilda and Zhaden.
"Or we'll gut yer friends right in front of ye."

Kiru clenched his jaw. They were caught, and just like the pirate said, he had no leverage. "Mutt," he said, turning his head to look at his friend.

"Yeah, Boss?" Mutt asked.

"Come here."

"But, Boss—"

"Now, Mutt," Kiru interrupted aloud, then clenched his jaw as he sent, *"This is the only way to keep Brunhilda alive for now. We'll figure something else out later."*

Mutt had his mouth open to say something else but quickly closed it. He nodded solemnly, then walked over.

Two gray-skinned men walked up behind their rather-smug dwarf leader and took the collars and cuffs from him. They then reached over and snapped each of the collars around Mutt and Kiru's necks. When that happened, Mutt's body slackened. His hair and nails shrunk as he gave an exhausted sigh.

Since Kiru was completely dependent on mana to move his disabled body, the psion went limp and fell to the sand. He couldn't even hear William speaking inside his mind.

"Are ye serious?! Yahahaha!" The dwarf laughed along with his subordinates. "The boy can't even handle a little trollstone!"

Mutt quickly knelt down and cradled Kiru's head. He was about to carry the psion in his arms, but the dwarf pirate spoke up again. "Hey, what ye be doin' there?"

"I . . . need mana to move." Kiru reluctantly answered.

"Pfft! What a bunch of whale shite," the gray dwarf scoffed. He drew his blade and pointed it at Mutt. "Ye there, orc. Drop this lying bastard and let 'im walk on his own two feet. That's an order."

"Uh, what?" Mutt asked, clearly confused.

"I said that's an order, slave!" the dwarf shouted and swiped his blade across Mutt's face, cutting his cheek and forcing him to drop Kiru to the ground. The dwarf then pointed his cutlass at Kiru. "Cease this charade, boy. My men and I don't like carryin' 'round dead weight, savvy?"

"I. Can't. Move." Kiru replied, emphasizing each word.

"Liar!" the dwarf shouted, then stomped hard on Kiru's calf. He growled and furrowed his brow when the psion didn't respond in pain. In his frustration, he stomped down again and again to no avail.

"I'm telling you the truth!" Kiru protested.

"Are ye now?" the dwarf asked through gritted teeth before stomping one more time on Kiru's leg.

There was a loud *snap*, and the psion's leg bent at an unnatural angle, now fully broken.

"Are you serious!?" Kiru asked angrily, though he didn't respond in pain to the clearly serious injury, an unintended perk of his lack of sensation.

The dwarf just stared in shock. "Blimey, ye were tellin' the truth, boy," he said as he leaned over Kiru. "It be as I said, though. We don't like carryin' dead weight, 'specially not some sickly limp noodle like yerself."

Kiru sighed. "So you'll take off this collar?"

"Oh, aye. After yer dead." He raised his cutlass with the seeming intention of stabbing Kiru straight through the neck.

Kiru's eyes widened, and his heart fluttered in his chest, unable to process what was about to happen. Had he failed? Was he going to die and leave his friends to be enslaved?

He closed his eyes and was about to shout that he was sorry to his allies, when Brunhilda screamed, "Parley!"

"Hm?" The pirate stopped his blade and looked over to her.

"I invoke the rite of parley. Ye be pirates, right? Nautical creed dictates that ye cease hostile actions and bring us before your captain," the paladin said.

"I know what parlay be, missy!" the dwarf snapped back. "It be clear, though, that ye don't." He raised up a crooked finger. "First, ye either must be a pirate or represent an organization that owns a vessel of their own to invoke such a thing." He raised another finger. "Second, just like what I told limp noodle here—" He kicked Kiru in the side for emphasis. "—ye got to have something I want: leverage. Ye clearly don't have that."

A third finger went up and his face turned deadly serious. "Yer not knowin' what yer askin' for when invoking parley with the Swordstrike Corsairs. Trust me when I say, ye don't want to see our captain. He's not as . . . pleasant as I am."

That painted a grim picture for Kiru. *This dwarf snapped one of my legs like a toothpick, and his captain is even more unpleasant?* Kiru thought.

Brunhilda wasn't deterred. She held her head up high and said, "I be Brunhilda Gertrude Lightsworn, niece to Jayson Craig Lightsworn, head jeweler and one of the three main leaders of the Merchant Federation in Stonereach. Our lives be of value and our deaths would bring about even more 'unpleasantries' than your captain can provide, sir."

Kiru was caught off-guard by how smooth and confident she sounded. Brunhilda was by far the worst liar of the group, some would say honest to a fault. *So, for her to say something so quickly and without a hint of doubt, she has to be telling the truth,* Kiru thought.

Brunhilda had told the group that her uncle was a merchant who specialized in rare gems, so that tracked. She hadn't said that he worked for the Merchant Federation, though. The Merchant Federation was a unique entity in its own. They were the undeniable top sellers and distributors of goods throughout the continent. Sure, there were other independent merchants, but none could compete with the Federation. Kiru didn't have any personal experience with them, but he'd read about them when he was at the academy library.

The stories weren't *all* good, though. The Federation was competitive—even downright hostile when it came to making sure they had the best supply of goods. Rumors of bribes, illicit materials, and sudden unaccounted for "disappearances" of their rivals abounded. Kiru had heard stories about a dwarven criminal business as a child. After finding the Federation's symbol in a tome at school, Kiru had at once realized that he'd seen it before. They were business partners with Vincent Constantine, the duke of Kiru's hometown of Bristleton. The Federation received half of all their metal ore from the mines at no doubt a discounted rate. Kiru had heard more than one disgruntled miner grumbling that the duke was receiving an extra "incentive" for the deal. *Given how rotten Ambrose was, I can't help but assume they were right,* he thought.

The dwarf pirate's face broke out into a crooked grin at Brunhilda's words. "Oh, the Federation? Haven't gotten to fight a Federation ship in quite some time." He turned to his men. "Ye hear that, boys? The lass thinks the Federation be scarier than our captain."

All the gray-skinned pirates grinned and shot each other knowing looks. Mutt furrowed his brows in anger while Zhaden flicked his eyes back and forth, seeming to try and find a way to escape.

The dwarf then snapped his head to glare right at Brunhilda with his beady, bloodshot eyes. "Why don't we show her just how wrong she be? What do ye say?!"

His men raised their weapons and shouted in approval.

"Alright, lass, ye will get yer audience. I, Hagish Saltbeard, first mate of *The Marauding Citadel*, accept yer plea for parley."

CHAPTER SIX

The Marauding Citadel

Kiru let out a quiet sigh of relief after Saltbeard accepted Brunhilda's plea, realizing then just how close he had come to dying. The psion then heard the dwarf pirate order his monstrous-looking men to carry the members of Pandemonium to their base, which was also in a cave. In Kiru's case specifically, they dragged his limp and broken body across the ground and into the cave. When they reached it, it was about ten feet tall and just wide enough to fit two people across, so they had to squeeze together when confined inside. The cultivators' nostrils were struck with the scents coming off the pirates. They smelled of body odor, salt, alcohol, and brimstone.

They soon discovered that the cave was in fact a tunnel as it began to turn into a descending, winding path. As they went down, the light went out altogether, and it was pitch black. Kiru knew it wasn't a problem for any of them except Zhaden, as the drakonid didn't possess any kind of darkvision.

They carried their prisoners easily as they moved single file. Kiru was in the back, and his bone-plate armor scraped against the stone below. Hagish drifted back to walk beside the prone Kiru, mocking and questioning him about his weakness. When he didn't answer and simply kept his head down, their insults started turning into cruel beatings. They kicked, cut, and punched Kiru all over, asking repeatedly if he could feel it. One kick in particular left a nasty wound on Kiru's cheek, causing a small, steady stream of blood to run down his face and body. While Kiru couldn't feel most of the blows, some of the strikes still caused him to cough. Once he even got the wind knocked out of him and was scared he wouldn't be able to breathe.

Brunhilda turned and protested that, under parley rules, they were not to harm Kiru.

Both Zhaden and Mutt bared their teeth to reinforce her point.

Hagish gave a crooked smile and told her that, since their prisoner couldn't feel anything, how could they be doing him harm?

The paladin tugged hard on the chain connected to her collar, yanking an unsuspecting pirate off his feet and making him fall face-first on the ground. Before anyone else could react, she wrapped her chain around the downed pirate's throat and gripped it tight. The thug let out a pained cough as she choked him. "Stop hurting him right now, or yer subordinate will pay the price."

"Oh, so ye be the one who'd break the parley, aye? What's to stop me from slitting his throat right now?" Saltbeard asked.

Mutt growled audibly, and his muscles tensed at the threat.

"I've got no patience to bandy words with ye," Brunhilda replied. "Ye know what ye be doing. Quit playing on technicalities. Leave my friend alone until we've spoken with yer captain and I'll release yer man here."

Saltbeard's cruel smile turned into a scowl. "Careful, lass. If ye keep givin' lip like that, I'll make sure yer end is nice and slow after yer parley is done," he threatened before nodding to his subordinate to leave Kiru be.

Brunhilda released her pirate in kind.

The man gasped and wheezed in a lungful of air as he rolled onto his back in relief. To Brunhilda's shock, Hagish stomped over, pulled the man's cutlass from his sheath, and stabbed him in the gut, impaling him to the ground.

The pirate screamed in pain. Every time he moved, the blade cut more into his flesh.

Hagish glared right at Brunhilda. "It'll be just like that. Savvy?"

She nodded before rejoining the formation, Hagish himself now gripping her chain, and with that, they continued down the tunnel to the echoing cries from the impaled pirate they left behind.

A chill ran up Kiru's neck at hearing his moans and pleas, the man eventually just begging for someone to end his suffering. That, coupled with the darkness of their surroundings, made Kiru truly grasp the cruelty of these corsairs. Thanks to the trollstone, the psion couldn't even communicate with William to provide him a mental escape, either. After a couple of more horrifying minutes in the dark, scream-filled tunnel, they all eventually started to see light off in the distance. They made a turn around the bend and were finally out. Kiru saw that they were in a large cove.

They were looking down on it from above at the top of a set of stairs that led to the beach below. Kiru was trying to keep his breathing steady so he didn't pay attention to every single detail of the place. Still, there were things about the area that were hard to ignore. There were many pirates moving about the beach, most of them walking away from a large, blood-stained pit dug into the sand below. The brown stone of the cove was porous, but it wasn't due to it being worn down by nature. No, breaking through various sections of the stone were random sections of buildings made of pure white marble. Some columns, a couple of walls with window holes, and even a section of a domed roof or two was visible. The marble appeared to meld seamlessly with the other stone as if they had been melted together.

The strange cove wasn't the most eye-catching thing, though. That belonged to the ship that was docked not far from the water's edge. Surprisingly, what looked to be numerous columns, walls, windows, and sections of buildings appeared in various locations on top of the vessel. It was the largest water vessel they'd ever encountered.

The wooden boat looked to be at least a thousand feet tall and half as wide. The length of the ship was even greater—a quarter of a mile, by Kiru's estimation. More than a dozen masts with multiple sails were adorned on its top with actual buildings interspersed in between them. Right in the center of the wooden vessel was a tower that stood taller than all the others. It was also made of solid white marble. Hundreds of gray-skinned pirates of various races were moving about, deconstructing various tents on the beach and taking smaller boats to get back to the domineering vessel anchored a few hundred feet out.

Kiru's mouth was wide open in utter shock. He could see that Zhaden had stopped moving too, his body eerily still as he took in the ship, until a corsair yanked on his chains to resume moving. *The Marauding Citadel* had sounded too grandiose a name at first when he had heard it, but now, he knew that it was perfect. Along the sides of the ship was the same massive painting of a giant black sword stabbing into a simple-looking red face with a pained expression. It was rather unsettling to see.

Hagish looked out to the ship with pride. "Ain't she a beaut, lads?"

"Aye, sir," the pirates all answered in unison.

The gray-skinned dwarf then turned to his prisoners. "Ye lot were good-enough fighters, so I would've let ye join the fighting pit below with the other slaves," he said, pointing to the large hole dug into the sand. The pirate then pointed a stubby finger at Kiru. "But after yer insistin' on keeping the limp noodle here and invoking parley, yer gonna wish ye had chosen the pits instead. Bind and gag 'em, boys."

Before the party could respond, the pirates holding their leashes shoved some nasty cloths into each of their mouths and secured them there with rope, which they then used to bind their wrists together. Then, Hagish began descending the stairs to the sand below. His men quickly followed, deciding to drag Kiru's compatriots along with him in another display of cruelty. The party, aside from Kiru, bucked and kicked but couldn't get themselves free. They continued to be pulled across the sand and to the water.

When they got to its edge, Kiru noticed Mutt's sharp canines actually were now cutting through the rope, but he wasn't able to spit out his gag before they tied another one over him. The pirates then promptly shoved a yellow powder up Mutt's nostrils on Saltbeard's orders. The blind orc sneezed and coughed in surprise, forcing it deep into his nostrils. After a couple seconds, he went limp and collapsed into unconsciousness.

So, at their captor's orders and a prod from an overly excited pirate's cutlass, they were all forced onto a small boat about as long as a canoe. It looked like the hundred other vessels that were going back and forth from the beach and *The Marauding Citadel*. While the others walked to the boat, Brunhilda being only tall enough to keep her head above water, Hagish had Kiru dragged up, submerging the psion's entire body in the water. Kiru bucked and fought to keep himself from drowning, but just before he was about to have to breathe in the salty seawater, he was unceremoniously thrown into the small boat. Kiru sucked in a deep breath of air from his nostrils as he lay prone on the small vessel.

Fortunately, Hagish appeared to be done with his antics for the moment and left Kiru to recover. The gray-skinned dwarf did look down at the shoreline where Kiru had been dragged, though. "Ye may not be able to feel anything, limp noodle, but ye sure do bleed like a stuck pig," he said remarking at the trail of blood that went across the sand and had pooled in the water by the boat before it was quickly washed away. Saltbeard's men chuckled at the dwarf's comment.

Though still bound and gagged, Brunhilda caringly helped Kiru sit up and held him to ensure he didn't fall back down. She grunted a question to Kiru, unable to speak from the gag in her mouth.

Kiru gathered from her looking at his awkward bending leg, that she was asking if he was okay. He nodded, only feeling the sting of his cheek where he was kicked earlier. It had been bleeding, but the saltwater seemed to have helped stop it. Now that they weren't being pushed forward at a forced march, Kiru was able to breathe a bit easier. Still, their situation was dire. They were without their powers and being taken to a literal mobile aquatic fortress. He bit down on his disgusting gag in frustration as he realized just how hard it was going to be to escape. Kiru also felt a bit empty as he missed William's voice inside his mind. Though the imp could be irritating, he was a part of Kiru—the literal fire inside him—and despite his issues, he'd been with Kiru longer than anyone.

However, Kiru did give a slight grim chuckle to himself when he heard one of the pirates on a nearby boat discussing with another that they'd heard that the *Citadel* was heading south. Though he would have *never* chosen to get aboard the pirate ship willingly, it seemed they were going to be taking the psion in the direction he needed to go anyway. *Maybe I'll find a cure for my injured core after all.* He did wonder though how exactly the ship moved. Sure, it had multiple sails, but the psion was reluctant to believe that it relied on wind power alone.

As they got closer, Kiru's question was answered. Along the bottom of the massive ship was a large groove with evenly spaced square holes. He noticed oars pulled in and lying on the grooves. Kiru's eyes widened as he deduced what they were for. *They're for their prisoners and slaves to row and propel the ship.* Kiru assumed, based on the pirates' overall cruelty and the fact that Saltbeard had mentioned fighting pits, that he and his friends weren't the first prisoners that had been captured. Kiru couldn't help but wonder how many poor souls were locked deep in the ship's bowels. Given the size of *The Marauding Citadel*, likely thousands.

The sleeping Mutt started to stir.

Hagish scowled in annoyance and ordered his men to "powder 'em all."

Before Kiru could protest, a gray-skinned orc reached into a small clay jar and slapped him in the face with its contents. Yellow powder went straight up Kiru's nostrils, and the psion rapidly fell into unconsciousness.

Kiru awoke, head aching. He wasn't sure how long he had been out, but he knew it had to be at least a few hours, as the sky's hue was now pink, indicating that the sun was setting. He found himself strapped down with his back against one of the large masts atop the hulking ship. The psion knew his trollstone cuffs were still attached as he still couldn't move or hear William inside his mind. Kiru turned his head to see the faint outline of two of his friends strapped down along with him. Zhaden was to his left and Brunhilda to his right.

"You awake now, Boss?" Mutt asked. Kiru couldn't see him but he sounded close, so the psion assumed he was on the other side of the mast.

"Yeah. Yeah, Mutt," he answered.

"Phew! Good thing. We were getting worried, weren't we?" Mutt said.

"Aye," Brunhilda confirmed.

"Indeed," Zhaden added.

Kiru was glad that all his friends were alright. Then he focused on his own body. One of his legs was still bent at an unnatural angle which made him wince when he saw it. He desperately wanted to realign the bone, but he couldn't do anything about that for now. Kiru then took a better look at their surroundings. He had to fight back a gasp—they truly were in the middle of what appeared to be a sprawling city on top of the boat. The name *Marauding Citadel* seemed to become more and more appropriate as he took in the vessel.

Kiru could see multiple multitiered apartment complexes, a building with a trail of meat-scented smoke wafting out from one of its windows, and what appeared to be a brothel. Numerous limestone structures that looked like posh homes were dotted throughout. There was also that marble tower that Kiru had spotted earlier from the cove. It had only one inconspicuous door at the bottom and a round, flat platform with a small point sticking out from its very center at the top, as if the tower had impaled a disc made of the same material as itself. Kiru didn't know what exactly it was about the building, but it made him feel very uneasy.

The psion noticed at least a hundred pirates moving about the different buildings up top. There were also some people without the telltale gray skin the Swordstrike Corsairs had. All of them wore shackles of some sort and their bodies were covered with wounds and bruises. Those whose faces didn't have looks of absolute despair were blank and devoid of emotion. All those people were doing some sort of laborious task or being dragged about by one of the pirates. It was clear that they were slaves and some of them had evidently been so for a long time.

"How long was I out? Can you catch me up on anything I missed?" Kiru asked his friends.

The three obliged. Apparently, they had awoken not long before he did, presuming that about five or six hours had passed since they'd been knocked out. Apparently, Saltbeard had also stopped by earlier and told them they would be seeing the captain "soon." The first mate added that it would be after he found someone to "wake the captain up."

Zhaden had noted also that the dwarf had cackled to himself before walking off toward the brothel, and the way he had said it had made them all wary.

Both Brunhilda and Mutt echoed that sentiment.

"He be a right creepy one," Brunhilda said.

The four cultivators just stayed there, strapped against one of the ship's masts. They tried to break free by squirming out or just by sheer force of will, but nothing was working. They had to try and do so when no one was directly observing them, too, which was admittedly difficult given the sheer number of people on board. Kiru did learn that part of Zhaden's tail was free, however, which did spark some hope and gave him an idea.

Before he could act on it, though, the smooth weather they'd experienced so far abruptly changed. There had been a gentle breeze pushing against the sails this entire time, but then it violently shifted. Despite there being no clouds in the sky, lightning crackled and struck. It wasn't normal lightning, either. Purple bolts sparked across the sky, and instead of fading in a flash, they seemed to freeze in place, illuminating the sky. Bolt after bolt repeated in this fashion.

Kiru looked over to Brunhilda to see if she knew what was going on, but based on her own bewildered look, she seemed to be as clueless as he was. Amidst the cacophony of dozens of lightning bolts striking mere seconds apart, Kiru heard one of the corsairs shout, "Gaarvstorm!" The party tensed as bells rang in alarm throughout the deck of *The Marauding Citadel*. Windows were instantly boarded up as people ran about in a panic to find shelter in the nearest building. Many of the pirates openly abandoned their slaves, giving their charges the opportunity to flee. None did, however, and Kiru could see them sprinting desperately in the directions of their masters, seeking the same shelter.

Lightning continued to strike, and the sails of the large masts were quickly drawn up, the corsairs struggling against the strong wind. Kiru was impressed by the pirates' efficiency and strength. The lightning bolts suddenly all concentrated until they formed a large ring that covered a large section of the sky.

"Brunhilda, what is a gaarvstorm?" Mutt asked, shouting against the wind.

Kiru was going to ask her the same. With the dwarf having close family who would risk these waters, she was their best source of information about any of the place's unnatural weather phenomena.

"It be a big ball of wind and thunder," Brunhilda shouted in answer.

Kiru looked back to the center of the ring. As if on cue, he noticed the wind gathering in the center of the ring, condensing into a spinning orb at least a hundred feet tall. The orb spun faster and faster.

"It be a good thing we be tied to this mast," the dwarf said.

"Why is that?" Kiru asked.

"Because—" Before she could finish, the lightning bolts immediately shifted.

All at once, they all turned downwards and struck the ocean in unison. Kiru closed his eyes reactively to the large flash of light from the impact. He then grimaced as the sound of dozens of bolts of lightning striking at the same time threatened to deafen him. He shook some of the ringing out of his ears and opened his eyes as soon as he felt the strong breeze he'd been feeling shifting directly *at* him. He gasped as he saw the water that had been forced upward from the lightning strikes flying directly towards the ship, each droplet containing a visible spark of purple electricity.

"Brace yourselves!" he shouted to his friends before closing his eyes and turning his head away. He knew there wasn't much they could do since they were all tied to the mast with him, but even averting their eyes and raising their shoulders to cover their necks could help.

Despite not being able to look at any of his friends directly, he trusted that the other members of Pandemonium had all done the same. Within seconds of his warning, *The Marauding Citadel* was hit with the full force of the gaarvstorm. Kiru's head was slammed against the mast, the pain of which threatened to send him back into unconsciousness, but he held on. He grunted in agony more than once as his face was struck by innumerable pellets of electrified water. And that was much less than the constant cries of discomfort Brunhilda and Zhaden let out. Even though Kiru was undoubtedly taking the brunt of the storm due to his position on the mast, the lack of physical sensation was saving him a lot of pain. Mutt was the luckiest of the group as his position behind the mast spared him much of the shock that his friends experienced.

The force of the wind battered him while the ropes held him in place—but then he felt fear flash through his gut. With his hands pinned down by the ropes, he couldn't secure his enchanted headband. The psion felt it being forced off of his head by the winds' strength. "No. No." He grunted, desperately trying to maneuver his head to keep it on, but it was to no avail. Only after a couple of seconds of him noticing it starting to loosen, it was gone, blown away so quickly and so far that Kiru lost sight of it. "NO!" he screamed, fear filling him. It had been blessed by the goddess Hlin to provide him extra protection and was a powerful boon.

Kiru bunched his lips in frustration and torment as he was still being struck by the crackling water. The strong, electrified, watery wind obscured much of the psion's vision, but he saw that his fate could've been much worse as a few humanoid forms flew past him. A couple of slaves and even a corsair too drunk or unlucky to find shelter were being carried away by the storm. The cries of multiple people in distress could easily be heard despite the fierce howling of the wind. Kiru was even struck in the chest by an unfortunate fish who'd been forced out of the water by the storm.

The strong and furious winds of the gaarvstorm continued for a minute straight, the force of the blast causing the entire massive ship to sway. Much of the wood creaked, but the vessel held strong against the storm's might. Then, as suddenly as the storm had appeared, it was gone. The ship, no longer being pushed by the wind, leaned back and crashed against the water, sending a sizable wave up from the impact.

After the *Citadel* settled, Kiru looked around. The sky instantly cleared, revealing the stars above. No wind was present either, so the massive ship was just floating about, not going in any particular direction anymore. The only evidence of the storm's passing at all were the erratic waters and the damage to the city structures on top of the ship's deck—of which there was plenty. Windows that hadn't been covered up in time were shattered, small puddles filled with crackling purple electricity were scattered everywhere, and more than a few broken, mangled corpses were spread around. Many of those unfortunate victims were slaves and most of their bodies weren't in one piece. Only a couple of sails hadn't been pulled up in time either, as evidenced by them still being down and torn to shreds.

Kiru did see the corpses of a couple of corsair nearby and noticed their cutlasses still on their belts. That did spark an idea in his head as to how to escape, but first, he needed to check on his friends.

"Is everyone alright?" Kiru asked.

The others all gave confirmation that they were okay.

"Oh no, Kiru, yer headband," Brunhilda said, looking at the psion's now-bare forehead.

He nodded. "Yeah, the storm was too much, and I couldn't grab onto it to hold it down."

Zhaden spoke up then, his tone more panicked. "What about your gemstone? Surely, one of these pirates will see the Ruby now and try to take it. Or worse, they may start to wonder about our true identities. We can't afford to be found out," he hissed.

Kiru grimaced at that. "That is a real danger," he said before an idea came to him. He lowered his head and shook it. His hair had grown long and had lost the red tinge at its tips. It was now solid black. Kiru's headband had kept it tamer and out of his eyes, but with that gone now, he could use his hair to at least partially cover the gem embedded in his forehead. "There. It's not a perfect solution, but it's probably the best we have right now."

"You said that your uncle travels these waters, Brunhilda?" Zhaden asked. "I must ask, why would he risk such danger if what we experienced is commonplace?"

"The Federation only rarely sails these waters—only twice a year at most. Still, that be a lot more than anyone else. The only reason the Federation even does it at all be because they charge a ridiculous amount of coin to do so."

Mutt shook his shaggy mohawk free of water before speaking. "But I gotta ask, why? I still bet it would be even faster to just send stuff over land."

Brunhilda gulped nervously before answering. "That be because, according to rumor, the Federation has dealings that aren't always . . . 'legal,'" she said, making air quotes with her bound hands as best she could. "Sailing through the Torn Empire may not be faster, but it ain't regulated either. Ye could say, me uncle be the black sheep of my clan," she admitted.

"Oh, so instead of being noble and devout cultivators like most of your family, he opted to be a businessman with ties to the black market?" Mutt asked, tone ambivalent—though Brunhilda flushed with embarrassment.

There was, however, a tense pause, since the other three understood.

"Aye," Brunhilda said. "Many have cut ties with Jayson, but my father has a . . . tenuous peace with him."

"Oh, okay," Mutt answered, still not picking up on her unease.

"Anyway," Kiru said, trying to change the subject, "I've got a plan to hopefully help us escape, so listen close." The psion quickly went over his idea, and the others agreed it was their best shot.

Kiru was about to start enacting it when Saltbeard came down one of the streets of the *Citadel*, a scowl on his face. He wasn't alone, however; the gray-skinned dwarf sat upon the shoulders of a cyclops, riding the monster as a mount. The cyclops was bound in chains and had multiple blades sticking out of its body, its mouth grimacing from constant pain. Kiru couldn't help but grimace too, mostly because where its singular eye should have been was a massive empty socket with a large blade jutting out of it. Not only was the poor creature in constant pain from the blades embedded in its skin, but it had been blinded as well.

The Marauding Citadel's first mate glowered at all the people running about the streets of the ship's deck and bellowed out orders to both corsair and slave alike. The dwarf looked up towards a banner lying limply at the top of a nearby mast. Seeing that it showed no evidence of a breeze, he stood up on the monster's back and shouted, "Man the oars!"

All the corsairs stopped for a moment before many of them quickly scurried up onto the roofs of some of the smaller buildings. Each roof had a large chest on top, and from each one, each of the pirates pulled out a large, oddly curved horn. One by one, they each blew, letting out a deep but somehow squeaky noise. They continued blowing their horns until the entire *Citadel* echoed with a strange cacophony.

Mutt growled in protest, his sensitive ears not enjoying the noise. It continued until a subtle drumbeat echoed from below. Then, remarkably, the hulking behemoth that was *The Marauding Citadel* began to move, clearly the result of Saltbeard's command. Kiru was stunned and intimidated by the fact that they had enough captured people on the oars to move the massive ship.

After it started going, the pirates started walking about the streets once again, focusing on cleaning up and repairing any visible damage—or, rather, forcing their bound slaves to do the work. Bloodstains were being scrubbed, glass was being swept, and even new wooden planks were being replaced. *As far as I've learned, the Empire is mostly desert, ocean, and some islands, right? How do they have so much wood to build this place, let alone do upkeep?* Kiru wondered. Though they were cruel slavers, Kiru couldn't help but be impressed with the corsairs' efficiency and sheer diversity. He'd seen humans, dwarves, elves, orcs, and even goblins amongst the crew. They all had that strange gray skin and monstrous-like alterations to their faces, though, so he knew there was something truly "off" going on here.

Despite their distance, Saltbeard locked his beady eyes with Kiru and gave him a malicious grin. Kiru could see him mouth the words "dead weight." He looked like he was about to force his mount to stomp over in their direction when a rather curvy corsair woman opened the door from a nearby building that Kiru presumed was some sort of brothel and started calling to him. The dwarf's focus immediately shifted to her, and his grin changed from one of malice to one of lust. Hagish kicked the cyclops and the monster groaned as it went to its knees and lowered its neck. The first mate slid off the cyclops, still holding its reins in hand and landed before the voluptuous woman before him with a bow. She gave him a suggestive smile and gestured for him to follow her in.

To Kiru's surprise, the dwarf tied the chains bound to the cyclops to a nearby wooden pole as if it were a simple horse before running into the brothel. The monster's mind was clearly broken, though, as Kiru didn't doubt it could've easily gotten free had it wanted to, but it instead stayed still with its palms and knees on the deck.

Since the dwarven pirate was no longer focusing on him, Kiru breathed a sigh of relief. Everyone else was running about, cleaning and repairing the ship. The corsairs seemed to not care about the dead as the psion saw them unceremoniously throwing corpses off the ship's deck and into the ocean. With Saltbeard no longer directly focusing on the party, Kiru started with Phase One of his plan. *Time to get one of the pirates closer.*

Unbeknownst to anyone aboard *The Marauding Citadel*, they weren't the only things traveling across the waters of the Torn Empire that night. When the psion had been dragged underwater, the blood that had dripped from him had sent a message across the ocean. An unseen force drew on the blood, and it surged across the water, picking up speed as it zoomed across hundreds of miles of ocean until it finally reached its destination: the mouth of a sea creature. When it tasted the blood, the monster's eye snapped open wide and let out a deep and baleful cry that was equal parts despair and madness, echoing out for miles. Those who served the creature matched their master's distress. The water vibrated as it sent out an order to them. Despite their anguish, they quickly complied with fervor.

They would find the source of this blood, and they would bring it to their master. Only then could they share their sorrow with all.

CHAPTER SEVEN

Vatrenex

Kiru's plan didn't get off to the smashing success he'd hoped for. Throughout the night, he'd pleaded to many of the corsairs rushing by to get his friends and him some water to no avail.

One thing he noticed was that he had started to feel a mystical tug despite his cuffs still being on. His core seemed to be connecting with . . . something off in the distance. Something that the ship was getting closer to. Having experienced that sensation before, only more mildly, Kiru instantly understood it had to be the liquid mental mana his father had told him about. No other explanation made sense. The possibility of finally fixing his core reinvigorated him.

Most of the corsairs either continued to ignore or threw insults at him for his repeated water requests. A couple of times, someone threw their ale at him and mockingly asked if he was still thirsty. Fortunately, none of them paid any mind to the ruby visibly embedded in Kiru's forehead; his hair seemed to be doing a good-enough job of hiding it. It wasn't until early morning when the sun's light had just started to crest over the horizon that Kiru was able to finally convince one of the clearly-very-hungover pirates to give him and his friends a spoonful of water. The monstrous-looking elf slurred that she would only do so if Kiru would shut up to spare her the headache he was causing her. The psion gladly agreed.

The members of Pandemonium had been stripped of most of their equipment before they had woken up to their current predicament, so they had nothing to cut the rope binding them to the mast. Kiru in particular had his weapons, mask, and section of bone armor that covered his torso removed, exposing his gaunt form. He still had his storage ring from his mother, but without access to mana, it was effectively just a simple piece of jewelry at this point.

While thinking about their own lack of equipment, Kiru was reminded of the blades that the corsairs carried. He quietly started discussing them with Zhaden, who was by far the most paranoid of the team ever since their time at the academy. Because of that, he was also the most observant. He whispered to Kiru that he recognized that every one of the Swordstrike Corsairs had at least a cutlass strapped to their belt, confirming Kiru's suspicions.

So, when Kiru was drinking his water, he made sure to be as loud and distracting as possible. The pirate scowled, expression turning into disgust at his exaggerated moans of pleasure while slurping it down. Meanwhile, Zhaden surreptitiously removed the pirate's cutlass from her belt with just his tail.

Then, the pirate proceeded to give each of the cultivators a spoonful of water without noticing her weapon was gone, and pointed a finger at Kiru, threatening to come back with the knockout powder if he so much as made another peep. The psion just smiled and nodded. Suddenly, the woman ran to the edge of the ship and promptly started puking her guts up. She'd clearly been hitting the booze too hard all night.

"Quickly," Kiru whispered to Zhaden.

The gold drakonid began very quickly cutting the braided ropes tying them down.

Just then, Mutt spoke up. "Hey Boss. We're being watched . . ."

Everyone went rigid at his words, halting all movement in order to conceal their attempt to break free.

"Where?" Kiru whispered harshly, his eyes frantically scanning from side to side.

"Mmm, look up," Mutt responded, sounding rather uncomfortable.

Slowly, carefully, they all gazed upwards. All of them let out terrified gasps at what they saw. Staring straight down at them and currently straddling the mast, upside down, were a pair of man-sized monkey-like creatures. Their limbs were too long for their frames and their heads were too small. Their bodies were covered in a layer of coarse gray fur while their bloodshot eyes and crooked sharp teeth matched that of every pirate member of the Swordstrike Corsairs.

The monkeys snarled before letting out a pair of bloodcurdling shrieks. They leapt down to the ground, one of them snatching the cutlass that Zhaden had tried to keep hidden in between his body and the mast while the other crawled over to the hungover pirate who'd just finished vomiting. The large monkey grabbed her by the hair and began to drag her over. She cried out in a mix of confusion and pain, but her protests were ignored. The one monkey came back to the other, who was now pressing the sharp blade of the stolen cutlass against Zhaden's throat.

"What are you damn dirty monkeys doing?! Lemme go," the pirate protested, not noticing that one of them currently had her sword.

The monkey who had hold of her hair clicked and trilled in response.

The corsair seemed to understand the creature, because she responded, "The prisoners?! Ah, they're fine. One of them just won't shut up. Now, lemme go or I swear that I'll cut off my hair and use my sword to gut you before making *you* wake up the captain," she threatened.

The monkey who was holding her cutlass hopped over and now pressed it against her throat.

The pirate instantly stopped moving as she looked down at her own blade. "My . . . my sword? How did you . . ."

The monkey trilled, and her eyes widened. "They stole it? No. That can't be possible. They were tied u—"

The two monkeys hissed. Then, the one who was still holding onto her hair pointed his free hand at the strange marble tower in the distance, the structure notably undamaged from the night's recent storm.

"Th-The captain?" She quivered. "That's not necessary. The prisoners didn't escape. So, no harm done, right?" she asked nervously.

The two monkeys grinned evilly. Then, together—and to Kiru's utter shock— they screamed out one word: "Vatrenex."

The Pandemonium members winced at the scream while Mutt gave a grunt of pain, sensitive ears clearly aching.

The primates' cries echoed throughout the mobile metropolis like a mixture of a declaration and a distress call, rivaling the horns that had sounded out earlier.

Everyone tensed.

The woman laid there, mouth agape in horror. Before she could say anything, though, both monkeys began dragging her across the wooden deck towards the marble tower. She began fighting desperately to break free, crying and begging to "not wake the captain." The monkeys weren't sympathetic or in the least bit deterred.

Unlike the previous call across the *Citadel* when the gaarvstorm occurred, the corsairs didn't panic and run for cover. It was quite the opposite. As if in a trance, the Swordstrike Corsairs began slowly filing out of the buildings above and from the quarters below deck to watch from the sidelines. It at first reminded Kiru of a funeral procession, but then he realized the pirates were speaking.

They were chanting, and they were saying just one word. It was the same as the monkeys had screamed: "Vatrenex." The corsairs who had gathered to watch their comrade at first started chanting low, but then their volume grew. Quickly, it turned into a loud and crazed fervor. That's when Kiru realized this was different. *This isn't like a funeral procession. No, this is some sort of sacrificial ritual.*

The dragged pirate kicked, bucked, and fought against the primates, but her strength wasn't enough. She flopped around and tried to rip her hair off her scalp to get away, but one of the monkeys backslapped her to stop. She coughed and spat a globule of blood on the right leg of her brown pants, then winced in pain. After that, she began begging and pleading for her comrades to come help her. None of them did. In fact, with their loud chanting, it was clear that they were quite pleased with the whole situation. Kiru even saw Saltbeard amongst the crowd, with his shirt off and pants half-off, giving the desperate, flailing woman a crooked grin.

"By Hlin's hardened helmet, what're they going to do to her?" Brunhilda asked.

"I don't know, Brunhilda, but it's clear that it's nothing good," Kiru answered. *I certainly don't want to get caught when we try to escape if they even treat a crewmate like some sort of sacrifice,* he thought.

Both the psion and dwarf continued to watch in horror and fascination at what was happening to the woman. Zhaden was on the other side so couldn't see what was happening. Kiru did hear Mutt wincing at the screams of pain, though, the orc likely "seeing" through his sense of touch.

After another minute, the chanting rose to a frenzy and at such a volume that the party couldn't hear anything else. The entire ship shook and rattled at the cries. Then, when the monkeys had finally made it to the tower's base, one of them grabbed the gray-skinned woman by her left wrist. The monstrous primate bit her hand with its sharp teeth, drawing a surprising amount of blood. The corsair screamed and tried to fight back by drawing her fist back to punch the monkey, but the other primate grabbed her wrist before she could do so.

Then, they picked her up and placed her injured palm against the white stone, deliberately smearing her blood across the marble. The carved stone doorway suddenly opened, and an odd pulse of energy surged out from it. It washed over everyone above deck, including the tied-up members of Pandemonium. Kiru recoiled slightly as the energy went through him. It felt . . . oddly familiar. It somewhat reminded him of mental mana, but it somehow left a . . . taste in his mouth. He didn't know how, but felt bitter and rotten, like something corrupted was emerging from within. It put Kiru even more on edge than he already was.

The last thing the psion saw of the injured corsair was her being thrown through the dark doorway. Her cries of fear and pain were suddenly cut short as the stone closed behind her with a resounding boom.

The mad chanting immediately stopped. *The Marauding Citadel* was eerily quiet, the only sounds that could be heard that of the waves and wind. It was as if everything was holding its breath. For minutes, all the pirates stared at the tower expectantly.

The only exception was Saltbeard, who pushed his way through the crowd and hobbled over to the Pandemonium members. "Still can't feel anythin', dead weight?" he asked Kiru before drawing out his cutlass and slamming the hilt of the blade against his forearm.

The psion just raised his eyebrows. "Does it look like I can?" he replied, doing his best to suppress his fear and not cower before the pirate. Meanwhile, fear mixed with growing excitement pulsed in his heart. He could sense they were getting closer. The ship wasn't heading directly towards the center of the Torn Empire, but they were nearing it, by his estimation. Though Kiru was unsure *how* he would get there, his resolve to get free had been boosted.

"Never hurts to make sure," the dwarf replied as he sheathed his blade.

"Oi, what be happening to that woman, ye villain? Why did those monkeys take her to that tower? What did she do?" Brunhilda asked.

Saltbeard shook his head and sighed. "There be only reason them damn monkeys would've done that to her. That woman made the greatest offense that any Swordstrike Corsair could. She lost her sword," he answered with his fingers tapping on his weapon's handle for emphasis. "Our cap'n be a cruel and bloodthirsty sort, and he has one rule 'bove all others: Never surrender yer weapon." He turned to face the marble tower. "That lass failed to keep her cutlass close, and now she be payin' the price."

The paladin gulped. "And what be that price?" she asked.

Saltbeard gave a crooked, toothy grin, "Oh, she has to go and wake the captain now. With him awake, ye will get what ye asked for, lassie. She'll disturb his slumber, and he'll come out to deal with yer little 'parley,'" he said, raising his fingers in quotations sarcastically at the word.

Kiru gulped nervously. Just then, the marble tower released another wave of corrupted energy before the door opened once again. Instead of the woman who had entered, out came a nightmarish being that made Kiru's blood run cold. At first, a gray and black sinewy arm emerged, its surface pulsating with veins of white, black, and purple light, each resembling twisted blood vessels. The hand, adorned with four sharp, luminous purple claws that looked like blades, clutched the doorway, etching four slashes into the marble.

Subsequently, the rest of Vatrenex unfolded before their eyes. Mirroring his left arm, each limb bore four glowing claws amid a dance of swirling magical lines. His skin was leathery, and the only clothing adorning his disproportionate, monkey-like limbs were a pair of tattered pants—identical to those worn by the corsair tossed into the tower, still stained with fresh blood. Vatrenex's elongated torso bore a conspicuous gouge pulsating with an eerie purple light that extended from belly to mouth.

The most unnerving aspect, however, was his head—which seemed metallic in nature, despite sharing the skin's hue. Two thick horns arched backward, culminating in sharp points. Instead of a traditional face, a helmet-like structure housed a single large red eye with a diminutive pupil. His mouth was utterly alien, split vertically rather than across. It reminded Kiru of an insect's mouth except without pincers. Then the captain yawned, revealing that the opening in his stomach was actually the bottom of his mouth, his teeth soon afterwards interlocking back in place to cover his torso.

Additionally, he wielded a formidable saber in his hand. It was nearly the size of Kiru and as black as the night, with the same pulsating lines of power as

Vatrenex's body, making the weapon appear to be organic. Towering over the onlookers at about seven feet tall, Vatrenex wielded the curved blade in his right hand, scanning the crowd with his one eye. He wasn't quite the size of an ogre, but he wasn't far off.

"Goddess' mercy," Kiru heard Brunhilda mutter under her breath, fear clear in her voice.

"Who has dared to disturb my slumber?" he bellowed, his voice deep but also multitoned. It seemed to echo, as if two people were trying to speak at once from within him. He spoke sharply and had a commanding aura. The effect was truly alien to Kiru, but just like the strange pulses he'd felt earlier, there was something . . . *familiar* about the monstrous, otherworldly captain.

Every member of the Swordstrike Corsairs on deck immediately took a knee and bowed their heads as if they were disciplined members of a traditional sect rather than the vile criminals they truly were. Any slaves they held in chains prostrated themselves, their bodies shaking in fear. Even the monkeys bowed before the captain.

"Cap'n Vatrenex," Saltbeard shouted as he stood up from a knee. "We have captured new prisoners who've petitioned for parley."

The monstrous being snapped his lone eye at the dwarf. His entire body then shifted at once to match the direction his eye was looking and began moving toward Hagish. Vatrenex swiftly began stomping over to the dwarf, his long legs' strides quickly eating up the distance, his black sword dragging across the wood of the deck, carving a furrow in the wood.

"And what is so special about them that we should even entertain a parley, Hagish?" Vatrenex spat out as he picked up the dwarf by the collar and raised the first mate up to his monstrous face. This was the first time Kiru had seen true fear on Hagish's face. The psion now understood why he had said that their captain was scary.

Understatement of the century, Kiru thought.

"She be from the Federation, sir," he hastily stuttered out in a nervous jumble.

"The Federation, First Mate? What business do we have with the Merchant Federation besides plundering and slaughtering them?" Vatrenex demanded.

Kiru noticed both Brunhilda and Zhaden tensing at the captain's words. He even heard Mutt give a barely perceptible little growl.

"The dwarf, sh-she be the niece of one of their leaders, sir. I thought—"

"You thought?!" Vatrenex interrupted. "You do not *think*, First Mate. You *do*. Specifically, you do what I tell you, and I told you to slaughter or make slaves of everyone we capture. I have no need for prisoners." With his last words, the captain angrily tossed Hagish like a doll, sending him skipping across the deck. He landed several dozen feet away, where he lay in place, groaning in pain. Now done with his first mate, the monstrous being that was Captain Vatrenex seemed to finally register the four tied up near him. Specifically, he locked onto Kiru's emaciated, broken form. The sun had now fully risen, and its rays now beamed down on all on deck, but Vatrenex's blade was still utterly devoid of any light. The captain growled, took two long steps, and got just inches away from Kiru's face.

Kiru breathed heavily through his nose, fighting back his terror. The scent of burnt ozone permeated from the captain, filling Kiru's nostrils. Just looking at Vatrenex directly in the eye was overwhelming. Kiru grunted slightly and fought these feelings as best he could, forcing himself to not cower.

"What is wrong with you? Your body is broken and . . . sickly. How are you even alive?" Vatrenex asked Kiru. The humidity from his breath was oppressive, the distinct scent of rot mixed in with the ozone.

Kiru couldn't exactly place it, but the creature seemed . . . wrong. He gave off an unstable, chaotic, and perverse energy, exuding the aura of an Emerald one moment, then that of a Silver the next. *Had he tried to ascend but failed horribly? Is he some sort of experiment gone wrong like what the cleric tried to do to Mutt back at the academy? Or is he some sort of ascended cyclops maybe?* Kiru thought rapidly as his brain tried to comprehend the being before him. Whatever the reason, the wrongness of the thing put him on edge, and he used the fear building up to fuel an angry retort. "I'm resourceful," he said through bared teeth.

"Haha! At least your spirit isn't broken. Most lesser beings tremble before my might." Vatrenex gave a hollow laugh before snapping back to be at eye level with the psion. "You are a curious one. You both nauseate and fascinate me. Tell me, what is that gem in your head?" he asked and began to lean a clawed finger in to touch the item.

"Leave him alone, ye filth!" Brunhilda spat.

Vatrenex stopped, then moved over to Brunhilda. "So, you be the one related to the Merchant Federation cowards. Tell me, what ails the sickly one?"

"Is this how ye treat those under parley? I say, ye be the cowards," the paladin retorted.

Vatrenex growled and grabbed the thick wood of the mast above the dwarf's head. His clawed hand clenched. He then pointed the tip of his massive blade to her throat. "Coward?"

"Hey, shadow asshole! Don't you tou—"

"Silence," the captain spat out, and Kiru heard him slam the pommel of his blade's handle straight into Mutt's temple. Kiru couldn't see him, but Mutt went silent, likely dazed from the strike.

"Mutt!" Brunhilda cried out, but that was quickly cut off when Vatrenex pressed his palm against her throat.

Kiru's eyes widened as the monstrous mouth on Vatrenex's torso began to open wide. He looked like he was about to literally bite Brunhilda's entire upper body off!

"My apologies for how my companions have treated you, O Great Captain Vatrenex. I will happily answer any . . . um, inquiries you may have," Kiru stuttered out. He was desperate to save his friends from this monster, and he knew from experience that those in power often liked to have their egos stroked.

Vatrenex stopped moving, and his lone red eye slowly turned to look at Kiru again. The captain let out a low growl similar to that of a cat purring and moved back to face the psion. "I see how you've stayed alive for as long as you have, Sickly One. You are the brains whereas the others are the brawn."

You have no idea, Kiru thought to himself.

"Fine, Sickly One. Answer my questions, or else I'll tear all of your friends limb from limb. For example," he said, and with a casual flick of his massive blade cut a good chunk off the tip of Zhaden's thick, scaled tail.

"Dragon piss," the drakonid hissed in pain as his tail spasmed reflexively. A stream of blood shot out, spraying all nearby. Some even landed on Vatrenex's face.

A sickly blue-green tongue as thick as Kiru's arm extended from Vatrenex's abdomen, and the captain licked Zhaden's blood and cooed, "Better hurry, Sickly One, or your troublesome friend will bleed out."

Kiru glanced to see that his friend's tail was bleeding a surprising amount from the wound. *I thought he could regrow it?* he thought. *Maybe he requires mana to replace his tail?*

Kiru's thoughts were interrupted when Vatrenex leaned in just inches from his face once more, the stench of his breath mixed with the odor of his skin nearly overwhelming him again. "Who are you? What business do you have with the Torn Empire? What use will you be to me if I spare you?"

Kiru gulped. While in Imakandi, the party had had some conversations about what to say for a convincing cover identity. Zhaden had learned during his rogue training that the best way to deceive was to mix in a bit of the truth as well. They also all knew that Brunhilda was a terrible liar, so it was best that she *didn't* do the talking. Though admittedly, Kiru was so distressed about his friend's injury, he almost completely forgot about their plans to only give half-truths. He was reminded when Zhaden said, "Tell him, sir," through gritted teeth.

Vatrenex growled at Zhaden's outburst and seemed ready to strike him again before Kiru spoke up. "Silence, servant! I'm the one speaking here!" Kiru then looked back to Vatrenex. "Now, to your question, I am the bastard son of an elf noble. I was given some sort of poison by my older sister that caused me to lose sensation in my body and caused it to waste away over time. I couldn't prove what she did, so, due to my affliction, my father disowned me despite being his only son."

Vatrenex's visage didn't change, giving the psion no indication as to whether or not he believed his story.

Kiru took a deep breath before continuing. "Before I was banished from Anor'Voren, I stole some of my father's items as well as discovered a way to work around what had happened. I now use mana to move my body." That sufficiently explained Kiru's condition and the high-quality gear they possessed while still hiding their identities and his mental mana. "Now, please, stop his bleeding, and I'll answer the rest of your questions. He won't make it otherwise," Kiru begged.

He could see Zhaden's head drooping to the side, and his movements were now sluggish as he seemed to struggle to stay conscious.

Vatrenex let out a set of clicks from his maw and turned his head ninety degrees while still facing Kiru. "Jackie! Mister!" he shouted.

A set of screeches rang out in response. Kiru turned his head to see the same two long-limbed monkeys shambling quickly over. The psion also noticed that all the corsairs were still on their knees with heads low. They were still waiting on their captain, not daring to risk his ire. The two monkeys made it over to Vatrenex, then bobbed and chittered excitedly.

"Stop the drakonid's bleeding, and get him a potion," Vatrenex ordered.

The two monkeys gave a pair of haphazard salutes before going over to the barely conscious rogue. One reached into a nearby wooden crate and pulled out a large glass jar with a white-green powder inside. It gave a sharp-toothed grin as it opened the jar, reached in to grab a handful of the powder, and slapped it straight onto Zhaden's open wound. It instantly stopped the bleeding.

The drakonid's eyes snapped open, and he shouted in pain, all traces of faintness seeming to disappear immediately. After a couple seconds of his screaming, the other monkey—Jackie, Kiru presumed based off how Vatrenex had addressed them—had shoved a potion vial straight into the rogue's mouth. Kiru could hear Brunhilda squirming a little, as she no doubt wanted to offer her services to heal but seemed too scared of Vatrenex to actually say anything. Zhaden coughed and gagged, but the monkey forced him to continue to drink. Within seconds, he seemed livelier and more energetic as health returned to him. His tail didn't regrow, but he was stabilized.

Vatrenex stabbed his black blade into the mast right by Kiru's face, obstructing his view of his friend. "He is stable, Sickly One. Now, answer. Why are these three accompanying a dying bastard elf, why are you in the Torn Empire, and why should I spare you?"

Now that Zhaden was no longer at risk of immediate death, Kiru continued with his fabricated story. "Zhaden and Mutt here are with the Twin Blades Mercenary Company. I hired them to accompany me, using enchanted equipment as compensation. Over time, we became friends." Kiru decided to go with that angle. It explained why the orc and gold drakonid were with him. Also, the Twin Blades Mercenary Company was an actual mercenary guild. It was the one run by the uncle of Joseph, the top Fist House student back at the Royal Academy. Kiru thought it was a good way to "mix in the truth."

The monstrous captain just gave Kiru a cold, blank stare, making him deeply uncomfortable. So, Kiru proceeded with his explanation in hopes that since the creature hadn't erupted into outright anger, he was on the right course. "Brunhilda is a childhood friend and has always looked out for me. We decided to go to the Torn Empire together to find rare artifacts of power and force my father to give me my birthright," he said.

Vatrenex rolled his eye. "Agh! You bore me, Sickly One. Why should I care about the desires of a petty child?"

Kiru paused for a split second. "Um, because . . . because Brunhilda's uncle is one of the leaders of the Merchant Federation, as she told you. They would certainly pay you handsomely for us to be returned unharmed. If you don't desire money, surely we can come to some sort of arrangement. What is it that you want?"

Vatrenex's vertical mouth spread wide, revealing more sharp teeth hidden deeper inside his maw. Then, he laughed. It was an unsettling thing to hear, as his hollow voice echoed and rebounded unnaturally. He dislodged his blade from the mast and placed his free hand on his belly as he continued to chortle. After a good minute of that, he composed himself and turned to face the ocean. "Corsairs!"

"Yes, sir," All on deck immediately stood and saluted in unison, with their hands pressed to their foreheads.

The captain raised his black blade and pointed to a structure off in the distance. "Make way to the wretched prison."

They all responded with an "Aye, sir," before running off in different directions as fast as they could, some to various masts to unfurl the sails, others below deck to get the slaves rowing faster. Within a few minutes, the ship had changed direction and noticeably accelerated speed.

"Jackie, Mister," Vatrenex bellowed as he walked to the edge of *The Marauding Citadel.*

The two monkeys chattered.

"Bring the sickly one to me."

The twin animals quickly loosened some knots to squeeze Kiru's thin body out from the bindings before tightening them once more to prevent the others from getting free. Kiru fell hard onto the deck, groaning and wincing as his head slammed against the wood. He barely had enough time to shake his vision clear before the two monkeys grabbed both of his limp arms and dragged him across the floor. Kiru's broken, crooked leg scraped across the wood, quickly starting to bleed.

The two monkeys then lifted the psion from under his arms and heaved him onto the guardrail. Kiru just laid there prone, only a couple of feet away from Captain Vatrenex. Kiru wasn't really focused on him, though. Instead, he was staring at the structure that the ship was quickly approaching. He *knew* that this was the center of the Empire—exactly where he needed to go. He was at once excited and frustrated. *Well, this is a double-edged sword. I've reached my goal but under the worst of circumstances,* he thought.

"Gaal'cothdreek-duun," Vatrenex said with an air of fondness.

Kiru's eyes widened as they neared. It was an island shaped like a large crescent. Unlike what he would expect from a tropical island, however, it didn't look like an oasis. Instead, it seemed to be made of coral and some strange purple metal. Grass, palm trees, and bushes had grown along the landscape. While the coral and plants looked as Kiru would have expected them to, their encroachment still couldn't conceal just how unnatural the reflective purple metal seemed to be. Also, the island's shape was . . . "off," for lack of a better term. Even from this distance, Kiru noticed three sharply pointed purple mountain peaks, their surfaces seeming to have been intentionally carved with foreign patterns. Their peaks seemed to resist the wear and passage of time.

Even without Vatrenex's words, Kiru could tell this was no mere island. These were ruins, and by his estimation from his studies at the academy, he reasoned they were at least centuries old. When he squinted, he was pretty sure he saw a round hole at the base of the ruins that looked like some sort of entrance, its perfectly round dimensions too precise to have come about naturally. Half a mile out, there was also a ring made of the same abnormal purple metal at was twenty feet tall and at least half as thick encircling the entire island. It gave the impression that it was there to keep others out—or to keep something in.

He sounds like he knows this place personally. If it really is centuries old, just how old is this pirate captain? Kiru thought to himself. Despite his growing concern, his heart raced in excitement. Even with the trollstone cuffs, his instincts reinforced that this place—Gaal'cothdreek-duun—was the very one that housed the cure for his damaged core.

Still, Kiru couldn't help but be thrown by its utterly alien look. Also, there was something else that Vatrenex said earlier. "You . . . called this place a prison. A prison for *what?*" Kiru asked, pretty sure he already knew the answer.

Vatrenex chuckled and gave the psion a grin that made him very uncomfortable. "Gaal'cothdreek-duun is a fortress that once was *my* prison. There is a magic device within that binds my brothers and me to this place. When the fortress fell to ruin, we intended to shatter that device to claim the power within." The captain then let out a low growl, his massive mouth shaking in anger, "Unfortunately, one of those cowardly arboth survived and activated the fortress' remaining defenses, forcing us out but keeping us tethered, unable to stray too far."

Kiru had just enough time to wonder what an "arboth" was when the monstrous captain raised his flashy great sword and slashed it upward. An arc of black energy was sent flying from it toward the island. It soared and seemed to be heading above the purple metal ring but broke apart as it struck a semitranslucent purple dome that suddenly covered the island, emanating from the ring. Kiru noticed a second barrier suddenly appearing in place behind the first one, reminding him of an onion with multiple layers. It looked like the outer edge of the ring projected the first barrier while the inner edge projected the second.

Vatrenex turned his lone eye to look down at Kiru. "You asked me what I want, Sickly One. I want to slaughter and dominate. I want to be free of this *Torn Empire*," he mocked. Then, he angrily slammed a fist into a nearby wooden crate, revealing all of Pandemonium's confiscated items. "I do not care for trinkets or weapons." He picked up the dragon bone armor and shoved it onto the psion's body so quickly that Kiru would've been impressed if he hadn't been so scared. He even took Kiru's mask and swords and roughly jammed them onto his belt, completely uncaring about the rare items. "Until I find one who can unlock or destroy the first barrier, I only want three things." He raised three sharp, glowing claws. "More followers, more slaves, or more tribute."

Kiru didn't want to ask, but he had to know. "Tribute for what?"

Vatrenex then gave the psion a wicked grin. At that, the clear blue water darkened. A set of roars and screeches rang out as dozens of massive tentacles surged through the water. They were so big that they even dwarfed the towering ship that was *The Marauding Citadel*, casting a shadow over the psion. "The barrier isn't Gaal'cothdreek-duun's only defense. To be granted safe passage to even go *by* it, the damned krakens require payment."

Faster than Kiru could process, Vatrenex grabbed him by the collar of his armor. "Your allies and mercenaries are . . . suitable to me. But do not worry, Sickly One. You also can give me something I want." The monstrous pirate took his gargantuan blade and deftly slashed Kiru's right check.

The psion groaned in pain, watching as his blood began spilling down into the water below. It also coated Vatrenex's blade.

The pirate captain chuckled and looked like he was about to drop Kiru when his blade pulsed like a beating heart. Vatrenex gasped as his one eye widened in shock. He shifted his long arm to move Kiru back over the deck.

"Mental mana," he said in a mixture of awe and anger. "How?"

Kiru's mouth was open. He had no clue what Vatrenex was talking about.

The captain growled. "Speak," he ordered as he squeezed tighter on Kiru's throat. Just as Kiru was about to respond, however, a horrible cry of despair sounded out from the other side of the ship, opposite where the krakens awaited. "Noooo!"

Vatrenex snapped his head back to the other side of the deck, moving Kiru back away from the water. The monstrous pirate gasped, showing the first inkling of fear the psion had ever seen on him. It only lasted a second before he replaced it with a familiar snarl and gave a low growl. "The Mourners."

Kiru turned his head to see what Vatrenex was looking at, and he furrowed his brow in confusion and also surprise. There, standing on the other side of the ship was a drakonid, his scales bleached white and his eyes bright red—an albino. The reptilian man wore only a loincloth, and his scales were covered in countless scars. In his right hand was a spear with the tip made of black and yellow bone. In Kiru's experience, drakonids didn't tend to have many facial expressions, but this albino specimen was doing a great job with his. He had a look of utter despair which seemed in sharp contrast to the confidence his muscular body and strong stance seemed to convey.

Vatrenex pointed his blackened blade at the drakonid. "How dare you trespass onto my ship? What business does your master have? Shouldn't he be off sulking in some dark corner, crying about how unfair life is? Leave now or I'll—"

The drakonid let out a scream, not seeming to have processed any of what Vatrenex had just said.

A chill ran down Kiru's neck, both due to how haunted the reptilian man sounded and the look of terror in his eyes. He was staring directly at Kiru as if he were the source of all his woes and he would stop at nothing to end him.

Vatrenex growled, his long tongue protruding from his vertical maw. "Begone," he said and swung his sword up, sending the same dark-slash technique from before at the drakonid. The slash surged forward in a blink. Remarkably, the drakonid managed to avoid being bisected, stepping to his right and only managing to lose his left arm. Despite the grievous wound, the albino drakonid wasn't fazed at all. He just lowered his bone spear and pointed it at Kiru, once again letting out an unintelligible scream.

Suddenly, a horde of people surged over the ship's deck behind the drakonid like a tide of ants emerging from an anthill that had been disturbed. People of all sorts of races followed the drakonid out. All of them were albino like him, wearing similar primitive loincloths or poor-quality hides. They all wielded various weapons of yellow and blackened bones.

"We're under attack! Corsairs, battle stations!" Vatrenex shouted. Since the pirates had already assembled on deck at their master's behest, no alarm needed to be rung. The pirates drew their cutlasses and charged forward as they shouted a battle cry.

The one-armed albino drakonid led his compatriots forward, his eyes never leaving Kiru. He changed the grip on his bone spear and hurled it with all his might before being stabbed in the gut by a corsair's cutlass. The spear's aim was true, however, and it flew right at Vatrenex.

The monstrous pirate captain was caught by surprise and struck in his right shoulder. To the psion's shock, Vatrenex was clearly in pain as a result. Seconds later, he dropped Kiru onto the deck.

The psion landed hard and winced as the back of his head bounced off the floor. The noise of battle filled his ears as literally hundreds of corsairs and the strange primitive albinos that Vatrenex had called the Mourners clashed in combat. Most of the people fighting were Silver and Gold, but there were at least a handful of Rubies as well, based off the power of their auras.

Vatrenex slammed the tip of his black blade into the ground as he took a knee. He gripped the bone spear embedded in him and broke it at the handle. The monstrous pirate's body continued to shift and distort as if both his bones and skin were made of clay in perpetual motion. The cause of his continuous morphing seemed to be the weapon stuck in him. Vatrenex would grow, shrink, become more masculine, then feminine, then seemed to be made of blocks. *What is he?* Kiru wondered. In addition to his form changing non-stop, the rank of power he gave off shifted even more erratically as well. He would seem like a Copper one moment, an Emerald the next, then blaze with the power of a Sapphire.

"Jackie! Mister!" Vatrenex called out.

In a matter of seconds, the lanky, disproportionate monkeys had made it over to their master.

"One of you, get him to the tower. I need his mana," Vatrenex said, gesturing to Kiru. "The other, get this damned bone out of me," he ordered.

Immediately, one of them grabbed Kiru by the hair and started dragging the psion roughly across the deck, staying close to the deck's edge to try and avoid the action.

Kiru gritted his teeth and did his best to fight against what was happening to him. Unfortunately, it wasn't enough. The monkey heaved with impressive strength, and more than once pulled out a small clump of Kiru's hair.

"Grr! Quit it!" Kiru barked.

It had been a good minute since the creepy simian had started dragging him across the deck, and the intensity of the fighting hadn't lessened at all. In fact, it had grown even more chaotic. Kiru had lost sight of his friends; they had still been tied to the mast, last he saw. He was scared that they had been killed but couldn't do anything to help them at the moment. He had to focus on getting away from the monkey and free himself from the trollstone before he could actually make an attempt to rescue them.

He did hear Vatrenex's shouts as he joined the fighting. Kiru even heard Saltbeard amidst the pained cries of his cyclops mount as the beast roared and trudged into the battle. Since Kiru was lying on his back on the ship's deck, his view of the fighting was severely limited. Bodies and weapons flew across the ship as the deck constantly shook amidst the fighting. The monkey was pulling him in a zigzag sort of pattern.

As Kiru thought back to what Vatrenex had said, his heart raced in growing panic and concern. Vatrenex hadn't *said* the word "psion," but it was clear from the moment he'd had his realization about mental mana that the monstrous-looking pirate captain knew something of Kiru's true identity and power. His situation was growing bleaker by the minute. He knew that he *could not* allow himself to go into that strange marble tower he was being pulled toward.

Despite his helpless situation, a primal drive pushed Kiru to fight, to do anything he could to prevent his certain doom. That was why more than once, he would jerk his head to the side, pulling against the monkey's grip. Even though most of his muscles had atrophied due to disuse over the last years, his neck was still very strong. He was still a Ruby, too. Both times he jerked, he forced the primate, stumbling and running, into a fighting cultivator. In both of those instances, the monkey—Jackie or Mister; Kiru couldn't tell the difference—managed to avoid getting injured. It would then come back and claim retribution on the psion. The first time, it just gave him a firm backhand. The second time, it bit out a chunk of his already partially cut-off ear.

Even with all of that pain, Kiru continued to frantically scan for another opportunity to thwart the simian. Despite the volume of the chaos, he gave a grimace of discomfort as he heard the monkey loudly munching away on the chunk of his ear as they were by the railing once more. All of the noise of battle was suddenly cut off at the loud sound of something striking the ship. Like with the gaarvstorm, the ship was rocked to its side slightly, which was no mean feat given that it was a city in size and scope. So, whatever hit it had to have been sizable indeed.

Despite his prone position, Kiru's eyes widened as he saw evidence of what that thing was. Tentacles at least ten feet thick and writhing about angrily emerged over the ship, dripping water onto the people below. He then remembered what Vatrenex said before the Mourner interrupted him: *The krakens require payment.*

"Oh no," Kiru said right before the massive tentacles began attacking the people of the *Citadel* indiscriminately. *Is it attacking because . . . because of my blood?*

With each swing of a tentacle, multiple people were swatted like flies, sent flying off *The Marauding Citadel* and into the water. The cries of battle and bloodlust quickly shifted into ones of panic and concern by both the Mourners and Corsairs. Amidst the cries, Kiru could hear Vatrenex: "Saltbeard, get down to the lower levels and get the slaves rowing faster!"

The psion's heart leapt slightly as he heard Brunhilda's crying out for him too. He couldn't see her, but it meant that one of his friends was still alive! Kiru didn't know what had happened to them after the fighting started, but he had feared the worst.

A good bit of the combat immediately stopped, and the people began to scatter as they had with the gaarvstorm. The horns were even sounded once again.

The monkey heaved, pulling the psion desperately as he tried to dodge both fleeing pirates and crushing tentacles. Kiru was conflicted as he didn't want to fall victim to the kraken, but he didn't want to be subjected to possible torture by Vatrenex, either. So, without thought as to what might happen, he fought even more against the monkey. Kiru managed to twist his head hard enough once as the ship rocked, which caused the monkey to stumble and get kicked square in the chest by a fleeing Mourner. The monkey screeched as it was sent flying over the deck. Kiru smirked at the creature getting sent to its doom. *Looks like the kraken will eat you instead, monkey,* he thought.

As if fate heard Kiru's thoughts, a giant tentacle blocked out the sun above him and came bearing down on him. A black slash cut through the air and cleaved the tentacle, the force of which caused the amputated section to crash down back into the water.

Vatrenex landed right beside Kiru, his one eye glaring at the psion. "You will not escape me," he growled at Kiru. His form was still alien and menacing, but he appeared notably thinner and much more exhausted than before, as he was breathing heavily. He also now only gave off the power of a Gold. As if in answer to the pirate's words, a guttural screech came from the water, more harsh and angrier than before, and four tentacles shot out from the water and above the decks with impressive speed. Vatrenex was able to raise his large blade and cut off another tentacle, but he wasn't fast enough to deal with the other three. The tentacles snapped forward like living whips, catching all in their wake.

Vatrenex, Kiru, and a nearby injured corsair were caught and lifted up, all of them now being squeezed tight by the monster. Kiru grunted. His dragon-bone armor was protecting him from serious damage, but his ability to take a deep breath was seriously impaired. As he was lifted up, his new vantage point allowed him to see that all three of his friends were fortunately unharmed and no longer bound. They had made it to the top of a pile of rubble that had used to be a building, away from most of the fighting. He could see that Saltbeard and his horrifying mount were nearby, however. The dwarf corsair's body was bruised in places, but those were the only noticeable injuries, showing he had remarkable resilience. He also saw that Brunhilda had turned and locked eyes with him. She was terrified. It was clearly not for herself but for Kiru, who was now in a sea monster's grasp.

Kiru's heart sank. *I'm done. There's no way out.*

"I'm sorry," he said.

Right at that moment, Vatrenex screamed and cut himself free.

The kraken that still had Kiru in its grasp gave a cry of pain and began to pull the psion and the other corsair it still had in its grasp down into the water before Vatrenex could use his slash technique to cut off its other tentacles. Kiru's heart seemed to leap into his throat, and tears started to well up in his eyes as he was dragged to the ocean below.

CHAPTER EIGHT

Descent

Time seemed to slow for Kiru as his body was pulled downwards and he caught sight of Brunhilda and Zhaden. The paladin's mouth was agape, sweat running down her face. The gold drakonid's reptilian eyes were open wide, and his teeth were bared in anger and terror.

Then, gravity and force took hold. Kiru's limp body began to be dragged down toward the ocean floor until he was turned upside-down. His heart raced as he descended faster and faster. Just then, his body crashed.

The force of the impact nearly knocked him out, but he managed to hold on. A second later, Kiru shook his head and blinked his eyes clear against the salty water that was stinging his bleeding ear. Despite how bright-blue the ocean had looked earlier, it was now a deep navy. Beside him was a bleeding stump of a tentacle on one side and the bound corsair on the other, his eyes bulging in terror. Kiru noticed no kraken bodies, but hundreds of writhing tentacles were all around. *Do they all belong to just one monster?* he thought.

It was only getting darker as he sank deeper and deeper into the depths. The stark silence of the water versus the loud rushing of air was very distinct. It left Kiru alone with his thoughts, completely ignoring the other victim sinking with him. The deeper he went, the further he sank into despair. The trollstone cuffs were still on him. He couldn't move, let alone swim to safety. The psion closed his eyes once again, overcome by sadness.

I've failed. I've come so far to fall victim to some pirates, he thought. *My friends are going to die. I'm going to die. The world is going to be overrun by death and destruction at the hands of the dragons, and my mother's sacrifice will be in vain.* Kiru scowled. *No. Even if I'm going to die, I'm going out fighting. What did Mother train me for if not to fight?*

Determination gripped Kiru's psyche, and he gave a slight confident grin as he gritted his teeth. *William would be so proud right now.*

A few seconds later, Kiru stopped moving, so he opened his eyes—immediately, that resolve was tested. Staring directly at him was a monster of legend: a kraken. The first thing that struck Kiru, aside from its immense size, was its alien eye, which was larger than the psion's entire body. It stared back at him with an otherworldly intelligence. It glowed a faint, bioluminescent blue. It felt as if the creature could pierce through the darkness and see into the very soul of the psion.

The giant squid's mantle—the bulbous part of its body—was enormous and pulsating with rhythmic contractions, keeping its position in the water with an eerie grace. The skin—a dark red-to-pink hue—shifted to reveal the sinuous movement of powerful muscles beneath. The kraken looked directly at him, then shifted over to his right. Kiru spared a glance to see the corsair who had been dragged down with him, the man's eyes distant and his mouth open. Dead. A thick trail of blood came from his open mouth.

The kraken used one of its many tentacles to somehow pull in that trail of blood towards itself. Its ten tentacles parted, revealing a black beak that had been hidden within the center of the writhing mass of limbs. Kiru watched as it sucked in the blood. He also realized that, with this monster only having ten tentacles and assuming all its counterparts had the same amount of limbs, there had to be at least a dozen krakens attacking the ship above. After a couple of seconds, the kraken stopped drinking the man's blood, seeming to come to a decision, and shoved the corpse in its entirety into its maw. The eerie silence of the depths was broken with the sounds of bones crunching inside the monster's mouth.

Kiru's heart raced. Still, he did his best to focus, hold onto his air supply, and not show this predator any fear. He couldn't move, but he would remain defiant until the end.

After only a few seconds, the deep-sea denizen had finished its meal and shifted its slightly glowing eyes back onto Kiru. It then moved one of its ten tentacles to probe at him. Kiru could see many of its suckers, each as big as his face. It went to poke his cheek, and Kiru responded by promptly biting the thing. He didn't draw blood, but he got his message across. It gave a sharp squeak of surprise before giving Kiru a low growl.

He refused to show it any fear, despite what he was feeling inside.

The kraken's eyes then shifted to slightly above him.

Kiru turned his head to see a small cloud of blood right beside him. He realized that it had come from his injured ear.

Like with the corsair, the kraken drew in the blood towards its beak. Unlike with the corsair, when the monster tasted the psion's blood, it suddenly went still. Its eyes constricted, and it made a high-pitched squeak that seemed to convey surprise and . . . curiosity? Somehow, Kiru knew that the creature was perplexed by him, or at least, by his blood. The kraken then loosened its grip on the psion just slightly before pulling him to be just inches away from one of its alien-looking eyes.

The kraken's pupil dilated, and it seemed to fully take in Kiru, measuring him on some unknown scale.

Kiru furrowed his brow and cocked his head in confusion, completely unsure as to what was happening. His eyebrows then raised in surprise as the word, "*Worthy,*" boomed inside his mind.

Kiru was shocked, so much so at what the tentacled monstrosity had done that he accidentally gasped, losing most of the remaining air in his lungs. A burst of bubbles escaped from his mouth before he gagged, but then he managed to compose himself. That composure almost immediately gave way, however, as his face visibly tensed. Kiru did not have much air left, and it was showing.

The kraken seemed to interpret something within the psion's expression, and immediately began carrying him through the water—though not toward the surface. Kiru grunted in concern, trying to send the message that he needed to go up, not across the water as the kraken was taking him now.

The monster ignored him, and within seconds, the darkness of the deep ocean gave way to reveal a wall of glistening purple metal. Kiru could see colonies of coral, kelp, and various fish now making their home in it. He realized that this was the purple ring that surrounded the island. Maybe it was the darkness, but it was so tall that he couldn't see its bottom. There was a round section of cloudy-looking glass in the center of the metal, and to Kiru's surprise, when the kraken touched it, it glowed with an artificial yellow light in recognition of the monster. The glass slid up and disappeared into the purple above, revealing a tunnel of glowing metal and light.

Swiftly and without preamble, the kraken compressed its body and launched both it and Kiru into the tube. In a flash, they were across the thick purple ring and past it. Kiru grimaced at both the speed at which he was being carried and at his growing lack of oxygen. He closed his eyes and pressed his chin against his chest. He felt himself being pulled across and then up abruptly. His heart raced in hopes that he would get more air, but his lungs were burning by this point. Anyone below Gold wouldn't have survived this long under these conditions, but fortunately, he'd withstood the shifting pressures.

The water pressure on his body became lighter and lighter, and he could feel the water warming against his face. He was scared that he wasn't going to make it, especially as he started to black out. Thankfully, a couple of moments later, Kiru was graced with sweet bliss as his body crested the water's surface, and he was allowed fresh air once again. He opened his mouth and gasped in deep, desperate breaths, increasingly grateful for each successive one. Most of the kraken's body and all of its tentacles broke the water's surface as it gave a shrill, clicking cry of pride that echoed for miles. It raised Kiru higher than all of its other limbs like a kid holding a trophy, and mentally shouted, "*Worthy!*" once more.

Kiru could sense it was the equivalent of a telepathic shout because he recoiled at the volume of the deep, booming mental "voice," and that all around the outer surface of the purple metallic ring, hundreds of tentacles shot up out of the water in response. Dozens of other similar cries echoed the kraken's and the booming mental voices of more krakens repeated the same word. They all shouted *"Worthy!"* in a tone that could indicate nothing aside from pure glee.

For that brief moment, time seemed to stop for Kiru. From his high vantage point, he was able to grasp where he truly was and what was happening. He was now inside the purple ring. Some strange, semi-translucent barrier was in between him and the island that Vatrenex claimed was his former prison.

Off in the distance, he could see *The Marauding Citadel*, with more than a few crushed buildings on its deck. Many pieces of wood along the ship's portside were either cracked or obliterated. Two of its many masts were partially shattered, though Kiru could tell the one his friends were bound to was intact. People were running about on the deck looking like ants from this distance, the sounds of combat still prevalent even over the kraken's cries. About a dozen tentacles surrounded the ship, their movements more like someone swatting at a fly versus true hatred. It was clear that while the krakens weren't thrilled with the ship's proximity, they hadn't tried to truly destroy the *Citadel*. While the vessel was the largest and the most impressive that Kiru had ever seen, it couldn't truly compete against the hundreds of monsters protecting the island.

Time suddenly came back to him in a flash as three of the tentacles surrounding the *Citadel* were suddenly cut off all at once by a very recognizable slash of black mana. That technique slashed through their thick flesh like it was paper and continued flying straight in Kiru's direction. In just a couple of heartbeats, it made it to the ring's edge. To Kiru's shock, the outer barrier that had intercepted the strike the first time the captain had used it was gone!

To his great relief, there appeared to be an inner barrier. As the technique broke against it, an unintelligible roar of rage came from the ship's deck. Even from such a distance, the psion was somehow able to notice the cultivator's hulking, abnormal form. He got the impression that the monster of a man had locked his gaze onto him and was staring maliciously at the psion even though Kiru couldn't see his face. In the next moment, the oars on the *Citadel*'s lower level began carrying them away from the island.

Then, the kraken abruptly let go of him. Gravity took hold of him, and he began to plummet. Kiru looked down to see the kraken had shifted its body so that its beak was now pointed upward directly at him. All he could do was let out a scream as the beak opened up and closed over him. He landed on a rough, wiggling mound of flesh that seemed to be the kraken's tongue. "No, no, no, no!" he spat out.

After a few moments of flailing, Kiru abruptly stopped to realize the kraken still hadn't swallowed him. In fact, its tongue was raised up to prevent him from falling deeper into its body.

"Hey, what's going on here?" he asked the kraken. All he got in reply was the beak clamping fully, taking away his only source of light. Kiru grimaced, wishing he could use Telepathy to communicate. Left without light to aid his vision, his other senses came to the forefront. The mouth was moist and hot, almost instantly causing him to sweat. The stench was also horrendous. Without fresh air to dilute it, the scent slammed into Kiru's nostrils. He dry-heaved a couple of times as the mixed odors of fish, salt water, human blood, and decaying flesh hit hard.

That dry retching turned into full-blown vomiting when the kraken's tongue wrapped tightly around Kiru, unintentionally rubbing pirate blood and fish guts against him. Before he had time to wonder what was happening, Kiru could feel that the kraken was moving, descending back into the depths, and by the feeling of his ears popping more than once, they were diving swiftly. Kiru wanted to question what was happening but saved his energy. For now, he was at the kraken's mercy.

It's like the thing's protecting me as we go deeper by giving me a place to breathe and keeping me safe from the water pressure, he thought. Kiru gave a chuckle at the realization but quickly stopped in order to conserve air. It may have been disgusting, but at least it was still breathable for the moment.

As they went deeper and deeper, Kiru thought about his friends. On the one hand, he was relieved to have gotten away from Vatrenex and the corsairs. On the other, he'd left them at the mercy of the pirates. With the trollstone binding him, there was nothing he could have done. He knew that on an intellectual level. Despite that, on an emotional level, his heart ached with survivor's guilt. He truly hoped they made it out. The horror on Brunhilda's face as he was pulled off of the ship had been chilling.

After another minute, Kiru went abruptly forward from a sudden stop in momentum. He was still wrapped up by the kraken's slimy tongue, so fortunately he didn't slam hard into its beak. Then he felt himself being tilted upwards as the kraken gently reoriented itself.

"What's going on?" he asked the monster.

In reply, it opened its mouth and launched his body out.

To Kiru's surprise, he wasn't greeted by deep ocean water. Instead, he was flung out a few feet to land on solid rock. Kiru coughed in surprise as he plopped on the hard surface. He blinked his eyes clear to find that he was in some kind of strange underwater cave. It was dark and damp, only about twenty feet long and half as tall. Half of the floor was taken up by a pool of flowing, salty ocean water with the other half being the stone floor which he quickly realized was actually coral.

Though Kiru did have darkvision, he didn't need it to examine the place, because it was illuminated by a green light. Kiru turned his head to see its source—a section of wall made of smooth metal. A door was carved into it, the center of the door had a strange, glowing, green symbol that Kiru had never seen before. The psion idly wondered if it was a rune, but in the back of his mind he didn't think so. Any rune he'd seen before had always had hard sharp angles. This strange symbol was complex and curving. *Maybe a lost language?* he thought.

His pondering was then cut off by a set of loud, blood-chilling clicks coming from the pool of water. He gasped and turned his head to see the massive, unsettling kraken eye staring directly at him from under the water's surface.

"Um, thank you," he said tentatively. "Why did you bring me here?"

The kraken gave a high-pitched cry. "*You are worthy. Now go,*" it sent before its large eye moved toward the strange metal door.

Kiru's frustration grew. "Hey, I'm grateful for you saving me, but I can't. First of all, one of my legs is broken." He nodded towards his grotesquely bent limbs. *Probably even worse now from your rough handling,* he thought but kept that to himself. "Second of all, these cuffs prevent me from using my mana, and I *need* it to move. Otherwise, I'm stuck here."

Kiru and the kraken just stared at each other. Neither blinked for a good minute. Though Kiru didn't show it, tension gripped his racing heart. He was at the kraken's mercy, and while he was hopeful it would continue to help him, he had no guarantee that it wouldn't abruptly change its mind.

Eventually, the kraken seemed to grasp Kiru's words and gave a set of subtle clicks from its beak. "*Help,*" it sent after it began to raise three of its tentacles out of the dark water and into the cave toward Kiru.

The psion's neck reflexively tensed in alarm at the tentacles at first, but he quickly nodded. A tentacle wrapped around each of his damaged legs. They squeezed tight and forcibly realigned the limbs with audible snaps of bone, making him especially glad he couldn't feel the pain. The teeth on the suckers bit down on the limbs, tearing through his clothing and clamping down on his flesh just lightly enough to draw blood. The third tentacle surprisingly laid over the first two and also bit down, this time on the other tentacles, causing thick rivulets of its own blood to pour over the psion's legs.

Both Kiru and the kraken's blood intermixed, liberally coating both of Kiru's legs. They began to visibly steam, and he gasped in surprise. Still, he didn't question the monster. His legs popped and shifted once more.

The kraken clicked approvingly before removing its tentacles from Kiru's legs. Kiru looked down at them and gasped in amazement. They were fully healed.

Just as Kiru remembered he still had his cuffs on, the kraken's remaining tentacle wrapped around his right wrist. It squeezed tight on the trollstone cuffs and shattered them, impressively leaving Kiru's wrists unharmed.

Kiru took in a deep inhale as if he'd been holding his breath this entire time as mana surged through his entire body once more, no longer suppressed by the cuff's effects. Chills ran up his neck as he no longer felt helpless. Tears welled up in his eyes in pure joy and gratitude. To go over a day without any power at all and to finally have it back again gave the psion both perspective and resolve. It made him realize that while he was indeed strong, he had clear weaknesses. He also resolved to *never* fall victim to trollstone again.

There was a sharp pain in his head, but he welcomed it because that meant that his activation of Telekinesis had worked. With just his mana, Kiru righted himself to stand up once more. His leg was healed, but his face was bruised, his lip was cut, he was missing some chunks of hair, most of his right ear was ripped off, and he had a couple of cracked ribs.

Something else familiar came back as well. "*Oh my gosh, Master. That sucked! I was stuck in your core, and I couldn't say or do anything! Never put on one of those things again,*" William pleaded.

Kiru smiled, happy to hear his familiar once more. "Trust me, William. I don't wa—"

"*Forget about that right now, Master. The kraken uses mental mana! Drink its blood, you fool, this is exactly what we've been looking for!*" William interrupted.

Kiru's eyes widened, and his heart raced at the realization. William was right. The monster spoke using Telepathy. It *had* to use mental mana.

"*Go,*" the kraken sent as it pulled its tentacle back into the water.

"No, wait," Kiru said as he put a hand out, but the kraken didn't stop. Most of its remaining tentacle was back in the water. "Crap," he growled out. His mind went through a flurry of thoughts. He was grateful for what the kraken had done and didn't want to hurt it, but a cure to his core's damage was right in front of him! He couldn't ignore that, and he couldn't take the chance on it leaving. So, without another word, he drew out his steel Fu Tao and sliced a small fragment off of the kraken's tentacle.

It shrieked in indignation at the blow, infuriated at Kiru's audacity after all it had done for him. The kraken let out a bestial hiss: "*Traitor! Unworthy!*"

Kiru quickly bent down to pick up the flopping, bleeding appendage, but just before he could suck blood from it, the kraken attacked. The massive monster surged upward. Its body was much too big to fit inside the small cave, but its sharp, black beak wasn't. It broke the water's surface in an attempt to bite Kiru in half.

The psion grunted as he almost lost grip of the chunk of tentacle and just narrowly rolled out of the way.

"Open the damn door!" William sent as Kiru stood back up and pressed his back to the metal surface.

Kiru was pressed against the smooth metal surface of the door, patting it desperately to try and find a way to open it.

The kraken took another snap at him, the vile rank of its maw quickly filling his nostrils once more, but it missed.

Before it could make a third attempt, Kiru pressed his hand on the strange glowing symbol on the door. When his palm pressed against it, it let out a *BEEP!* before sliding open. With his weight pressed firmly against the door, Kiru promptly fell backwards as it slid into the wall and gave way. The psion landed on his back, and the kraken cried out in anger and lunged to bite him again. Kiru raised his head to see the door rapidly sliding back in place just in time. The kraken's beak slammed hard against the strange metal, but it was remarkably durable, only denting instead of breaking it.

Kiru heard the monster cry out in anger again, but no other attacks came. Feeling relatively safe for the moment, Kiru turned back to his hand to see that the section of tentacle for which he had risked was still in his grip. He grimaced to see it still wriggling like a worm. Fortunately, it was still bleeding, too.

"Hurry Master. Do it!"

Fighting against all of his instincts, Kiru closed his eyes and shoved the bleeding stump into his mouth.

CHAPTER NINE

The Heat of Battle

Brunhilda had gone through a whirlwind of emotions in the past few minutes. She had seen plenty of deadly creatures on her travels with her friends, but this strange one-eyed thing passing itself off as a pirate captain was the truest definition of a monster she had ever witnessed. He reminded her of the ogre exile back in Mutt's homeland with its abnormal, grotesquely large mouth. Unlike that ogre, the slit that was Vatrenex's maw was vertical and nearly split it in two like a zipper.

There was also something about him that was just . . . wrong. It hurt her to look at the thing for too long. Her uncle Jayson had told her stories about the terrible pirates and cutthroats that called the Torn Empire home, but he'd never mentioned a horror like Vatrenex—just the gray-skinned pirates and maddened bloodthirsty residents of the various islands in the Southern Sea. Both of which were now fighting each other on the ship they were bound to.

While that was distressing, the most heart-wrenching thing was what had happened to Kiru. In the chaos that followed, she turned to her other friends. "Zhaden, Mutt, Kiru be needing our help. We gotta get out of here. Mutt is there anyway ye can find him?"

A crazed albino man only wearing a loincloth charged at the bound Mutt, screaming "Despair!"

She turned to see Mutt giving a wide grin. From Mutt's positioning, she could admit the pirates were smart in keeping his feet from touching the wooden deck. She wasn't sure if they had done that intentionally or not. Despite that, amidst the orc's excitement for a good fight, he seemed to have subconsciously put his feet to the back of the wooden mast he was tied to. That mast was connected to the rest of the deck which Brunhilda presumed allowed the blind orc to "see" what was going on. He didn't need mana to sense. He could detect the literal hundreds that were fighting all around him . . . and also where Kiru was.

"Guys, I know where the boss is. Stabby, get ready," he said to Zhaden as the crazed pale islander neared.

The drakonid just grunted in affirmation.

Before the man could stab Mutt through one of his eyes, the orc snapped his head and snatched the spear with his powerful jaws, redirecting the weapon away from his body and into some of the ropes binding them to the mast.

The man stumbled forward as he was pulled off balance, and Zhaden used that opportunity to kick him in the side of his left knee. The crazed man's leg gave way, and he collapsed to the ground, losing grip of his weapon.

In an impressive display of dexterity, Mutt—with the spear still his mouth—dislodged the weapon and began cutting the ropes that bound the three. In a matter of seconds, all three of the cultivators were freed and landed on the ground. Their bodies tingled as blood flowed through them more readily since they were no longer being constricted. Brunhilda looked at Mutt with admiration, and the orc gave her a big grin, but they didn't have time to marvel at their newfound freedom or Mutt's grace. Fighting was going on all around them, and no one was their ally.

The islander that Zhaden had kicked had gotten back up. He pulled out a crude obsidian dagger from who-knew-where and lunged at the gold drakonid, the look of horror on the man's face never changing. Brunhilda knew Zhaden was always on the lookout for danger so was able to easily strip the weapon from the man's grasp and slit his throat with it. Blood gushed from the wound, and to the dwarf's surprise, he didn't try to staunch the bleeding. Instead, his look of terror changed to one of bliss. Brunhilda couldn't be sure, but she thought he heard the man say "thank you" before he collapsed to the deck with a smile on his face. It was puzzling, but the paladin didn't have time to think about it currently; there was danger all around.

The three members of Pandemonium huddled down by the mast in hopes of being less noticeable. They still had their trollstone handcuffs, so techniques were out of the question, but with their overall fighting prowess—being at Ruby—and Mutt's senses, Brunhilda felt confident that they could find their friend before it was too late.

"He's being taken to the stone tower by one of those monkeys along the deck's edge. We just need to get over there and hug the edge, and we should be able to find him," Mutt said.

"The prisoners!" an orc corsair shouted. "Capture the—grr!" His cry was cut off by a spear to the throat.

"Move," Zhaden urged. Keeping low, the three wound their way through the fighting. Their progress was delayed more than once by someone noticing them and them then having to fight them off. Fighting was significantly more difficult for Mutt and Brunhilda. Brunhilda was used to having her shields, and while Mutt was a very competent fighter, he'd grown accustomed to using his techniques. His familiarity with the spear he'd wielded was clearly lacking, based on his movements. Fortunately, the dagger Zhaden had taken from the dead islander was just what the gold drakonid needed. He almost exclusively fought with short blades, only rarely using a garrote, so he did most of the fighting.

Despite him doing most of the heavy lifting, Brunhilda and Mutt were both Rubies, and they weren't pushovers. Most of the pirates were Gold or lower, so their brute strength was sufficient for those foes. Most was not *all*, however, and that didn't take into account technique usage. Slashes sent from swords and projectiles fired from spears all made of the same black mana that Vatrenex had used were recklessly fired amidst the fighting. To the paladin's surprise, the same type of technique was used by both sides. She didn't have time to think much about it, as the trio had to focus on *not* being struck by the magical attacks as they scrambled to find their friend.

Wherever the techniques launched by the opposing forces struck, the black mana destroyed all it touched. Bones and muscle were rent, wood was shattered, and stone was obliterated. Many pained cries mixed in with the shouts of fighting from those who'd been hit by one of the devastating techniques. Brunhilda wanted to put herself in front of her friends as a paladin of protection, but without her techniques, both Zhaden and Mutt ran interception, instead deflecting or guiding the arms that wielded the weapons releasing the techniques.

Finally, she and the others reached the deck's edge and found their stolen items. Even without being able to use mana, it soothed the dwarf to have her items again. Mutt didn't carry much on his person, so the orc was able to focus on keeping anyone from attacking his friends while Brunhilda and Zhaden reequipped themselves. Once ready, they scanned their surroundings again. Brunhilda was surprised that with such violence and death, the numbers hadn't seemed to decrease. A steady stream of pale people of varying races adorned with tribal gear swarmed over the starboard side while even more corsairs exited from the buildings and from below deck to meet them. It was clear that the pirates would win eventually as it looked like the Crazed were being slowly pushed back, but it wouldn't be without cost.

Unfortunately for the trio, their presence hadn't gone unnoticed. One of the creepy monkeys seemed to appear behind them and let out an ear-piercing screech, alerting others to their presence.

Vatrenex finished bisecting a warrior and turned to lock his malevolent red eye on the three. He pointed his bulky blade at them as six orbs of swirling purple and black mana formed around him. "Prisoners escaping. Capture them!" he ordered before shouting "Voidflare Barrage!" At his words, the six orbs flew towards the three cultivators.

The hairs on Mutt's head tensed like those of a cat. "Get down," he said as he tackled his friends to the deck. The orbs zoomed right over them and struck the wooden railing behind them with a series of quick *thooms*.

Brunhilda looked up to see six perfectly round holes left in their wake.

"Move!" Mutt shouted once more as he pressed his friends back.

Though Mutt's senses far exceeded those of the other two, Zhaden's sense of danger was still superior—in his own opinion, that is. The gold drakonid, while unsure *exactly* of Kiru's location, knew that their chances of locating him were growing slimmer the more they stayed where they were at. "We need to get to higher ground. We'll be able to find Kiru easier and have a modicum of safety," he whispered quickly.

"Aye, but how're we supposed to do that?" Brunhilda asked, her eyes scanning the amassed foes closing in.

"We need to clear a path to the buildings in the distance," Zhaden answered as he gripped his blades, the links on his cuffs pulled tight. "I'm just not sure how yet."

"Oh! I know. Sneaky Turtle!" Mutt said with a wide grin. Sneaky Turtle was one of the formations Pandemonium had come up with back at the Royal Academy in preparation for the Warrior Games. Kiru would stop using Telekinesis on his body while Mutt held him up and Zhaden guarded his rear. Brunhilda would be up front with both shields at the ready, luring any foes close. Then, Kiru would use his Telekinesis technique on the dwarf to launch her forward and clear a path.

"Mutt, dearie, we need Kiru to do—"

"Sneaky Turtle!" Mutt interrupted as he shouted cheerfully and picked up one of his allies in each arm and charged forward—the opposite of sneaky. He held Brunhilda by the back of her chest-plate and jacket and shoved her forward like she was a living shield while he held Zhaden by the waist, forcing the drakonid to lean forward and cover their rear as Mutt barreled ahead. Both ally and enemy were caught *very* off-guard by Mutt's impromptu action, but despite their surprise, Zhaden and Brunhilda were accustomed to their friends coming up with crazy plans. The drakonid recalled that Brunhilda often called the strategies Kiru came up with "cockamamie."

So, even with Mutt not consulting them, Zhaden rapidly adjusted to the circumstances. Based on the fact that Brunhilda wasn't complaining and their momentum hadn't stopped, he presumed the dwarf had made peace with it as well. He gave a quick peek back to see the stalwart paladin with her two shields braced as she plowed through her unsuspecting enemies, her strong arms easily pushing them away. Satisfied, Zhaden turned back and continued to cover their rear as the gold drakonid deflected retaliatory strikes from the pirates. A couple of times, a corsair had attacked with a projectile slash technique that Vatrenex had used. The drakonid, seeing the power of the captain's previous technique, had shouted for Mutt to dodge in a certain direction instead of electing to try and fruitlessly deflect them.

In just over a minute, Mutt had pushed them through the thick of the fighting and into the city proper, unharmed. Even without access to his beast mana, the orc was an impressive athlete. Zhaden and Brunhilda were then quickly thrown onto the roof of a nearby shop before Mutt jumped up to join them. Even though the orc had done all the running, it was the other two who were breathing heavily.

"Mutt, I like ye, but dunnae do that again," Brunhilda said.

Mutt gulped. "Oh . . . Sorry, guys."

Their brief pause was cut short by a shout. "Chaos Rift Slash!" From the ground, a thick line of black mana surged forward, its size rivaling that of Vatrenex's. It was taller than the small building the three were standing on.

Zhaden leaped forward as the technique split the wooden structure in two and joined his friends on the left side.

The right side of the building crumbled, and they could see the source of the power down below. There, grinning up evilly at the three, was Hagish Saltbeard, his serrated cutlass in hand. Even with their trollstone cuffs on, they could feel the aura of power coming off the first mate. He was a Sapphire and Zhaden knew was far beyond their abilities, especially with their lack of techniques.

"Ye three have gone and made 'nough trouble. As ye can tell, we be a little busy. So be good slaves and come down and surrender. Cap'n's orders," the dwarf pirate said.

At his words, an entirely forgotten-about threat returned. The air vibrated as a cacophonous set of shrill cries and roars filled the air and gigantic tentacles taller than the ship and thicker than its many masts surged from the ocean. They dropped thick streams of water, and the first mate had just enough time to say, "Damn!" before the fleshy appendages attacked *The Marauding Citadel* and those onboard in a reckless frenzy.

The tentacles crushed buildings, broke masts, and whipped out at any unfortunate person in their wake. Many people were smashed by their sheer force, and a large number were wrapped up and pulled off the ship and into the deep ocean below. Even though many fled to avoid the monstrous appendages, Zhaden saw much of the fighting on deck continued as the tribal albino people were unfazed by the creature. The gold drakonid had a quick thought as to what exactly an albino drakonid was doing so far from New Draconia but didn't have time to ponder as wood and stone debris flew at them. To Pandemonium's benefit, a pair of tentacles came crashing near them, one of them whipping into a three-story stone building and forcing it to fall towards Hagish—and toward them as well.

Brunhilda jumped onto Mutt's back. "Mutt, I changed me mind. Take us outta here now!"

"You got it, Brunhilda," Mutt said as he wrapped his muscular arm around Zhaden's waist once again.

Zhaden wanted to protest that he could move on his own, but he was too late as the orc had jumped on top of another building and run across it with them in tow. There was another corsair up there, but she was only a Silver—by the time she'd turned around to see Mutt, the orc had already promptly sent her flying off the structure with a heel kick to the sternum. Zhaden could hear Saltbeard's harsh voice shouting something from below, but it was muffled by the sound of the collapsing structure. Mutt kept running as the ground shook and jumped through the aperture of another building.

He crashed into a bedframe, snapping it into pieces before the others got to their feet. Mutt only groaned slightly and stood up.

"Sorry for losing my temper. Ye still be a bloody idgit, but I be grateful for ye," Brunhilda said as she jumped up and gave Mutt a kiss on the cheek.

The orc's green cheeks darkened as he blushed.

Zhaden wasn't paying them much attention. He had quickly rolled to his feet and was cautiously scanning outside. "There's a cloud of debris where the building collapsed. I can't see the first mate, but I doubt that was enough to take him down. We need to stay hidden so that we can find Kiru." The dust was swiftly settling, but it was hard for him to discern what was going on. "Mutt, check from the other opening. Has Kiru reached the tower?"

Mutt stuck his head out, first sniffing loudly, then clicking his tongue, using echolocation to help his scan the surroundings. Sounds of death, destruction, and battle filled the *Citadel*, and the orc growled in frustration. The sounds of the tentacles wildly striking the ship likely didn't help, either. He did eventually discern his location, however, likely helped by having known his last position.

"He hasn't made it to the tower yet, but this is not good. We're a lot farther from the boss than I thought. He's by the railing, being pulled by one of those freaky monkeys," Mutt said. The orc's senses were top-notch, so it wasn't often that he missed his mark when tracking someone.

The chaos of the battle below may be too much for him to handle, Zhaden thought. Before he could say anything, though, a giant clawed hand smashed through the room they were in, sending the three crashing into another partially ruined building.

There were a couple of loud cracks as well as a series of consecutive thumps as the three hit the structure, turning it to a giant pile of stone rubble. Mutt rolled on the ground and roared in pain as he grabbed his left wrist. It was bent at an odd angle—clearly broken.

Zhaden stood up slowly. There was now a large gash over his left eye, blood flowing down it and covering half his face. It made it difficult for him to see from that eye, and his heart began to beat faster as he had to move his head about more frequently to ensure there were no more enemies in their immediate vicinity.

Fortunately, Brunhilda had suffered only minimal injury, her hardy constitution, armor, and shields up to the task.

Zhaden saw that the trollstone around Mutt's wrist had broken as well, the stone crumbling off both arms as he stood up. Though in clear pain, he defiantly snapped his head at their incoming foe.

Saltbeard was now trudging over to them on the back of his now-mutilated-and-blinded cyclops mount. The dwarf pirate gave them all a wicked grin, displaying his sharp, crooked teeth. *The Marauding Citadel*'s first mate didn't even look injured from the building having fallen on top of him earlier, the only evidence being a layer of dust over his body and debris in his white facial hair. "I've had enough of yer antics. Yer parley is done. The cap'n said to capture ye, but he didn't specify with how many limbs," he said, then tugged on one of his mount's reigns.

The cyclops raised its right hand to swipe down at the cultivators, but the three weren't helpless. Mutt had mana now, too. Bracing his broken wrist to his body, Mutt hopped forward and activated three of his techniques. A thick layer of brown fur grew all around his body, even covering his milky-white eyes, giving him a bestial appearance. Dweller Bear's Fur gave him a layer of protection that rivaled even medium armor. His already-large tusks and teeth grew even longer and thicker, becoming more pronounced as he activated Gnoll's Bite.

Lastly, he gave a savage, defiant roar with Bounder's Howl. The final technique conveyed the prideful ferocity of a predator, striking at the psyche of those it targeted.

Saltbeard tensed, but after a few seconds managed to scowl right back at the orc. His mount was another story. Zhaden assumed the poor cyclops' mind had been broken long ago, so its ability to resist Mutt's howl technique was much lower. The monster's mouth went agape, and it lowered its arm as it took a couple of nervous steps back.

Brunhilda readied her shields and scanned for where the ominous tower was located. She sighed in relief when she noticed it was only a couple of blocks away. Just as she was about to turn back to face the monster and first mate, her ears were beset with a guttural, angry cry coming from the water. Then, she saw four more tentacles emerging over the ship's deck as if they were being pulled up by some magnetic force.

One of the tentacles was quickly amputated by the familiar-looking black slash, but the other three didn't falter. They snapped down like vipers and wrapped tightly around their newest victims. Brunhilda's heart sank.

"Kiru," she said under her breath.

She noticed that Vatrenex and another corsair were also caught but didn't pay them as much mind. The paladin was focused on her friend.

"Oh mighty Hlin, goddess of protection, safeguard my friend," she uttered to her goddess in desperation.

Brunhilda could only stare. She knew that none of them could reach Kiru in time. She watched in growing horror as the tentacled monster—whatever it was— raised him up. Her blood ran cold as she locked eyes with Kiru. Despair gripped her heart as she knew there was nothing she could do. She noticed Vatrenex cut himself free but kept her primary focus on Kiru. The psion's eyes were full of relief and sadness, seemingly glad that they were okay but resigned to what was about to happen to him.

Though she couldn't hear him amidst the utter chaos around them, she could read his lips. Brunhilda watched him say "I'm sorry" before the two remaining tentacles pulled him and the corsair crew member below the water.

CHAPTER TEN

Turn of the Tide

Brunhilda wanted to fall to her knees and cry. *Kiru was gone*. Thankfully, her thoughts were interrupted by Saltbeard kicking and swearing at his frightened mount.

"Quickly, my friends! We must get away while the pirate is preoccupied," Zhaden hissed as he backed away, frantically scanning their surroundings with his one open eye. He clearly didn't notice the monster taking Kiru.

"Sounds good to me," Mutt said as he picked Brunhilda up with his uninjured arm and he and Zhaden began sprinting towards the ship's railing. He seemed not to have noticed, either.

"No. No, stop. Stop, ye idgits. Trying to get Kiru be pointless," Brunhilda said as she bucked, tears now flowing down her face in thick rivulets.

Zhaden and Mutt clearly picked up on the fact that something was wrong and knew they needed to figure out what was going on before continuing to rush through the urban combat zone. "There," Zhaden hissed, pointing to a dark alley out of Saltbeard's line of sight.

Mutt nodded, and the two quickly rushed over and crouched behind debris and some wall outcroppings; Brunhilda was still crying.

"What do you mean in stopping our pursuit of Kiru? What did you see?" Zhaden asked, his tone urgent and his eyes constantly searching for enemies.

"What happened, Brunhilda?" Mutt asked as he rubbed one of her shoulders, concerned more with her emotional well-being than anything else.

Brunhilda sniffed a couple times before saying, "Kiru . . ." She shook her head. "He be gone. I watched whatever monster be attacking the ship grab him and pull him over."

"Oh no, not the boss," Mutt said sadly.

"Are you certain it was Kiru?" Zhaden asked.

"Of course I be certain," Brunhilda responded in an angry hiss.

Zhaden wasn't bothered by her tone. He seemed to be too focused on keeping them alive. "Then our objective has changed," he said.

"Changed? Kiru's gone. It be over," Brunhilda said.

"If he is truly gone, then we must warn the Great Alliance. The people must know about the upcoming dragon invasion so they can prepare," Zhaden countered. "You are a paladin of protection, so you must understand."

Brunhilda felt herself going through a series of emotions in a few seconds. At first, she was angry, feeling he'd insulted her, but she quickly realized that his words weren't meant with malice. So, despite Zhaden's lack of tact, Brunhilda quickly resolved to follow what he'd said. Her goddess was that of protection, and she would honor Hlin by doing the same.

She sighed before nodding. "Aye, ye be right. What do we do then?"

"We take advantage of the chaos, sneak down to the lower levels, and find a vessel to commandeer. If possible, we should capture a pirate who could sail us back to the continent," Zhaden answered. "Mutt, can you use your senses to find us the safest path to the lower levels?"

"My arm's broken, not my senses, Stabby. So, I got you," Mutt answered, with a thumbs-up.

Then, without ceremony, the three began running along the city streets, careful to avoid detection as they worked towards the nearest way down. They did run into a couple of corsairs who were badly injured, but Zhaden easily dispatched them, his training clearly better than the pirates'. Fortunately, they'd avoided running into Saltbeard thanks to Mutt's heightened senses and Zhaden being on high alert, constantly checking their surroundings. They eventually reached a passage, but it was right by the most intense area of the battle where there weren't any buildings—just open deck and masts. There was about a hundred feet between them and the stairway going down. A metal grate covered it, keeping any corsairs from fleeing or any invader from going deeper.

"I got it," Mutt said. "Since I have my mana back, I should be able to cut that thing open. Ready?" he asked.

"Ready," the two replied.

Then, they ran out, easily dispatching combatants from both sides as they made their way over to the grate. Mutt activated Fenrir's Claws, and his nails elongated and sharpened. He then began swiping away at the metal, easily cutting into it, only being slowed down by its thickness. Brunhilda knew Mutt would be able to cut through, though she didn't know if they'd have enough time.

Hurry up, Mutt, she thought impatiently. Both Brunhilda and Zhaden guarded the orc in the meantime. While the two may still have had their trollstone cuffs on, at least they had their gear back. That may not have been everything, but with their skill taken into account, the paladin couldn't help but feel a little more secure as she knew it could make all the difference.

Brunhilda bashed in the nose of a pale orc islander with her steel shield before thrusting the pointed end of her mithril shield into the neck of an elf corsair.

Zhaden spun and knocked a thrown spear out of the way with his tail. He hissed, as it was clearly still painful from where it had been partially cut off, but while it wasn't as long as it used to be, it was still usable. Then, all the fighting stopped at once as a chorus of clicks and shrill cries echoed all around the ship, everyone stopping as they acted on some sort of primal instinct. Before anyone dared to move once more, everyone's minds were attacked by a series of telepathic shouts all ringing in unison: "*Worthy!*"

As if time were running in slow motion, Brunhilda and Zhaden turned to the ship's port side, where Kiru had been pulled over. There, they could see hundreds of tentacles in the water, spread out for kilometers. Even more notable was what she could see off in the distance. There, past the ring of purple metal that surrounded the strange island made of the same material, was Kiru. His form was small, but she knew deep down that it was their fate-defying friend. She could see he was being held up by one of the monsters like some sort of vaunted hero.

The paladin's heart soared to see him alive. Despite her protests, they had come to the Torn Empire to reach the center and heal their friend. There was supposedly a connection between this place and his psionic heritage. Seeing the monsters praise him and call him worthy made Brunhilda realize that Kiru was right and that he was okay.

"He . . . made it," Zhaden said in a blend of awe and disbelief.

"Aye," Brunhilda said before wiping her nose with a gauntleted wrist.

In her mind, Hlin spoke softly to her: "*Thine compatriot and my acolyte is spared from death currently, but not from danger. He must undertake a trial, and once he begins, he must endure it alone.*"

Brunhilda was both relieved and concerned for her friend. She trusted her goddess and Kiru's abilities. *Nothing we can do to help him now, save pray.*

"Who made it?" Mutt asked, unable to see what was going on.

A hideous cry of utter outrage came from Vatrenex. Despite their proximity, he didn't notice the cultivators as his attention was solely fixed on Kiru. The pirate captain raised his bulky blade up in the air with one arm, chaotic black mana pumping through the weapon's veins as if it were alive.

Brunhilda knew that Vatrenex was about to release another Chaos Rift. On instinct, she pushed through the people to get to the hideous creature. *I failed Kiru once. By Hlin's might, I won't fail again.*

"Chaos Rift—" As the captain swung down his blade to complete the technique, Brunhilda was there. "Sla—' he said but was immediately cut off as the paladin shoved her shield forward to bash into the captain's hand, knocking the technique's trajectory off course.

The slash was bigger than they'd seen before, and it zoomed through the air, cutting through three nearby tentacles with ease. It continued forward, its momentum uninhibited, flying in Kiru's direction. To Brunhilda's relief, she had knocked its aim off, and it missed him. She felt a little silly when the technique also hit a barrier but was surprised to see that the barrier she'd first seen was gone; the one she had just witnessed was a second barrier. Even if her efforts were unnecessary in the end, she still felt proud for having defended her friend. That pride was immediately cut short as she was struck by a backhand with the force of a raging bull, sending her into unconscious.

Brunhilda woke up in a dimly lit area, the only illumination being a subtle red glow coming from a gem on a pedestal in the center of the room. She shook her head, and focus came back to her mind. Thanks to her troll blood, she had remarkable healing abilities, but she still coughed out some coagulated blood after her first big breath. Vatrenex had hit her hard. Once she'd settled down again, she took in her situation and surroundings more fully. She was bound once again, except this time, she was hanging to a stone wall by her wrists, and she still couldn't access her mana, meaning these cuffs had to be made of trollstone as well.

There was no rushing wind, no sound of crashing waves, and not even the salty scent of sea water. The only noise was the slight rattling of her chains. The paladin deduced that she had to be in some sort of dungeon, the dimensions of each wall about twenty feet by her guess. Mutt and Zhaden were bound to her left. Both were also gagged, their urgent cries to her muffled by the fabric stuffed in their mouths. But she quickly found out what they were trying to warn her about.

"It seems yer finally awake, missy," Hagish Saltbeard's rough voice echoed out.

Brunhilda snapped her head to find the first mate walking out from behind the pedestal, a wicked grin plastered on his face, which was even more ominous now in the red light.

"What do ye want, ye villain?" Brunhilda asked.

"It's not what *I* want, lass. It never be what I want. It be what the cap'n wants," he answered as he casually walked forward. As he got within a few feet, he drew out his blade and pressed its tip to her chin. "And what the cap'n be wantin' is answers. Understand?"

"Aye," she answered. "Why are my friends gagged, and why ain't yer captain here himself to ask me?"

The pirate pursed his lips as if in thought. "Ye be a funny one, lass. Ye said ye understood, but then ye go and ask a question instead of answering one. Ye don't get to ask questions or make demands of the Swordstrike Corsairs, savvy?"

She nodded.

"Good, now, the cap'n won't be pleased if ye keep that up. Ye don't need to know why yer friends are gagged. Ye just need to know—" He stopped speaking and pulled his blade away from Brunhilda's chin to stab it in Mutt's right eye.

The orc screamed in pain through his gag.

Zhaden grunted, recoiling in shock.

"There be consequences for yer lack of cooperation," Saltbeard finished, his crooked grin returning.

"Oh, gods, no." Brunhilda quivered. "Stop. I understand, now, please," she begged, tears streaking down both eyes.

"Good," Saltbeard said before yanking his blade out of Mutt's now-ruined eye with a squelch. "It nae matter anyway, lass. He still can't see. Haha!"

Mutt groaned before rapidly breathing loudly through his nose, grunting with every exhale.

"Ah, cease yer whining, ye ninny," the pirate said.

"Can I—" Brunhilda started to ask but immediately stopped.

Saltbeard snapped his head to her, then patted her on the cheek. "Oh, ye were about to ask me a question, right?"

Brunhilda didn't say anything; she just stared at the pirate.

Saltbeard gave her a thumbs-up. "Ye *are* learning, lass. As a reward for yer effort, I'll make sure his socket won't fester," he said, then reached into his pocket and pulled out a bottle of booze. He then tore a ragged piece of cloth from one of his pant legs, doused it in the foul-smelling liquid, and shoved it forcefully into Mutt's bleeding eye socket.

The orc snapped his head back and groaned loudly from the newfound pain. His jaw tensed, and he bucked his head in a fruitless attempt to get the cloth out. It was enough to make him shake his already-broken arm even more. With a loud snap of bone, Mutt's arm broke again, and the orc passed out from the pain.

Saltbeard, undeterred, reached into another pocket and pulled out another item. It was an eyepatch, and he snapped it over the packed-in socket where Mutt's right eye once was. "Now ye look like a true pirate, haha!" The first mate laughed at the unconscious orc, then turned his head back to Brunhilda, clearly trying to goad her.

The paladin scowled, glaring angrily at the man who'd injured her beloved, but she refrained from asking or demanding to let her heal Mutt. *That's what Saltbeard wants.* "I'm ready to give yer captain his answers whenever he likes," she said with careful deliberation, intentionally avoiding anything that would sound like a question or demand.

"Good," Hagish said and then walked right back up to her face, exhaling his rancid breath in her face. "I'm going to undo yer cuffs now. Any sudden ideas of trying to fight or escape, and it'll be more than just an eye yer friend will be losing. None of ye will make it out of this tower alive," he threatened.

Brunhilda nodded. Hagish gave off the aura of a Sapphire. There was no way she could take him on all on her own. She did raise an eyebrow at something he'd said though. *Tower?* she thought. Brunhilda then raised her head up to see they were indeed at the bottom level of a massive, hollow tower. She quickly realized this was the very one that they'd seen one of the corsairs forced into like a sacrificial lamb in order to "wake up" the captain. A shiver ran down her spine at that realization. And now she knew *why* there was no light. A spiraling, chaotic vortex of mana hovered high above them, like a rain cloud, exuding the same strange power that Vatrenex had earlier. *What type of mana be that?* she thought.

Saltbeard undid the last cuff and Brunhilda plopped to the ground, which was also made of stone, and rubbed at her hurting wrists. Despite the pain, having access to her mana once more made the paladin breathe easier. The feeling of having been detached from her mana was a hollowing one, and it was something she *never* wished to experience again.

Saltbeard put a rough hand on her left shoulder and shoved her towards the center of the room. "Grab the blade," he ordered.

She stumbled forward and fell to her knees. *Blade?* she thought. *What blade he be talking about?* She quickly stood up and found she was only a couple of feet from the pedestal with the red glowing gem, only to discover that the pedestal wasn't a pedestal at all. It was Vatrenex's massive blade, which was nearly as wide as Brunhilda and even taller. The weapon pulsed just slightly, doing so after every five or so seconds, like a slowly beating heart.

Brunhilda shook, instinctually afraid of what might happen. She looked back to see Hagish looking at her.

He was standing next to Mutt and casually pressing the tip of his blade to his bare chest.

Mutt was breathing heavily, still unconscious while Zhaden kept looking back and forth from the pirate to Brunhilda.

The paladin knew she didn't have a choice. *Hlin protect us,* she prayed before reaching up and wrapping her hands around the blade's grip. Her hands immediately tightened as if in a seizure, but in contrast, the rest of her body went limp, her eyes rolling to the back of her head. Horror struck her—she wasn't alone in her own mind.

Brunhilda gasped as she opened her eyes. She knew that her focus had been forcibly drawn inward. During periods of meditative cultivation and prayer, she would often be drawn into the place her instructors had informed her was her "mind's eye." Brunhilda had constructed a pristine temple made of flawless granite and marble with an ornate statue of Hlin at its center. For some reason, the marble had more black spots and streaks marring it, but it didn't affect the aesthetic at all. White, sourceless light illuminated the room. It was a place that would've brought the paladin much comfort had the darkness not come in.

Brunhilda pressed a hand to her heart and visibly recoiled when she caught sight of the center of the temple. Staring at her from atop the statue of Hlin was Vatrenex—only he wasn't as Brunhilda knew him. Instead of legs, he had innumerable tentacles. He still had long arms, but they bent at multiple sharp angles. His skin was no longer pallid gray but solid black with white dots subtly interspersing like stars in the night sky, and the horns on his head were gone. His brain was now visible, reminding Brunhilda of William.

The reason she knew without a doubt it was still the pirate captain was his face. He still had the vertical slit mouth, though it only went down to his chin now. His single red eye focused intently on the dwarf, bearing down on her like a predator about to pounce. He growled like a jungle cat as his gaze locked with her. Goosebumps ran up Brunhilda's skin as she saw the horrifying creature. Her lip quivered in fear. She hadn't known what to expect when Saltbeard had ordered her to grab the blade, but it certainly hadn't been *this*.

"I see that my true form doesn't fail to impress," Vatrenex said as he opened his arms dramatically, his skin wriggling and his limbs bending at odd angles.

Brunhilda took a step back. She knew it was pointless, but she couldn't help herself. "Hlin protect me," she uttered.

The statue Vatrenex was wrapped around pulsed. The monster's form distorted slightly, and he shrieked in pain before growling again. His tentacles quickly spread and squeezed. The statue shattered from the pressure, and the glow immediately stopped as its pieces fell to the ground. The monster snapped his eye back to the dwarf.

"That was unwise," he said.

The darkness behind the creature spread, completely covering and obscuring the half of the temple behind him. "Your false god cannot save you," Vatrenex spat out, his form growing and distorting until he reached the ceiling. His clawed hands crashed hard against the floor, his lower half completely obscured by the malevolent darkness.

Brunhilda started backing away, slowly at first but quickly turning into a full-on sprint.

Vatrenex followed.

Brunhilda eventually made it to the wall at the end. With nowhere left to run, she turned and readied her fists. They began to glow with her mana, but before she could do anything about it, one of Vatrenex's massive hands wrapped around her entire torso. He pinned her arms to her body and slammed her to the wall. Then, he lowered his eye to be down on Brunhilda's level. "Your companion has void-touched mana. He uses mental mana yet is clearly not an arboth. How?"

"Void-touched? The void be a myth. I dunnae what ye be talking about, and I dunnae know what be an arboth," she grunted. "Kiru be a psion. He's had his mental mana core for years, and he hadn't left his homeland when I first met him. There be no way he has mana from the void."

Brunhilda had heard of the void in one of her many religion classes while back in her homeland. The void was a supposed realm of darkness where monstrous horrors made their home. There had been theories as to its existence, but any attempts to verify such claims had never come to fruition. The soundest working theory by those religious scholars adamant about the void realm's presence was that it was what remained of the primordial darkness before life was created.

"So, he lied," he growled, not believing her.

"It be the truth. He be a psion. *That's* how he uses mental mana," she retorted.

Vatrenex cocked his head to the side, "Psion," he tasted the word. After a few seconds, he refocused back on Brunhilda. "It is clear you believe his deceptions, but I tell you, wretch, he is no true inheritor of mental mana. That is something only arboth wield. He is a thief, and I will deal with him," he said as he glared directly at Brunhilda. "Now," he growled, "submit!" and his hand squeezed tighter. It also began stretching, each of his clawed fingers wrapping around her body like a constrictor.

Brunhilda strained as she fought against the grip, but it felt hopeless. The still-expanding hand reached as far as her head now, threatening to completely encase her. Dread seized her heart as she felt her mind slowly slipping as Vatrenex's hold tightened. She thought of her goddess, of Mutt, of Zhaden, and of Kiru. She felt like she'd let them all down. Unlike Kiru, she didn't have a natural penchant for getting out of trouble. She was the clearheaded, cautious one of the group. She wasn't the one who decided to become a living lightning rod whilst attached to a dragon.

Thinking of her friend and that cockamamie plan of his brought a small smile to her face despite the grim circumstances, giving her a small measure of comfort. She couldn't do anything now, but she had faith in her friend. Hlin saw his value, and so did she. Somehow, Brunhilda just *knew* that he would get her out of this.

Despite her consciousness slowly fading, Brunhilda managed to give the monster a confident smile. "Ye have invoked pandemonium." With that, her mouth and face became completely engulfed by his massive fingers, and she was overcome by the black.

Vatrenex finally seized control of the dwarf's mind. In an instant, he took in everything: her thoughts, hopes, dreams, and memories. He learned everything there ever was to know about this foolish paladin, Brunhilda Lightsworn. Indeed, her ally, the thief she knew as Kiru, genuinely believed he was a "psion." It also appeared that he'd been playing them for fools this entire time, or he was completely unaware of the truth of his abilities and heritage. Vatrenex was perplexed as to how in the centuries since his imprisonment in these waters, a non-arboth had managed to steal the ability to use mental mana and spread it to progeny.

He knew for a fact now that the man had mental mana. Vatrenex had made contact with the thief's blood, confirming it. While the captain had been surprised at first when he discovered that from Kiru, he was even more so about the dwarf he'd taken control over. Her mind wasn't eroding. When Vatrenex found a new host, his powers would quickly consume them on contact. This dwarf wasn't being dissolved, however. He looked to the black orb surrounding the paladin. *How?* he asked himself.

He neared the orb once more and noticed that there were tendrils coming off it—tendrils that he hadn't created. Vatrenex used his eye to follow where they went and discovered that they had connected to the pillars the dwarf had created in this visual construct of hers. *She's connecting to chaos mana, but* how? *Could it be . . . ?* He had thought of the most likely reason and tried to refute it, but after only a few seconds, he found the evidence undeniable. The mental construct of Vatrenex gave a wicked smile before projecting himself out from inside his new host's mind.

Though the conflict between Brunhilda and Vatrenex took at least a few minutes inside her mind, it was a battle that only lasted four seconds in the outside world. Mutt woke up not long after he'd passed out to witness in horror through his sense of touch her body visibly mutate and morph. Her skin turned a dull gray as her limbs shifted, growing and rearranging themselves with the unpleasant snapping of bones. Black vessels spread across her skin and bulged. Much of her clothing tore as her body transformed. Most of her armor remained intact but bent as it was forcefully changed from the inside.

The swirling cloud of black mana above them spiraled and turned into a small tornado. It struck Brunhilda. Instead of sending the dwarf flying, however, she absorbed it, bringing the mana inside her. It seemed to Mutt that she was somehow cultivating. After a few seconds the mana retracted from Brunhilda's morphed body, rising back up to resume its slow spinning up at the ceiling of the dark, hollow tower.

A chill ran up Mutt's spine as he sensed his beloved. She was all *wrong* now. She even smelled different.

Her body abruptly stopped moving. Even her breathing halted. She then snapped her head, revealing that she was no longer herself. Her face had warped into a hideous visage. Though Mutt couldn't see, he could sense how she'd changed, and it horrified him. She now only had one vertically slit red alien eye that took up nearly half her face. Her button nose had been replaced by a pair of vertical slits. Her mouth was too wide as she grinned, revealing row after row of sharp teeth like that of a shark.

"Hello, Mutt," she said in a voice that was no longer hers. It was distorted and monstrous as if she and Vatrenex were speaking at the same time. Then, a pair of curved horns erupted from her temples and partially encircled her head. She now stood eight feet tall, her arms and legs stretched out. The thing that had possessed the dwarf raised its bulky, curved sword on its shoulder and walked toward the orc. It removed the gag from Mutt's mouth, then put a hand on his chin, licking its lips. "Do you approve of my new form?"

As long as there wasn't a fight going on, Mutt was by far the calmest person in Pandemonium, but this enraged him like nothing else ever had before. He let out a growl. "What have you done to her? Let her go! I'll kill you."

The monster before him just grinned and squeezed its face tight until he stopped talking. It tsked. "There, there. Do not worry, Mutt. Your mate is safe, as long as you cooperate."

Zhaden managed to rend his gag with his teeth and speak. "I take it that you are the same Vat—"

"Quiet, you," Saltbeard spat out as he slammed the pommel of his blade into the rogue's gut.

The creature snapped its head to Zhaden. "Ah, the drakonid. I have seen your kind before. I have some of your brethren as my thralls, but I confess, I've never seen a gold one before. As to your intended question, yes. I am the same Vatrenex. I will allow you one more question."

Zhaden nodded nervously. "Gratitude. You told my companion—" He gestured to Mutt. "—that our friend Brunhilda would be safe as long as we cooperate. Will you elaborate as to *how* you're keeping her safe and what exactly happened to her?"

"Haha! But of course, Zhaden, but of course," Vatrenex replied in mock joviality. "What you *need* to know is that I require a host in order to engage with others. Your friend here," Vatrenex said, "happened to be an ideal candidate. As long as I live, she will live. If you try to kill me, your friend will die an agonizing death, her mind and soul torn to shreds."

Mutt gasped at the words, even with Vatrenex's vice grip still on his face. Seemingly amused, the monstrous captain let him go.

"Wha-What are you?" Mutt asked, his tone filled with grief and despair.

"I am Vatrenex the Marauder, Ruiner of Gaal'cothdreek-duun, leader of the Swordstrike Corsairs, and the most powerful of the Harbingers," the monster answered proudly before turning back and leaning over Zhaden. Vatrenex towered over the bound drakonid. "Now, let's talk."

Zhaden was caught off-guard by what Vatrenex had said. The information had both given the drakonid a better understanding as to what happened but also baffled him even more. Most of the captain's titles were odd, to say the least.

"What is it that you wish, sir?" he hissed, lowering his head in deference.

Vatrenex seemed to coo in approval, almost purring like a cat. "You and Mutt will be the Swordstrike Corsairs' newest war slaves in our crusade. You will each have a special purpose in the fights to come—"

"Or what?" Mutt cut in. "How do we know that Brunhilda's really alive, huh? Her scent is gone completely. For all we know, you're lying to us."

"How dare ye—" Saltbeard pulled his cutlass back to remove the orc's other eye, but Vatrenex stuck his huge, curved blade out in between the dwarf and orc, stopping the first mate.

"This dwarf's memories tell me that you are a thick-headed one," Vatrenex said, pointing to his skull. He then shifted over, his monstrous face now looming just inches from Mutt's. "Fine, if you need proof, here you'll have it," the captain said before his face grotesquely shifted. Vatrenex's gray skin vibrated and stretched as if being pulled by some unseen force. His lone eye was tugged to the right, and his mouth bent and warped unnaturally. After only a few seconds, Vatrenex's face had split in two. The right side was the horned gray visage of a monster. The left was that of Brunhilda, with her regular tan complexion and purple hair.

The two faces were wearing completely different expressions, the monster's snarling and observant, the dwarf's quivering and terrified. Zhaden was truly horrified by the sight.

"Mutt? Oh my gods, Mutt, what be happening?" the left side of the face asked, the side of the mouth moving completely separate from the right.

Mutt gasped, and his whole body tensed as he shifted his focus to his beloved. "Brunhilda, is that you?" he asked.

"Aye," the left side of the face answered. She seemed to be unable to move her head, but her eye quickly gazed at her mutated body leaning threateningly against Mutt. "Please tell me what's going on, Mutt."

"I allowed your mate to bear witness that you are indeed alive, wench," the monstrous right side answered. "I brought you back to the surface but for a moment. Consider yourself fortunate."

Inside the shared mental temple that was Brunhilda's mind's eye, the dwarf felt the monster's grip, which had previously been loosened, tighten once more. She felt her focus blur, but she resisted as best she could. It wasn't much, but she shook and fought against the monster's control. It was more than she could have before. Unlike earlier, she could now somehow feel a connection between her mind and the intruder. *Perhaps, it be because I've experienced the suppression once before now?* She didn't have enough time to contemplate, however, as the mental projection of Vatrenex gave an angry growl and took complete control once more.

Outside of Brunhilda's mind, the left face that bore her features let out a small gasp before going slack. It was as if the monster possessing her had experienced a stroke. The right side of the face snapped and twitched. Vatrenex let out a confused grunt before repeating the same snap-and-twitch action. Nothing happened. Vatrenex put a clawed hand up to the left side of his face, feeling the feminine dwarven features still present.

"Everything alright, Cap'n?" Saltbeard asked.

Vatrenex was annoyed and didn't hide it as he replied only with a glare. The monster then refocused his gaze back on Mutt to find the orc having the audacity to smirk at him.

"What is the source of your amusement, orc?" Vatrenex growled.

"You can't change back," he answered. "I thought your face was ugly before, but even blind and with one eye gone, I can tell that you are the most hideous thing I've come across," he said.

The monster cocked his head to the side. "Do you think I concern myself with beauty?" he asked before slamming Mutt's body back into the wall with his aura. *None of my other hosts have ever given me such a stable aura. Good,* he thought. Vatrenex was now able to give off the aura of not only a Sapphire but the highest tier within the Sapphire rank. Only those who had reached Tier-Two Sapphire could outwardly project their shrouds to become auras. Vatrenex grinned evilly.

Meanwhile, Mutt gagged and choked, unable to speak.

"We agree to your terms," Zhaden shouted hastily. The fearful but apparently cunning drakonid seemed to have been taking in all the information and deducing what he could from their exchanges. He seemed to be a sharp-witted one unlike his simpleminded orc friend.

Vatrenex retracted his aura, and Mutt gave a deep sigh of relief.

"If you swear on your core to keep our friend safe," Zhaden continued, "we will agree to serve as your slaves."

Vatrenex glared at Zhaden from his one open eye, as his right mouth growled, "War provides no guarantees of survival or success, but I will agree to keep your friend as safe as I can. In exchange, you will submit yourselves to be my slaves. I cannot swear on my core as others of this realm can," Vatrenex said, then raised his vein-covered blade, pointing its tip at the drakonid, "but I swear on my blade as captain of the Swordstrike Corsairs. This is the greatest of oaths that we can make on this ship, and it is an honor that I rarely bestow. Understand?" He didn't tell them *why* he couldn't use his core for the oath. They didn't need to know.

The drakonid's face wasn't the most expressive, but his tail moved through a variety of patterns in a way that made no sense to the Harbinger. Before he was about to shout in annoyance, the drakonid finally spoke up. "We . . . agree to your terms," Zhaden hissed reluctantly, nodding in acknowledgement.

"Excellent," Vatrenex replied with a grin before looking over to Saltbeard, "Undo their bonds from the walls but keep the trollstone on."

"But, Cap'n, ye haven't—"

"I have spoken, First Mate," the monster spat out.

Saltbeard's eyes opened wide, his mouth agape in fear. "Aye, sir," he said, then began quickly freeing both Zhaden and Mutt from the wall cuffs.

Vatrenex lifted his curved blade towards one of the dark walls. A doorway that had blended in seamlessly with the wall instantly opened, letting in the bright light of day into the hollow tower.

"Guards!" Vatrenex shouted.

The guards visibly tensed before they each turned to face inside. "Aye sir?" they nervously asked. Upon seeing Vatrenex's new visage, they recoiled but quickly composed themselves, presumably to avoid angering him.

"Take our newest pair of war slaves down to their quarters," Vatrenex ordered. He noticed the orc clutching one of his wrists, and the memories of the dwarf host informed him that it had been broken previously. "Get the orc a bone-mending remedy as well. We need his arm strong for what I have planned for him."

His newly acquired slaves both shuddered before lowering their heads to avoid the monster's gaze and began limping over towards the doorway and out of the nightmarish tower.

After they exited, the door closed, leaving only Vatrenex and Saltbeard remaining inside the monster's dark abode. The dwarf sheathed his cutlass and rubbed his hands nervously.

"Beggin' yer pardon, Cap'n, but why didn't ye make them take the vow? And what happened with the paladin there? I've never seen any fight against yer control 'fore."

"My appearance is none of your concern Hagish!" Vatrenex snarled. "My control is absolute. It always has been and always will be."

"Of course, Cap'n." The dwarf quickly bowed his head in submission.

Vatrenex let out a low growl but had been placated enough by the dwarf recognizing his place. "As for your first question, it is because those two are . . . special, like this dwarf here," he said, looking down at his new body that he had transformed to his liking. "I recognize that I need them untainted by my direct influence. I have not found a more suitable host in centuries—" *Despite her face not reverting back,* he thought only to himself. "—and I believe it is from their time spent near that thief they call Kiru. They have been 'primed,' so to speak."

"Truly, sir?"

"Indeed," Vatrenex replied.

"Is that why the krakens spared the limp boy? What be so special 'bout him? Is he why the Mourners attacked?" Saltbeard eagerly asked.

"You assume correctly, First Mate. Gaal'cothdreek-duun's first barrier is gone. I could tell when I tried to kill the boy from a distance. The first barrier has prevented me from retaking the fortress for countless years. Zis'Piel and his Mourners sudden attack also proved our new slaves' value. I sense that an end to our constant stalemate is finally near, Saltbeard. The tide is about to turn. With these new slaves under our control and Gaal'cothdreek-duun's first barrier finally dismissed, it is time we finally end the stalemate between my fellow Harbingers and I."

"Ye mean?" Saltbeard asked.

"Yes, First Mate," Vatrenex said before looking up to the swirling cloud of mana above them. "We go to war. It's time we claim the entire Torn Empire for ourselves."

Both the monster and gray-skinned dwarf gave wicked grins, eager for the bloodshed to come.

CHAPTER ELEVEN

Gaal'cothdreek-duun

The bleeding tentacle in Kiru's mouth oozed thick, tarry blood, making him feel as if he was drinking liquid metal. The tentacle flopped as if it were alive and had a mind of its own, but Kiru bit down harder, causing more blood to squeeze out. Then, before he could reflexively spit out the foul-tasting stuff, he swallowed.

Despite the lack of physical sensation below his neck, Kiru could sense the power inside the blood as it traveled down into his stomach. The liquid was laced with mental mana, and Kiru somehow *felt* his body absorbing it, the power inside it leaving his gut and traveling across his blood vessels before reaching his meridians. As the power flowed, Kiru could tell it was moving steadily, but there was a slight resistance as if it were a thick syrup. Based on how gritty the blood was, he wasn't necessarily shocked.

When the power from the kraken blood finally made contact with his meridians, however, that was a completely different story. The mental mana inside the kraken's blood surged upward towards Kiru's cracked mental mana core as if drawn in by a powerful magnet.

"*Oh . . . crap*," William said a split second before the blood contacted the damaged core.

Kiru's entire body went rigid as he was beset by a wave of simultaneous pain and euphoria. His eyes rolled back as he visualized his core. He watched as the orb of swirling, condensed mana, bisected by a large crack that was leaking out white mental mana was suddenly struck by the kraken's blood. All of the liquid was drawn to the core, landing directly on the large crack. The blood continued to flow until it completely covered it.

Eventually, the blood formed a full patch, completely sealing the crack. The psion was reminded of how the kraken had healed his limbs. Once all of the blood had been drawn in, the entire core glowed brightly. Kiru breathed a deep sigh of relief and brought his focus back to his body.

He spat the tentacle chunk to the ground, then rubbed the back of his head. "William, I think it worked," he said aloud as his body relaxed.

"*I think so too, Master,*" the imp replied, but there was still some doubt in his voice. "*How do we check? I don't want you to summon me and break your core. I'm wonderful to have around, but not necessarily worth destroying yourself for when you can still have me inside here.*"

Kiru smiled. "*Easy. I just need to see if activating a technique hurts,*" he sent via Telepathy.

"*So . . . did that hurt?*" William asked.

Kiru's grin widened. "Not one bit." He then clenched his fists in excitement. He was back! He then shouted in triumph, unable to help himself.

"*Fuck, yeah!*" William echoed his jubilation. "*Now, get me outta here! I'm ready to stretch my legs.*"

Kiru smiled and did just that. Though it wasn't necessary, he guided William to appear in front of his chest. It was a habit he developed back when he was at the Royal Academy in the Kingdom of Blades so as to avoid anyone suspecting his psionic identity. He felt it was a good habit to maintain, just in case there were prying eyes.

The orb of red light grew and gathered until it morphed, shifted, and coalesced into the form of his familiar. William's body appeared, revealing his emaciated form, his red skin tight over his bones. His most notable feature was, as always, his head with the top of the skull missing, exposing his pink and wrinkled brain.

Kiru was used to the grotesque sight, so he didn't bat an eye. He caught William with his left hand, the imp landing firmly on his palm.

William puffed out his chest proudly and looked down his long-hooked nose at Kiru, assessing him like a judge. "Well done, Master," he congratulated.

"Thanks," Kiru replied, both grateful and amused.

William nodded, then jumped up to his usual perch on Kiru's shoulder.

Kiru then turned around to see where exactly they were, and both William and he discovered that they were in a metal tunnel. It was dimly illuminated by dots of green light spread randomly about. With the dented door behind them and the kraken behind it, they had no choice but to go forward.

"Where do you think we are, Master?" William whispered.

"Below the island," Kiru answered. "That pirate captain called it a fortress. A prison. It definitely wasn't natural, what with all the purple metal I saw. I have a sinking feeling that we are at the bottom of it."

"Ugh," William said as he shook a little. "That guy was the creepiest thing I've ever seen, and that's counting that fat, furry ogre that tried to eat us with his belly mouth."

"Agreed," Kiru replied, before pressing on.

For the first time in centuries, Mal'throk awoke. The warden of Gaal'cothdreek-duun let out a haunting inhale as his singular red eye opened once more. Mal'throk coughed wetly as he slowly forced himself to stand, his tentacles weak from injury and disuse. His body, once powerful and grand, now looked pitiful. He was physically connected to the fortress' power source—the Chaos Core—via pipes that were made to control most of the ship. This is what kept him from deteriorating.

Mal'throk had taken extreme measures in order to ensure those damnable Harbingers didn't take over Gaal'cothdreek-duun. After the fortress broke, separating it from the hive mind, those wretched experiments had attempted to revolt. In order to stop them, he'd activated all of the fortress's last-resort defensive measures, from the twin barrier ring to even releasing the damned krakens to keep all but an arboth from entering, hoping that one day one might help him reclaim their people's glory. After all, only an arboth could wield the mental mana needed to get past the outer barrier. Before placing himself into a state of stasis, he was notified that they'd crashed into an ocean of whatever realm they'd landed.

"If I'm awake, then that means . . ." he trailed off in realization. Mal'throk did his best to move to the fortress' control panel, where hundreds of screens lined the wall. Many of them were cracked or dull—evidence of the ship's damage, as well as the fact that he'd had to divert much of its power to sustain himself. Much wasn't all, though, so when he pressed his long finger into a socket, he activated what power was left to the Gaal'cothdreek-duun.

The warden took in another deep inhale as his mind connected with the fortress. His ability to perceive and control his people's stronghold had been severely limited by his injuries and his diverting of the ship's power. Still, he was able to locate the lone being who'd entered. Mal'throk cocked his head in confusion. *That is no arboth*, he said. This was an intruder who'd somehow made it past his defenses. He had to monitor.

The tunnel wasn't long, and Kiru and William soon found its exit. As they neared, the metal grating underneath them became more uneven. Kiru looked down to notice strange root-like growths interwoven through some of the grates. He was unsure of what they were, so he continued on and tried to put them out of his mind. Then, they reached a round, open doorway in a glowing red wall. He took a step through and entered the bottom chamber of the fortress.

Kiru felt as if the red light was something thick and tangible as they passed through it, and they arrived in a nightmarish, alien place. "Did you feel that?" he asked William.

"Yeah," the imp answered. "Where in the abyss are we?"

"Vatrenex said it was both a fortress and a prison. He called it Gaal'cothdreek-duun. Maybe this was the prison part?" Kiru suggested. The chamber they walked through was all twisted metal, shattered glass, and eerie, red illumination. It was large, with a vaulted ceiling at least a hundred feet tall. Multiple columns spread out evenly across the chamber, the second floor visible behind the upper halves of the columns. The air was heavy with the mixed scents of decay, blood, and salt water. It reminded Kiru of some sort of ruined cathedral.

The metal walls, once sleek, now bore scars and fractures, the remnants of some forgotten battle. Numerous tunnels dotted the walls, leading further into the unknown. Tendrils of fleshy roots snaked along the metallic surfaces, occasionally pulsing with an otherworldly rhythm. The grated floor was now a labyrinth of jagged edges and rough, uneven surfaces. Here, the floor was overtaken by the roots.

Broken machines and consoles were scattered about, glass screens cracked and flickering with ghostly echoes of strange symbols. The sound of dripping water resonated throughout the chamber, one small stream gently pouring out from one of the second-floor balconies into a small pond below.

"Master, I gotta ask. If Vatrenex was a prisoner here and he's been alive for gods-know-how-long, what else might be stuck here?" William said.

As if in answer to his rhetorical question, a couple of guttural barks came from one of the tunnels to the right.

On edge, Kiru drew his two blades.

William gulped. "You know, Master, your core actually wasn't so bad of a place to stay. In fact, I'd like to be in there right now. It's not that I'm scared—not one bit. It's just that I think I'd be more useful to you in there, you know what I mean? With me being inside your core boosting your perfect recall, it would be dumb for us not to do that, right?" William said. The imp was clearly terrified, but Kiru knew he wasn't about to admit it.

Given their current situation, Kiru agreed that placing William back inside was the wisest decision.

After he did that, Kiru heard the Mask of Fenrir moving just slightly on his belt. It wanted to be put on, and Kiru did so. Even if he would have to fight off its bestial influences, he reasoned he needed every advantage he could to survive in this foreign territory. Kiru's half-elven senses were impressive, but with the mask on, his senses of smell, hearing, and ability to tell when danger was near were far superior. After the mask's enchantment activated, Kiru was practically struck backwards by the complexities of the numerous scents assaulting his nostrils. He had to shake his head a few times to adjust to the onslaught. A moment later, his right ear twitched slightly as it picked up the noises that echoed throughout the room.

Kiru could hear rhythmic tapping of something approaching on the metal floor coming from the right, where he'd heard the barks emanating from earlier. Though he had no clue how far down he'd been taken, Kiru knew that he needed to go up. That would be his way out. *Once I'm outside, maybe I could find a ship to use? That way, I can go and locate my friends,* he thought. For now, unsure of which tunnel led upward, he chose one of the lefthand ones, his only logic being that he heard none of the intimidating noises that had come from the right side and that the smell coming from the one he chose was the most tolerable of all of them.

The dark tunnel wound about. The sparse red lights cast elongated shadows, making Kiru more on edge than he already was. Each step felt like trespassing on forbidden ground, disturbing the equilibrium of the foreboding place. Occasionally, he heard squelches underfoot, making him realize that the roots he'd seen were actually more like tendrils of flesh—or veins, even. Kiru grimaced at the noises. *At least we're not going further down,* he thought.

Amidst all of the squelches of moving flesh, he thought he noticed an eyeball opening along the wall beside him. He quickly turned his head in alarm, but then saw nothing watching him.

"Do you think it's one thing watching us or more?" Kiru asked William via Telepathy.

"I'm not sure, but I don't like it either way," William replied.

Kiru agreed. That feeling of being watched but finding no evidence kept recurring until the psion finally emerged from the tunnel he'd chosen. He discovered that he'd gone from one large chamber to another. Where the first reminded him of a ruined cathedral, this one was like a strange metal swamp. It was roughly five times as large as the previous room with a giant warped metal pillar in the center that looked like a tree of some sort, on an island surrounded by a lake of bright green bubbling acid, giving the entire place a subtle green glow amidst the darkness. Numerous crooked metal pathways led across the lake of acid to the central tree.

Clusters of metallic debris were strewn around in all directions, along with what looked to be willow trees made of flesh. Kiru's eyes widened as he saw a small crab scurrying in the distance. Thinking about food reminded him of how hungry he was, and he took a careful step toward the crustacean. His hopes of having crab for lunch were abruptly shattered, however, when the "flesh willow" snapped down at the crab, wrapped it up with one of its branches, and lifted it towards the top of its stalk. A mouth quickly appeared there, and the tree chomped down on the unfortunate creature, devouring it rapidly with a set of sickening crunches.

"The fuck?" Kiru whispered.

"What in the abyss is that?" William asked.

"Your guess is as good as mine," Kiru replied. His mask-enhanced hearing finally picked up on sounds coming from behind him. The psion took a step back, his blades ready in a defensive stance. He was taken aback to see a single eyeball on a stalk protruding from the metal wall on his left. The eye didn't react to his noticing it. Instead, it continued to focus on Kiru, unblinkingly.

"Um, hello?" Kiru said.

"Are you getting a bad feeling from that thing, Master?" William asked.

"Yep," Kiru sent back.

Suddenly, he heard a series of snarls from nearby to his right, emerging from the tunnel he'd come from, growing increasingly closer. A pile of metal creaked loudly to his right, and he turned to see a large paw cresting the metal's surface. It was quickly followed by a head and finally the rest of the creature. The thing Kiru saw before him was a bizarre blend of a wolf, a lion, and an octopus. It certainly favored a wolf in its overall bone structure, but it had purplish skin, a mane of small wriggling tentacles, and six yellow eyes arranged in a semicircle along its head and mouth, all now focused on him. It smelled of tar.

The monster snarled, and Kiru took a step to his left just as another one of the creatures emerged. *It seems they're just like regular wolves, hunting in packs*, he thought. The two bared their teeth at the psion and slowly stepped toward him. One even growled, revealing that their mouths opened out in four flaps like a flower's petals. Kiru's ears twitched as he picked up a noise behind them. *Clever,* he thought. He could tell there was a third wolf about to ambush him, using its compatriots' noises to hide its movements.

Just as the one behind him pounced, leaping up from behind a metal bush, Kiru spun and used "Hammer The Boards." The hook of his blade caught the thing unawares and cut right into its throat. It let out a pained cry as Kiru continued his momentum, swinging the wolf off of his weapon and into its allies. The creature landed on one of them, but the third was able to leap directly at Kiru. He met it with "Sweep The Barn," deflecting the beast, before eviscerating it with his other blade, killing it.

The other two beasts stood back up, the one Kiru had previously injured somehow managing to staunch the blood dripping from its wound slightly with some of the tentacles that served as its mane. Kiru smirked, feeling a bit of his mask's bestial influence but also excitement that using his mana no longer hurt. *I've missed this,* he thought. So, when the wolves came, he didn't use another sword form. He used a technique instead, throwing the beast into its compatriot. The second wolf was knocked off-balance and fell into the pool of acid.

The beast shrieked in agony as its body began to dissolve, but Kiru didn't pay it much mind. He was still focused on his final opponent.

"He looks like he's gonna lunge," William warned.

Taking those words seriously, Kiru bent his knees and readied himself. The psion was prepared and sidestepped the creature as it lunged. He then performed a variation of "Caught Fish," embedding the hooks of his blades deep in the beast's mouth. Using the built-up momentum, Kiru pulled hard on them and yanked up. The blades easily cut through the creature's mouth and the right side of its face. Gouts of dark blood erupted from the wounds, but its pain was cut short as Kiru reoriented his blades to point both hooks upwards, ending its life with "Clean the Ceiling."

The Fu Tao bit deep into the thing's skull with a set of crunches, and its body went limp, falling hard onto the metal ground.

Kiru just stood there, breathing hard.

"*That was awesome!*" William cheered.

Kiru nodded and grunted in agreement. The feeling of having had his core repaired was indescribable. To be able to fight again and without any pain . . . he had to agree with William, it *was* awesome. His joy at that revelation was cut short, however, when he heard movement. Kiru snapped his head up and braced his blades.

It was the mounted eyeball he'd seen earlier, which had now extended out about a foot longer than previously, still staring intensely at Kiru. The eye's pupil was constricted, somehow conveying a sense of rage.

"*I don't like how it's looking at us, Master,*" William sent.

"*Agreed,*" Kiru sent back.

As if the eye had somehow heard their telepathic conversation, it twitched and Kiru's mind was beset with a sharp, high-pitched noise.

Kiru gritted his teeth and fought against the force. The noise was assaulting not only his brain but his mental mana core as well.

"*Abyss, no!*" William shouted, and the imp formed a protective barrier inside Kiru's mind, instantly providing a great deal of relief.

Emboldened by his familiar, Kiru glared at the eyeball. "*Get out!*" he shouted via Telepathy.

The eye recoiled at Kiru's rebuff, seeming to have been caught by surprise.

Kiru let out a wolf-like growl, thanks to the influence of his Mask of Fenrir, and cut the eyeball from its stalk before it could try and attack him again. The remaining portion of the stalk recoiled like a worm quickly getting sucked into a small round hole in the metal wall. Kiru was going through a series of emotions at that moment—anger, fear, excitement, but most of all he felt . . . good. Maybe it was his mask imbuing him with the confidence of a predator. Maybe it was due to just being able to move again or having had his core repaired.

The psion quickly dismissed those possibilities, though. It was something else. "What is this place, this Gaal'cothdreek-duun?" Kiru was starting to like this place but wasn't sure if he should be or not.

CHAPTER TWELVE

Oasis in the Nightmare

Kiru's familiar was confused. *"What are you talking about, Master?"* William asked.

"The creepy pirate with the big-ass sword said it was a prison and a fortress."

Kiru snapped at his familiar. *"I obviously know that. Just what kind of fortress has lakes of acid, six-eyed flesh-hounds, predatory trees, and oh, weird eyeballs that use mental mana, hm?"* While the psion was excited about exploring more, despite the danger, William was starting to really grate on his nerves.

"I . . . don't know," the imp admitted.

"That's what I thought. Just think about what you're going to say before always spitting out the first thing that comes to mind, alright? I know you mean well, but you're not being helpful right now, okay? Try to be smart about things. Be useful," he sent.

William didn't say anything for a good while before giving a begrudging *"Okay."* Kiru felt bad for his reprimand but didn't have time for niceties. They certainly weren't safe where they were right now. Kiru walked over to the corpses. He shook one with his foot and idly wondered if it was a sacred beast. "Well, if Vatrenex is any indicator of the type of denizens in this place, I shouldn't be surprised," he said before looking around. "Now, where do I go to get out of here?" he asked.

"I'd say go to the pillar on the island, Master," William answered.

"What? Why do you say that?" Kiru asked.

"Well, we gotta go up since the kraken brought us down. That metal pillar has what look like some lights and windows. I figure that must be for a reason. I haven't seen any stairs up since we got here so far, so I bet there are some inside the pillar," William explained.

Kiru thought for a moment, stunned by his response. *"That's actually a reasonable and well-thought out idea that can be of some use, William. Thanks."*

"I know I have good ideas. I'm smart too. I can be useful," the imp muttered as he conveyed the image of him crossing his arms.

Kiru sighed, feeling bad for what he said earlier. *"I know, William. You're very smart, and right now I need your intelligence to get us out of here. I'm sorry for what I said. You're a great companion,"* Kiru sent, trying to extend an olive branch.

"Really?" William asked.

"Yes," Kiru replied.

"So, I'm the perfect familiar?"

"You have your uses, but that doesn't mean you can't be better." Kiru replied. He could tell that William was about to protest, so he added, *"We* both *can be better, okay?"*

The imp sent the mental equivalent of a nod to Kiru.

With their somewhat promising lead, the psion then began to move towards the large pillar. The pathways along the lake of acid were crooked and winding. Some were made of metal, others from winding tendrils of some cross between bark and flesh, by his guess. Scattered about the lake were innumerable metal outcroppings. Nearly every one of the weird metal boulders had some form of plant life on it. From what Kiru could tell, they were either those terrifying carnivorous willows or some strange metallic mangrove tree. The foliage from the latter looked like yellow porcelain cups, all of the "leaves" facing upward as if to collect rain from the nonexistent sky. The foliage was also dense, obscuring much of the dark cavern above.

Kiru discovered that he had remarkably solid footing, despite traversing a path floating over acid. He reasoned that the materials that made up the path must have been surprisingly resistant to the acid, as there was no indication of weakness at all. He was grateful for that, because he wasn't interested in taking a dip in the bubbling liquid.

Soon, Kiru discovered that the closer he got to the central pillar, the more potent the vapors from the acidic lake became. At first, it was just minor, only bringing a foul smell to his nostrils. Eventually, it started to make him cough. Then, his eyes watered as they began to burn. Despite being a Ruby, his resistance only went so far. He covered his hand over his mouth and began coughing loudly as he searched for a way forward through the dense fog coming off of the acidic fumes.

Kiru snapped his head to the right when he heard a strange trilling noise coming from the trees. Primal instinct kicked in, and he forced himself to stop coughing because he didn't trust that whatever made that noise wasn't hostile. Kiru rushed back to hide behind a nearby pile of metal that he'd just walked by. The fumes weren't as strong here, so he was able to breathe easier as well.

Slowly, carefully, he peeked his head out towards where he'd heard the strange noise. For a while, he saw nothing, other than the nightmarish mangrove-like forest amidst a lake of acid. Eventually, however, he noticed movement among one of the metal trees. He eventually spotted a lizard-like creature about the length of his forearm, not counting its long tail, with a pair of yellow eyes on each side of its face. On its back was what looked like a colony of mushrooms.

Kiru watched as the thing moved along the branches of the tree until it was just inches away from the acid. His eyes widened as he saw the odd fungus pulsating and glowing, the fumes from the acid seeming to be drawn to them. He nearly let out an audible gasp as the lizard literally cleared the entire area within a five-foot radius around it of fumes. Once it was done, it let out another trill before climbing back up the tree and hiding in one of the cup-like leaves.

Kiru looked around the forest, noticing the predatory, leafless willows, and an idea came to him. "*William, I've got a plan,*" he sent before summoning out his familiar once more.

"What is it, Master? Do we cut down these trees to help us make a clear path?" William asked.

Kiru shook his head. "I'm thinking a stealthier approach is in order." The psion then proceeded to tell the imp his idea. William wasn't a fan of it but reluctantly agreed. A couple of minutes later, Kiru watched as the imp was halfway up the metallic tree, and grumbling in frustration as he climbed. As William neared the leaves, the four-eyed lizard stuck its head out to peer over at him. It cocked its head and trilled curiously at the imp.

"Get over here, you," William growled as he thrust his hand out and used his own version of Telekinesis. Though strong, his body wasn't tempered like the psion's, but it was enough.

The fungal lizard began to float in the air. It snapped its head from side to side and its body wiggled, clearly in distress at its lack of control.

William cackled. "Hahaha, yes. You are nothing compared to my might, little worm. Ow!" He cried out as the lizard snapped its whiplike tail, cracking him in the face. The sudden pain broke his hold over the reptile.

The lizard leaned over the branch and hissed at the imp.

William growled right back.

That was when the lizard's friends showed up, just as Kiru had been hoping for. Emerging from amongst other cup-like leaves were about fifteen more of the four-eyed creatures.

"Retreat!" William shouted and began rapidly climbing down the tree, the reptiles following close behind. The imp leaped off the tree and used Telekinesis on himself, flying back over to Kiru.

The lizards let out a series of angry cries that sounded like a bird chirping crossed with a pig squealing, echoing throughout the subterranean jungle. Many of them stayed on the tree, but seven larger lizards, including the original one

William had goaded, leapt onto the ground and charged. Kiru was impressed by their speed, but he was still ready.

The psion pulled out his psyslime blade and used his mental mana to levitate it above his palm. As William landed on his shoulder, the reptiles were quickly closing the distance. With a flex of his will, Kiru forced the psyslime to change shape, morphing from a blade to a net, and launched it towards the incoming creatures. The lizards scattered, but one got caught in his trap. As the remaining beasts neared, Kiru decided to use more of his Telekinesis, forcefully knocking them away one by one.

Two reptiles were accidentally knocked into the acid, letting out sounds of pain as they were melted alive. Unlike the flesh wolves, these things had been minding their own business, and he wanted to spare as many as possible. Seeing them get liquefied was not a sight he enjoyed.

"Master, can't you force out your technique in a big wave or something?" William asked.

"Not effectively," Kiru grunted amidst uses of Telekinesis. "While I can use my technique on more than one target such as keeping myself up and dealing with these lizards, it's better if I concentrate on a single source per use instead of firing a large wave."

Just as he finished his explanation, one of the lizards managed to get past his barrage. Demonstrating remarkable athleticism, it whipped its tail hard against the ground to launch it up to reach eye level with Kiru. While midair, it spun and hit Kiru's left ear with a *whack*.

"Graah!" Kiru grimaced, then growled, his mask's influence growing. "Stupid thing," he spat out before kicking the lizard with a Telekinesis-enhanced boot.

The fungal lizard let out a wet gurgle and was sent flying back into the fog, its body breaking apart into fleshy pieces from the force of the blow. The other lizards paused in their charge as bits of their dead comrade rained down on them. The psion only needed one to be alive for his purposes, but he knew he could find more colonies to collect from.

Kiru pulled out his steel blade, no longer caring about sparing the beasts' lives when he suddenly heard something. The Mask of Fenrir was enhancing his already-excellent sense of hearing, and his now-hairy ears twitched as he heard not one but two different sets of noises coming from deeper in the acidic fog. The first was a set of clicking noises off to his left and the other was a chorus of deep, inhuman groans farther away but directly ahead of him. The psion took a step back and pointed his blade to the left.

Out from the fog came a colony of hideous, blue-green, crab-like creatures, each with a single pink eye. Each one's eye was located on a different part of its body, no one crab being exactly alike. One had it on top of its shell, another on a leg, and the one in front on one of its claws.

"Ugh!" William grimaced at the sight of the creatures.

The "ugly crabs," as Kiru dubbed them, appeared to be scavengers, just waiting for their next meal. They came crawling out amidst the metal and vines of the pathway and voraciously began eating the scattered remains of the fungal lizard Kiru had punted. The remaining reptiles turned and hissed at the crabs. The pink-eyed crustaceans clicked their mandibles and claws in response, showing they were ready for a fight.

Content to let the two sets of creatures fight it out, Kiru slowly began leaning down to get his net and trapped lizard. That was when the moaning grew significantly louder. Both the crabs and lizards froze.

"What was *that?*" William asked.

His question was immediately answered as a set of purple glows appeared from deeper in the mist. Both the crabs and the lizards immediately began to flee to their hiding places. While the crustaceans were able to get away, the lizards needed to make their way back to a tree. They turned and leapt towards a nearby one, but none of them succeeded. Of the four remaining lizards—not including the one Kiru had trapped—only two were even able to attempt a leap. Neither of them made it to their target. One of them got too near to one of the carnivorous willow trees and was caught midair by one of its tentacle-like branches and gobbled up.

I did not expect that, Kiru thought.

The other lizard was bit down upon by what seemed to be a glowing mouth made of purple light that shot out from the fog. The mouth was still connected to . . . something, and it was pulled back like it was on a string, bringing the lizard with it. The other two lizards were seized by a pair of black tentacles that slammed them down with enough violent force to squash and kill them both instantly. The lizard in Kiru's net was now frantically trying to get out of its bonds, cutting its scales in a desperate attempt to break the metal psyslime.

Sensing that whatever was in the fog was bad news, Kiru quickly picked up the net, using Telekinesis to keep the lizard trapped, and backed up, keeping his blade pointed at his unseen foe. On the one hand, he wanted to run. On the other, the more curious part of him wanted to know what this thing really was.

"Hey, you know, Master. If you wouldn't mind, I think it would be better for you to recall me again now. To allow me to keep your core safe from—" William gulped. "—whatever that thing is."

Kiru shook his head. "*Whatever it is, I don't want to alert it to our presence from the light that comes from summoning and recalling you,*" he sent via Telepathy. "*And no talking, just Telepathy for now.*"

William gulped again before nodding nervously at Kiru.

It only took a few more seconds for the source of the light to become visible through the fog. Kiru gazed upon the strangest thing he'd seen to date. It was a dark, ominous creature with characteristics resembling both plant and animal. It had a spherical body that was purple and luminescent, with multiple glowing purple orbs embedded within it. Extending from its body were numerous dark tentacle-like appendages that extended in all directions. The lower tentacles had small "threads" coming off of them, making them appear to be more like roots. The strange being was floating, its roots just inches above the ground. It was about Kiru's height.

It let out a set of dissonant moans, and it was met with a reply by another abomination that Kiru saw behind it. The psion could see that the purple orbs were semi-translucent as he noticed the lizards inside them flailing about and being dissolved before his very eyes.

"If you wanna put me back in right about now, for your own safety purposes, I'd completely understand," William sent.

The creatures let out a chorus of howls and began floating in Kiru's direction. They weren't fast, but they weren't slow either, moving at a good pace comparable to the psion power-walking.

Kiru backed up, blade in one hand and the bound lizard in the other.

"Tactical retreat?" William asked.

One of the abominations flicked its black tentacles at the psion.

"Definitely," Kiru said and jumped to the right.

The other then attacked in a different way. The orbs proved to be very malleable because one of them extended out, stretching far from its body and turning into a mouth.

Kiru ducked under the attack and swiped upward at the extended "mouth" in an arc. He cut through the purple substance, causing the end to fall off and land by him with a wet *plop*. It reminded Kiru of gelatin as it broke apart and jiggled.

The abomination recoiled, brought the purple substance back inside it, and gave an even more bloodcurdling cry. Both creatures then redoubled their attacks on the psion. One of them struck out at William with a tentacle, but Kiru recalled his familiar before that could happen and took the blow on his right shoulder pauldron. The blow was strong, but Kiru's armor took it, the dragon tooth on it managing to cut the appendage as well.

The creature gave another howl of pain as it pulled back its limb.

Emboldened by his Mask of Fenrir's predatory instincts, Kiru thought he might fight the thing now and show it who was the alpha. That was until he saw the thing regrow its tarry black tentacle as if it was nothing. He turned back to run only to find another one of the abominations blocking his path. Kiru used Telekinesis to cause it to fall into the acid, but to his dismay, it only floated above it.

So, facing an alien foe who could regenerate in a subterranean jungle with an acidic lake and fog, Kiru did what any reasonable person would: He ran. He had wanted to test his idea with the fungal lizard and the acidic fumes before implementing it, but he didn't have that luxury anymore. He forced the psyslime net to bind the small reptile tight until it could no longer move, then wedged it between the teeth of his wolfish oni mask, the fungi on its back facing out. With the ways to the front and the back both blocked, Kiru ran to his left, his feet slamming loudly against the path as he sprinted away from the monstrous things and moved deeper into the fog.

"*Master, are you sure about this?*" William asked.

"*We're going to find out,*" Kiru replied via Telepathy. To the psion's great fortune, his idea proved viable. The absorption ability of the odd mushrooms on the lizard's back proved effective enough to clear away all the acidic fumes around the psion's face. It kept his airway and face free of the caustic substance, but only for a few inches around his head. It wasn't the five feet that he'd seen the lizard make before, but it was better than nothing. Still, it rendered his vision minimally effective. Kiru also had to fight the mask's influence to not eat the bound lizard. The psion found it repulsive, but the beast mana flowing through his senses thought otherwise. The need to run for his life, however, overcame that urge.

Kiru ran deeper into the mist. He heard the skin of his hands beginning to crackle, and he looked down to see it reddening and bubbling.

"*Uh oh, we gotta hurry,*" William said.

Kiru agreed. He looked around, trying to get a sense of where exactly they were. They had been running for a couple of minutes along the winding paths, getting out of the way of more abominations emerging from the fog, dodging strikes from the carnivorous willows lying in wait to ambush him, and narrowly avoiding the attention of a pack of flesh-wolves by forcing his feet to levitate off the ground so as to not make as much noise. The only reason he could tell that the creatures were near was the sound of their snarls and the glowing of their six yellow eyes visible through the fog.

It was not long after that point that Kiru had believed that he'd lost the trail of the abominations. The psion wondered if it was noise that attracted the things since he'd been much more quiet when just barely levitating. Kiru then thought to levitate himself high above the fog, but when a giant shadow and accompanying deep cry flew above him, he thought better of it. *Don't need to get the attention of whatever that thing is,* he thought.

"*See Master, this is where a real powerful blast of Telekinesis could clear a path in this fog for us,*" William sent.

Kiru grunted in frustration at his familiar's words. Despite the possibility of there being some sort of dangerous flying creature above the forest he was in, the psion realized he was out of options. He was lost, and his body was being broken down by the acidic fog. His armor was holding up for the moment, but he didn't know how long it would last. Even the lizard was more lethargic than before. The psion readied his blade and lifted himself up out of the fog using Telekinesis.

To his great relief, he found the pillar was only two hundred feet away. He then gazed upwards to catch sight of a pair of long, segmented creatures that looked like a cross between a whale and a millipede floating near the ceiling of the massive cavern. The things were about twenty feet long and at least half as wide and had gray skin with splotches of rusty brown. They were munching on some faintly glowing blue moss that was growing on the ceiling and, by the sounds their mouths were making, Kiru reasoned that one of the two was the source of the shadow that had flown over him earlier. *At least they seem docile for the moment*, he thought, relieved there appeared to be at least one herbivore in this nightmarish place. He still wasn't going to lower his guard as he wouldn't put it past the large creatures to be omnivorous.

"Master, can we get to the pillar now? I feel exposed, and I don't want those things to find us again," William sent.

Realizing how vulnerable they indeed were, Kiru flew above the forest, reaching the central pillar in a matter of seconds. To his surprise, the area immediately around the pillar was free of fog, like there was an invisible barrier keeping it safe. "It's like an oasis in this nightmare of a place," he said.

Having now emerged from the acid fog, the lizard inside the jaws of his mask began to squirm about some more.

When Kiru began to drool at the prospect of eating the thing raw, the psion realized it was time to take off his mask. He removed the fungal lizard from it, then commanded the psyslime net to loosen, allowing the reptile to scurry away to find another tree. Kiru then undid his mask, freeing himself from its effect and feeling his eyes, ears, nose, and mouth reverting to their normal appearance.

The psion, now just feet away from the pillar, took a much closer look at the place. It was a large structure made of metal and glass. Brown, fleshy roots snaked up and all around it and strange mushrooms grew all over it. On the ceiling around the top of the pillar was more of the subtly glowing blue moss he'd seen those floating worm whales eating earlier. Kiru hadn't noticed the moss when he'd seen the structure from a distance. With the roots and mushrooms, the pillar looked like some strange attempt at making an artificial tree. The bottom of it was partially collapsed on the left side, the structure seemingly stabilized and still standing due to the entangling roots all around it.

"Where's the door?" William asked.

Kiru carefully scanned but couldn't find one. "It's likely seamless, like when we found the entrance to this place. With all these fleshy root things covering most of it, I doubt we can find one, let alone get it to open," he said.

"So, how do we get in? Are we going to cut a door?"

Kiru shook his head. "No, this place is already more damaged than I realized. I don't want to affect its integrity any further." He then noticed some of the oddly arranged windows. "But we can probably break those."

William laughed giddily at the idea.

Kiru sheathed his steel Fu Tao before telekinetically altering his psyslime once again. This time, instead of a net, he made it into a maul. The psion then walked over to the nearest window. It was slightly above him, and he was able to reach it with the weapon. A majority of it was covered in the vines and roots that surrounded the pillar, but there was enough of an exposed area for Kiru to squeeze himself through. So, he lined up his weapon, reared back, and swung. *DONG!* The window rang like a bell as it cracked.

Kiru winced at the noise, surprised at the window's toughness. While his body wasn't physically strong in the classic sense, the force behind his mana-infused movements was significant. To see the glass only crack versus shatter proved just how strong it was. William chortled at the failure, but Kiru paid him no mind. He just needed a few more swings. His heart raced, however, when he heard the moans of what he presumed to be multiple abominations in the fog. "Uh oh, apparently I just rang the dinner bell," he uttered.

"*Hurry!*" William urged.

Kiru didn't need to be told twice. He smashed into the window three more times in succession, with renewed vigor, each strike eliciting more haunting moans from the jungle around him. After the third hit, the corner of the window finally shattered.

He'd thought his swings were loud at first, but the sound of the glass breaking was *deafening*. More cries echoed throughout the fog mixing in with the howls of the flesh-wolves, as if in answer to the noise. Kiru snapped his head to scan his surroundings and noticed telltale purple lights off in the distance and moving quickly toward him. He was pretty sure he saw some of the wolves' yellow eyes too. Not wanting to waste any time, he sheathed his psyslime and forced himself into the opening he'd made.

He jumped shoulder-first to squeeze in, but his momentum abruptly stopped—even though his body was thin, his bulky bone armor wasn't.

"*Master, come on! Hurry up*," William insisted.

"I'm working on it," Kiru grunted back. He started to shimmy himself into the tight space, slowly making progress to the point that he got his first arm free. He then heard another moan from much closer. Kiru looked back to see that multiple abominations were indeed just cresting out of the fog. That was when he *really* started to wiggle his way in, forcing his way forward, his heart loudly racing. After a few seconds, he heard the sound of cracking in front of him. He looked down to see small segments of the glass scraping against his armor. The pressure of his body and the force of his movements seemed to be breaking it even further.

Kiru gasped as he realized the small pieces of the window that were still connected to the frame were what was impeding his progress. He pushed harder to try and get in, but he had become stuck. *I gotta break this*, he thought before he saw a couple of the tentacled monstrosities just fifteen feet away from him. "Crap," he spat out.

"*This is not good, Master*," William sent. "*We can't fight them. Use the Brainstorm!*"

Not seeing any better option, Kiru did. His core sent mana along his body, gathering charge and lacing the electricity along his unfeeling nerves before bringing charged mental mana back into his core. Once there, he concentrated the mana-laced electricity until it coalesced together. In just a second, the psion was ready and fired the technique directly from his core and out of his forehead. "Brainstorm!" White electricity shot out from him. In a flash, it hit the nearest tentacled abomination and spread out to link and attack four more creatures trailing behind it. The monsters all writhed in place from the technique, and their bodies started smoking.

Kiru had just a moment to take it in before the concussive boom of the technique forced him to recoil. The force was strong enough to break the remaining glass fragments and send the rest of him into the partially ruined column. His body slammed against the metal ground with a *thunk*, and he quickly turned it into a roll to get himself in a standing position. Not daring to see if the abominations survived, Kiru unsheathed his blades once more and hastily moved deeper into the column away from the window, hoping to find answers within.

CHAPTER THIRTEEN

Be Useful

Like most of the underwater fortress, the inside of the column was dark, metallic, and full of those same invasive roots. Unlike outside, however, it was remarkably clean and well-preserved—at least, the part of the tower that *hadn't* been destroyed. After Kiru moved out of the small room he'd fallen into, he quickly rushed deeper into the column.

The next area he found himself in was a large circular chamber that appeared to be the central room of the tower. As soon as he entered, the doorway behind him slammed shut. Kiru turned back to see a metal door blocking his way back that seemed to have moved out of a groove. For just a moment, he was in complete darkness before glowing green and red symbols started to appear all around him in quick succession. The psion gripped his weapons tight, unsure if another threat was coming.

Thankfully, nothing came, and after about ten seconds, a hundred or so lights appeared along the walls and structures in the central chamber, fully illuminating it. It indeed was a large, mostly round room that was maybe three hundred feet in diameter, by Kiru's estimation. A good third of the room was taken up by a giant pile of rocks, metal, and possibly glass, all covered in a network of roots. Along the undamaged walls were multiple doorways identical to the one Kiru had just come from. He counted seven in total.

"Well done, William, you were right to bring us here," Kiru said.

"*It's about time I was recognized for my value,*" the imp sent, clearly feeling smug.

Kiru just rolled his eyes before he continued to analyze his surroundings. The central chamber had six large glass tubes both taller and larger than the psion set up in two parallel rows. Each tube looked to be some sort of giant vial, all of them holding some sort of liquid in them, illuminated by a green light from below. Kiru recoiled slightly as he got a better look at what else was inside them: bodies. Warped corpses of monstrous-looking beings. After a moment's hesitation, Kiru carefully crept forward to examine them further. The smell of formaldehyde hit his nostrils as he neared the closest one. It looked to be a pale giant rodent nearly the size of a dwarf. The rodent had a hunched spine, a long snout with buckteeth, tiny slits for eyes and a large hole on each side of its head instead of classic ears. Kiru also noticed that it had two tails and multiple wires attached to its body from the top of the vial it floated in.

"What do you think that is?" William asked.

"Your guess is as good as mine. Probably some unlucky prisoner here," Kiru said, wondering if the thing was like that before it was put into the tube. *Was a rat experimented on and made to look like that, or was it studied because it was like that already?* he thought. The psion then noticed a glass and metal panel to the left of the vial. There seemed to be buttons carved into the glass. Unsure but curious, Kiru pressed one of them. The glass panel immediately came to life, glowing a bright green and illuminating all the buttons, each one showing a strange, curved symbol similar to the one on the door that Kiru had slapped to get into this fortress.

A strange noise suddenly came from the panel, sounding like someone was gasping for air while trying to slurp water at the same time before the panel turned red and flashed. Something else beeped and flashed red for a moment from the wall opposite from where Kiru had first entered, and then a small spark shot off from the panel, and it went dark. "Okay, so it looks like this thing is out of power . . . but what was powering it?" Kiru asked himself before he looked over to where the beeping had been coming from.

There, he saw a stone obelisk about as wide as him but slightly taller. It had sharp angles, and the top of it seemed to be broken from how rough and uneven it was. It was right by the wall, and a massive mirror was mounted above it, larger than any Kiru had ever come across.

"My guess is that thing," William said.

Kiru moved a few feet forward, in awe of such craftmanship. He saw his reflection in the mirror too. He noticed that his right ear was still severely damaged. It had healed over in the day since the monkey's attack, but it was now an uneven chunk of flesh. Kiru grimaced at the sight and touched it. *It's at least functional and doesn't hurt,* he thought, trying to comfort himself. As he neared the obelisk, Kiru felt himself being drawn to it. Given how dangerous this place had been so far, it put him on edge. *Is this a trap?*

Once he got within touching distance, the thing began to hum slightly. Kiru jumped back, but the humming didn't stop. That was, until a spark shot out from a hole in the wall behind it. The top of the obelisk flashed red twice and beeped before the thing seemed to shut off. Kiru took a step to the side and looked behind the structure, from where the spark had shot out.

There was a hole about the size of Kiru's arm in the wall just under the mirror. A thin piece of black metal was visible in its center, extending all the way to the obelisk, partially embedded in the structure. On the left of the hole were more veiny growths, which had clearly expanded into the hole where the metal originated from. Kiru's darkvision allowed him to see inside to find it was a mess of tangled-up knots and wires.

Since I'm stuck in this hostile place, the more information I can get, the better. Those tablets are my best chance to access anything that can help. From what I can tell, I need the obelisk to work to gain access to the information on them. Now, I'm no engineer, but the sparks and messed-up knots coming from inside that hole seem to indicate that those growths are affecting it somehow. Problem is how do I get back there? Kiru thought. He pondered that conundrum while he investigated the rest of the central chamber. To double-check, he pressed on one of the glass tablets by another floating body. Just like with the weird giant rat, it flashed red and the obelisk beeped before it lost power.

With confirmation that it wasn't just one panel that wouldn't work, Kiru looked at the corpse in the giant tube beside him and raised an eyebrow in confusion. While he had a feeling the thing was in fact dead, it seemed to be made of some strange reflective metal rather than something he'd qualify as an organic material. Its body was composed of sharp angles, and it had two eerily faceless heads. They were literally just featureless spheres. He spotted no genitalia, either. *It looks like a construct,* Kiru thought, reminded of Daisy Directory, the one that handled the Royal Academy's introduction for new students. She possessed a featureless, plain-white body, the only indications that she even was a "she" being her name and the feminine manner in which she spoke.

Kiru went to check the other doors in the chamber. Getting more familiar with how the prison worked, he pressed a palm to the light glowing on each door. Of the six doors that weren't the one that he'd just come from, three opened. One was full of debris, as the room had collapsed in on itself. The second beset the psion with a foul odor as soon as he opened the door. His gut clenched and he was grateful his stomach was empty as he dry-heaved from the stench.

After managing to muster his resolve, Kiru looked into the room. In the center was the source of the smell. There was a pile of rotten remains in a heap that went nearly as high as the ceiling. He couldn't discern any distinct body parts as it was all just a mess of indistinct gray and black flesh. Even William made a disgusted noise in Kiru's mind.

Along one wall though were three shelves. The bottom two shelves had brains in jars of preservative fluid, reminding the psion of the corpses in the central chamber. It was what was on the top shelf that intrigued him, however: glass orbs containing various liquids. Kiru didn't know what they were, but he could sense the mana coming off of them.

"Those could be useful," Kiru said.

"Oh, Master, do you have to go in there?" William asked. *"I really don't want to have to smell you if you get any of that rotten filth on your clothes."*

Kiru sighed. "William, you're inside my core. You can't smell me. Also, what did I say about thinking things through and being useful?"

The imp paused. After ten seconds of silence, he said, *"I . . . guess those vials could help, and it could be worth it, even if you happen to get some smell on you,"* the imp sent, clearly begrudgingly.

"Good. Also . . ." Kiru said, then stuck out his left fist and activated Telekinesis. Carefully, precisely, he lifted and pulled in each glass ball one by one and loaded them into the storage space on his enchanted ring. ". . . I don't have to go in the room anyway," he continued. "See, you just need to think things through. That's when you're useful."

William grumbled inside Kiru's mind.

Kiru felt bad for being so blunt with his familiar, but the imp's impulsive nature often seemed much more a curse than a blessing to him. All the childish and unnecessary comments just compounded Kiru's stress at the moment. He was in a hostile location—he didn't need William chattering away on top of it. *I need William to either help with providing options or to not speak at all so I can think.*

With no way to identify the strange glass orbs, Kiru left them in his ring. He hoped that if he could bring power into this area, it may help him in that endeavor, but for now, the safe bet was to leave them stored away. Kiru walked away from the horrendously smelling room, and to his fortune, the door closed behind him.

The final door that opened gave the psion the most hope. It revealed sparsely illuminated stairs leading up. Up was the way he wanted to go. Still, he needed to get information and didn't want to rush headlong into a trap. So, he went back to the obelisk.

Kiru reexamined the hole where the rod that presumably powered the obelisk came from. There was no way to get to it. The doors that did open didn't connect to the area that he saw, though he was able to deduce that the invasive growths were likely the cause of the issue. Without a better option, he raised his psyslime blade and cut at the thin length of root about as wide as his pinky, leading into the hole. For how small this piece was, it was remarkably durable. His psyslime blade barely scratched it.

Kiru grunted and swung down again. It cut deeper but didn't detach it. *I'm going to have to saw into this thing,* he thought. A smile grew on his face as that gave him an idea. He let go of his psyslime and directed it to float in the air beside him. With a flex of his will, he altered the blade's shape into that of a round saw. The psion then directed it to spin and carefully ordered the blade forward. It began to cut into the small root much more quickly. After about thirty seconds, it finally managed to cut off the root. The blade began to hit the metal wall, sending sparks before Kiru called it back. He leaned down to touch the severed piece of root. It made a crinkling noise like dry leaves underfoot.

"It's weaker now," he said. Kiru noticed that it was still intact, though. Part of him had hoped it would just wither away, but clearly, more work was required to remove the rest from whatever powered the obelisk, as it clearly was still entangling it.

"Now, how do I get rid of all those roots back behind the wall?" Kiru asked himself as he pondered what to do next.

"*I'll do it,*" William said.

"How?" Kiru asked.

"*I can fit in there and claw away at the roots interfering with the rod. It's the best idea I can come up with,*" William replied.

"Now *that* is useful," Kiru sent excitedly. He then summoned William out from his core once more and placed the imp on his palm. For once, William didn't say anything, he just furrowed his brow and turned to face the hole. Kiru sighed.

"Hey, William, I'm sorry for being rude earlier. It's just been *really* stressful here, you know? Almost getting eaten by a kraken three times, getting chased by a monstrous abomination, nearly getting dissolved by acidic fog, and then getting chased by even *more* abominations can wear down anyone's nerves," he explained.

The imp just crossed his arms and stayed silent, still not deigning to look at Kiru.

Kiru sighed again. "Look, I know you didn't mean anything bad. I—"

William stuck a palm out. "No, no, Master. You want me to be useful. You've stated it multiple times. I'll show you useful," the imp growled right before quickly leaping off his hand and scurrying inside the hole.

William was angry—angrier than he'd ever been with Kiru. He knew that Master was stressed being down here, but that didn't give the psion the excuse to harass him. William had always said what was on his mind, and *now* Master wasn't okay with it? *And why does he keep telling me to "be useful?" I'm always useful,* he thought as he climbed through the small hole. "Just look at this idea. If I hadn't said anything, Master would still be trying to find a way to clear these roots that made it back in this hole," he grumbled quietly under his breath to keep Kiru from hearing. "Sure, there've been times when I should've given things 'more thought' before I said anything, but that's part of my charm," he continued to mumble.

After a few more seconds of squeezing his form through, he made it to the other side of the wall. It was just a small area of crawlspace for this strange piping. There was only about six inches in all directions, but he could see the metal rod was part of a system like pipes and branched out in four different directions: up, down, left, and right. In the center area from which the rod spread out was where the suspected problem originated. There was a large ball of tangled-up roots there.

William smiled. *I'll show him useful,* he thought. The imp then began clawing away at the roots. He groaned and grunted with effort—they were a lot tougher than he'd suspected. After Master had weakened them, William expected that removing the rest would be a breeze. Unfortunately for the imp, that was not the case. Still, he was determined to make Master eat his words, so he kept at it.

For at least an hour he clawed at the knot. Kiru asked William if he needed help, but the imp vehemently refused to even acknowledge the psion, his focus not wavering on his task. He had heard Master say something about taking time to cultivate while William was working on his mission, but he didn't pay attention to the psion's words. His goal was too important. *I'll make him regret thinking I'm not useful.*

William growled at how slow his progress was. He then thought about how Master had used his techniques to aid him since they entered this tower, such as Telekinesis to change his weapon into a spinning saw. It gave William an idea. The imp raised his right palm and shifted fire mana into it.

Before Kiru's fire mana core had been shattered, the psion had recklessly created a half-baked technique called Hot Hands. While Kiru could no longer use fire mana, that didn't mean William couldn't. The imp's red palm heated up until it turned orange. He then pressed it on the knot. The growths instantly began to burn away, turning into ash. William cackled like a villain before the realization hit: *Wait, I could have done that from the very beginning?* In just a minute, he burned away all the growth surrounding where the pole branched off, revealing a glowing diamond at its center. The diamond was black and flawed with white cracks.

The imp's eyes widened at the sight, and he accidentally touched it in his effort to thoroughly remove every piece of the material that had encased it. A spark crackled from the glowing gem, and William's vision went white as he was flooded with chaotic power. The imp's mind felt like it had been taken elsewhere as his vision cleared and he found himself standing on a floating round disc. Master was standing opposite him—only it *wasn't* Master, not completely.

It was a strange silhouette of Kiru, as if a simple sketch of him had somehow come to life. Its eyes were empty but who it was supposed to represent was unmistakable to the imp. For some reason, even though he knew it wasn't Master's, he could tell it represented him, for some reason. So, in a way, it *was* Master. All around the two, a chaotic storm swirled. Flashes of multihued lightning bolts could be seen amidst the clouds surrounding them. Above them, in the center of the strange hurricane William was now in, was a starry black sky—only the stars were moving, shifting about like they were insects.

He looked back at Master's silhouette, the man's empty eyes staring blankly at him. Master raised an arm to reach out to the imp and took a step forward, but

William scowled and jumped back. "I don't need your pity. I will show you useful," he said, flexing his thin arms. "I will be powerful . . . I will be the most powerful familiar there is. I will become so useful, that you will feel like a fool for having doubted me," he spat out. The surrounding storm closed in rapidly. Before he could say anything else, he was struck by four different lightning bolts at once, each a different color.

The imp was immediately flooded with chaotic power. He became . . . *more.*

Kiru kept trying to apologize to William, but the imp was continuing to ignore him. He could see William clawing away at the roots and making slow progress, similar to how he'd done with his blade before he turned it into a spinning saw. After a few minutes of fruitless attempts, he decided he would do something useful with his time, namely rest and cultivate. Kiru reasoned he was in as safe a place as he was going to be for a while, so it was worth the risk. He was still hungry too, but without any viable food options around, he'd just have to deal with it. It also helped that he had his mother's storage ring which contained plenty of water, so thirst wasn't an issue.

Kiru rested his back against one of the tubes containing a corpse, deactivated his Telekinesis, closed his eyes, and started to cultivate. He immediately gasped as mana rushed into his body with shocking ease. Normally, he would describe cultivating without any dreaming minds nearby like sucking thick syrup through a straw. This, however, was like warm water rushing into him of its own volition. Kiru didn't even need to bring it inside him. It was as if he was standing under a raging waterfall.

Normally, his body would have to filter out the mana in order to have anything usable, as mental mana wasn't abundant in most places. Kiru believed he was pretty efficient in his cultivation abilities, but it still took him time to build up sufficient stores. The mana in this place, however, was . . . different, to say the least. First off, there was plenty of mental mana, which really threw Kiru. He'd never found any place other than the academy's library with as much of his mana type readily available.

The second thing was that the mental mana was laced with . . . *something—* another type of mana. Kiru went to his mind's eye to envision the mana he took in. He could see the white thread of mental mana being drawn to his core, but attached to the top of it was another thread of mana, this one shimmering in a kaleidoscopic pattern that was hard to look at. Kiru wasn't sure *how* he could tell, but he somehow *knew* that the multicolored mana was somehow controlling the mental mana.

While he was examining the mana, the psion could sense that the mana he was intaking was coming in so fast that it would eventually overwhelm him. With a flex of his will, he closed off his meridians and core. After that was taken care of, he refocused. *Now, how do I filter this out?* he thought as he contemplated the strange wild mana.

Fortunately, he quickly found a solution. He simply reached out with his will and ordered the mental mana to separate. And instantly, like a zipper being unzipped, the mental mana began to detach itself from the other mana and be brought into Kiru's core, filling him with the magical power. In just a few seconds, his core was already one-quarter full. *This is amazing.* The psion had roughly estimated that when his Ruby core was full he would have twenty-four hours of movement available. *Barely need any cultivating at all to refill myself here!* He would've been ecstatic had the strange, multicolored remaining mana not started to cause issues, acting erratically, moving and shifting about in an unpredictable pattern. Normally, when Kiru cultivated mana, he would filter out anything unnecessary through his meridians without issue. This mana didn't behave that way, acting like it was alive with a will of its own. It snaked, twisted, coiled, and bent as it soared across Kiru's meridians. He kept trying to exert his will over it, but as soon as he focused on where it was in his body, it would dart away, making him miss it somehow. He struggled at it for five minutes, then ten. After fifteen minutes of trying and failing, the psion had an idea. After the mana moved into the meridian of his right arm, he focused on that meridian itself. He temporarily forced it closed off by "barricading" it with a wall of his mental mana.

The chaotic mana still twisted and contorted uncontrollably within it. When Kiru focused on it again, the mana tried to surge across his body to escape his targeting, but when it neared the wall of mental mana Kiru had made, it was forced back as if by magnetic repulsion. With its escape route blocked off, the psion was able to target it with his will.

To his surprise, while the mana still twisted and writhed, once he got a hold of it, he was able to control it if he exerted his will carefully. It was the mental equivalent of holding a slimy, wriggly worm in between two fingers. Too much effort and Kiru feared the mana breaking apart into two separate pieces. Too little effort, and it would likely slip out of his control. There was a problem, however. *Now that I have it, how do I get it out?* he thought.

He was used to mana just filtering out of his body naturally; he had never guided any foreign mana out intentionally before. *Well, there was that poison laced with mana back in Imakandi when I saved Mutt's sister,* he mused, *but this is different. Back when I first started cultivating, many of the other village children had waste products coming out from their pores when they cultivated. Can I force this weird mana through my pores somehow? Maybe, but I don't know how to do that. My meridian doesn't have an exit point.*

Although, technically . . . his right arm meridian *did* have an end. It was the concentrated round bottom in his palm. With no better idea, Kiru started to shove the strange mana at the end of the meridian. He grunted as his arm shook with the effort. Fortunately, he was successful in getting a small bit out after a few seconds. It was like shoving thick taffy through a strainer, but after ten minutes of focused work, he was nearly finished in forcing out all the strange mana.

"What is this mana?" Kiru asked out loud, sweat pouring down his face. Just before he got the final piece of the strange mana to emerge from his palm, Kiru felt both the segment and his mental mana core going intensely bright inside him as the two suddenly radiated power. The force of the surge was too much for him to handle. It made his eyes roll into the back of his head and his body fall limp to the side. His core pulsed erratically like it was about to explode, and his mind was transported somewhere else.

The psion's vision cleared to see that he was now standing on a flawless, round piece of white marble flooring. After looking at the ground and his feet, he began to scan the environment. The first thing he noticed was that he wasn't alone. What was standing across from him was hard for the him to comprehend. It was William but not like he was used to seeing him. The imp was somehow two-dimensional, like he was made from a cut-out piece of paper.

He couldn't explain the imp's strange form, but he realized that it was some kind of avatar for him. Before he could ask him any questions, the telltale sounds of lightning hit his ears. He quickly turned his head back and forth to see that they were surrounded by a vortex of swirling black clouds, as if they were in the eye of a storm. It looked like they had about twenty feet of space between them and the clouds in any direction, with intermittent, multicolored bolts of electricity providing both color and illumination to the intimidating sight.

Though there was no wind, Kiru could tell that the clouds were slowly closing in on them like a constrictor coiling around its prey. The psion had no idea where exactly he was, but based off his familiar's avatar, he figured it was some sort of mental space. *Maybe William's own Mind's Eye?* he thought. *Didn't know he could do that, but I guess it makes sense.* Kiru noticed that there was a small string connecting his mental mana core to William's chest as well.

Then, he raised an arm and took a step forward. "Hey, William, watch out for those clouds," he said.

The imp looked comically angry and jumped back, raising a fist in the air and chattering some unintelligible gibberish that Kiru couldn't understand. William then flexed his arms in a poor display of strength.

A split second later, Kiru's body went stiff and he jerked his head forward as he felt the connection between William and himself go taut. *If he moves any farther back, it's going to break,* he thought. *Am I about to lose William as my familiar?* Kiru hesitated, not wanting to scare the imp away, but he was stumped as to what to do since it seemed they couldn't communicate properly. It was as if he and William were in the same space, but there was a filter in between them, affecting how they perceived each other. It was during that moment of hesitation and real-ization for Kiru that the storm clouds got too close and touched William.

Four bolts of lightning, each a different color, snaked across the clouds like they were alive somehow and the imp was their prey. One hit his exposed brain and another hit his chest, while the final two struck each of his boney legs.

Kiru's vision went white once more as he felt the chaotic lightning's power via the connection he had with his familiar. His physical body convulsed as if in a seizure from the lightning's strange effects. As he shook, he realized that the bolts, while all different, each shared one thing in common. *They're all made from that same weird mana I was filtering out,* he thought.

Yet before he could dwell on it further, the surge of power stopped, and his focus was forced back to his real body. As he opened his eyes, Kiru gasped as if he'd been holding his breath. He found himself lying on the cold metal floor of the central room of the tower once again, his mouth wet from twin trails of drool. "W-William?" Kiru coughed out as he reactivated Telekinesis to force himself up. After his familiar didn't answer for a few seconds, the psion turned his head to face the hole where the imp had crawled into. He wasn't there. Still, it was a small space, and Kiru wanted to make sure that something hadn't happened. So, he started walking over to the area. He only made it a couple of steps when he heard the sound of someone clearing their throat behind him.

Kiru turned back to see a being that was unmistakably William but remark-ably different as well. The lower half of the imp's body was now just a small white cloud, his tail no longer there, either. Unlike his typical bony, hunched-over spine, he now boasted a muscular physique with even some veins bulging out in some areas. William's face remained mostly the same except for three key differences: his eyes were slightly larger, his teeth were now big and white, and he had facial hair.

How in the abyss did William grow a mustache? Kiru thought as he examined his familiar. His new pointy black mustache was oddly bent and crooked, mak-ing it appear not like true hair at all. The final and possibly most concerning change was William's brain. It was still pink and exposed like before, but it was now three times taller than before, and on top of it was a red eye, staring unblinking at the psion.

Kiru opened his mouth to say something, but was truly at a loss for words, thoroughly thrown off at his familiar's new form. He expected the imp to flex his muscles and brag about his new body and for a giant cocky smile to form on his face.

Instead, William crossed his arms over his chest and pressed his lips in a thin line, looking disapprovingly at Kiru. While his two eyes squinted at the psion, the eye lodged in his brain was shifting up and down as if scanning him. "Hmph, so much wasted movement. Tell me, what is the use in standing there gawking at me like some sort of starstruck child?" William asked. Kiru had never heard the imp sound like this before. Instead of a bloodthirsty little demon, he was more like a strict elder back in Kiru's hometown of Bristleton talking down to an unruly disciple.

Kiru raised his eyebrows. *"Uh . . . William, is that you?"* Kiru asked via Telepathy. Though he instinctually knew it was his familiar, he couldn't help but ask.

William rolled all three of his eyes in response. "Such a useless question. You clearly know it is me, Master, just as I can sense that you are you," he said before shaking his head side to side and tsking. "Wasting your mana to use Telepathy to ask something so pointless. Honestly, there are so many better things to spend mana on—at least thirty-two different options by my calculations alone. If we're going to make it out of this ship, we are going to have to improve your mana expenditure and cultivation rank."

The psion's eyebrows were now raised all the way up to his hairline in surprise. He expected the little demon to be bursting with pride, but the derogatory way William was speaking toward him was completely foreign to him. The psion could sense through their connection that the imp truly believed that he could improve Kiru's cultivation. "Okay, hold on. There are multiple things we need to clarify. First off, what happened to you when you went into the hole to clear out the growth? Second, how do you know how to improve my mana usage and cultivation ranks? Last I checked, you only knew how to get me to Gold at best— also, my efficiency at mana expenditure is quite good for my rank," he said defensively.

William flared his nostrils and grunted. "It will save time to just give you the information instead of us wasting time talking about it. We have a long way to go in order to reach our goal. Bring me back inside," he said.

Kiru paused for a moment, unsure if he wanted to let the changed imp back into his core.

William appeared to pick up on Kiru's caution and grumbled, "We've already been over this, Master. I am me. I swear on the very mana that created me that I mean you no ill. In fact, I mean to help. Let me be useful."

Kiru's core could sense the weight of the imp's oath and knew it to be true. So, eager to figure out what in the world had happened to his familiar, the psion recalled William back into his mental mana core. In an instant, Kiru was flooded with new knowledge he couldn't have dreamed of acquiring. There was so much to learn!

CHAPTER FOURTEEN

Knowledge Is Power

As soon as William was fully brought back inside his core, Kiru was inundated with a vast amount of knowledge. His eyes rolled to the back of his head from the sheer volume of it.

"Hmph, it appears this is too much data for you to absorb all at once," William said inside his mind before the influx seemed to be suppressed, as if a floodwall had been erected, allowing only a little information in at a time. Kiru blinked his vision clear as his mind began reviewing the information that he'd just absorbed. He quickly realized that what he'd gained was William's memory. Kiru gasped as he "saw" what had happened to the imp over the past few minutes: his tearing-up of the growths, using Hot Hand, and touching the glowing fragment under it all. Kiru then saw where William had been transported to after making contact—the same mental space that Kiru had been sent to. Then, William was struck by that unknown power.

There was no new information after that, so William then began speaking: *"I was flooded with new information and power, the same power that the transmitter I made contact with is made of—chaos mana."*

"Chaos mana?" Kiru asked—he'd never heard of that before. Sure, he'd heard of techniques that had been described as chaotic before, but that was it. But he wasn't fully surprised, as he'd heard of all sorts of strange mana types before, such as Royal and Laughter.

"Yes, Master, chaos mana," William replied. *"It flooded my body and transformed me. I could feel it trying to corrupt me, but my mind resisted its effects. The rest of me resisted as well, because I didn't want to be forcibly changed, but I wasn't as effective on that front, as you can see with my changed body. Though my form is different than before, I believe it is an improvement. My physical capabilities are far superior to my previous ones, and I can fly now, too."*

Kiru quietly listened to the imp. Based on how William was acting and even the lack of his usual thirst for violence, the psion wasn't sure his mind *wasn't* corrupted, but he kept that to himself.

William didn't seem to notice Kiru's doubt because he kept on speaking. *"Now that you have seen the evidence, it is time I teach you even more of what I've learned."*

"Even more?" Kiru asked just before letting out an involuntary gasp as William shared more information as if the mental floodwall had suddenly been lowered, allowing more knowledge to rush into the psion's mind. His eyes widened and his heart sank as he learned where exactly he was and the horrors that called this place home. Gaal'cothdreek-duun was indeed a prison, but it was so much more. It was a ship—a flying fortress city whose inhabitants used it as a base of operations to conquer those they deemed lesser.

It reminded the psion of *The Marauding Citadel*, only much more advanced. The place was hundreds—and, in one area, thousands—of miles wide in nearly all directions. The beings that inhabited it, the arboth, were a warmongering people who roamed around, enslaving and experimenting on all of those who were unfortunate enough to cross their paths. The realm they inhabited was one that Kiru had never heard of: the Void. His mind was flooded with visions of millions of humanoid cyclopean creatures with too many tentacles roaming about the place like termites in an underground network.

He got a distinct image of an army of thousands disembarking from the ship in a space that looked like a starry night sky and attacking a pod of whale-like creatures in a fierce battle. Another image appeared of the creatures that survived being taken down below in chains. The next showed the tentacled creatures torturing and experimenting on the things. A few red eyes squinted gleefully while the other arboth seemed to gaze at the horrific scenes with academic interest.

"Enough!" Kiru shouted, stopping the tide of images from coming in. He looked around and breathed heavily. It was all too much. The horrors he'd witnessed were so much worse than even things the old William could have come up with. From the glimpses he'd been given, Kiru believed the things that had called this place home were even worse than the dragons. "We're really fucked, aren't we?" Kiru asked, now realizing the full scope of the terrible situation they were in. From what he'd gathered, he was in the ruins of some nightmarish prison ship that was thousands of miles deep and hundreds of miles wide. Oh, and that ship was almost completely submerged in the ocean. The only reason it appeared to be an island when Kiru had first seen it from the outside was that just the very tip of the structure had broken the surface of the sea.

"No, Master, our situation is not as dire as it may appear. Though the arboth that once inhabited this place were undeniably cruel, I believe we should be able to escape," William sent.

". . . How?" Kiru asked, clearly skeptical.

"As I said, I have absorbed a lot of information, too much for you to take in at once, apparently, but I should be able to slowly impart to you what I've learned over time from the transmitter," the imp replied.

"The transmitter? Was that the glowing crystal thing you touched?"

"The very same, Master. It has granted me much knowledge, and with knowledge, comes power," William said. *"This entire ship has conduits of mental mana spread throughout it. It once powered this vessel after it was cut off from its main source of power."* Kiru was about to ask the imp how he knew that when something new happened.

A blue semitranslucent screen appeared in his vision. On that screen was a map of Gaal'cothdreek-duun. Kiru observed a complicated network of rooms, cells, and tunnels that was mindboggling to look at. Then he realized that this was a shrunken-down version of where he was standing. There was even a glowing triangle slightly pulsing, indicating his exact location.

"This is a map of the level we are currently in," William explained.

Kiru nodded, though there was one thing that bothered him about the map. *It's way too nice. I don't notice any of the damage or strange growths anywhere, let alone the forest that surrounds this tower,* he thought.

Seeming to read the psion's thoughts, William continued to speak. *"Of course, this is the original map of this level. Level 6."*

"Only Six? Wow, we may not be as deep down as I thought," Kiru said.

"Six is the bottom level. Observe," the imp said before the map shrunk down even further, revealing the entirety of the ship as a whole. Just as Kiru had witnessed in his visions, it possessed gargantuan proportions bigger than any city the psion had ever heard of. As William had said, there were five more levels above them, each one unique and massive. It was shaped like a spinning toy top, like the ones Kiru played with as a kid. It was smallest at the bottom, gradually increasing in width as it went up before narrowing again at the top, ending in a fine point. Then, before Kiru could say anything, half of the projected map of the multilevel fortress city and prison flashed red and disappeared, as if it had been cut vertically down the middle with a crooked blade, each floor with different amounts remaining, as the break wasn't a clean one.

"What happened?" Kiru asked.

"According to the data I've collected, some event tore Gaal'cothdreek-duun from their realm suddenly and without warning. The ship couldn't fully handle what happened and was split in two. I was also able to get an updated map from the last remnants of the transmitter," William replied.

Kiru tried to return to the hole where William had gone, but the screen followed his eyes. "William, can you make this screen go away?"

"Of course, Master," he said, and the screen went away. *"For future reference, with me inside your core, you now have the ability to call up information I have stored."*

"Good to know," Kiru said as he looked to where he'd sent William before his transformation. No glow was visible back there, confirming the imp's words that the "transmitter," as he called it, was no more.

Testing his ability to call up the screen, Kiru willed it to appear once more. The zoomed-out map of the damaged fortress came into view. He felt like he knew how to control it based on intuition. *Is it because of my mental mana? Or because of William's presence in general?* he thought as he focused back on the Level Six. Unlike before, the map now displayed a much-more-accurate depiction of the current layout, with the acid lake and all. There were still sections that were either blurry or blacked out, but it was a great improvement.

"How long has this place been down here?" Kiru asked, not expecting an answer.

"From the data I have gathered, approximately 4,625 years have passed since this place went down to minimal function."

Kiru snapped his head. "Four thousand years?! How can that be? It's only 925 Post-Ragnarok. Even if this place pre-dates Ragnarok, how can it be here? Alterra hasn't been around for *that* long."

"According to my calculations, Master, there must be some sort of dilatory effect. Time passes quicker here. It appears to go approximately five times faster here, which is good. That gives us five times longer to get out and save the other members of our party," William answered.

Kiru's eyebrows raised. "Wow, that's really useful information, William. Thank you. How exactly did you get that knowledge?"

Though recalled inside Kiru's core, the psion could tell William was pleased by the compliment but he didn't want to show it. Apparently, there still seemed to be some hard feelings based on his response. *"Hmph, of course, Master. I was useful, am useful, and always will be useful. As for how I acquired the exact information, I took it from the ship's logs. Here,"* William sent before the map was replaced with a series of notifications. They were all in the same swirling alien script Kiru had seen earlier, so he couldn't understand it, but then William seemed to translate it for him.

Name: Gaal'cothdreek-duun
Status: Damaged
Connection: Severed from Source Mind—Auxiliary Power Engaged. Chaos Core at 85%.

Warning! Containment Breach!
Enacting security measures. Locking down Levels 4, 2, and 1.

Warning! Harbingers #1-4 have escaped.
Authorization required for auxiliary power to enact emergency measures.

> **Warning!** are Prisoners have escaped Level 6.
> Enacting security measures. Releasing Guardians. Guardians insufficient. Engaging Automatons. **Error.** Automatons have insufficient power. Redirecting hostile forces.

> **Warning!** Severe damage taken to Level 3. Unable to lock down.

> **Warning!** Hostile forces are taking over Level 3.

> **Warning!** Level 2 has taken 65% damage. Hostile forces will break through in 54.2 seconds. Hostile takeover imminent. Emergency measures requested. **Error.** Authorization required before emergency measures can be performed.

> Authorization given. Enacting emergency measures.
> Emergency measures in effect. **Error.** Due to significant power demands, all other services aside from life support will remain active. Chaos Core must undergo dormancy to recharge before more auxiliary power functions can restart.
> **Last Data Point Entered:** 4625 Years Ago

Kiru sat down again, his mind reeling from all the data. "So, I'm going to have to travel hundreds, if not thousands, of miles through a multilevel prison from another realm that is full of monsters in order to escape. I'm assuming there is a way to get out of each level? William, how long do you think it will take to make it to the top?"

"There should be ways to traverse each level, Master, and by my estimations, we should be able to make it in one to five years," William replied. The imp then changed the screen in Kiru's vision to show the map of the sixth level once again. This time, it had a glowing blue line starting with Kiru's location, highlighting a path to take.

"One to five years," Kiru repeated, breathing heavily. He just sat there silently for an unknown amount of time, processing that fact. But he knew he needed to get moving. The longer he waited, the greater the chance his friends would die. On top of that, he still had his main quest to acquire his father's items, reclaim his throne, and save the continent from having to suffer an invasion of dragons. In the end, Kiru comforted himself knowing there was nothing he could do about it now. This was his situation, and he had to make the most of it. *At least with the time dilation, it won't be as long for my friends.* "Well, I guess I'll finish cultivating, and then we'll head out."

"While I do agree that cultivating is useful, I believe there are more things to address first before we leave this tunnel," William sent.

"Such as?" Kiru asked.

"I wasn't exaggerating when I said I can help improve your mana expenditure and rank, Master," the imp said before giving the impression of a giant grin. *"Knowledge is power, and I've got a whole lot of knowledge for you."*

CHAPTER FIFTEEN

Ruby Tier Two

Among the myriad of changes that Kiru was experiencing from this transformed version of William, the most welcome was this absolute plethora of new information. With William's current hyperfixation on being useful coupled with Kiru's perfect recall, the psion knew his understanding was about to reach new heights. After he finished cultivating and removing the thick tar that was chaos mana from his body, he was ready.

"So, after combing through your memories and sorting through the new data I've acquired from the fortress, I have come up with a way for you to reach Tier-Two Ruby like Mutt has," William sent.

"Really? Please, go on," Kiru said excitedly. He was personally a bit bothered that William could search through his memories now—that was entirely new—but he didn't let it show. He was too intrigued on how to advance at the moment.

"As you previously discussed, Tier Two is all about filling every part of your body with your mana at once: every organ, muscle, bone, tendon, and every drop of blood to create a new equilibrium in your body. That will allow far greater reservoirs to be available and a level of control you have never experienced," the imp explained. *"Mutt is so simpleminded, he didn't realize what the leokin had done for him to accomplish that feat, not until you pointed it out to him."*

"The mini meridian?" Kiru asked.

"Precisely, Master," William replied. *"Now, as you spoke about with your friends back in the desert, you could simply just submerge your entire body with mana until it is full. This may be the one place in all of Alterra to allow you to do so. However, I would advise against that. Why? Because I learned how the arboth reached Tier-Two Ruby, and it's not so dissimilar from what happened to Mutt. But it's more precise and should allow for even greater technique control. Plus, I believe it will help your transition to Sapphire that much easier."*

"You know how to get me to Sapphire?!" he asked incredulously.

"Not currently, but I believe I will in time. We need to get to Tier Two first. If the method I've devised doesn't work for whatever reason, then we can try the more basic approach," William sent. *"Now, do you see the glowing symbols above the doors?"*

"Yes," Kiru replied.

"You need to dislodge the paneling and remove the crystals providing the white illumination," the imp said.

Eager to get the process started, Kiru stood up and drew his psyslime blade. He moved over to one of the white symbols above the door, floated up to it using Telekinesis, and used his weapon to cut the panel open, eventually dislodging and removing the metal section altogether and revealing a small glowing orb. On instinct, the psion knew it was a mental mana core, barely at Silver. "Why is this up here?" he asked William.

"I was unable to learn the specifics, but it's something to do with mental control. I did learn that the arboth take the cores from those they find weak and unable to progress," William explained.

Kiru grimaced at the barbarism. *Can't do anything about it now,* he thought as he removed the Silver core. He repeated the process with the one other mental mana core he could find in the walls. They were of different sizes but of roughly equal power. Also, both of them had sharp edges, like the cores had been squeezed too tight and their forms had paid the price.

"Good, good," William sent. *"Now, remove the core from the head of that arboth over in that test tube there behind you."*

Kiru turned back to see one of the floating corpses and scowled. He really didn't want to have to smell the bloated body but quickly strengthened his resolve. He walked over to the giant tube that William had indicated. Inside was a bloated mass of tentacles. Kiru had seen what a living arboth looked like in his visions, and the dead one fit the description. It had one vertically slit red eye with a mouth turned in the same direction. Its brain was large and exposed without a skull, reminding Kiru of William. He paused for a moment, wondering if that was significant, then decided to ignore it.

It had a thick, snakelike body other than its two arms. Aside from that, there were an uncountable amount of extra smaller tentacles coming off its body, taking up a large amount of the liquid inside the container.

Kiru saw the same large tablet beside the dead arboth. "Hey, William, since you drained that transmitter dry, do you know of another way to power this on so I can read it? I'd like to learn more if possible."

"There is no need for that, Master. I will show you what it said," the imp sent. Then, information appeared in Kiru's vision beside the floating corpse.

> **Name:** Subject 042103
> **Race:** Arboth
> **Rank:** Silver
> **Mana Type:** Mental
> **Path:** None
> **Status:** Deceased

"Also, I have some more information to share," William added before more text appeared in Kiru's vision.

> *One of the four main races of the void, the arboth are a warlike people who seek dominion over all. They believe themselves superior to all life due to them being the only race in existence to use mental mana. As such, they believe they must bring order to the chaos that is the void. They intend to conquer and subjugate all to their will.*

Kiru just stood there dumbfounded for a few seconds. "Wh-what?" he managed to get out, surprised to see the information just appear in his vision instead of being projected out from the tablet.

"Oooh, this is useful," William said in awe at his own display. *"Master, whenever you need me to identify something or someone, just say 'Imp's Label.'"*

"Imp's Label?" Kiru asked curiously.

"Yes. It's not a technique . . . exactly, but this may be one of my most valuable discoveries to date."

"And you can identify someone's mana type from a distance?" Kiru asked skeptically. Determining someone's cultivation ranks wasn't too hard unless they were actively suppressing it, but figuring out mana types was much harder.

"Not yet, but once I do, it will be even more useful. For some, I'll know what mana type they have based on the data I acquire. And, I can add more information as our knowledge grows," the imp replied, undeterred.

Kiru nodded, finding the idea quite useful indeed. But more important was the description. "William, how can this be? The text said that arboth are the only race in existence to use mental mana, but I can use mental mana too. Am I . . . an arboth?" he asked, looking in terror at the floating tentacled corpse.

"Your biological data does not support that idea, Master. From the information I've gathered, about the arboth, they very much believed in the superiority of their mental mana users. They were all elites and wouldn't allow any who weren't pure like them to use their sacred power," William replied. *"Perhaps your ancestors stole their power, or maybe they were the results of an experiment gone wrong?"*

Kiru's eyes widened at the suggestion, his perfect recall reminding him of key things that had been said previously. Once when he'd spoken with Hlin, she told him that he'd "stolen from the void," referring to his psionic abilities. And Vatrenex seemed to recognize his power, too. The ship captain's shape didn't match the silhouette of the dead arboth, but he was certainly alien enough that Kiru didn't have a hard time believing that Vatrenex could have been from the void as well.

Then, thinking about his patron deity, an idea struck Kiru. He closed his eyes. "Hlin? Are you there?" he asked. The room around him buzzed for a moment as if the power was about to be cut off, but then there was nothing. Kiru couldn't explain why, but he sensed that the goddess was being blocked from communicating with him.

"William, I think you may be onto something about my ancestors," Kiru said.

"*Of course I am,*" the imp replied as if that were obvious. "*Now, collect the core.*"

Kiru then grimaced as he knew what he needed to do. He changed the shape of his psyslime to a maul again and swung at the glass. It easily shattered with one crack, spilling the foul liquid and the mushy corpse of the arboth on the ground below. The fetid smell hit his nostrils. It was like rotten fish mixed with preservative chemicals. Still, Kiru changed his weapon into a dagger and got to the grisly work of dissecting the body. Fortunately, his intuition was right, and the core was in the center of its exposed brain. Like the others, it was at Silver and a strange shape.

"*Good, now summon me out and give me those cores. While I'm working on them, cultivate and refill your core until you are at full capacity,*" William ordered.

Kiru did as bid and allowed the floating three-eyed imp to take the cores and float off to a different section of the room. When the psion asked what he was doing, William just waved him off. Trusting his familiar, Kiru focused on his cultivation. After a few minutes of cultivating followed by ten or so more minutes of Kiru forcing out the chaos mana from his palms, William floated back over to him, the three cores in hand.

When Kiru questioned him, the imp went on to explain that he suspected that when the leokin bit down on Mutt, the sacred beast's mana must have formed a bridge with his own mana to contact the orc's meridian, creating the "mini-meridian," as Kiru classified them. The mini-meridian then served as a conduit to allow the swifter distribution of mana as well as likely improve the ability to intake mana, though the latter was not currently a problem for Kiru. William also explained that for Kiru, the core fragments would serve as the "teeth."

Kiru grimaced as he connected the dots regarding what was about to happen next. *Good thing I still can't feel,* he thought. For the next half hour, Kiru let William float around him and push the sharpened core fragments into specific parts of his body, partially embedding them. The psion had to take off his armor to reveal his form; despite his lack of muscle and fat to provide any additional barrier, the imp seemed to work with high precision, not once striking bone. Kiru knew that William, being his familiar, had intimate knowledge of his meridian locations as well, which likely also helped.

In the end, Kiru had eighteen pieces of mental mana cores partially embedded in his body in different places: three in each arm and leg, three in the left side of his chest, and three in his abdomen, each trailing a small amount of blood. The imp floated around Kiru and gave him an approving nod. "Good. Now, pull more mana in from the environment, but instead of doing it specifically into your core, do it the way you originally learned."

Kiru was surprised by the guidance but did as bid. Instead of pulling mana directly in from his head to his core, he began drawing it in as all commoners of the Kingdom of Blades learn—pulling it in through his entire body. It was a wholly inferior method to what William had taught him back when he was only a Bronze, but this time, Kiru almost instantly understood what the imp was trying to make happen. The standard method required Kiru to draw in mana from every pore, then carry it along his body and meridians towards his core. The body would naturally filter out a large majority of the mana, losing much of what was valuable in the process.

With the embedded core pieces and the abundant mental mana in the environment, however, that was not the case. The core pieces functioned essentially as large pipes, funneling even more mana into his main meridians. When the meridians seemed as if they were about to burst, Kiru started filtering the mana out through his palms and feet where they terminated. He guided the heart and intestinal meridians to filter out that way too until he had only mental mana remaining in his body. Per William's instructions, Kiru repeated the process until all six of his main meridians could contain no more, being full to the brim with mental mana.

Beads of sweat went down the psion's forehead as he struggled to keep it all in. *It feels like the mana is going to explode out of me*, he thought.

"Well done, Master. Now, I need you to draw in more, but this time only pull in through the core fragments embedded within you," William instructed.

Kiru grunted at the task. He knew that normally such a request—drawing mana in through eighteen different spots at once—would be near-impossible. He was confident he could do it this time, though. After many discussions with his friends in the past, he was aware that his ability to control mana was extremely impressive, especially after he guided the mana-laced poison out of Mutt's sister's body back in the orc capital of Dissé. He pulled more in through the core pieces alone. To his surprise, once they were full, it was much easier for them to filter out any chaos mana compared to the rest of the body. *I guess it's because they're cores made from mental mana*, he thought. He repeated the process one more time until the fragments could hold no more mana.

Then, it happened.

Kiru's entire body glowed white with power. He closed his eyes at the sight and gritted his teeth, shaking uncontrollably. He dared not use any of his mana. He realized he was ascending. Then, suddenly, like a dam had burst, mana leaked out from every one of his meridians in a wave. Kiru could sense the magical energy flooding his body, seeping into every organ, muscle, bone, tendon, vessel, nerve, and cell. He could sense it flooding through and out the core fragments as well, spreading mana over his skin.

It's like a protective shield, Kiru thought. The light eventually began to dim, allowing him to open his eyes once more. As the light continued to progressively lessen in intensity, he was able to better observe his body. The embedded cores, which had been jagged and rough protuberances that were now flat and even with his skin. They pulsed with light a few more times before they seemed to sink into him, disappearing under a layer of skin that grew over them in a blink. After a few more seconds, the glow was gone completely, leaving Kiru's thin body unharmed and sitting in lotus position as if nothing had changed.

"What . . . What happened?" he asked William. Kiru knew, but he was still processing.

The imp crossed his arms like an ancient sage and grunted. "Close your eyes and examine your cultivation, Master. Look at your mana inside your body."

Kiru did so and gasped at what he found. Though he had his mana running strongly along his meridians and in his core, he could sense the mana *everywhere* now. Goosebumps raised along his neck. He still didn't have true physical sensation from below the neck, but he could tell that mana had permeated every part of his body, including all of his skin. He couldn't feel in the classic sense, but the awareness and sensation of mana throughout him, was damn close. On top of that, he had new meridians. *Eighteen* mini-meridians. The psion could tell instantly that he could move his mana faster now and with much greater control. Other cultivators at his rank could never compete with this.

He stood up in order to test his newly formed channels but then stopped himself, realizing what he'd just done. "Wait . . ." Kiru trailed off. "I just stood up."

"Yes, and?" William replied.

"William, I'm not using Telekinesis," Kiru said.

The imp furrowed his brows and opened his mouth to speak, but closed it again, for once at a loss for words. Both just looked at each other in amazement, and eventually, William broke the silence. "You . . . you can feel again, Master?" the imp asked, his stern visage finally beginning to break.

Kiru, breathing heavily, looked away from the imp and back to his own body. He started moving each limb and finally, *walking*. His mental core was in his brain, and his core sensed mana. As such, he "felt" but in a different way. Kiru began to laugh, and tears started to well in his eyes. He understood what was happening.

Instead of the normal electrical currents running along his nerves, he now had mana! He wasn't using a technique to move himself anymore. The average person didn't have to think "Move!" to do so. They just moved.

Kiru realized that he'd essentially revitalized his body—especially his nervous system—and provided a new "power source," so to speak. The psion knew instinctively that his nerves could still conduct electrical signals, but it was still impossible for him to move his body that way. But, with his mana, it was unnecessary now. Again, his newfound ability to feel wasn't like anyone else's. With the mana providing him an avenue for his touch sensation, it was both more blunted and somehow more detailed all at the same time.

But walking around and manipulating his limbs was extremely easy. He now understood his body at a level he couldn't have even imagined before. He could sense his heart pumping, his muscles moving, and even his nerves twitching. Outside his body, however, felt more dulled compared to before his spinal injury. It was akin to wearing thick gloves all over his body. He could touch things, but even with his fine control, the pure tactile sensation of contact was greatly muted. The psion wasn't bothered at all by that though. *Some* sensation is far better than none!

After a few minutes, Kiru realized that William was waiting on him. "Oh, right," he said as he turned to his floating familiar. "William." Kiru paused with tears welling in his eyes. In a flash, he zoomed over to the imp. Kiru could tell William was surprised, but before he could respond, the psion wrapped his arms around him, embracing him tight. "You are the most useful familiar ever! No doubt about it!" he laughed as he squeezed. "Thank you! Thank you! Thank you!"

"Grah, Master, let go," William protested. Yet for all his new bulk, he couldn't push the psion off of him.

Kiru chuckled after a few more seconds and finally let go.

William brushed the nonexistent dust off his shoulders and snorted. "Hmph, what was the use of that gesture, Master? While I do appreciate how useful ascending and fixing your paralysis is, laughing about it like a deranged school child and risking our location being broadcasted is truly unwise. We need to be smart about this information and power we've acquired. We need to use your enhanced power and my knowledge about this ship and mental mana to stay alive and escape this place."

"Oh, come on, William. This is the safest place we've found so far. Plus, shouldn't we celebrate our accomplishments?" Kiru asked.

"I do not see the use," the imp replied. "I think it is far better to focus on our next goal."

Kiru just pressed his lips together. *Is this because of the Chaos Core? Or is this because of how hard I've been on him recently?* he thought, remembering that William was typically the most boastful and celebratory member of Pandemonium. He understood the imp's sentiment about being loud, but he didn't think it a bad idea to at least smile and give a hug. Before he could say anything though, his stomach let out a very loud growl, reminding him that he hadn't eaten anything since the single bite of tentacle that he'd cut off from the kraken.

"At least your stomach seems focused on our goals," William muttered. "It appears that we need to find you some sustenance, Master. Recall me into your core. It's time we get moving and test our newfound abilities."

CHAPTER SIXTEEN

Unshackled

The first thing Kiru did was repeat the use of Imp's Label on the other two floating corpses he'd seen earlier.

Name: Subject 051864
Race: V'keth
Rank: Bronze
Mana Type: Time
Path: None
Status: Deceased

V'keth are one of the four main races of the void. Most are devoid of emotion, relying on logic to help them discern the mysteries of their home realm. Their origins are unknown and are made of a strange metallic-like substance. They are a reclusive race who desire to learn and observe from a distance. It is thought that they originated from automatons who gained sentience and independence.

"I wonder," he said before looking at the humanoid rat creature and willing Imp's Label to appear with his mind instead of touching the information pad by the rat. To his joy, it worked.

Name: Subject 073096
Race: Quist
Rank: Silver
Mana Type: Darkness

Path: None
Status: Deceased

Quist are one of the four main races of the void. They are scavengers and would rather flee than fight. Though not known for their durability, they are known for their speed and stealth capabilities.

Tier Two is really showing its worth, Kiru thought as he took in the information. He was also shocked at the revelation of something called "time mana." The psion knew that Ruby was one of the rarest of all cultivation ranks out there. Most cultivators, even the skilled ones, never made it that far. Kiru discovered that in terms of raw power, while Ruby was higher than Gold, it wasn't as dramatic a difference when someone reached the higher rank. Tier Two wasn't supposed to be a major shift either. That clearly wasn't the case for the psion, though.

Some more information that William had acquired from Gaal'cothdreek-duun's stores of data about Tier-Two Ruby trickled in; as Kiru read it, he came to realize that it was more of a foundational stage for most of the cultivators who dared to reach for higher. Tier One improved your soul and mind, which did help the body as a secondary effect, while Tier Two purely improved your body, priming a person to be able to reach the next stages. A cultivator would still improve in strength from Tier One to Two, but it wasn't drastic. While the psion couldn't deny that the information made sense about it being more of a foundational stage with not much major benefit for most cultivators, most was not all, and Kiru was undoubtedly one of those exceptions.

He was eager to test his fighting and techniques. He'd spent enough time in the safety of the strange pillar and was ready to move on. "William, can you generate a way to get out of here?" he asked.

Voice monotone, William said, *"Analyzing map. Correlating with new data from recent travels. Updating map. Generating path. Path confirmed."* At his words, a blue arrow appeared in Kiru's vision in the top right corner. *"This arrow will act as a compass to point you along the correct path. I, of course, will aid you directly too, Master."*

Kiru looked at the strange arrow. It was pointing back in the direction of the room through which he'd entered. He turned, but the arrow still pointed in that direction. "Hey, William, why aren't we taking the stairs that I saw? Aren't we supposed to go up?" Kiru asked.

"A valid question, Master. While you were cultivating, I took some time to investigate that stairway. Unfortunately, too much debris had crashed down and blocked the way up entirely. The stairs only wind up a couple times before they are completely obstructed."

Impressed at the imp's intuition and the new guiding arrow in his vision, Kiru quickly moved over to the door. Fortunately, as he neared, it opened on its own. It was quiet once more, with nothing moving about outside. Still, to be safe, Kiru looked out past the broken window he'd come through. One of the abominations was floating along the edge of the fog.

Kiru sighed. *"Do you have an idea how we can take that thing without using Brainstorm?"* Kiru asked William via Telepathy. Brainstorm was a powerful but flashy technique, and the psion didn't want to draw the attention of more abominations.

"Hmm, based off the data I analyzed from your memories, those things have both incredible reach and two main methods of attack," William replied. *"Their tentacles—"* A circle highlighting some of the appendages appeared in Kiru's vision. *"—and what I've concluded to be their stomach."* This time, the central part of its body glowed. Kiru remembered how some sort of gelatinous appendage shot out from one of the abomination's honeycomb-like holes.

"Well, that makes sense," Kiru sent back. "If it's the thing's stomach or something like that, it does explain why I saw one of those lizards get dissolved alive when it swallowed the reptile. Still, I don't know how to beat it. When I cut off one of its gelatinous appendages extending out from its stomach, my blade just phased through it."

"I am aware, Master," William said. *"That's why I propose an alternate method."* The imp sent his plan into Kiru's mind.

The psion smirked. Trusting his friend, he began to squeeze his way out of the safety of the pillar. It wasn't the most graceful exit Kiru had ever made, but he was able to get himself out a lot smoother and quieter than his attempt to go in. After he had, he once again checked his surroundings. Satisfied when he didn't notice any other creatures, he bent his knees to keep his form low as he attempted to close the distance with the abomination.

Though it didn't have any discernible eyes, it seemed to be able to sense Kiru as it gave out a cacophony of angry moans and turned in his direction after he got within twenty feet of it. Its numerous tentacles began flailing about as it began to move towards him.

"Imp's Label," Kiru sent to William as his eyes locked on the monster.

Name: Chaos Abomination
Race: Monster
Rank: Gold
Mana Type: Unknown
Path: Unknown
Status: Hostile

Kiru absorbed all that information in the blink of an eye, a perk from William's "technique."

"It's weaker than you. Do it, Master!" the imp encouraged.

The psion reached his hand out and used Telekinesis. His mana was directed from his core down his neck and out his arm before it struck the abomination.

The monster's momentum immediately halted, its form wriggling but unable to move closer to Kiru.

"Excellent, now you know what to do next," William sent.

Kiru nodded before he pushed his arm out again and flung the monster back. It was no longer over the metal flooring, but directly above the acid lake. He had shoved it only a few feet away where the fumes weren't too thick, so he could still see. It still couldn't move towards him, but he noticed it retracting its lower tentacles towards his body.

The psion grinned at the sight as it seemed he had found the strange foes' weakness. The abomination kept trying to move but still hadn't overcome Kiru's control. Before it could try anything, though, he snapped his arm downward and sank the monster deeper into the acid. The strange moans turned into a series of high-pitched shrieks. This only lasted a moment, however, before it was completely submerged.

Kiru's arm continued to shake as he held the thing under his control. Then, a large bubble formed where he'd dunked it. When it popped, Kiru felt the creature slipping from his grasp, dead. He smirked, proud of what he accomplished. William had theorized that, while strong and seemingly resistant to the fog, the creatures weren't *entirely* immune to acid.

If William's new ability to analyze and discern whether certain creatures were truly below Kiru's cultivation level, then they shouldn't be able to resist his Telekinesis when using it directly on them. With Kiru no longer having to use his mana constantly in order to simply move himself, he could now focus more of it on attacks, making them stronger.

"I'm glad my idea was correct, but, Master, we cannot dally. We have more data to gather," William sent.

Kiru sighed but wanted to help build a good rapport with this new William. So, he just asked, "Such as?"

"Finding a safe way out of this fog. Do you remember what I previously discussed with you about using your mental mana on Telekinesis to create a path by forcing the air to move in a giant wave?" William asked.

"Yes." Kiru nodded, his perfect recall bringing up the conversation in his mind.

"I'd like to test that too," William said before the imp imparted more new information directly into the psion's mind from his core.

Kiru gasped as he took the information in. "On the . . . air? Telekinesis on the air?" he asked in shock.

"There is mana all around us constantly. Why can't *you use your technique on the mana in the air?"* William sent back.

Goosebumps ran along Kiru's body. He quickly moved over toward the direction the guiding arrow in his vision pointed him. He was just inches from the fog, safe from its harmful effects but only just barely. He focused on the fog. It helped Kiru that he could see it instead of trying to just visualize "air." With his mind, the psion reached out towards the mana in the air. He quickly recognized the mana making contact with his skin, but he couldn't seem to make a connection with anything past that.

"Hmm, only a partial success, I see," William spoke up, sounding very analytical. *"It looks like we may need to consider flying above the fog again and chance those giant millipedes possibly chasing us in order to avoid it."*

"Actually, I have an idea of my own," Kiru sent. *"All this new knowledge you've been giving me has helped me think more about what I can do. It's like I've been wearing weighted training equipment my whole life, and now I'm free. With more of my mana at my disposal, I'm unshackled, and I think I know how to be safe from the fog."*

Then, Kiru began using his mana to guide the air that was making contact with his skin, to move. Round and round it went over his body, picking up speed and gathering more air around it until the psion had generated a dome of spinning air around himself. Kiru laughed a little at this, still riding high from the elation of regaining sensation in his body. *What else can I do?* he thought in excitement. The psion drew his blades and readied himself before entering the fog.

CHAPTER SEVENTEEN

Breaking the Beasts

Boom, *boom! Boom, boom! Boom, boom!* The drums continued to beat in the same rhythm. Zhaden rowed to their beat, along with the hundreds of slaves chained to the bottom of *The Marauding Citadel*. Most were only at Silver, so it wasn't hard for him to keep up the pace. To Zhaden's annoyance, after the first hours of nonstop rowing, Saltbeard graced them with his presence, personally monitoring their progress.

The monstrous captain seemed to notice Mutt's strength, as eventually he ordered him to row two of the massive oars by himself. This task was monumental considering that everyone else was either assigned to a single oar or with a partner, with only those Gold and higher truly being able to handle one on their own. Zhaden wasn't sure if Vatrenex assigned Mutt two purely for efficiency's sake, however. The drakonid noticed a slight look of trepidation in the monster's eye. *Is he scared of Mutt, or is it related to the connection Brunhilda has with him?* he pondered.

Zhaden only tentatively agreed with Mutt's assessment that Brunhilda had somehow resisted the monster's control. He wasn't fully convinced, but that presumption was further validated when Zhaden noticed that Vatrenex now wore a simple metal mask covering the left side of his face—the side that was Brunhilda's face. The gold drakonid wanted to speak with Mutt, but the blind orc was assigned to the very front of the ship while Zhaden was towards the middle on their first day, and he hadn't been able to converse with Mutt since.

After twelve hours of rowing, they were finally ordered to stop. Zhaden, Mutt, and the rest of the slaves were all relieved of duty and forced to their quarters near the bowels of the ship. Each of the prisoners was forcefully marched in a narrow line, just inches from each other. As they made it to their quarters, the stench of body odor made Zhaden grimace. *I can only imagine what Mutt must be going through, with his enhanced sense of smell,* the drakonid thought.

The portion of the ship that housed their cells was much shorter than the others Zhaden had seen so far. It had no windows, so it was dark, only illuminated by sparse lanterns. Some straw littered the floor, along with puddles of urine. The pirates placed about ten prisoners into each cell, barely giving anyone room and forcing all in there to huddle together in order to sleep. They were each given a cup of water and extremely stale bread for nourishment. Zhaden scarfed down his portion all in one go as he walked into his cell, doing his best to ignore the taste and how difficult it was to chew.

He also did that so quickly due to the looks of greed and starvation many of his cellmates gave him as he entered. A couple were visibly angered that his bread was gone, likely having intended to rob him. The gold drakonid wasn't scared, though. He was a Ruby. Zhaden was exhausted from his exertions, but he knew that those inside his cell were in the same state. The other prisoners in the cell could feel Zhaden's power, too; he wasn't hiding it. That also seemed to deter them from attacking.

This pattern continued for three days by Zhaden's estimation, with no way he could communicate with Mutt. None of the other prisoners spoke with him much either, seeming to be scared of his power. Every day, his doubts grew about their situation. *He said we were important tools, so why are we being treated like the other slaves?* he thought. There was a notable change to Zhaden's psyche on the fourth day. *Maybe we are important but still expendable. Maybe that outburst with Brunhilda's face was a ruse! Yes, that has to be it! That's why he didn't swear an oath!* Just as the thought came to him, a voice echoed throughout the quarters.

"Evenin', slaves," Saltbeard said.

Zhaden bared his teeth and even heard Mutt let out a growl in the distance.

"As most of ye may have noticed, we got some new additions to the flock a few days back," Hagish said. "Cap'n Vatrenex thinks there's too many of ye as the orc and the goldy can do the work as ten of ye useless lot. "So, he gave me an order, see? The cap'n be feeling generous. He said whoever shares a cell with the blind orc or the gold drakonid and kills 'em gets to be freed and join the ranks of the corsairs. Think of getting a hot meal, yer own place to sleep, and plenty of people to sleep with if ye catch my drift? Anything's better than being forced to row fer the rest of yer days, aye? Ye have five minutes."

Zhaden's eyes widened and his heart began to race. He quickly scanned his cellmates and found them to all look utter shocked. They all gazed into each other's eyes before slowly turning to Zhaden. It was as if they were drowning and his death were their life raft. There was a shout in the distance, followed by the familiar sound of Mutt roaring, and then the first person lashed out at him.

A rail-thin elf pulled out a crude shiv from within his hair and lunged toward Zhaden, but he was too weak and the drakonid too prepared for his attack to work. Zhaden grabbed the elf by his wrist, twisted his arm, and took the blade from his hand. In a flash, he stabbed the elf in the neck with his own weapon before kicking him into a bald human, who had been trying to take advantage of the moment.

Zhaden didn't want to kill these people. They were victims like him, but they had made their choice. Unlike his friends, Zhaden didn't have as much reservation about killing. The life he'd chosen to live as an assassin and as Kiru's ally came full of risk. Death was a part of it, and death didn't play favorites. Zhaden had grown close to an orc scout during his time in Dissé, and even with how anxious he was to ensure her safety, death took her as well. In truth, Zhaden was still grieving that loss, but the events of their recent journeys had provided sufficient distraction.

Though it couldn't bring Ebysso back, killing enemies did bring the gold drakonid a bit of comfort, whether he admitted it or not. The first attacker clutched his neck as he rapidly bled out on the floor. Besides the one that got knocked back, none of the other slaves paid the dying elf any heed. Zhaden snarled. "Good," he said before jumping forward to meet them. Though his tail had been partially cut off, he still had most of it, plus it was slowly growing back. He jumped and spun, swinging it out and slapping two prisoners hard enough to knock them on the flat of their backs.

Zhaden stabbed another prisoner in the heart before pulling out his weapon and throwing it at another who charged at him. The shiv was crude and unbalanced, so his throw wasn't as precise as it otherwise would have been, but it still caused the woman coming at him to stumble as it carved a large gash across the left side of her face. The man he'd stabbed in the heart just before coughed and clutched his bleeding chest before falling flat on the ground. Meanwhile, he caught the stumbling woman by the throat in his claws, which he squeezed, quickly killing her on the spot. She twitched and gurgled as her blood poured down her neck and soaked her body.

The other prisoners visibly recoiled from the gruesome display, their wills broken, yet the drakonid was without mercy. They had tried to kill him, and he wouldn't allow them another opportunity. *I will not let anyone stop me from escaping,* he thought as he flicked the blood off his blade. *I will kill them, and when the time is right, I will escape. Kiru is dead. Brunhilda is too. Escape is our only option.*

Vatrenex was standing on the edge of his ship observing the small island not far from the vessel. There was a sizable volcano at the island's center, and it constantly discharged lava and ash, creating twin molten rivers flowing down and darkening the sky above it. The cloud of ash extended for miles in all directions, making it appear like it was night even though it was midmorning. Ash also rained down in a constant cascade, giving the place a truly infernal look.

Vatrenex gave a faint smile upon seeing the island. He had tempered many a corsair at this place, and the two new cultivators he'd acquired were the most promising he'd had in centuries. Thinking about the orc and gold drakonid made the left side of his face twitch slightly.

"Quiet," he growled as he gripped the mask covering it. "This damnable dwarf is proving much more of a nuisance than I expected," he grumbled.

Somehow, the thief she called a "psion" had influenced the other three in his party with his mana. It made the trio the perfect candidates for new hosts. They didn't degrade from the chaos mana like the others, but their resistance was a problem. *Once I have them all under my control and shatter the prison's power source, the dwarf and her friends won't be able to stop me,* he thought. *The more I mold them like the others, the less they will be able to resist. They won't know the difference between themselves and my brothers.*

"Er hem, Cap'n." Saltbeard cleared his throat as he neared Vatrenex.

The captain turned around to see his first mate. Behind Saltbeard were the orc and gold drakonid. Both were scowling and covered in a layer of dried blood. "I see that the two of you succeeded in your first bit of training last night," he said.

Vatrenex saw the drakonid's tail stiffen and his head cock at an angle in apparent confusion while the orc's nostrils flared.

"Training?!" Mutt growled. "You promised us safety!"

Saltbeard went to strike Mutt, but Vatrenex put a hand on his shoulder to stop him. The monstrous captain stared at Mutt and cocked his head. "Did I? No, I promised that your mate will be safe as long as I'm alive and you continue to be my slave, orc. *Your* safety was never guaranteed. You will serve me as I temper you to become the best weapons you can be, or I will make her body a husk and have one of you be my host instead."

Mutt's mouth hung open and Vatrenex gave a cruel smile. The simple orc didn't know that the captain needed them all to live for his plan, so he bought the lie. Vatrenex then glanced over to Zhaden. The gold drakonid was watching them with a discerning eye before quickly scanning their surroundings. *I don't like his eyes. Brunhilda's memory tells me that he is a paranoid one. I will use that weakness and break him.*

"First mate," Vatrenex said.

"Aye, sir?" Saltbeard asked.

"Undo their shackles and have them follow to resume their training," he ordered before looking to the two Rubies. "Your training continues, slaves. Orc, you will row the drakonid and my first mate over to the island." At that, Vatrenex's gray flesh morphed and expanded until he'd formed a membranous wing under each arm, much like a bat. Then, he flapped his arms down and ascended with a whoosh before flying over to the island.

Ten minutes later, the others joined him, Mutt being the only one to row, per Vatrenex's instructions. The three stood there in front of the captain, waiting on his next command.

"Saltbeard," he said.

"Aye, sir?" the dwarf responded.

"Take the drakonid and go hunt us some dinner. Make sure to keep the eyes intact," he ordered.

Saltbeard's face went "Oh!" in recognition before nodding and shoving the drakonid away from the others and towards the volcano.

"Now, orc," Vatrenex said before the wings he'd formed faded away and he hefted his massive blade, "we train."

"You want me to fight you? Why?" Mutt asked warily.

In truth, Vatrenex had been thinking about what to do with the two slaves. He believed he had a solution, but he needed them to be more than just his slaves. "If you defeat me, I will relinquish your mate from my control completely. This I swear on my blade," he said.

No sooner had he finished saying that that Mutt launched himself at him, full-force.

Vatrenex was ready, however. The captain met the orc's claws with his massive blade, intercepting his strike, as well as his follow-up attack. Mutt attacked with a reckless ferocity, but Vatrenex continued to block his blows with his blade as if it weighed nothing at all. Mutt went to bite his shoulder, but the monstrous cultivator sidestepped him, kicking him in the stomach for good measure. Mutt went flying back, bouncing off the hardened black lava rock. "Impressive strength and aggression, orc, but you lack control."

"My control is fine. It was enough for me to beat a Sapphire before you," Mutt retorted before letting out a Bounder's Howl technique.

As the soundwaves shot out toward Vatrenex, his eye widened in surprise. His entire body began to ripple as his shroud protected him, the technique harmlessly washing over him. When Mutt stopped, Vatrenex tapped his horned head. "You forget, I've searched through Brunhilda's memories. I know that the 'Sapphire' you fought previously wasn't a true Sapphire. You may be a Tier-Two Ruby, and even an exceptional one at that, but you are no match for one who is truly above you. Let me show you our gap in power."

Then, he unleashed the power of his aura directly onto Mutt. The blind orc was forced flat to the ground. He groaned as he futilely tried to fight back against the pressure. The ground under him began to crack and threatened to give way and fall into the sea. Only then did Vatrenex let up.

As Mutt gasped for air like a beached fish, the captain walked over to him and slammed his blade into the ground right by his head and leaned down. "You have two choices before you: Serve me as my loyal acolyte and keep your beloved alive inside me, or resist and lose her forever . . . while still being my slave."

"But what kind of choice is that?" Mutt asked.

Vatrenex fought back a smile. *He is beginning to despair. Good.* "One where she will be alive, Mutt. Now, accept me as your new leader. Not even your Kiru can stand up to me."

The orc just laid there breathing heavily for about half a minute, but Vatrenex kept his gaze fixed. "I'm not a very smart guy," Mutt said. "The only things I really even give a crap about are fighting and hunting. But the boss, he's very smart. I will follow you as one of your corsairs for now, but I won't accept you as my true leader . . . not until you've defeated the boss." He lifted his head to the monster.

Vatrenex began to chuckle, continuing until it became a mad cackle that lasted for a minute straight. "You truly believe that boy can pose a real challenge to me? His body is so weak and broken, I'm surprised he's even alive."

"The thing is, I don't know how. I just know that the boss is *really* good at overcoming the odds," Mutt said. "And I don't have to know how, I just trust that he'll figure it out. So, that is my condition. I will accept my position temporarily as long as you continue to keep Brunhilda and my friends safe until you face the boss. I've already agreed to be your slave, but I will be your willing acolyte as well until the time comes. I won't find a way to find some loophole." He offered his arm. "This I swear on my core . . . if you're not too scared to take the challenge."

"Aye, me as well," Brunhilda called out from under the mask.

"Grah! Silence!" Vatrenex shouted as he pressed a hand over her side of his face. The monster scowled, glaring hatefully at the audacious orc before him. *How dare they think so little of me?* Then, realization struck him, and his scowl turned into a hateful smile. "I accept these terms," he said before ripping the mask off the left side of his face, revealing Brunhilda's visage. "This I swear on my blade." He then clasped wrists with Mutt, as they each gave sharp-toothed grins to one another.

What absolute fools, Vatrenex thought. *They didn't even specify how I would face this Kiru, if he's even alive. I will bend them to my will like the beasts they are.*

CHAPTER EIGHTEEN

Toads & Training

Saltbeard led Zhaden up towards the volcano and then around it to the other side of the island. After they'd crested the ledge, Zhaden scanned their surroundings, but he didn't notice anything significantly different about this side of the small island versus the other. "What are we hunting?" he asked the dwarf pirate.

"Toads, Goldy, and a lot of 'em," he answered. As if beckoned, a three-foot tall, gray and black toad jumped out of the ash not far from Zhaden. The creature croaked and lashed its tongue at the gold drakonid like a whip.

Zhaden was ready, though, and blocked it with his Bloodstep Stiletto. To his surprise the blade just bounced off the tongue, not even wounding it. Instead of retracting the tongue, the toad just slung it down and struck Zhaden's chest. Fortunately, his armor took most of the brunt of the hit, but the tongue did manage to cut into the leather. *The tongue has a blade at its tip?* he thought before leaping to the side to avoid another blow.

Before the toad could attack again, Saltbeard rushed over in a burst of speed and stabbed the small creature in its open mouth. The creature let out a sad cry before its entire body went limp and it died. "Ashen toads," the pirate said before he pulled out his cutlass. "Annoying little buggers. Their bodies be covered by a thick layer of hardened ash, including their tongues. Their main weakness be inside their mouths. That's where their flesh still be soft."

"And I'm correct in the assumption that, based off your captain's words, you intend to eat them?" Zhaden asked.

"Oh, aye. Their hearts taste delicious while their stomachs help our brewers' fermenting process. They also be good for alchemy purposes," the dwarf said before putting the dead toad in a pouch he wore. Judging by how it didn't change size, Zhaden assumed it to be some sort of storage device. "Yer job be to kill a hundred of 'em, plus a bull toad."

Zhaden sighed, realizing this was going to be unpleasant.

It took Zhaden the better part of an hour to kill the hundred toads. He was riddled with wounds and his leather was falling apart. The greatest challenge he faced was that the toads had thermal-based senses, so, in the heat of the day, they could always find him. That also dispelled his illusory techniques. He had contemplated using his Nightmare technique once to subdue a number of them in one fell swoop but held off against it as he'd yet to encounter a bull among the species and wanted to save it in case he needed a trump card.

The gold drakonid had hoped that the Sapphire first mate would help, but unfortunately, Saltbeard was content to follow him and pick up the dead in his storage bag. Zhaden's friends always told him how jumpy he was, but with how regularly he was being attacked at the moment, plus the constant falling of ash, his paranoia had reached a whole new level. He had to force himself not to overreact at every movement.

He eventually did find a bull toad higher up on the volcano. It was twice the size of the other toads he'd seen, and it stood on a ledge with its back against the volcano, preventing anything from sneaking up from behind. Zhaden prepared to use his Nightmare technique but thought better of it in the end. He was concerned about the possibility of it damaging the creature's eyes, since apparently they were what Vatrenex was looking for. *Also, it will be better to have it for when I can find an opening to escape,* he thought. When he remembered again that the toads sensed by heat, an idea came to mind.

Zhaden picked up a recently killed toad before Saltbeard could get a hold of it. It was fortunately still warm. He took the garrote in his belt and tied it tight around the dead toad. He then threw it in the bull toad's view. Its eyes instantly snapped down toward the corpse flying about fifteen feet away from it. In a flash, it lashed out its tongue and snapped it at it, looking for an easy meal. Unfortunately for it, the meal stopped mid-flight as Zhaden held on tight. Both the toad and the gold drakonid were stuck in a tug-of-war, but Zhaden didn't intend it to be that way for long.

Since the toad's tongue was still out of its mouth, its vulnerability was exposed. With his free hand, Zhaden expertly flung his stiletto at the creature, striking true. Blood squirted out from the wound, activating its enchantment and teleporting Zhaden right there. The bull toad let out a croak of surprise at the orc's sudden appearance before he shoved the blade up into its brain, and its body went stiff.

After all of that, Zhaden began to hobble back in the direction they'd come from, his left hand clutching a gash in his right arm. Saltbeard followed behind him, clearly not planning on offering any aid. After the two had crossed over a ledge to reach to the other side and began descending to where the boat was docked, they were greeted by an unusual sight. Vatrenex and Mutt were each sitting on large rocks a few feet from each other and having what seemed to be a civil conversation. The monster's mask was off, revealing Brunhilda's left half, which was also awake and apparently taking part as well.

"The technique is called Fenrir's Claws. I don't get how I'm supposed to use it but not make claws," Mutt said.

"Just because that's the name of your technique doesn't mean you can't manifest it elsewhere," Vatrenex responded.

"Mutt, what in the abyss is going on here?" Zhaden hissed angrily. *This monster is responsible for Kiru's likely death, he's wearing Brunhilda like a suit, and Mutt is just casually talking with him, like it's no big deal!* Zhaden thought.

"Stabby, we've added more terms to our agreement," Mutt said before explaining what he and Brunhilda had discussed and sworn to with the monster who had possessed and altered her body.

I can't believe it. What utter lunacy! I don't have proof that Kiru is dead but we can't put all our hopes in the faint chance that he survived. We can't swear an oath to this monster! We should all be thinking of a way to escape and warn the nations of the Great Alliance of the incoming invasion.

"I . . . see," Zhaden finally said as he noticed Mutt's warm smile towards the part of the face that was still Brunhilda.

Mutt cannot let go. He will do anything to keep Brunhilda alive. He just can't accept that she's gone. That is a monster, not our friend.

Despite his frustration, the gold drakonid kept his face calm and forced his tail to wag slightly from side to side, so as not to betray his true thoughts. Zhaden had accepted that it was up to him and *only* him to get away. Still, he needed to put on a good show and not anger the monster or his first mate. They were both Sapphires and could easily kill him. "I feel that it is unnecessary for me to also agree to those additional terms. I've already agreed to be your slave. What difference does it make if I make an oath?"

"Because it means you will serve me willingly and not oppose or undermine me," Vatrenex said. "I am aware that our prior agreement left some . . . loopholes that could be exploited. For example, you swore to be my slaves in my upcoming crusade, but you didn't say for how long. I aim to rectify that. If your Kiru is as powerful as your friend claims, then it shouldn't be a problem for you in the long run."

This time, Zhaden's tail did stiffen in alarm. That was *exactly* what he was fearing. He did not want to wager his entire life on Kiru freeing them. He realized that he was trapped, and he had only one chance to escape.

"Mutt, you fool!" he cried before activating his Nightmare technique. A wave of shadow shot forth from his body, coalescing until it formed a massive ghostly dragon, which let out a terrifying roar before its shadow surged out in all directions.

Zhaden put all he could into the technique. He was injured already, so he knew he couldn't engage in a protracted fight. He hoped the element of surprise would be enough to hold off the two Sapphires and Mutt. Zhaden couldn't trust his friend anymore, either, so the orc wasn't spared from the technique's fury.

Mutt screamed out in terror, but Zhaden heard nothing from the two Sapphires in the darkness. He gritted his teeth and, ignoring his injuries, ran towards the boat. He made it to within a couple feet of the vessel when he heard someone shouting behind him.

Feeling imminent danger behind him, Zhaden rolled to the right and narrowly dodged the technique, which cut through the air where he'd been standing. The black slash continued forward and easily severed the small boat. Suddenly, however, Zhaden turned his head back to see his Nightmare technique being bisected. In the middle of the clouds stood the monstrous Vatrenex. The right side of his face was glaring at the gold drakonid while the Brunhilda side was limp and seemed to be asleep.

Vatrenex hefted his massive blade on one shoulder and wagged his finger at Zhaden. "If you will not be my willing acolyte, I will ensure that you're beaten until you are my most obedient weapon instead," the monster said, and his red eye bulged slightly.

Zhaden's already-injured body felt the force of Vatrenex's aura slamming down upon him before he lost consciousness.

The gold drakonid woke up feeling both sore and disoriented. "What? What happe—" He stopped short as he gained awareness of his surroundings. His entire body was bound once again, except this time both of his arms and legs and his tail were strapped down by steel cuffs and chains instead of trollstone, other than the shackle around his right wrist. His back was pressed against a wooden board, making him feel like some science project. He looked around to find himself in a strange room made of glass. He knew he was back in *The Marauding Citadel* because he could spot concentric wooden boards surrounding the glass room in nearly all directions.

On the other side of the glass was what looked to be an alchemy lab of some sort. It had no windows, but a couple of artificial mana-powered light constructs were embedded in the ceiling. A gray-skinned gnome was busily working among the multiple tables there, going back and forth, mixing different concoctions while he muttered to himself.

The gnome's ears had been cut off, and he wore thick leather goggles with black lenses, obstructing the drakonid's view of his eyes. The gnome seemed to realize Zhaden was awake and monitoring him, and he gave the drakonid a sharp-toothed smile in response. "You're awake. Good, that means we can begin," he said in a dry, squeaky voice.

Zhaden's body tensed as he tried to break his restraints, but it was no good—the lengths of chain were wrapped tight. Also, while he noticed that many of his cuts and gashes from the ashen toads had been healed, he felt notably weaker as well. *What is happening?* he thought.

The gnome tsked. "I see you've noticed that your strength is currently not what it once was. That is to be expected." He then looked down to a notebook and scribbled something in it. "Moving on, Captain Vatrenex informed me that you were the one to thank for all the ashen toad specimens I've been given and sustained many lacerations in the process." The gnome then turned away from Zhaden and ignited a flame under a glass beaker containing a black liquid. "The ashen toads have all sorts of beneficial chemicals that can be extracted. One of them is pretty insidious."

"Enough of this! Set me free, gnome!" Zhaden hissed.

The gnome continued talking over Zhaden, completely unfazed by him. "One of them is from their tongue barbs specifically," he said as he took a rolling pin and rolled it over a long, cut-off toad tongue nailed down by the edge of a table. When he did so, a yellow, viscous substance oozed out of the barbed tip and into a small vial underneath it. The gnome raised the vial towards one of the lights. "It is a slow-acting stamina venom. It doesn't start working until a couple of hours after contact with the bloodstream. Once it does start to take effect, however, the venomous compound can linger for days. Even one as strong as yourself would be significantly weakened by it, especially with how many cuts you received." The gnome then turned his face back to look directly at Zhaden and gave a wide grin. "That gives me plenty of time to get you properly prepared for my revenge."

"Revenge? What revenge?" Zhaden asked.

Though Zhaden couldn't see the gnome's eyes under his thick black goggles, he could tell the he was confused, based on how he furrowed his brow.

The gnome grunted and waved his hand dismissively at Zhaden. "You scaleys have such strange facial structures that it's hard to read your lips and tell what you're saying." He pointed to the stump of what remained of his right ear. "This is what I'm getting revenge for. I was deafened by the Cult of the Hushed. Those bastards literally destroyed my eardrums and would've taken my tongue too had the captain not saved me in time.

"Ever since I recovered, I've vowed to get vengeance on that accursed cult. That is where you come in. The captain informed me that you and your friends are the key to winning his war against his brothers, who lead the other factions in the Torn Empire, and rallying them to his cause. Besides us corsairs, there are three cults who rule." The gnome lifted a finger. "The first are the Mourners—you encountered their lot earlier when they attempted to raid our ship." A second finger went up. "Next are the Joyful, possibly the most annoying and crazy of the cults." A third finger. "Last are those accursed members of the Hushed."

The gnome scowled as he named the last cult. On the one hand, Zhaden was genuinely interested in learning more about Torn Empire. On the other hand, he'd much rather have been free. As the alchemist rambled on, he tried to subtly loosen the bindings with his tail. Unfortunately, the stamina venom was affecting his coordination too.

The deaf alchemist fortunately didn't notice as he continued. "The captain believes it's time to unite all under his banner and take back his power. The crew has been talking about how the first barrier went down for the first time, and, based on Vatrenex's actions, it does appear to be a sign that things are changing. The captain informed me that each member of your party are key to defeating and dominating each of his brothers. You will be the instrument used to destroy the Hushed, but you need some improvement before then. That is where I come in." A predatory grin spread across the gnome's face.

Zhaden's body went stiff at the gnome's words. He stared at the man on the opposite side of the glass, his heart beating rapidly. He hadn't made any significant progress in loosening the chains with his tail, so he was at the gnome's mercy. He quickly remembered all the terrible scars Mutt had received when he was experimented on by the mad cleric back at the academy and gulped.

As if to confirm his suspicion, the gnome looked over to the beaker of bubbling black liquid. "And it looks like my first concoction for you is just about finished." On cue, the bubbling immediately stopped, and the liquid settled. The gnome rushed over, turned off the flame under the beaker, and removed the glass. Zhaden reasoned that either the glass had somehow already cooled down or the gnome had remarkable heat resistance.

Before the drakonid could ask what he was doing, the gnome had pushed open a seamless door in the glass box that Zhaden hadn't noticed, and stepped inside. The alchemist then quickly shut it and checked to make sure that it had closed completely.

Zhaden's heart raced as the gnome neared. Maybe it was adrenaline, but the sudden fear seemed to increase his control over his tail. An idea came into his head. *Once he gets close enough to try to force the potion down my throat, I'll knock it away with my tail.* Unfortunately for Zhaden, the gnome stopped about five feet away from him. The alchemist then heaved the beaker forward in the drakonid's direction.

The glass container actually flew over Zhaden, the sound of glass loudly breaking behind him confirming that it had shattered. The rogue grinned at the alchemist. "You missed," he mocked, making sure to overemphasize his mouth's movements to help the gnome understand him as best he could.

The gnome wasn't focused on him, however. Instead, he placed a thick, leather mask over his mouth with three different metal cannisters attached to it for him to breathe through. Thick gray smoke that smelled like a mixture of damp earth, ash, and blood rolled from behind the bound drakonid and over his body. His eyes immediately watered, and his nostrils burned. Zhaden began to cough as he unintentionally inhaled some of the substance, which immediately began to rage inside his body, forcing him to cough reflexively and unintentionally breathe in more of the foul substance. Zhaden flailed about desperately, trying to free himself and get some fresh air in his system.

There was something inside the concoction that had turned into a gas. Zhaden could feel it moving about like some sort of parasite squirming around inside his body. Despite the gold drakonid's best attempts, he couldn't escape. Eventually, he had to breathe again. Like a man who'd been too long underwater, the drakonid let out a large inhale and even more of the foul substance entered him, combining with what he'd already breathed in to become stronger. Zhaden coughed and even vomited once as his body tried to force the foreign gas out of him.

After a few more torturous seconds, the pain left, all of a sudden. In the blink of an eye, he could breathe easier now, even with all the foul black gas around him. "What?" was all he had time to say before his body began to stiffen, like he was turning to stone. He became more and more rigid until he lay prone, mouth open. He could still breathe but just barely, and his eyes were able to move about frantically though he was unable to notice anything in the smoke surrounding him.

Then, suddenly, the gnome walked up to him, staring at him through his thick goggles. "You see, this is what you would've eventually experienced from those toads. I just made it happen a lot quicker," the gnome said before raising a finger. "Now," he said as he rubbed his hand together excitedly, "time to enhance your body."

Weevil Jutherford paused while writing down his notes about his latest experiment. Currently, he was satisfied with the results. Going from a lowly gnomish servant for a dwarven sect, to prisoner after the corsairs had raided their ship, to lead alchemist of the pirates was something Weevil was certainly proud of. Though chaotic, the people of *The Marauding Citadel* functioned very much like a sect in his eyes. Weevil had improved leaps and bounds under the service of his captain and master over the decades and had even gained enough favor to have his airtight glass chamber built for him.

His captain had tasked him with subduing and improving slaves before. The alchemist had a number of failures but more successes over the years. The gnome's greatest was the mental toxin he'd made to coat the blades in order to weaken the will of the cyclops that the first mate used as a mount. From there, Weevil had grown to become a master of poisons and toxins and had elevated himself highly within the corsairs to become head alchemist. He had crafted many deadly toxins for the corsairs to use in their raids over the years, tailoring the brews specifically for their opponents. That's why the Hushed had targeted him when he went to one of the brothels and deafened him, and that's why he hated them.

He was so proud of his position that he would do whatever his captain ordered, which is why when Vatrenex asked him to enhance this drakonid's sight, he eagerly worked toward that goal. When Weevil was told that the scaley would be vital in taking down the Hushed, he did so with gusto. Normally, he preferred to work with poisons rather than doing pure enhancements, but what was requested was not outside the scope of his abilities. So, Weevil decided to train the drakonid's body using some poisons of his own design.

The captain had said that Weevil's subject had two glaring weaknesses: his lack of darkvision and his overall paranoia. The first was easily dealt with. Ironically, the ashen toad samples that he collected helped with concocting this as well. First, Weevil took six intact toad eyes and crushed them with a mortar and pestle. Then, he added one milliliter of kraken ink, the burnt remains of three dwarven eyebrow hairs, precisely one drop of liquid mercury, and twelve grams of volcanic snail moss. Once he swirled them together, Weevil placed them in a glass syringe and attached the barbed tip of one of the toad tongues to the end to serve as a needle after he had sterilized it with a flame.

Once finished, he injected it directly into his subject's eye.

"Subject showed standard reaction to the potion's introduction," the alchemist muttered as he wrote. "Severe pain, moderate discharge of blood and ocular fluid, and cries of displeasure." Weevil was extremely grateful for the paralyzing effect of his gas. It still perplexed him as to exactly *how* someone could scream so much even with the compromised lung function that the paralysis brought. He reasoned to study that in greater depth later.

Time went by, and Weevil continued to collect data. He noted all the minor, nuanced information that his subject presented in response to his experiments. The drakonid gave much of the desired reactions. That intrigued the gnome even further as to his experiment's implications.

"After approximately two hours of adjusting to the new material introduced into subject's eye, full metamorphosis had been successfully achieved," the alchemist said as he finished his notes and looked up at his bound subject. The drakonid was looking around the room, the paralyzing effect already having worn off, his eyes now two orbs of solid black. Weevil knew through previous experiments that the subject could now not only see in the dark but detect heat signatures as well. The gnome had made sure to add that last part to ensure that the drakonid was as deadly as possible.

The paranoia was harder to deal with. Normally, Weevil would've administered one of his typical concoctions with a drop of his captain's blood to suppress the slave's will, like he usually did, but Vatrenex had explicitly told the gnome *not* to use that secret ingredient. That puzzled Weevil for a bit, but after an hour, he discovered that poison *was* the answer for this problem. While the subject was still immobilized, Weevil poured a fear-enhancing potion directly into the drakonid's open mouth. Since the captain plainly told Weevil *not* to use his blood, he decided to try something else—a piece of the captain's skin that had been cut off from a previous fight. Weevil had preserved it in formaldehyde for such an occasion. If he couldn't remove the fear, he would *amplify* it and direct it to be useful. After the alchemist did some conditioning—or "more training," as he liked to call it—the drakonid was now truly terrified of his captain and would do whatever it took not to be the target of Vatrenex's ire.

"Upon visualization of the captain's image, subject's entire body notably shakes with fear and he begins muttering about how he 'must get away.' The subject will turn his head in the opposite direction of the drawing of the captain in order to avoid looking at the image," the alchemist spoke as he continued to write. "Based on the results, I conclude that the subject is significantly improved. While he may not yet be a loyal servant eager to obey, the data supports that he doesn't need to be controlled. He just needs to be aimed and released."

CHAPTER NINETEEN

Traversing the Depths

Kiru moved about the nightmarish acidic swamp with much more confidence than he had just a few hours earlier. With William's ability to analyze, coupled with his own new lack of restraint, Kiru was experiencing a true power-high.

A lone flesh-wolf emerged out of the fog. The creature leaped out to sneak-attack Kiru, but the psion was quick enough to roll out of the way just in time. *Guess my orb of clean air didn't go unnoticed*, he thought as he readied his blades and turned to face the creature. "Imp's Label."

Name: Flesh-Wolf
Race: Monster
Rank: Gold
Mana Type: Unknown
Path: Unknown
Status: Hostile

Kiru grunted as the information quickly appeared and was absorbed by his mind. He believed he could handle the animal, but suspected that it wasn't a lone wolf as none of the others he'd dealt with had been. He didn't have enough time to equip his Mask of Fenrir to increase his senses, though, so he had hoped this new ability of William's would've given him some new information as to how to more adeptly handle this foe. As if his familiar had read his thoughts, different parts of the wolf's body suddenly became highlighted in his vision with some text appearing beside each.

The first was a spot behind its head.

> **Previous combat data points to this being a vulnerable area.**

Its abdomen glowed blue and gave the same information.
The next was inside its mouth as it bared its teeth at Kiru.

> **Data from previous corpses shows the inside of the mouth to be much softer and more vulnerable.**

Finally, its left elbow was highlighted.

> **Abnormal conformation based off of previous data, with significant scar tissue present. Area highly vulnerable.**

"What the—?" Kiru uttered as his brain took all that information in after only a second.

"*Talk later! Attack its left elbow, then go for the back of its head,*" William sent.

Trusting his companion, Kiru moved to do just that. He charged, using Demon's Inciting Strike at the wolf's elbow.

The creature let out a sharp cry of pain as it fell onto its chin, as it was suddenly no longer able to support its own weight.

Kiru spun and used Dragon Ascends the Sky, slicing across the wolf's neck before finishing it off with a downward stab of his dual blades right into the glowing spot behind its skull. There was a crunch of bone and a soft cry from the creature before it stopped moving under the weight of Kiru's blades. Kiru just took a few deep breaths to calm his racing heart. *Glad I was able to finish it off without any real techniques.*

"William, what was that?" he asked.

"*I . . . I don't know how, but it seems that, as I integrate more with you, Imp's Label has become even more effective,*" the imp replied.

"I'll say!" Kiru said. His mind boggled at the implications of his being able to see weak points and get real-time analyses and recommendations for battle plans. "Do you know what this means, William?"

"*I do. It means that my usefulness should never come into question again. I calculate a 212% increase in your battle prowess with just this new tool alone. If you want to help improve my analytical capabilities further, I suggest you gather me more data.*"

Kiru furrowed his brows, wondering exactly how he could accomplish that. Meanwhile, he didn't notice that they had new guests approaching until he felt his sword dip toward the ground. Kiru looked down to see a colony of ten of those strange one-eyed crabs scurrying across the corpse of the dead wolf, hurriedly clawing at it and stuffing their maws with its flesh. And one of them was now quickly climbing up Kiru's arm.

"Grah!" Kiru shouted out unintelligibly as he swung his blade to remove the crustacean. Unfortunately, he accidentally flung the crab directly onto his face. "Grr! Dang it! Get off," he cried as he reached up to rip it off of him.

The crab was determined, however, and pinched Kiru's upper lip in defiance.

He cried out in pain. His sense of touch on his face and neck weren't dulled, so the discomfort was heightened. The psion bit off the crab's claw in reaction, forcing it to lose its purchase and be flung off into the acid a few feet away. Kiru snarled as he broke the shell with his teeth, his mouth filling with crab meat and blood.

"*Data Acquired. Information gained on subject: void crabs.*"

"Uh, what?" Kiru asked.

"*Well, Master, you were useful too. It seems that ingesting biological matter of a specimen allows me to gather more data on them, such as with those crabs. I'm able to interpret their biological information to learn more about them and even their history. Well done,*" William grunted in approval. "*Use Imp's Label on one of the crabs.*"

Kiru looked at one of them shoving the wolf meat down its gullet.

Name: Void Crab
Race: Beast
Rank: Bronze
Mana Type: Void
Path: None
Status: Neutral

Biological evidence suggests that these were once simple crabs but have been warped over time due to persistent exposure to hostile mana. Their shells are more durable than normal crabs, but due to the sporadic placements of their eyes, many likely don't survive into adulthood.

Kiru's eyes widened. "Wow!" William's ability to somehow produce more information about the creature based on the blood of its counterpart truly stunned him. He could now see its mana type and even got a small snippet of the crabs' evolutionary history.

"*You know what else would be useful to consume . . .*" William trailed off without saying.

He didn't need to. Kiru knew exactly what he was implying. The psion looked down at the monstrous flesh-wolf and grimaced. The thing smelled like tar and its thick blood trailed over it like oil—not something Kiru really wanted to ingest. He sighed. Wanting to help his familiar and work to further mend their relationship, he dipped a blade into one of its wounds and licked the blood off of it. The substance was foul and sizzled a little when it touched his tongue; it didn't burn exactly but it wasn't a pleasant experience, either.

Once he'd closed his eyes and choked it down, William spoke up again.

"Data Acquired. Information gained on subject: umbrafang. Updating information on beings previously identified as flesh-wolves."

Kiru then used Imp's Label on the dead creature.

Name: Umbrafang
Race: Monster
Rank: Silver
Mana Type: Chaos
Path: None
Status: Deceased

Biological evidence shows a strange heritage for these creatures, none of which contain any canine blood despite their similarities to wolves. Rodent-like and cephalopod biomatter are the two primary sources, somehow mutated and spliced together. Data on those two different groups of animals suggest that the umbrafangs are ambush predators and prolific breeders. Their skin is similar to that of mollusks but much more thick and durable, giving them resistance to the harsh environment of the acidic fog in the swamp.

"Wow, that *was* useful," Kiru said.

"Agreed," William sent back.

Before the psion could say anything else, his ears picked up on a familiar howl off in the distance. His previous scream of pain from the crab had alerted more umbrafangs to his location. Fortunately, due to his increased knowledge and power, Kiru was able to circle his previous location and either avoid or kill the umbrafangs that he'd alerted by quickly slicing their throats and leaving them to bleed out and hopefully distract any other predators. Kiru only took some minor scrapes from the conflict. The psion waited behind a large boulder for a couple of minutes, but after no other creature aside from the void crabs appeared, he rushed forward and collected a couple dozen of the crustaceans into his mother's storage ring. Though he didn't need as much food and water, thanks to his higher cultivation rank, Kiru still needed some sustenance. After five or so minutes, he was back to moving his way out of the swamp, following the arrows that William had provided for him in his vision.

For the imp's sake, Kiru did go off the path a couple of times to collect more samples. The first thing he did was cut off the tip of a fungal lizard's tail and swallow it. Kiru did his best to avoid tasting any of it, but a couple drops of blood touched his tongue, tasting ironically like a mushroom. He learned that they were called spowts, as well as more information about them. William asked Kiru to ingest a piece of one of the predatory trees, but when the psion noticed small finger-like baby trees taking over the backs of some of the spowts, he thought better of it. *I do not need to have that growing out of me.* When he caught sight of one of the trees snatching up an unsuspecting spowt from a nearby rock and chewing it up, that further reinforced his resolve. *Seeing how it just grabbed its prey, I'll just settle with calling them graspers for now.*

After that detour, Kiru was able to make it out of the acidic fog with William's guidance, finally dismissing the protective sphere of Telekinesis around him. Kiru took in a deep sigh of relief. The air was still foul and smelled of sulfur, but there was something refreshing about being free of direct danger. Despite his newfound relative safety, however, Kiru still proceeded with caution, his blades out and at the ready.

The psion was fortunately unbothered by any more foes for the next half hour and eventually made it back to the large chamber from which he'd originally entered the prison. He needed to return to the area, according to his map, as it was on the way to the location that would help him ascend to the next level. Bringing the map back up, he found that this was one of its blurrier sections. Kiru knew he needed to proceed to the right side of the chamber to find the spot to go up; he just didn't know which of the ten doors on the lower level he should choose. Not seeing any better option, he decided to go with the leftmost door on the right wall.

The door slid open, revealing a large hallway similar to the one he'd just come from but with much more grime and fewer of those root-like growths. It was also better illuminated with more orbs of artificial light set into the ceiling. Kiru pushed himself onward, his senses sharpened. Eventually, doors and other corridors started to branch off from the one he was in. Unsure which way to go, he suddenly felt a distinct calming sensation coming from a door about half a mile ahead of him.

Kiru couldn't explain exactly why, but he felt drawn to the place. So, despite William's protests, the psion quietly but quickly moved over to that door. He pressed his palm against it; fortunately it registered the blood on his hand, even though it had dried. The door beeped and slid open with a hiss. Mist rolled out over Kiru's feet, and he was greeted with a strange sight: a bath!

Inside a twenty-by-twenty-foot room, a large bath was set into the middle of the floor, covering most of its span. The walls around it were made of the same purple metal he'd seen outside, covered in numerous intricate, swirling carvings. The room was illuminated by the pool itself, with some odd light source shining through the bubbling cream-colored liquid which was the source of the mist. Kiru could sense that the bubbling bath itself was the source of the calming energy.

Despite that, Kiru wrinkled his nose in disgust. The smell was even more foul than the acid fog!

"It's like old fish and burnt hair," he said as he clenched his nose and turned his head away, wondering if he could use Telekinesis to somehow block his sense of smell.

"*Master, let me look at it*," William said.

Kiru gladly summoned his familiar, not wanting to get any closer if he could help it. To his surprise, William wasn't affected by the odor in the slightest. Instead, the imp floated over to the bubbling liquid and scooped a handful directly into his mouth. All three of his eyes widened for a moment before he turned to Kiru. "Master, you must bathe in this."

Kiru stared at him, started to respond, and then stared for a moment longer. "*Bathe?* Are you kidding me, William?"

"Not at all," William said, shaking his head. "This fluid contains potent regenerative properties for those who utilize mental mana. A few hours in this, and all your exhaustion and physical wounds will be gone."

Kiru raised an eyebrow at that. He'd been ignoring much of his exhaustion due to the constant danger he'd been in, but when William brought it up, the reminder hit Kiru hard. He had only a few superficial physical wounds, the worst being the cut on his lip from the crab pinching him, but there was nothing debilitating. Still, with the near-constant stress and fighting, the thought of a reprieve hit Kiru hard.

"Can this door be locked behind us so that nothing can ambush us?" he asked.

"Indeed," William said. "From my analysis, all you need to do is press your palm against the door on the other side when it closes behind you."

Sure wish I'd figured out how to block smell, he thought. Despite the foul odor, the possibility of a break was too tempting to pass up, so he stepped in and locked the door behind him.

"I sure hope you're right," he said.

To Kiru's joy, William was indeed right. He didn't know what the liquid was exactly, but it did as intended. Even with its gross smell, it soothed and relaxed his body, mind, and even his core and meridians. He quickly fell asleep after immersing most of his body into the tub, awaking a full twenty-four hours later, according to William.

The room served as Kiru's temporary base of operations over the next few days, letting him become inured to the smell and eventually able to ignore it. He would move along the winding corridors in hopes of eventually lining up with William's map once again but always had to go back to rest and recover as he found that the tunnels had too many monstrous inhabitants to handle. The psion sustained himself by eating the void crabs he'd killed and collected. For water, he fortunately still had plenty stored in his mother's storage ring. Kiru also discovered that the two glass orbs that he had found back in the pillar were not as exciting. They were both full of water, each laced with a type of mana, changing its color and appearance. One was laced with mental mana, and the other with chaos mana. Kiru figured that he could use the former to help both with cultivation and in fighting dehydration. He would have to carefully consider how best to use the other vial.

Normally, he would have been distressed about going through winding corridors in the dark for days, unsure what was happening to his friends, but the knowledge there was a five-to-one time dilation effect and his perfect recall, made up for it. He was never lost and, though he wanted to hurry for his friends, he couldn't help them if he was reckless and died. He'd encountered a number of different creatures along the way, mostly umbrafangs, void crabs, and abominations, and had even gathered more information about them. More than a few of the tree-like graspers were apparently growing in the rooms and in some of the tunnels, and Kiru had to deal with them. They were surprisingly resistant to his Brainstorm technique, but he was able to cut them apart when they struck out at him; while their finger-like branches whipped out blindingly fast, they weren't very durable. So, changing his psyslime to a spinning saw that doubled as a shield easily took care of them.

"Oh, come on, Master. Take a bite of that thing," William pleaded.

Kiru looked at the cut-off pieces of branches scattered about. Their skin-like hue and the hideous nature of the strange plants made him even more uncomfortable about ingesting them than umbrafang blood. The psion could see the usefulness in doing so, though. So, as a compromise, he let William do the job himself in order to gain the knowledge of about the graspers. They discovered graspers were actually called fleshing trees, a name that made Kiru shiver, and surprisingly enough, the abominations were called just that—void abominations.

It was midway through the fifth day when things took a notable change, and it had to do with the creatures that called the prison home. Kiru dealt with a few umbrafangs at least once a day as he explored the tunnels, trying to find the spot his incomplete map indicated was the exit from the bottom level. As he'd been moving deeper and deeper into the tunnels, the frequency of encounters only grew. Both he and William surmised that it meant they were getting closer to their nest. Kiru had gone through enough tunnels too that they had figured out their location according to William's map. It just so happened to coincide with the direction they were now moving in, which was also closer to their target goal, an exit up to the next level.

Since they were getting closer to danger, Kiru put his mask on again. With his sense of smell renewed, his nose picked up the oily odor of umbrafang down the hall to his left. Their lair was that way, while his map pointed him to proceed forward. At a crossroads, he decided to go and deal with the monsters first. He didn't want to leave a potential threat behind him.

The tunnel he now crept down was covered in gore and fecal material. *Yep, definitely their home base,* Kiru thought. As he got closer, he could see a large doorway to his right. The psion noticed large claw marks all along the edges, indicating that a door had once stood there. Carefully, he peeked around the edge to observe what was inside. The room was a large, cave-like place full of metal debris, bones, corpses of various creatures, and at least a dozen umbrafangs. The most striking thing, however, was what illuminated the room.

Set in the ceiling was a giant water tank that nearly covered it completely. Two different pipes connected to the tank, one of which was partially broken and leaking a constant stream of water onto the floor from which the umbrafangs drank. Inside the massive tank was what looked to be a large whale. Kiru couldn't be sure, as he'd never seen a whale before, only read about them. The tome he read from did have a drawing, as well, and it looked similar to the being in the tank but with a few key differences. First, it was glowing a bright blue-green. Next, it had hundreds of long, glowing whiskers growing everywhere off of its body. Lastly, it had spots of orange dotted along its flesh as if its body contained stars.

Imp's Label.

Name: Subject 726341
Race: Nebulor (Juvenile)
Rank: Gold
Mana Type: Gravity
Path: Voidwalker
Status: Dormant

Nebulor are one of the four main races of the void. They are nomads and the main rivals to the arboth. While the arboth desire order and unification, the nebulor stick to the tenets of freedom and independence.

Kiru gave a subtle gasp at the information and pulled his head back out of the way before any of the umbrafangs could spot him. *"William, did you see that?"* Kiru sent.

"Yes, Master. I process the data even faster than you do. What is the use of that pointless question?" William replied.

Kiru rolled his eyes at his companion and suppressed a groan. *"Fine, then do you think that if I break the tank, it will no longer be dormant? I want to open it up to flush out all the umbrafangs at once."*

"Given the length of time it's been in dormancy and the status of the holding tank, I put your odds of actually reviving it at 4%. Still, even if it doesn't live, breaking the tank will improve your odds of success of eliminating this colony of umbrafangs to 94%."

Kiru nodded. *"Guess I don't have a choice, then,"* he sent before running into the room. Immediately, the dozen umbrafangs all locked onto him, each growing, the tentacles that made up their manes flaring up in anger. Kiru noticed a particularly large umbrafang on a tall pile of flesh and bones—their leader, he presumed. A few of the creatures came charging at him, but he didn't fight them. Instead, he leaped and used Telekinesis to help him fly up to the tank in the ceiling.

Kiru looked down to the monsters below him. They were looking up at him with their beady yellow eyes and snarling. He smiled, feeling free from danger at the moment. Then, he changed his psyslime into a drill and started working on the thick glass. The umbrafangs continued to growl and focus on him, but he paid them little mind. It was only a couple of minutes until he started to notice cracks starting to develop. He smiled behind his mask at the progress, but then his ears picked up the sound of metal bending.

Kiru looked down to notice that the umbrafangs were now scaling the wall, their claws pressing into the metal. "Crap," he spat out and then put even more effort into his drilling. He had originally intended to break the glass carefully to allow him to dodge the juvenile nebulor's body. He hoped the creature's body and the large amount of water holding it would either kill or debilitate the umbrafangs enough for easy elimination. When he saw them closing in, though, he knew he had to improvise. He forced his drill to move faster and faster.

More cracks started to form along the glass as soon as the psion saw the umbrafangs had clawed their way to the ceiling. With a groan of effort, more cracks started to spread.

"Master, I detect the structural integrity is irreparably damaged. We must flee," William sent.

Right after the imp's message, one of the umbrafangs leaped off from its position. It clamped down on Kiru's left foot, and while it didn't do much damage to him, the sudden addition of weight plus its momentum forced him to fall faster. As he fell, he called his psyslime back to him and knocked the monster off of his leg. But Kiru unfortunately wasn't fast enough to do that *and* stop his descent. So, immediately after he beat the umbrafang off him, he landed in a large pile of scrap metal.

To his credit, Kiru stood back up immediately, his dragon-bone armor fortunately providing him enough protection. All the umbrafangs that were on the ground surrounded him, completely ignoring the damaged tank above them. Water started to shoot out from the cracks like rain, but still the monsters didn't take their eyes off the psion, clearly eager to devour him. Kiru quickly scanned his surroundings.

They have me on all sides. I can't go up because the tank is there. I also can't use Brainstorm since that'll hurt me too with all this water around. How can I protect myself from every direction until the tank cracks? he thought. *If only I could make my psyslime shield me from all sides.*

Kiru's eyes widened as an idea came to him.

Some unknown signal seemed to pass for the umbrafangs, because three of them leaped towards him at once.

With no time to lose, Kiru mentally ordered his psyslime into a brand-new configuration, a protective sphere that encompassed his entire body, leaving him in complete darkness. Just then, there were three consecutive thuds against the metal. Just as he'd hoped, they didn't even leave a dent. For the next half minute, Kiru would hear the occasional bang of a likely probing attack from one of the umbrafangs—but nothing significant.

Kiru forced his breathing to slow. He knew he had a limited supply of air and would eventually have to open up a section of the slime to allow more in. It was just at that moment that a new, loud, clearly stronger force struck the top of his protective orb.

"It appears that the tank has finally cracked," William sent. *"By my calculations based off the dimensions of the tank, you should be able dismiss this dome in approximately 5.4 seconds."*

Really?! That fast? Kiru thought to himself in amazement. He was stunned for a couple of moments until he realized he'd forgotten to count down. So, he silently began, giving himself a few extra seconds to be safe before dismissing his psyslime, forcing it to change shape back into his Fu Tao, and launched himself up in the air with Telekinesis. There was still water streaming down along the edges of the tank, but fortunately he was inside the center. Looking down, much of the detritus and buildup inside the umbrafang den had been washed away, the water rushing out of the sole entryway inside the spacious room. While it looked that some of the monsters had been caught up by the sudden flash flood, Kiru counted ten of the original pack still present, and grunted in frustration at only two having been dealt with. The psion had expected more to have been washed out or killed. *Must be because I lost the element of surprise,* he thought. Kiru did notice a leg sticking out from under the dormant or possibly-now-dead nebulor, clearly crushed under its massive bulk. *Guess the nebulor was too big to avoid entirely.*

Kiru did notice that the biggest of the umbrafangs had remained unscathed. It and the rest of its pack were looking up, glaring hatefully at the psion, all of their thick, hairless hides glistening from the sudden downpour. Noticing both that and his relative dryness, Kiru smirked.

"Time to let loose a little," he said as a small spark of electricity crackled off his body.

The psion channeled his mana quickly until electricity sparked off of him. Concentrating it to just around his head, he fired a Brainstorm at the umbrafang's alpha.

The monster didn't dodge in time and was struck full-force by the electrical technique. It didn't stop there. The water and metal conducted the Brainstorm with ease, and in the blink of an eye, everything that was touching the ground was electrocuted, even the nebulor. Kiru continued the technique for five seconds before dismissing it. When he did, all of the umbrafangs were smoking husks. In an impressive display of strength, the alpha was still standing, but evidently that was the extent of it as its legs wobbled and it breathed heavily, seeming not able to move.

"A wise and useful way to save on your mana expenditure, Master. I approve," William sent. *"Since that umbrafang is currently weakened, I suggest using Subjugation on it. Having an extra ally could come in handy."*

Kiru nodded in agreement and slowly descended to the umbrafang. As he neared it, he could see that the creature was still stuck looking up, clearly dealing with the lingering effects of his technique. That was fine for Kiru, however, and he placed a palm against its head and activated Subjugation. In a matter of moments, the creature's mind was under his control. The remnants of his Brainstorm technique left its body too, which caused it to stagger and relax.

Feeling pleased, Kiru smiled. He then noticed a large shadow suddenly forming behind him. He turned, "Uh, William, what percent chance did you say the nebulor would awaken?"

CHAPTER TWENTY

Whale of a Time

Both of the nebulor's large eyes moved to look directly down at him as it let out an otherworldly, haunting moan. It started deep and shook Kiru to the bone before ending in a higher pitch. Kiru couldn't be sure, but the thing sounded as if it were . . . curious.

He sheathed his blades and put his hands up. "Hi there, I am Kiru. Can you understand me?" he asked.

The nebulor made a vibrating noise, but the psion couldn't tell whether or not the whale could comprehend his words. Kiru was leaning towards the theory that it had at least *some* understanding of what he was saying, as Imp's Label had told him that the nebulor were one of the four main races of the void. With that being the case, he presumed at least a basic intelligence.

"I suggest using Telepathy. Hopefully, communicating directly to his mind should help bridge the gap," William offered.

"I mean you no harm," Kiru sent to the nebulor as he took a step forward and reached out his hand to touch it—which seemed to be the wrong choice.

As soon as it had received his message, the nebulor's eyes widened and the floating creature immediately recoiled from him. It trilled rapidly, which soon turned into a guttural grow, making Kiru's body shake once more.

"Okay, you did not like that," he said out loud as he took a step back, making sure his hands were out and his tone of voice soft so as not to set off the whale creature any further. *"William, that backfired. What do you suggest now?"* he sent.

"Um, that was . . . unexpected. I advise making your way towards the exit slowly. Make no sudden moves," the imp replied.

"If you want me to leave, I'll just go out of the exit here, and you'll never have to see me again," Kiru said, taking William's advice. He then took a step towards the doorway but stopped as the creature gave out a shrill cry conveying anger. At the same time, a heavy mana signature appeared in front of Kiru like a pillar. The ground before him suddenly started to sink in as if struck by some unseen force.

"*From my analysis of its vocal patterns, it is growing increasingly hostile to you. That wasn't a warning shot. It just missed its attack. That was its gravity mana. Another attack is imminent in three seconds,*" William sent.

"What?!" Kiru exclaimed, then let out a groan and fired a Brainstorm at the nebulor.

It gave a loud cry of pain and snapped itself up before a wave of mana rained down on the creature, forcibly removing the technique from its body. It looked back down and glared at Kiru, letting out a clicking growl.

Kiru drew his psyslime and launched himself forward at the nebulor, changing his weapon in midair into a spear to stab the whale. He wasn't fast enough, however, and was swatted like a fly by the nebulor's tail. The psion was sent flying and crashed into one of the metal walls with such force that he was partially embedded in its surface.

"*Master, it's charging. Force yourself down,*" William pleaded.

Fortunately, Kiru wasn't dazed from the strike, and while he no longer needed Telekinesis to move, he could still use it. And that was precisely what he did, flinging himself down to the ground and narrowly avoiding getting swallowed whole by the nebulor. He didn't land gracefully, however, falling face-first onto the wet floor, but adrenaline helped him override the pain and quickly get back up. He readied his spear to jump and stab the whale in its exposed flank.

Most of its head was stuck in the wall, but it shook and freed itself in the blink of an eye, sending ruined pieces of metal flying in Kiru's direction.

He had to abandon his attack and leap to the side to avoid being struck. He had just enough time to notice a giant hole in the wall with a purple glow before the nebulor struck again. It hit Kiru with its gravity attack, and this time, it didn't miss. The psion slammed against the wet metal with such power, it was as if a giant had stepped directly on his back. Within a couple of seconds, the floor around him caved into the pressure until there was a circular indent all around him.

"This thing sure is strong for a Gold," Kiru growled as he forced himself to slowly stand against the pressure. While he could move, it was much restricted. Kiru knew that if he didn't find a way to stop this technique and soon, he was in trouble.

The nebulor glared at the psion and clicked angrily.

"Any ideas, William?" Kiru asked.

"*Indeed,*" the imp sent back.

Time seemed to slow down in Kiru's mind. Something glowed off to his left. He saw that it was the subjugated alpha umbrafang that the imp had highlighted in his vision. Kiru had honestly forgotten about doing anything with it, given how quickly everything had spiraled out of control with the nebulor. Though Kiru had subjugated it, the monster still had its natural survival instincts. It had stayed off in a corner doing its best to be out of sight until called upon.

"My analysis of this thing shows it needs a direct line of sight to use this suppressive gravity technique. Use the umbrafang to distract it long enough to throw your spear at it. Once you hit it, use it as a lightning rod to enhance your Brainstorm like you did with the dragon in Imakandi. Ready?" William asked.

Kiru didn't fully understand how the imp had managed to slow down his perception of time, but he wasn't in a position to ask. He didn't really care at the moment, either—he needed all the help he could get. Time sped back up in his perception, and with a mental command, he ordered the umbrafang to charge the nebulor.

The whale-like being opened its mouth wide, revealing innumerable metallic teeth that looked like hair, indicating it intended to swallow Kiru whole. Before it could do so, though, the umbrafang leapt off a pile of metal scraps and bit down into its thick flesh. The nebulor gave out a high-pitched cry of pain as its focus was diverted to the monster savaging it, freeing Kiru from its oppressive gravity attack. The nebulor smacked the umbrafang off with its flipper, the wolf-like beast landing hard with an audible cracking of bone. It went limp.

The whole interaction only lasted a few seconds, but that was all Kiru needed. The psion heaved and threw the spear with all the might he possessed. With a boost in speed and guidance from Telekinesis, the weapon struck the nebulor in its right eye.

It recoiled in pain as glowing ocular fluid liberally spurted out from the wound.

Kiru didn't let up and fired another Brainstorm, this time directly at the psyslime weapon. The metallic slime easily drew the technique in and conducted it deep into the nebulor's body and brain. The spear seemed to amplify the damage as the creature let out a harsh, shrill cry of distress. The bulky creature appeared to not be able to manipulate gravity to hold itself up anymore, and it fell down and crashed into the already-damaged wall behind it. It hit the wall as if it was a siege engine, and where there was previously just a hole, now almost all of the wall collapsed into pieces, revealing an equally large room behind it.

Kiru stopped his technique and stood there breathing heavily for a bit. He hadn't grown accustomed to using Brainstorm in such close succession before, and it drained him. *I'm glad I can move without Telekinesis now. Pretty sure multiple casts like that would have wiped me out a few days ago.*

Fortunately, the nebulor wasn't moving anymore, so Kiru was pretty sure it was dead. Just to confirm though, he asked, "William?"

"The creature is dead, Master. I detect no signs of life," William replied.

"Good," Kiru said before taking his mask off and staggering toward the corpse. When he got close enough to it, he willed his psyslime weapon to come back to him and forced it to change shape before he sheathed it. As he continued to move up the pile of debris the creature was on, he eventually crested the top and got a better view of the now-exposed chamber. "Oh, shit," he said.

The room they'd broken into was just as massive but much more dangerous. It was dark, only sparsely illuminated by a solitary red orb of light on one wall and by some purple light coming off a bubbling black pool that took up a good third of the floor space. There was what appeared to be a large, ominous, spiraling staircase on the opposite side of the room, hovering around the pool were four abominations, each of them wriggling and contorting as if their shapes hadn't solidified yet.

Worst of all, there was a fleshing tree, and it was massive. The thing was bigger than any of the others Kiru had seen, rivaling the nebulor in both size and width. Unlike the others as well, the thing was always moving constantly wriggling and twitching, despite being rooted to the metal floor, as it scanned the room for new prey, letting out terrifying shrieks every few seconds.

William spoke up in that same monotone way when he was analyzing something, interrupting Kiru's train of thought, "*Scanning layout. Scan complete. Updating map.*" In Kiru's vision, a glowing arrow appeared, pointing straight up the staircase. "*Based on this room's layout, I can state with certainty that the path to the next level is on the other side of this room.*"

Kiru pursed his lips in frustration. That staircase was just feet away from the base of the massive fleshling tree. Then, one of the shifting abominations eventually solidified its form and moved over to the large tree. Predictably, the tree picked up the abomination and swallowed it whole. What was not expected, however, was what happened next. The tree munched and chewed audibly before suddenly spitting it back out after a few seconds. The abomination seemed to be unharmed but now had multiple pale growths coming off its body. It then promptly exited the chamber through a nearby doorway into the maze-like series of tunnels.

"*Interesting,*" William sent.

"Did that thing just pollinate the abomination?" Kiru asked.

"*Indeed, Master. Based on its sheer size, this looks like the oldest fleshing tree we've encountered so far. It may be the progenitor of all the others we've observed on this level,*" William sent. "*The abominations appear to be unwilling hosts for the fleshing tree, acting like bees would for flowers, spreading its seeds throughout this place. Also, this place appears to be the source of the abominations.*"

Kiru looked back at the bubbling purple-black pool and saw a misshapen clump of goo being spat out from the fluid. It landed with a wet thunk and began to wiggle and roil. In just a couple of seconds, a small black tentacle started to grow. "You're right," he said. Fortunately, despite their loud entrance, the abominations weren't moving towards them and the giant fleshing tree couldn't reach him. So, he was relatively safe for the moment. With the abominations not being fully focused on him or even fully developed, Kiru was confident that he could slip past them without any difficulty. The problem was the tree. The psion could tell the thing was too fast and too aggressive for him to simply ignore and slip past.

Placing a hand on the nebulor's corpse beside him, though, he did have an idea. "William, what do you think?" he asked.

"I can already imagine what you're thinking, Master. While it would likely work if you were at Sapphire, I do not believe you can perform it at your current capabilities," the imp sent back.

"Really? Why?"

"I've reasoned that you want to launch the nebulor's corpse directly at the tree to distract it. If that is so, I believe it to be too much for you to lift. Based off the data I've accumulated about them and this one's dimensions, it must weigh at least two-thousand pounds. Even at the upper echelon of Ruby, you cannot lift a literal ton," William explained.

Kiru gripped the pommel of his psyslime weapon and looked down at the malleable substance. "You know, using the slime as a protective barrier was very effective. I'd never used it that way before. How well do you think it would withstand—"

"I calculate a 98.7% likelihood of failure if you use the slime as a protective orb around yourself. While it could withstand direct strikes from the branches, it will eventually break down if the tree just picks you up and tries to chew you. Its teeth will either break the slime, or you will have to open it up to get air, leaving you vulnerable."

Kiru grimaced.

Before the psion could say anything else, though, William continued, *"However, that idea is not without merit. Hmm, calculating."* After only about five seconds of silence, the imp picked up where he left off. *"Success! I have discovered a plan that has a 96.7% chance of success. Observe."*

A semi-transparent image of Kiru's psyslime blade appeared in his vision. It then changed into the shape of a large orb, which then flew over the growing abominations and directly into the fleshing tree's mouth.

"Based on my assessment of your current capabilities, Master, you should be able to easily control the psyslime within a span of twenty feet. Once you allow the tree to swallow it, you simply will the slime to transform into a spinning saw and bisect it from the inside," William sent. To punctuate his point, a glowing image of a round saw blade popped out from inside the tree.

Kiru thought it was a reasonable plan—better than the one he'd come up with. There was one problem, though. "How do I get close enough to control the slime? The branches on the thing must be at least twenty feet long by themselves," he said.

"I have thought of that too. While you cannot move the entirety of the nebulor's corpse, if you cut off a large piece, you could move that. Using that as a barrier to shelter behind should buy you enough time to enact your plan," William said.

Kiru sighed and looked at the giant corpse behind him. "This is going to get messy, isn't it?"

"*Undoubtedly.*"

After taking an hour to cut through a thick enough portion of the tail, Kiru, covered in the creature's blue blood, enacted the first step of his plan. To make sure that he had no enemies behind him, he used Brainstorm on the growing abominations. While he had been slicing into the nebulor, William had figured out that the pool spit one of them out every twenty-five-to-thirty seconds. Since they didn't appear to be "fully matured," they easily succumbed to his technique.

With roughly half a minute until another abomination appeared, he drew his psyslime, still in its Fu Tao form, and proceeded to move the hunk of ten-foot-tall nebulor flesh ahead of him like a bulwark. The giant tree, despite having no eyes, locked onto him, its hissing mouth drooling thick globules as it seemed to focus on his location. As soon as the first branch whipped out at him, Kiru pressed his body against the large area of whale flesh to keep himself safe.

Kiru's makeshift shield shook as it was struck but held as the assault continued. Now it was time for the second step. He forced the slime to contort into an orb and threw it up and over the nebulor toward the tree, rolling to the side to maintain his line of vision and activating his Telekinesis on the slime, forcing it to fly toward the terrifying plant. The large fleshing caught it before it could be forced down its mouth, but it actually moved to place it inside its maw on its own.

Kiru smiled in satisfaction, but before he could make the psyslime change shape, one of the fleshing tree's many branches that weren't involved in feeding it were still thrashing.

"*Roll forward!*" William sent.

Trusting his familiar, Kiru immediately did so, avoiding a series of strikes where he'd just been standing. Realizing he had just a split second before he would be struck at again, Kiru reached out with his mind at the orb he could see was just about to be out of his sight.

The slime turned into a round, serrated saw blade that cut through the stalk of the tree in all directions with a wet squelch. The giant fleshing tree's near-constant screeching came to an abrupt halt as it let out a chocking noise, and all of its whip-like branches went limp at once. Without any ceremony, the thing fell over to the side, completely bisected.

Kiru let out a sigh of relief, and he began to casually walk over towards the dead tree. He was honestly surprised with how easily he'd been able to deal with it. "Well done, William. How'd you know I was going to be safe going forward when all those branches were striking out so quickly?" Kiru asked.

"Analysis," the imp answered like it was no big deal.

Kiru just exhaled at William's explanation. Whatever that Chaos Core thing that powered the ship once upon a time was, it had really changed his friend. While undeniably useful and improved in a lot of ways, Kiru wondered if William was truly still in there or not. He had tried to probe him during his times recovering in the strange pool room they found, asking if the imp had enjoyed the frequent fighting and violence and if he missed his old body, but William had been either vague or dismissive to his questions. The psion would have to try again to truly understand what had become of his familiar but not right now. Even with the fleshing tree dealt with, this room still wasn't safe, with abominations being spewed forth every half-minute.

Kiru turned his psyslime back into its typical hook-blade form and sheathed it once again and started his way up to the next level. He had only made it a couple of steps, however, when he heard movement behind him. The hair stood up on the back of his neck, and his heart sank as he turned to see the source. The fleshing tree wasn't dead.

The top half that Kiru had amputated was now freed from its stalk and using its numerous branches to move around. It was snarling and seemed to be focused in the direction of the nebulor's corpse.

"Did you expect this to happen?" Kiru asked telepathically.

"Negative," William replied.

Carefully, Kiru stepped back to continue up toward the next level. His second step must not have been quiet enough, though, as right after he did so, the now-mobile giant fleshing top snapped towards him. Just milliseconds after it did so, it gave a blood-chilling screech and charged toward the psion using its branches as legs.

Kiru felt like his heart was about to leap into his throat. "Oh, shit!" he spat out before taking off as fast as he could up the spiraling path. There weren't any actual stairs, just one smooth incline that was easy for Kiru to sprint up, but that also helped the thing behind him make headway too. Aside from the sounds of his breathing and footsteps, Kiru's ears were full of the crashing noise of the fleshing behind him.

The path up was now completely dark, but it fortunately didn't inhibit Kiru, thanks to his darkvision. As he ran, he stole a glance behind him and saw the thing taking up the entire width of the tunnel and quickly closing the distance. Realizing he could move faster by levitating, the psion used his Telekinesis to float and fling himself far off, zooming enough ahead that the fleshing was out of sight. As he ascended, William scanned the tunnel somehow and told Kiru that the structural integrity of the spiraling path was at less than 50% percent, and there were notable cracks along the walls. It gave Kiru hope that it would collapse under the monstrosity's weight. *And if it won't, I'll make it happen.*

Quickly, he made it out of the tunnel into the fifth level and landed on the ground. He didn't have time to take it in, though, as he knew he had just a few seconds before the fleshing would be on him. He could hear the tunnel breaking apart by the constant sounds of shattering stone and metal, but they weren't louder than the fleshing's screeching.

It's going to make it out before the tunnel collapses, he thought and then reached out with all his might at the tunnel walls. The cracks along them rapidly spread out, and the tunnel began to shake from the force of his Telekinesis. Just as the crawling giant fleshing tree crested the corner, the psion ripped large chunks of the tunnel wall free and began throwing them at the predatory plant creature with all his might. Despite the creature's bulk, it was forced back under the constant barrage of sharp, heavy debris. The fleshing was forced to back away to avoid the makeshift missiles for only a couple of seconds, but that was all the time Kiru needed.

With the tunnel already collapsing and Kiru accelerating the destruction with his technique, it fell right on top of the fleshing just as it began to charge once more. The fleshing plummeted, careening down amongst the falling debris and crying out hideous screeches along the way. The noises continued for another five seconds but were cut off abruptly with a boom.

Kiru sighed and nearly collapsed to his knees in relief. There was blessed silence from below, and he could only hear his own heavy breathing. That relief was cut short, though, when his ears picked up the sounds of a familiar haunting chorus of moans off in the distance.

CHAPTER TWENTY-ONE

Weapon of War

Vatrenex stood on top of his tower overlooking the sea. His personal quarters were *The Marauding Citadel*'s tallest building, only rivaled in height by the ship's masts. As such, his view was unparalleled. Vatrenex was once the leader of the Harbingers, an elite fighting force who were bound by cruel masters, now fractured into four disparate groups. With the first barrier to their former prison now gone, Vatrenex now knew that he had to force his brothers to serve him again. Only together could they take down the second barrier and destroy Gaal'cothdreek-duun's power source that kept them tethered to these chaotic waters.

"Now that I have the right weapons to wield, it is time to wage war once again," the monstrous captain uttered to himself. His underling alchemist had reported positive results with the experiments on the gold drakonid. Vatrenex had intended for the gnome to be a slave when he'd raided a Federation vessel all those years ago, but when he saw the hate in the alchemist's eyes, the captain knew he had potential. Now, that potential was coming to fruition for Vatrenex as he saw their destination coming into view.

It grew larger as they got closer—a large, crescent-shaped island with thick mangrove swampland taking up most of its surface and a line of dead volcanoes along its back. It was the Whispering Isle, the home of one of his brothers, Plio, and his followers, the Hushed. The dead volcanoes served as a barrier, preventing anyone from approaching in any other direction but the swamp. While any mangrove swamp would be considered difficult terrain for any army to invade, with the extra defenses the island had, it was practically impossible.

Vatrenex growled in annoyance as he beheld the island, reminded of his previous attempts to conquer the Husheds' homeland. There was a large tree in the island's center that looked like a blackened husk. It radiated Plio's power and allowed the swamp to withstand and even repel *The Marauding Citadel*'s cannons. It also caused the plants of the swamp to regrow unnaturally fast, preventing the corsairs from simply cutting through. A couple of times over the centuries, Vatrenex had attacked directly, and those were the only times Plio would make his presence known.

Damn that cowardly rat, Vatrenex thought. *We Harbingers were meant to conquer, but he hides, afraid of this world that is ripe for the taking.* Though he knew he was much stronger than Plio, his brother had a home advantage, and he had never been able to defeat him there. The captain of *The Marauding Citadel* clenched his fist and scowled. Unlike Plio, though, Vatrenex had been working to improve himself over the centuries. All four of the Harbingers possessed the Chaosbind technique which allowed them to take over a host body, but the captain had managed to evolve it into something more. He had discovered a way to use the technique to take over a victim, dominating their psyche while still being in complete control of their body. The only catch was the being that he dominated had to cultivate chaos mana like himself.

Like me brothers, he thought as his scowl turned into a sadistic grin. *I will take control of them all and finally have the means to free myself from this sea. I just have to defeat them first.*

Vatrenex looked down to the city below, and his grin widened. *And I now have the means to finally best them.* There was the gold drakonid, his newest weapon, the final piece of the puzzle he needed to defeat Plio.

The reptilian rogue was shackled and frantically looking around. While others saw an unstable cultivator bound in chains, Vatrenex saw a cannon ready to be fired. He just needed to aim him correctly. The ship dropped anchor half a mile from the island, as there was a coral reef that spread out and prevented any ship the *Citadel*'s size from getting too close.

Vatrenex took that as his cue; the monster leaped from his tower and landed with a boom. All of the people around him were visibly startled, but the worst off was the drakonid. Upon turning and seeing Vatrenex, his mouth dropped open, his pitch-black eyes full of fear.

Zhaden began desperately heaving and tugging on his chains, doing his best to rip them from the corsairs' grasps. "No, he's here. Must get away. I must get away," he grunted in clear panic. Despite his strength, it wasn't enough to contend with five Golds on each side of him.

Vatrenex's monstrous half-face gave a wicked grin as he stomped towards the drakonid, his blade in his left hand and resting on his shoulder. The closer he got, the more Zhaden shook until eventually, he went completely still, like a baby fawn. Vatrenex used his free hand to grab Zhaden by the throat and lifted him up to eye level, his strength easily forcing the ten Gold corsairs down on their knees.

"You want to get away, do you?" Vatrenex asked the drakonid.

Zhaden didn't answer, his face paralyzed by fear.

"Then I will give you your chance," the captain said before forcibly turning Zhaden to face outwards. "That is the Whispering Isle. It is your new home if you can survive." Vatrenex's mouth opened all the way down to his chest, revealing his numerous teeth. "Release him!" he barked to his subordinates who rushed to do as bid. Once they detached the trollstone cuff, Vatrenex drew the drakonid within centimeters of his face. "But know you will *never* be safe, Zhaden. My men and I will *always* hunt you."

Zhaden still kept completely still, not even seeming to breathe. Vatrenex would have to praise his alchemist for the sinister concoction that had broken the stubborn rogue's mind.

Vatrenex's long blue-green tongue started moving out from his chest and over to Zhaden's left hand, where it placed two daggers in it before making the hand close around them and retracting.

"Enjoy your freedom, while it lasts. Now, run," he said before spinning and throwing the rogue off *The Marauding Citadel* and towards the Isle.

Zhaden felt the wind whooshing past his scales as he soared through the air. As his momentum petered out, gravity took effect, and he began to fall. His body plummeted and would crash into the shallow coral in seconds. Despite the imminent danger, now that he was no longer right by that monster, the drakonid felt relieved and ready for what was to come.

Just milliseconds before he would make impact, Zhaden tucked his head under his forearm and oriented his body. It was just in time, too, because when he did drop on the coral, instead of hitting it face-first and breaking his body, he managed a roll, using the momentum of his fall to help him spin and land on his feet unharmed. His body and leathers were wet, as there was still a thin layer of salt water in the shallows, but that didn't deter him as he knelt with a blade in each hand and scanned for any threats. None could be seen ahead of him.

Quickly, he looked back to *The Marauding Citadel* a few hundred feet away. Fear gripped his heart again as his black eyes locked onto Vatrenex standing on the deck, the monster's single red eye fixed on him, a malicious grin plastered on his face. But what the gold drakonid could now see under the surface disturbed him even more. Whatever the gnome had done to his eyes, it had given Zhaden the ability to see the heat coming off the bodies of living things. Yet when he looked at the monstrous captain, he saw heat only from two places—from inside Vatrenex's maw and his blade. Brunhilda's exposed half-face had no heat at all.

That confirmed it for Zhaden—Brunhilda was dead. *That's why Vatrenex couldn't swear that he wouldn't do us harm*, Zhaden thought as he averted his eyes. He knew logically that the blasted gnome had artificially elevated his fear of Vatrenex to a ridiculous level, but just because he knew it didn't take away from the fear.

A horn then bellowed, and Zhaden saw a section of the *Citadel*'s hull open, lowering itself as a drawbridge to land on the water. Standing inside the open section was the first mate, flanked on each side by half a dozen corsairs and twice as many chained slaves, many of whom had crazed looks in their eyes. The corsairs radiated malicious glee and the slaves, pure desperation. All of them were focused on Zhaden.

"The hunt be on, lads," Saltbeard shouted as he drew out his cutlass and pointed his blade at the rogue. "Any corsair who captures the scaley will be promoted. Any slave of theirs will get to live fer another day."

Zhaden didn't focus on the pirates any longer. He turned back and sprinted toward the isle with all his might. He heard another horn blare behind him and shouting as the corsairs and their slaves chased after him. To his horror, he heard Vatrenex calling out to him, saying that he'd "better run fast!" That reignited the primal fear that had been imbued in him, and he somehow seemed to move even faster.

Zhaden expertly leaped and climbed as he navigated the winding roots and thick foliage that was the mangrove swamp. About twenty feet in, he made a sharp turn to the left to break any remaining line of sight of him from the ship and activated both his Silence and Invisibility techniques in tandem. For the next minute, he pushed himself deeper and deeper into the swamp, moving about chaotically, as the trees and roots made it impossible to go in a straight line for more than about ten feet.

Utilizing his training and his desperate need to get away from Vatrenex, Zhaden moved about with impressive speed and grace, the only evidence of his passage being the occasional scratches his claws made into the trees and the rippling of water when he needed to step on a partially submerged root to continue. His techniques helped him push through so impressively, he would have been extremely proud of himself, had not he been so terrified. Eventually, he found a particularly large mangrove tree with a large opening at its base. Thinking it was the best place he could find for now, Zhaden quickly rushed into the hollowed-out tree base and scanned his surroundings, listening for any hunters who might be following him.

He stood in water just below his knees as he crouched and used his senses to constantly check for any foes. Zhaden still kept both his techniques going. His heart rate slowed and his breathing calmed slightly in relative safety, and that's when he realized the utter lack of noise coming from the swamp outside. There was nothing—no chirping of birds, no croaking of frogs, no buzzing and trilling of insects that one would expect from a swamp. He couldn't even hear the corsairs from afar.

Zhaden opened his eyes to observe the swamp once more. The area was so thick with plant life that no wind blew through it, making the place completely still. It was as if the whole place were frozen in time. The unnatural quiet made him uneasy. *Isn't this place called the Whispering Isles? Shouldn't there be at least some whispering?* he thought.

Then, Zhaden noticed a partially submerged set of tangled roots about ten feet away. As the subtle ripples from his legs moving hit the roots, it revealed something underneath, from which his newly improved eyes picked up a heat signature. Just as he registered what it was, someone leapt out from the water towards his hiding spot, a dagger in one hand and a hatchet in the other. Not wanting to be caught in his current spot, Zhaden silently rushed out of the tree and began climbing up it before the person could make it. *I'm both invisible and silent. How did they detect me?* he thought. He was confident in his ability to get away, but then he saw the person send out a familiar-looking black slash of mana in his direction.

Zhaden took in a sharp inhale and threw himself to the side off the tree. As he fell back, he saw the mana strike at the spot he'd just been in, nearly bisecting the tree. His back landed roughly against the uneven roots amidst the water, but his cry of pain was only detectable from the bubbles coming from his mouth. That moment of distress quickly passed, though, as he pushed himself back upright with his tail, his body still invisible but the water clearly signaling his location.

Zhaden still had his daggers in hand, which was a good thing because his attacker was on him almost instantly, with blinding speed. Zhaden barely managed to get his weapons up and block the strikes. This instantly dismissed both of his techniques, revealing himself fully. The two combatants stood there, each glaring at the other, weapons locked.

Now that his attacker was standing still for a moment, Zhaden was able to see who they were. It was a thin human man who stood a good foot shorter than Zhaden, his features gaunt and his eyes sunken in. He gave off the aura of a Gold and was adorned in shoddy rags and a haphazard blend of furs, some in significant decay.

"You disturb the water. You disturb the trees," the man said in a dry, harsh voice that sounded like he hadn't spoken in a century. He then bared his crooked teeth. "You are loud."

While the man's strength was impressive, especially for his stature, Zhaden could tell that he was stronger. The rogue pushed his attacker back a few feet, planning to use his longer proportions to his advantage in order to defeat this foe.

"The master hates noise," the man growled and swung his dagger up, sending another slash technique.

Zhaden just managed to narrowly spin out of the sudden attack's way. He used the spinning dodge to his advantage and turned it into an attack of his own, tripping the man with his tail. He fell on the flat of his back in the water, the splash echoing around the clearing. Despite his position, he flailed wildly with both of his weapons in hand, in a desperate attempt to ward off Zhaden from dealing a fatal blow. He failed.

Zhaden grabbed one of the man's wrists and removed his hatchet from his grip as he spun him around to lie on his stomach. The man screamed as his face was forced underwater and did his best to try and stab Zhaden with his remaining dagger by reaching up behind his back, but was quickly subdued when the drakonid stomped down on his elbow. Zhaden then took the hatchet and buried it in the back of the thin man's skull with an audible crunch. Immediately, the man's body went limp, and Zhaden moved away from him, breathing heavily while adding his attacker's dagger to his belt.

As he played the fight back in his head, the unnatural fear grew even stronger in his mind. *The technique the man used . . . I recognized it. That wasn't coincidence. He used the same technique as Vatrenex. But why?* he thought before a realization struck him and a chill went down his spine. *That must mean he works for Vatrenex!*

"Oh gods, how could he have found me so soon?" he muttered fearfully, the terror now gripping him overriding any instinct to remain quiet.

Then, as if his words had flipped a switch, the unnaturally quiet swamp filled with noise. Whispers came from every direction, their words and source indiscernible. Zhaden pressed his back against a nearby tree and began checking for any new foes. He didn't know where exactly he was in the swamp at first, but amongst the whispering, he heard screaming and shouting as well as the clanging of metal striking metal ahead of him. *The corsairs are there; that must mean that's the direction of the coast and . . . him,* he thought.

Despite the dangers of the swamp, Zhaden refused to head in the direction of that monster. So, he turned the opposite way and moved deeper into the swamp and island.

For hours, Zhaden pushed forward. He met many more of Vatrenex's ragged, skeletal assassins, sometimes two or three engaging him at once. Afterwards, he would loot their bodies when he had the chance and find small water skins and dried-out bugs in his foes' packs, which he consumed for sustenance. Over time, the whispering grew louder, eventually to the point where he could understand them.

"Nowhere is safe. Vatrenex will find you. He will wear you like a skin suit, just like Brunhilda," they whispered insidiously.

At that, Zhaden abandoned all attempts at stealth in order to move even faster. He was exhausted and overheated in the humid swamp, forcing him to pant like a dog to try and cool himself down. His fear was the only thing that kept him sharp. During times when he had to slow down, he heard the corsairs behind him, cutting through the thick foliage and shouting hatefully. That would instantly get his heart racing once more and reignite his desperate flight deeper into the island.

The swamp gradually became darker and darker as the day progressed. That didn't stop the drakonid. Even with the difficult terrain, he was moving about at a rapid pace, only forced to stop when the swamp assassins would try and ambush him. His heat vision rendered their attempts pointless, however, as he was able to spot them well before they could harm him. By the time the sky turned pink, Zhaden had killed at least a hundred of them and made it to a clearing.

Feeling at least a modicum of safety, he fell to one knee. Almost all of his stamina had been spent by this point. As he tried to force his racing mind and heart to calm down, he noticed that the incessant whispering had abruptly stopped as well. It was as if he had passed an unseen barrier. The large clearing had no visible ground, only thick roots that spread out in all directions, making an uneven floor. In the center of the area was a giant black tree, from which all the roots were growing. It would be more accurate to call it a husk because it appeared to be completely burnt to a crisp, like it would crumble to a pile of ash at the slightest touch. There were no leaves, as it looked to be cleaved in two by a giant diagonal slash, leaving a hollow opening at its top.

Zhaden didn't know how the tree was still standing but didn't question it. *Maybe I can hide inside there and recover my strength,* he thought as he slowly walked towards the it, feeling delirious. With the tree having nothing near it. It would provide the tired drakonid the ability to see a threat from any direction. After all the constant fear and tension, he finally felt some relief. It was too much for his body to handle any longer and before he could reach the tree, he passed out from sheer exhaustion.

CHAPTER TWENTY-TWO

Victory

Zhaden awoke with a gasp as he heard the loud sound of trees crashing behind him, followed by cheers of triumph. His black eyes widened as he realized what that meant. *They aren't too far away*, he thought as he stood back up. He didn't know how long he'd been out, but it must have been at least a few hours as it was nighttime now. Despite the dark, the clearing was well-illuminated by the clear night sky and the twin moons. Zhaden noticed how much better he could see in the nighttime even without the moons' light, another benefit his eyes now had. He would never be grateful for the torture he'd suffered at the hands of the gnome alchemist, but that didn't mean he couldn't use the results to his advantage.

Feeling at least a little recovered from his unintentional nap, he began jogging toward the center of the clearing toward the strange tree husk. His ears picked up no other noise or life immediately around him, which gave him a small degree of comfort. That was the case until he made it to be within a few feet from the strange tree. As he neared, the whispering returned, only it was different than before. Whereas it had previously come from innumerable sources in all directions, there was now only just one voice and it was coming directly from the tree.

"No, no, no. Too loud. Leave, intruder," the voice said in a harsh tone that was a mix of a wet squelch and a squeak.

Zhaden paused and readied his weapons. Every time he'd heard whispering, he'd eventually had to deal with an assassin. After a minute of silence, nothing happened, though. *It doesn't attack me like the others. Is this a trick?* he thought. *Maybe I can go around it?*

The sounds of violent combat suddenly erupted from the swamp behind Zhaden—apparently the corsairs hunting him were gaining ground. He didn't know if this tree was a different entity, but he didn't have time to give a lengthy explanation. He would try to go around it if he could. "I mean you no harm," he said and took a step to the side instead of back.

"Loud," the voice whispered back, angrily. Then, from inside the hollow opening on the top of the tree, a figure leapt out and descended toward Zhaden.

The gold drakonid leapt away to avoid this new foe, who landed where he'd been standing without a sound. Zhaden gazed at this enemy who gave off a sensation similar to the other assassins he fought but different at the same time. The biggest and most obvious difference was his appearance. The figure was a pitch-black humanoid rat creature. His form was hunched over, reminding Zhaden of Kiru's familiar. It wore no clothes, with long arms and disproportionately short legs and a single large red eye. The rat had no discernible genitalia but for some reason seemed like a male.

Zhaden gasped at the obvious similarities between this thing and Vatrenex, his heat vision also picking up on the fact that it only exuded heat from the same two places: the single dagger he wielded, and his mouth, which was steaming.

The rat man's lip shook. "You are loud, and you are a liar. Die!" it hissed as it lunged at the drakonid with incredible speed.

Zhaden leapt to the side but wasn't fast enough to avoid the strike completely as the dagger cut easily through his leather and sliced across the scales of his side, drawing blood. He was surprised that something with such short legs could move so quickly but didn't have time to dwell on it.

The rat man redirected his lunge with his tail and turned to come right back at Zhaden.

The drakonid jumped in the air and activated Duplication, forming three illusory copies of himself midair. All four of them threw one of the collected daggers from their belts at the rat. Though only one was real, Zhaden hoped it would be enough to at least confuse his opponent for a moment.

"Time Step," the rat man shouted right before he suddenly disappeared, reappearing right at the spot where he had originally landed by the tree. He glared at Zhaden. "You made me loud. Curse you," he growled.

Zhaden and his duplicates all turned to face the rat man. Panic gripped him once more, though he did his best to hide it. *This is another of Vatrenex's followers, but he has techniques that I haven't seen before. I have to kill him quick before the others catch up with me,* he thought as he drew out another looted dagger from his belt and readied himself.

The rat man radiated a chaotic mix of fear and hate that made Zhaden stagger. His opponent was a Ruby like him, but the malice he radiated made the drakonid nervous. One of his arms shook, betraying any attempts to hide his fear. There was another loud crashing of trees off in the distance, and the rat glanced in its direction, somewhat nervously. Zhaden didn't have enough time to question that look before his foe turned back to him and hissed, "True Darkness." The rat man's body seemed to dissolve before Zhaden's very eyes, turning into pitch-black smoke that quickly encompassed the entire clearing.

Fortunately, Zhaden's new eyes were perfectly suited to dealing with it as he was able to spot the warm light of his foe's blade, cutting through his illusions and making its way toward him. Zhaden parried the dagger and sliced across the rat man's belly before turning and kicking him in the back of the head.

The rat man staggered. He put one of his long arms to his head as Zhaden went to stab it through the neck. "Chaos Step," he whispered before disappearing from the drakonid's sight once again.

Zhaden stumbled forward as nothing stopped his momentum and then quickly looked around. Then he heard "Chaos Rift Slash," from above him. Zhaden looked up to see his foe had somehow been teleported scores of feet away up in the air and was firing a massive version of the offensive technique at him. Knowing he had no way to block it, he began running with all his might to avoid the oncoming strike. His wound tugged at him, giving him a clear warning if he ran too recklessly. He ignored it, though, in favor of his immediate safety.

The wound was forced open even more, causing blood to more readily spill down his side. He grimaced, but it was worth it because he was able to avoid the technique that cleaved many of the roots in two. He pressed a hand to his wound and looked up to find his foe. The rat man was falling directly in his direction, just twenty feet away. Zhaden threw three daggers at him at once, but the rat man uttered, "Time Step," and vanished from his sight. Before Zhaden could move, he felt a sharp pain in his gut.

Blood leaked out from his mouth, and he looked down to see the rat man's black dagger partially embedded in his abdomen. He followed the arm attached to the blade to see the rat man staring hatefully at him with his one eye, his hot breath smelling of decay. Zhaden felt his body start to go weak, the blade clearly causing some internal bleeding. He was about to give in, to let death embrace him, when he heard a voice in the distance.

"Zhaden!" Vatrenex bellowed.

Though the voice was far away, the rogue knew it was undoubtedly him. That unnatural fear gripped him again, bringing focus and sensation to his body as if it refused to let him die. *I can't die. I must get away from Vatrenex,* he thought.

"Vatrenex!" the rat man gasped and tried to pull his blade free from Zhaden.

The gold drakonid grabbed him by the wrist, preventing the blade from coming free. Zhaden knew he had to kill the rat man before he could flee. Otherwise, his foe could tell Vatrenex where he was going. Zhaden still had one thing he hadn't tried. "Nightmare," he hissed. From the cracks between his scales, dream mana emerged and coalesced above him until it formed the silhouette of a shadowy dragon, which roared and fell upon the rat man with fury.

The rat man screamed and writhed, but Zhaden didn't let go of his wrist. He knew that if he let go, he would likely teleport again. After half a minute, the nightmare disappeared, and the rat man was on his knees.

The rat breathed heavily and looked up at Zhaden with a mixture of confusion and fear in his eyes, "That technique was not one of Vatrenex's. Who are you, and why do you serve him?"

Zhaden's eyebrows raised, completely thrown by the unexpected question. "You, you do not serve that monster?" he asked, but before he could get an answer, he felt a sharp pain in his back.

Vatrenex stood back up on top of his tower monitoring the progress of both his men and his newest weapon of war during the night. The slaves and low-ranking corsairs that he had sent in as fodder were making slow progress, but it was at a better pace than any previous raiding party he'd ever sent to attack the Whispering Isle. They were fighting Plio's Hushed forces as well as some retaliatory strikes from the mangrove trees when they cut their way through a thick area of them, but they weren't being massively overwhelmed. Vatrenex knew that it was because many of them were distracted by an even greater threat—his weapon, Zhaden.

He only ever noticed glimpses of the drakonid amidst the thick mangroves, but occasionally caught a glimmer of his golden scales. Vatrenex never sent his aura out into the island because that would alert Plio, and he was not ready to do that yet.

It was easier to monitor his corsairs as they intentionally felled trees to allow their captain to keep sight of them. Throughout the day, Vatrenex would order his first mate to send more slaves and soldiers to reinforce the fighters when their numbers were dwindling and also to ensure that the path deeper into the swamp was maintained as the mangroves had a habit of rapidly growing back where they had been removed. Zhaden didn't seem to do any major damage to the trees, which pleased Vatrenex. *That means he's not alerting Plio to his presence as he focuses on the fodder I send in. Good,* he thought.

Despite the promising start, Vatrenex started to grow frustrated as day turned to night. He had not spotted Zhaden for hours. "If he is dead, then I will have to act now," he growled. Before he went in there himself, he did one more thing. He shouted. "Zhaden!" His voice boomed over the entire island. Vatrenex remembered the drakonid's utter terror back when they were on deck and believed that his voice would force him to act. He knew that Plio would hear him but wagered that he wouldn't react as long as he didn't cross the physical threshold of his domain.

Vatrenex's luck held out, and it worked. After only a couple of more minutes, he noticed that the mangroves were no longer moving of their own accord. That meant Plio was distracted.

"It is time," he said, barely containing his glee before a pair of hideous wings grew out from his body. Vatrenex then readied his blade and deliberately dropped, making it halfway to the deck before his wings caught the wind and he flew forward between the buildings of the *Citadel* and towards the isle at impressive speed.

Once he had physically entered the swamp, he could sense his brother's power and fortunately, it wasn't focused on him. Vatrenex soared towards the nearest contingent of his soldiers. He could see they were arrayed defensively with their cutlasses at the ready in one hand and torches in the other. He extended out his aura and was able to sense three of Plio's followers hiding in the trees surrounding his corsairs.

"Chaos Rift Slash," Vatrenex shouted before swinging his blade in a horizontal slash. His technique arced through the air with rapid speed, zooming across the air before anyone else could register it.

The flying slash cut two of the Hushed in half as well as carved straight through a large swath of the thick mangroves like they were paper. The third Hushed cultist was struck by Vatrenex's blade directly, and they were blown into pieces by the sheer force of his swing. Vatrenex's blade pulsed in delight and greedily drank in the blood of his latest victim. He stood on top of the tree by the pool of gore that remained of the Hushed he'd just struck and slammed the tip of his blade into the thick tree so as to make a loud crunch to get his soldiers' attention.

The clearly frightened corsairs all turned to look at the source of the noise, and their beady, bloodshot eyes widened in surprise upon seeing their leader there.

"The captain is with us!" an orc corsair with half her face covered in gruesome scars cheered.

Vatrenex dislodged his blade and pointed it in the direction of his brother's aura. "Push forward, corsairs. Our time of victory is at hand!" he declared.

The corsairs all gave a loud, triumphant cry in response before they began going forward once more, reinvigorated by their captain's words.

Vatrenex used his powerful technique to cut through acres of trees and quite a few people, and nearly made it to the center of the swamp in a matter of seconds. While he had carved a path, many roots still remained. Since none of his troops had any discernible movement techniques nor could they fly like him, it still made their progress—while significantly faster than before—slower than he desired. So, Vatrenex decided not to wait on them. They weren't his concern, anyway. They could all die horrible deaths as long as he defeated Plio.

He flew below the tree line and retracted his aura to not alert his brother, only using his eyesight to find them. Once he reached the swamp's edge, he saw the clearing and the central tree that was Plio's stronghold. He hid behind a large tree and kept his form low to observe the scene unfolding before him. The drakonid was holding his own against Plio. It appeared that the rat's current host matched Vatrenex's new weapon in rank, which certainly helped. They both fought with impressive speed, making it even a little difficult for Vatrenex to follow.

He forced himself to stay still and patiently wait despite his blade pulsing in bloodlust. He knew that, even though his rank exceeded Plio's, the rat was undoubtedly faster with his ability to teleport. Vatrenex needed to strike when his brother couldn't flee, when he wouldn't see him coming. Then, he saw it. The drakonid, even with his broken mind, was able to come up with a clever strategy, using his body to trap Plio before unleashing his trump card—the Nightmare technique—to subdue him. To make it even better, the rogue's body obstructed Plio's sight from Vatrenex.

After carefully aiming the tip of his blade at the optimal angle, Vatrenex surged forward as fast as he could and stabbed Zhaden straight through his back, avoiding the rogue's spine but spearing his blade out from the drakonid's abdomen and cutting off Plio's hand.

In a blink, a giant black blade erupted from Zhaden's gut right beside the dagger. The blade surged forward, cutting the rat man's arm from his body. Blood now rushed out of Zhaden like a fountain as he vomited up the fluid.

His legs went limp, now only being held up by the blade impaling him. He wiped his mouth and weakly forced his eyes open. He saw the blackness of the one-eyed rat man dissolve before him, fading away until an elf covered in rotten rags and faded furs was left in its place. The elf was even more withered than the men Zhaden fought but had the same attire and look about him—he was clearly in league with them.

The elf clutched the stump of an arm to his chest and looked over Zhaden's shoulder. "Thank you," he uttered before a monstrous hand reached out above Zhaden and grabbed the elf by the head. The hand squeezed, and he cried out in pain but only for a couple of seconds before his eyes rolled back, and his head popped like a melon, covering Zhaden in blood and brain.

The blade impaling Zhaden tilted down, forcing him to slide painfully off and land on the flat of his stomach onto the elf's headless corpse. He weakly turned his own head to see the hulking Vatrenex standing over him. The monster reached over Zhaden and grabbed the black dagger that had just been inside his gut. The drakonid watched as he gripped the small weapon and raised it in the air.

"Yes! Finally!" he declared, gripping the pommel tight. "Chaosbind." The black dagger then let out a whining noise and Zhaden noticed steam coming off the weapon as if it had been heated and was now rapidly cooling. "You, Plio, are mine," Vatrenex said at the dagger, which still glowed warmly.

Zhaden gasped in realization as all the pieces clicked together in his mind. The weapons were alive—cursed—and somehow would take over their wielder's minds and corrupt their bodies to be their own. And it looked like these cursed weapons had gathered followers and were in a constant state of war to rule over the Torn Empire. He gritted his teeth in frustration at the timing as he realized it was too late. He was significantly weakened from the wound, and he knew it would only be a matter of minutes before he bled out. Besides, with Vatrenex so close, his unnatural fear paralyzed him from doing anything, making him go still, like a scared fawn.

The drakonid's eyes bulged as something unexpected happened, though, Brunhilda's visage sprang back to life. As soon as the dwarven half of Vatrenex's face started to move, Zhaden's heat vision detected warmth from that side. "Vatrenex, ye villain!" Brunhilda said. "Ye swore to keep my friends safe."

"Quiet, dwarf," Vatrenex growled back. "I swore to keep you and the orc safe as you were the ones to agree to the oath. I said nothing about your friend here, as he wasn't part of it. Our agreement holds firm. Now, begone!"

As quickly as the dwarven face had come to life, it went cold and still, now completely devoid of life.

The sight of Brunhilda's defiance gave Zhaden a shocked clarity. He'd been so positive that she was dead earlier, but her appearance this time clearly wasn't a ruse by Vatrenex. *That means Brunhilda truly is alive in there. I can save her! All I have to do is make the body drop the blade,* he thought as a mad plan came to his mind, his blood loss, and adrenaline temporarily overriding the fear of Vatrenex he typically would have had.

When he had been stabbed by Vatrenex's blade, Zhaden lost grip of his weapons, and he'd already run out of looted blades on his belt. However, he still had his rarely utilized garrote. Zhaden was extremely competent with the weapon, to the point that he could put it to multiple uses that few would ever expect. *I'm sorry I could not do more for you, my friends,* he thought as the monster leaned down to stare right into Zhaden with his large red eye.

Vatrenex held the dagger containing his brother in his right hand while he wielded his great sword with the other. He turned his hand and presented it openly to Zhaden like a gift. "If you wish for your fear to be over, take it. If you do not, I will ensure that your terror is magnified for all eternity," Vatrenex threatened, his mouth opening all the way down his chest and revealing his horrifying tongue.

Zhaden knew he couldn't touch the blade and had pushed back against his fear for the moment. So, he weakly lifted his head toward the dagger before suddenly snapping it the other way and biting down on Vatrenex's wrist with all his might. Black blood sprayed all over his face, but the drakonid wouldn't let go.

The monster screamed in pain, and Zhaden heard him dropping the dagger, though Vatrenex maintained his grip on the sword. Before the captain could retaliate, Zhaden tore his mouth off of the monster's injured wrist, and with his last burst of strength, pulled out his garrote and snapped it like a whip at the dropped dagger. The loop he'd made at the end of the metal wire tightened around the dagger's pommel and Zhaden snapped it at the creature's already-injured wrist, easily cutting through the remaining tendons and damaged bones remaining.

Zhaden watched Vatrenex's left hand plop to the ground, separated from the blade, and sighed as he gave a bloody grin of relief. His body relaxed as he looked up at the face of his foe, glad that his hold over Brunhilda would now fade. Brunhilda may be without a hand, but it was better than being forcibly controlled. The relief disappeared the moment Zhaden saw Vatrenex's face. The monster was smiling broadly, the mouth opening all the way down to his abdomen. Zhaden was confused as to why . . . until he noticed Vatrenex's other arm. While Zhaden had amputated one hand, the monster moved his other to maintain a grip on the weapon that was the parasite's true body.

"Thank you, Zhaden," Vatrenex said, no longer showing any signs of discomfort from his wound.

Zhaden furrowed his brow, unsure why the monster was thanking him. He then gasped as his body went stiff. He felt a sharp, wriggling pain travel up his arm. Though he was now fully rigid, he could still move his eyes. What he saw made his blood run cold. The black dagger had somehow stretched and coiled, twisting down and along the garrote wire until it penetrated the drakonid's palm. *How?* he thought.

"You do not have to make *direct* contact with a Harbinger weapon. We cannot be forced upon a new host. We just need to be used by a *willing* wielder," Vatrenex answered Zhaden's unvoiced question. "Goodbye, Zhaden."

Zhaden's vision went fuzzy. He wasn't sure what he was seeing now, but Vatrenex appeared to be gone, replaced by the monstrous rat man he'd just fought—Plio, from what Vatrenex had said. Zhaden wanted to speak, but his body was still frozen. He felt a strange warmth wrapping around him and noticed black tendrils coiling up his body. He wanted to fight, he wanted to scream, but he was too weak and his mind too foggy. After only a few more seconds, his mind faded to black.

CHAPTER TWENTY-THREE

Up and Up

About time," Kiru muttered as he saw the platform lower. The fifth floor was completely different from the bottom level but just as dangerous. However, despite that, he found the place much more annoying than lethal. Even with the utter darkness, none of the threats felt greater than the nebulor or the giant fleshing tree below. The entire place looked to Kiru like it was the inside of one giant machine. Gears laid dormant along the walls, giant pistons extended down for miles in concentric rows looking like columns, and various glass cylinders adorned with dull crystals on top were spread about in random places.

William had informed Kiru that the fifth floor was what was called an "engine room," and it had once served as a beacon to conduct power to the entire prison ship. At random times, one of the pistons would move too, causing a metallic echo. William informed Kiru that they needed to proceed to the center of the miles-long room to the "control hub" in order to get to the fourth floor.

Just as with the bottom level, though, this level had changed dramatically from the original map that William had received. There were winding paths of metallic debris, and the entire place was covered in a pasty, dark grime which made the metal room look more like a cave. The darkness was much more difficult for Kiru to see through, as well. William informed him it was because the fifth floor had an unnatural abundance of darkness mana, which made it supernaturally dark, thus making it difficult even for people with a modicum of darkvision to penetrate.

It was also incredibly difficult to open a pathway here. When they reached the central control hub, William was able to interpret the alien text and decipher what was needed. Apparently, the crystals spread haphazardly along the chamber's walls would activate when illuminated by light, each crystal giving its own unique color. If you illuminated them in a certain pattern, they would do particular things. To open an elevator up, they needed to light the colored crystals in order: blue, red, green, yellow, then pink. Kiru also had to have them light up exactly one second apart from each other.

He thought that would be impossible, given the supernatural darkness, but then discovered a solution. He found that there were crystals atop the metal structures that made up the control hub, and once a day, they would let out a loud boom and release a palpable wave of darkness mana in all directions. It served as some sort of cue for these small glowing creatures to emerge and illuminate the entire chamber. They would fly from one side of the chamber to the other and consume the darkness mana as they did so, their glows slowly dissipating the more they ate until they disappeared completely.

So, with a rough plan in mind, Kiru traversed the entire dark chamber to find the specific crystals needed to activate the controls to help him go upward. The sheer scale of the fifth floor made finding the crystals and the symbols showing the correlated colors time-consuming to say the least, with the monsters making it take even longer. The glowing beings that Imp's Label identified as "Iridescent Plankton" provided the solution to illuminating the crystals. They discovered that the creatures only came out once a "day" as the crystals atop the control hub seemed to be overflowing with the darkness mana by that point. So, it took Kiru some time to capture enough of them and put them by the crystals. He caught fifty over the course of many days and wrapped them up ten at a time in either a cloth bundle or the hides of some umbrafangs unfortunate enough to find him. He had to conceal them because he needed to light up the crystals at precise moments; if he didn't, the plankton served as beacons for the other monsters to come as the small creatures seemed to be the main source of food for the other denizens of the floor.

Abominations, man-sized void crabs, a darkened variant of umbrafangs, fleshing trees, and even a new type of monster—one that William classified as a "darkness specter"—kept him always on high alert. The specters were essentially black blobs that blended in with the environment, indistinguishable from the innumerable gunk-covered pieces of metal. They were very fast, could change their bodies' morphology, and could only be killed when their small, condensed core was broken. And on top of the troubles of dealing with occasional monster attacks, William pointed out that in some of the crystals' locations, there were flaws in the machinery they were connected to: displaced gears, rotten piping, and missing liquid in the vials under the crystals. So, on top of finding the crystals, fighting off monsters, and trying to collect a light source to illuminate the crystals in a very specific order, Kiru and William had to play mechanic and do their best to "fix" the machinery so that it would work as intended.

All in all, it took Kiru two whole weeks to solve the puzzle that was the fifth floor. He suspected it would have taken him years had it not been for William's aid. Since the imp could understand the language of the arboth and had a base understanding of the floor, it saved Kiru a lot of time that would've been wasted in trial and error. Kiru knew his psyche would've been significantly impacted having to spend more time in darkness, as even just the two weeks he'd been stuck had been draining.

When he placed the bags of glowing plankton in place, Kiru used some fallen, disused wiring to tie onto the bags and bring it back all the way to the central hub. He had to use *a lot*. With William's precise timing and guidance, Kiru was able to utilize Telekinesis to get the crystals to light up in order, as intended. As each crystal was illuminated, the cylinders of fluid underneath began to bubble, which caused the crystals to ring out in a distinct tone. The nearby gears and pistons then began to move in kind, which led to a small round platform descending from the ceiling, bringing with it a beacon of purple light from the level above.

Kiru's efforts hadn't gone unnoticed, however, as he heard a chorus of monstrous cries echoing from all over the fifth level. Kiru generally only had to fight monsters occasionally, but now, a horde had been disturbed. Monsters and beasts of all shapes and sizes that had evolved in this dark, quiet environment charged to attack the new sources of light that had intruded upon their home. Kiru noticed two different specters were quickly shifting toward him on one side while at least five abominations rushed at him from the other, the light from above serving to make him a prime target for their fury.

Kiru grimaced. He'd hoped for an easier time up, but it seemed that the monsters were going to get in his way yet again. *Well, I don't have to wait for the platform to come to me. I'll just go to it*, he thought, before using Telekinesis to rapidly elevate himself. An abomination whipped a tentacle at him, but he cut it off with his blade. The two specters also extended their amorphous bodies to grab him, but when they were touched by the purple light above, they shrieked and recoiled as if burned.

Kiru smiled as he continued to fly up, and landed on the platform. It dipped a little from his added weight but held and even stopped its descent, which made him smile. Then, there was a loud crashing sound of glass breaking from the chamber below. Kiru leaned over to the side to see a pack of umbrafangs crawling all over each other and scaling the wall where the red crystal hummed and glowed. One of them had slashed at the bubbling glass canister of liquid underneath, and the fluid was spilling out rapidly. The crystal began to dull.

"Master, I calculate abrupt failure of this platform in 1.3 seconds," William sent.

Kiru's eyes widened. In a split-second decision, he snapped his gaze up to the hole in the ceiling above and leapt with all his might, using Telekinesis to send him flying upward faster than he'd ever gone before. It was about fifty feet ahead of him, but Kiru managed to fly through with a *whoosh* and make it to the fourth floor just before the floor abruptly closed with a loud clang of metal on metal.

The light was so bright to Kiru that it was blinding, and he had to close his eyes shut as he crested the fourth floor, causing him to temporarily forget about maintaining his Telekinesis, and he abruptly fell after making it fifteen feet into the air. He crashed hard onto his back, letting out a gasp of air which forced his eyes open, exposing them once more to the blinding light. Kiru winced and raised his arms up reflexively to cover himself. He groaned, and it took a solid ten minutes for his eyes to grow accustomed to the new source of light.

When he was finally able to process what he was seeing, he realized "source" was the wrong word. There were many, many sources of light on this floor. Whereas the fifth floor was a set of pitch black, grime-covered, metal ruins, this floor was a bright metropolis. He stood on top of a hill overlooking a massive, sprawling cityscape made up of large stone, metal, and glass towers, each with a ring of purple light placed seemingly at random. There was a giant glowing purple ball of light like an artificial sun shining so high from above that Kiru couldn't tell how tall the floor was.

The city below was completely devoid of any life. The only things that Kiru noticed were metal purple statues placed randomly on street corners, each of them looking like knights and standing in the same pose with their blades held up at their sides. The knight statues had no faces, just what looked like hoods, with hollow, black spots where their faces should have been. Kiru could see that while the city was in much more pristine condition than the engine room floor, it wasn't perfect. A good portion of the buildings were now just piles of rubble, while some still remained partially intact and glowing. Aside from the completely artificial nature of the place, Kiru could also see the same roots that covered the bottom floor were here as well, spreading over a good third of the city below. They grew over roads, buildings, and even a few of the statues. That's where most of the ruined part of the city was located.

"What is this place?" Kiru asked.

"My data shows that this level is known as 'the Database.' It serves as both conduit and repository of information that the arboth had gathered over the millennia."

"You mean those buildings somehow hold information?" Kiru asked before giving out a whistle. "That's a lot of info." He then looked at the empty city once again. *How come all the other levels I've been to have changed so much but this one so little? Also, the other two levels had creatures. Why aren't there any living things here?* he thought.

His blood ran cold when an idea came to him. *What if all the creatures on this floor are hiding from something?* A giant deadly predator was not outside the realm of possibility with how dangerous the prison ship had been thus far. So, Kiru immediately crouched down behind a large stone cube nearby and carefully scanned the environment again, checking for any sign of movement, even making sure to reexamine the skyline. He did notice what looked like strange turrets or ballistae lining the walls in even increments, roughly a hundred feet from the ground and thirty feet apart, by his estimation. *Guess flying high over everything is a no-go. Maybe I can find something to test if they're operational?* he thought.

After a minute of careful searching, Kiru finally spotted some movement in the city below, after all. It was another abomination. It seemed that strange, tentacled monsters were on every level, like terrifying cockroaches. Kiru observed the abomination floating down one of the city streets at a casual pace, not chasing or running from anything. It passed by one of the knight statues, one of the ones without any roots growing over it. As soon as it was in front of it, the dark hole where its face should have been came to life. Where there was only black, there was now a swirling kaleidoscopic vortex.

The metal knight proved it was not just a statue as it walked off its pedestal and lowered its blade to point at the abomination.

The abomination gave a chorus of haunting moans before lashing some black tentacles out at the knight.

The metal knight easily cut away at them with a couple of swings of his large blade.

Then, the gelatinous mouths extended from the abomination's pores. Three of them reached out and bit down on different parts of the knight's body.

The metal began to sizzle, but the knight didn't seem fazed. Instead, it proceeded to walk forward towards the abomination, lift its foot, and stomp down on the monster. There was an audible squelch as the abomination was turned to goo. Kiru watched as part of its gelatinous form was sent flying straight up, like a popped pimple. It reached so high that it crossed the threshold of the turrets, and the psion witnessed two of the things instantly turning and locking onto the fragment's position. In the blink of an eye, the turrets fired two orbs of black mana and vaporized it into nothing.

Well, it looks like they are *operational,* the psion thought as his eyes widened at the display of the turret's abilities, almost entirely forgetting about the before he caught more movement on the ground below. Kiru saw what remained of the abomination falling off the knight, seeming to turn into liquid as it splashed on the ground. The knight's armor was unblemished. Then, as if nothing had happened, it marched back to its pedestal and resumed its pose.

Kiru's eyes widened at the impressive display. *So that's why the place is free of monsters,* he thought.

"*Hmm, useful data,*" William said.

"*What did you pick up on?*" Kiru asked via Telepathy.

"*Judging by the average size of the abominations we've encountered, I calculate that thing to be eight-to-nine feet tall. From the data I've acquired from the bottom floor, I believe I have more information on the things as well,*" William sent before a box of text appeared in Kiru's vision.

Name: Arboth Automaton
Race: Construct
Rank: Error
Mana Type: Chaos
Path: Error
Status: Dormant

Arboth Automatons are elite constructs designed for warfare. They are the second-greatest success ever created by the arboth.

Strengths
Durable metal bodies
Hivemind - Whatever one automaton observes is shared with all the dormant ones to help them adapt.
Adaptable - While on their pedestals, all automatons share data with their comrades to shape their bodies as needed to most ideally defeat their foes in combat.
Determined - Automatons will not stop until their target is eliminated or they are destroyed.

Weaknesses
Limited range - When possessing no pilot, automatons can only go half a mile from their pedestal port.
Limited function - When possessing no pilot, automatons only have one function: to eliminate all within their effective range.
Limited detection - When possessing no pilot, automatons will not be able to detect any hostiles unless they pass through their field of vision or what they're protecting is under threat. They will periodically check areas previously targeted.

William also sent data regarding the pilot. Apparently, if there were any arboth around, they could wear the constructs like a suit of armor. They had somehow crafted the things to respond to their specific physiology. *It was a good thing that they all appear to be dead then*, Kiru thought. *And if the automatons were their second-greatest success, what was the first?*

Feeling like he didn't want to know the answer, Kiru quickly asked William to show him how to get up to the next level and closer to freedom. In response, William generated a map of the fourth floor and an arrow pointing in the direction Kiru should go. Fortunately, since the level had changed so little since the map had been made, it was extremely accurate.

According to that data, there were two possible paths to ascend to the next level. The first was what looked like a gigantic covered slide in the center of the wall opposite Kiru. He didn't notice any stairs there, so he wondered if it was only meant for travel down instead of up. The other option was a round platform like the one he'd used to help him get out of the fifth level. It was located on the left side of the futuristic city. Unfortunately, it was the third of the level that was a pile of ruins and covered in the common viney overgrowth, so that wasn't an option. That left only the other two on the opposite side of the abandoned city.

Seeing as there was no other choice, Kiru stealthily moved down into the city below. As he descended and entered the Database proper, he shifted from building to building, using the shadows coming off of them to help him hide. He continued to follow William's translucent map in his vision to aid him, careful to avoid the detection of any automatons. With no detectable life whatsoever—not even any animals, insects, or sounds of nature—the psion felt a deep sense of unease.

It was only about ten minutes into his journey when he noticed another abnormality to the place. The buildings themselves weren't true buildings at all. Kiru quickly realized that while, from afar, they looked like metal and glass fortresses and domiciles, they were actually strange obelisks. That quickly dispelled any lingering doubts that this Database was truly a city.

Kiru only discovered that fact by pure chance. He had stuck to the shadows, making sure to be out of an automaton's line of sight when he noticed a crack in the wall of the structure he was leaning against. A purple light shone out of it, and when Kiru peeked in, he saw that it was full of subtly glowing glass walls that touched the ceiling of the roughly fifty-foot black metal building. Kiru was unsure why, but they looked like massive library shelves to him, despite their inability to hold any books.

Too curious to leave it alone, Kiru forced himself through the massive crack and into the structure. He looked around once inside. He found no other way in or out, so Kiru reasoned that the thing wasn't intended for someone to be inside. The chaotic way that the glass walls were arranged reinforced that notion.

"Master, do you think . . . ?" William asked.

"Yeah," Kiru said knowing what the imp meant without even saying. "These walls look like bigger versions of the things we saw by those cannisters of floating corpses back in that strange tower in the acid swamp." Without any prompting, he reached out and touched one of the glass walls.

Another box of text appeared in his vision.

Database Archive 0705
Select Information option(s) to request:
-Database Layout
-Mana Types of the Void and Their Users
-Recipes Using the Gray Matter of Quist
-Inferior Species Behavior Patterns

"Request?" Kiru asked in confusion.

"*Yes!*" William answered, sounding truly excited for the first time in weeks. "*Master, this place can give us new and useful information! Just will 'accept' in your mind, and we can absorb all of it,*" the imp pleaded.

Kiru furrowed his brow. He was wary of potentially opening himself up to any influence the fortress had, but he trusted his evolved familiar. Kiru also knew that he had to take some risks if he wanted to improve his situation. And so the psion willed himself to accept the information with one caveat—the third option. He had seen what a quist was: one of those rat men. Kiru *did not* want to learn how to cook their brains or eat anything's brains ever. Surprisingly, when he did that, his body went stiff for just a moment, but while that happened, his mind was flooded with new information. He instantly learned the behavior patterns of three different races: Quist, V'keth, and the Nebulor. He'd also learned about the six mana types that originated from the realm known as the Void: darkness, chaos, time, void, gravity, and mental mana. Lastly, while he already had a detailed map of the Database from William that conveyed the locations of the obelisks and automatons, it hadn't stated everything's purpose.

Kiru now knew that the obelisks were all numbered, and each was a repository of knowledge for one who could access it—a failsafe and a swift way to train new troops without having to invest much time into them. Kiru realized that they could also be used to indoctrinate others as well and had a sinking feeling that was exactly what the Arboth did. There had been over three thousand of the obelisks on this level during the height of the Arboth Dynasty.

Kiru smiled as all that knowledge was out there, ready for him to take it.

Before he could say anything, though, William spoke up. "*Why didn't you get the recipes, Master?*"

"Because it wouldn't be useful," the psion responded, using the imp's own logic as a counter.

The imp gave a *"Harrumph!"* via Telepathy, but before he could say more, there was a loud crashing noise of stone and metal to Kiru's right.

The psion snapped his head to see one of the automatons peering at him from the other side of the crack Kiru had entered through, a swirling vortex of colors under its hood with a central bright light, which seemed to serve as the thing's eye and also seemed to be staring directly at him. There was a long, heavy silence. Then, some of the wall around the crack began to crumble. The automaton reached into the crack and began opening it wider with impressive strength.

"William, what's happening?" Kiru asked as he drew his blades.

"You've triggered its threat response. Attack is imminent," William answered.

"But how? There's no way it could've seen me inside this," Kiru said.

"The only logical explanation is that you've placed what it's guarding under threat," the imp replied.

Kiru's heart raced as he put together what that meant. "These obelisks and the information they contain . . . the automatons are guarding any intruders from accessing them," he said as he backed away from the construct forcing its way inside.

"From the information I was able to gain from the bottom floor tower and the data we've acquired based on their behaviors, that supports that conclusion," William sent.

The automaton had now made its way fully inside the hollow obelisk. It made a series of mechanical clicks and warbling sounds before it suddenly charged at the psion. The nine-foot-tall construct swung its sword, which was nearly the size of Kiru, at the psion with terrifying speed.

Kiru rolled to the right, nearly hitting one of the glass walls. He backed up into a tight corner, hoping to limit the automaton's ability to strike at him. Kiru reasoned that since they were made to protect the obelisks and the information they stored, the constructs would have to be careful to not damage the glass. He was wrong. As soon as its blade struck the ground, it instantly used the momentum from its weapon bouncing back up to help it swing again in a wide horizontal arc, eliciting a few sparks. The large sword shattered one of the glass walls as it continued its forward motion.

Kiru was just barely able to put his blades up in a guard position and intercept the blow. While he had prevented himself from being bisected, the strength of the swing sent him flying back. Kiru flew straight through another glass wall before landing hard. Kiru wiped a layer of drool from his mouth, glaring at the automaton that was turning to face him.

"Okay, so that idea didn't work. William, use Imp's Label to find me a weakness," Kiru said.

Various parts of the metal construct began to glow in Kiru's perception. Its various joints, neck, and face all gave off a subtle orange light. Despite their size disparity, Kiru let out a sigh of relief. Seeing its weak points gave him a confidence boost. It was also a bipedal weapon user—Kiru's ideal foe. Still, this wasn't an opponent he'd like to have a drawn-out fight with.

In the span of a breath, the psion had formed a plan. When the construct took its first step toward him, Kiru concentrated mental mana in his legs, then used it to propel himself forward with a burst. The construct had just enough time to raise its great sword up when Kiru was in striking range. Using Demon's Inciting Strike, he amputated its right arm at the shoulder joint. As he was falling, Kiru spun and managed to sink the hooks of his blades on the edge of its metallic hood.

With gravity along with the momentum from both his charge and spin aiding him, Kiru was able to slam the automaton down on its back with a loud boom. The force of the impact shattered the remaining glass walls around them, removing all sources of light other than the one from inside the automaton's hood. Before it could strike at Kiru again, he quickly removed his blades, changed his grip, and began furiously punching the central orb inside the hood. With his weapons' sharpened guards.

It was like hitting thick glass. It didn't immediately break, but his blows eventually began to crack the orb. The automaton gave a mechanical groan as the light started to dim. It raised its remaining arm to swipe at Kiru, but the psion struck too fast. In just a couple of seconds, he'd already gotten six strikes in and by the seventh, the orb shattered. The light inside the automaton went black, and it went limp as it let out a last soft dying moan.

CHAPTER TWENTY-FOUR

A Friend

Kiru stood atop his foe, reveling in his newfound strength. He didn't ever want to stop. He wanted more power, and not just for the sake of his quest.

After being so useless and weak after his injury in Bristleton, he never wanted to feel that way again. His new power seemed to have awakened a primal urge within him to get more, to make sure those that abused their strength could *never* do that to him again.

William's evolution and the new information he had acquired had allowed Kiru to reach new heights. He wanted to reach even higher. "Hey, William?" he asked.

"Yes, Master?"

"Is every obelisk in this Database like this, a cache of information like the tower on the bottom floor?"

"Each obelisk has its own set of data. While there may be some overlap, each one is unique in what data they specifically have accumulated. So, while they don't possess a shard of the Chaos Core like the tower, they do contain caches of data that could be accessed by the arboth who once worked in this prison," William replied. *"I believe this information will be beneficial to our cause. The more knowledge I acquire, the better our chances of survival."*

"Good," Kiru said as he moved away from the automaton. "Then we're about to take a lot more information from this place." Kiru moved toward the crack in the wall with a new sense of determination.

William seemed oddly caught off-guard by what he'd said. *"Ah . . . y-yes! I completely concur. We need to acquire as much information as possible."*

Kiru peeked out from the crack to make sure the coast was clear. He switched to speaking via Telepathy in order to maintain as much silence as possible. *"I don't want to just randomly pick a spot to strike at. There are literally thousands of obelisks here."*

"Two-thousand-twenty-one, to be exact," William interjected.

"Could we use the map you took from the bottom floor?" Kiru asked.

"No. However, the information that we downloaded from that obelisk involving the Database Layout does indeed have what we need," William said.

Kiru's heart raced with excitement. He quickly found a tall, thin obelisk away from any automatons and their lines of sight. Kiru then nestled in the shadow that the structure provided. *"Good, then pull up the map,"* he sent. A moment later, a sprawling, miniature, three-dimensional map of the Database appeared before him as if resting on an invisible table. All of the two-thousand-plus obelisks as well as the nearly three-thousand automaton ports were present. The map instantly updated to show the damage that they'd seen on the lefthand side of the place.

"Okay, I want to find obelisks that have information regarding the cultivation of mental mana, specifically reaching to Sapphire and above," he said. Nineteen different obelisks lit up. *"Good. Now I also want to find obelisks that contain information on mental mana techniques and their usage."* Five more obelisks illuminated. Kiru gave a small smile and nodded. After William had suggested different ways he could use his Telekinesis technique, such as creating a protective dome of air around him, he thought about what else he might be able to achieve. He hoped the Database would provide even more answers.

After the twenty-four obelisks were identified, Kiru had William pull up any useful information each might contain. There was a plethora of subjects that he found tantalizing such as "Expanding Mental Mana Technique Range" and "Arboth Essentials to Achieving Sapphire." There was another called "Growing Techniques" which sounded intriguing. One of the obelisks even had information on how to combine techniques.

As soon as William got him the directions he needed, Kiru began carefully making his way to the nearest one. Apparently, that one had information about transitioning to the second tier of Sapphire. Upon reaching it, Kiru searched it for a defect or crack in order to enter. Unfortunately, its surface was pristine, without a single flaw.

Thankfully, William was scanning as well. *"Master, my examination of the obelisk has revealed a small number of minute cracks in the wall."*

Different spots on the wall were now illuminated. Kiru noticed a group of cracks conglomerated in one area. Seeing it as his best chance, he drew his psyslime weapon and had it change form into a two-handed maul. "William, how long do you estimate we have before the nearest automaton comes after us? I'll be ready since we know I can cut it down, but I want to know."

"Based on their size, speed, and that the nearest one is 0.2 miles away, I estimate we have roughly two minutes and sixteen seconds," the imp replied.

Kiru nodded. *That should be plenty of time,* he thought before pulling his maul back and swinging with all his might. The obelisk was much tougher than he'd thought. Not only was he not making as much headway as he'd like, but the sound he'd made seemed to have alerted a nearby automaton. Even now, he could hear a whirling engine and the rhythmic sounds of metal on stone.

Kiru's nostrils flared and he swung once, then two more times, causing a two-by-two-foot hole to appear, revealing the purple light of the glass information storage devices within. Not wanting to lose any more time, he jumped down and squeezed himself through the hole. He made it through ungracefully, landing almost flat on his face, but he didn't care. He was racing against the clock. Kiru quickly got back up and began racing through the obelisk, touching each of the haphazardly arranged glass walls to find the information they were looking for, which he did in about a minute.

Database Archive 0921
Select Information option(s) to request:
-Grappling Fighting Methods Using Tentacles
-Neurological Chemicals That Aid in Cultivation
-Darkness Mana and Its Weaknesses
-The Threshold Between the Two Pillars of Sapphire

Kiru smiled as he read the list of information. He willed "Accept All" in his mind. With the sudden influx of information, Kiru lost all sense of time of the outside world. He learned how to fight with tentacled appendages—interesting enough but useless to him. The next thing he learned was a little weird, but he could get at least *some* use from it. Phenethylamine was a potent chemical found in brain tissue that helped improve the cultivation of mental mana. It was also found in chocolate, which sounded *much* more appetizing.

The information about darkness mana was intriguing but also not that helpful. He was surprised to learn that darkness mana and shadow mana were two entirely different types, though. Thankfully, after that, his brain started absorbing the information he desired. Somehow, he could tell that he'd learned about a quarter of the total information about the Sapphire rank he needed but was only able to parse out a vague sentence from it: *All physical bows to the mental.*

Kiru was confused by that but before he could learn more, his connection was abruptly cut off. His eyes refocused as the information wasn't going to his brain anymore, and saw that the glass wall he had been touching was no longer there. Instead, there was now just a pile of glass under a black piece of rubble. "Huh?" he said before turning in the direction of where he had come from. Instead of a small hole, there was a giant opening larger than he was tall. Standing in its center was another automaton, both hands gripping its long sword.

Instantly putting together what happened, Kiru furrowed his brow. *Crap. I wasn't fast enough. The force of it making its way in must've launched a piece of rubble in here,* he thought before readying his blades.

"*Abyss,*" William growled in Kiru's mind once again. "*That was going to be such useful information.*"

Kiru prepared himself to rush in and take down this new foe the same way he'd beaten the other guardian. He would close the distance, take out an arm at the shoulder joint, then go for the vital points in its chest and face.

To his surprise, however, the automaton didn't try to attack him with its blade. Instead, it grabbed a piece of rubble with its right hand and threw it at Kiru with tremendous speed.

The psion jumped to the side, crashing through another wall of glass to avoid the projectile. He didn't have time to tend to any cuts or bruises, though, as the automaton continued to throw more rubble at him. Kiru jumped and rolled before deciding to deal with the assault head-on and knocked a piece of rubble out of the way with both of his blades. With a momentary clear path forward, Kiru charged. Since he didn't have time to concentrate his mental mana in his legs, he couldn't use the solitary burst of speed like he had previously. Despite that, he was quickly closing the distance.

The automaton continued to throw things at the psion, even resorting to ripping parts of the wall off. It forced him to move about in a serpentine pattern, but the psion was still making progress. It wasn't until Kiru got within ten feet that the automaton used its blade, instantly stopping its attack pattern and moving its free hand to re-grip the weapon. It swung in a horizontal arc but couldn't hit Kiru as he jumped above the blade.

Then, he swung at the thing's shoulder joint like he had before, but instead of cutting into it easily, the pair of blades met resistance and only left scratches. He realized too late that the joint was now covered completely in purple metal armor, no longer exposed.

"What?" he asked aloud as he landed behind the construct and outside of the obelisk. His ears picked up on the sound of the construct's body moving, and he managed to get his blades up just in time to block its next strike. Boot met blade as the force of the thing's mule-kick sent Kiru flying.

Kiru's back struck against the outer wall of another obelisk a block away. Fortunately, he was still durable enough to take the hit and remain conscious. Kiru spit out a small amount of blood and blinked his vision clear, seeing the automaton charging toward him, its blade tip pointed directly at his gut.

"William, what exactly happened there?" he groaned out as he pulled his body free.

"*The automaton seems to have changed its attack pattern based on the data from your previous battle with the other one,*" the imp replied monotonously.

"Oh, yeah," Kiru said in frustration, "I guess they do share information like that. That must be why my strike to its shoulder didn't work. It changed its body based on how I defeated the other one."

"*The data we have strongly supports that.*"

"Looks like we'll have to do this one differently," Kiru said and used Imp's Label once more. Just like before, multiple spots on its body were highlighted in his vision—its cavernous opening of a face and numerous joints, specifically. The notable exceptions were its shoulder joints, now encased in a layer of the same purple metal. Still, there were vulnerable spots aplenty. Kiru readied his Fu Tao as the automaton continued to charge.

As the tip of its large blade neared, the psion acted. He hopped to the side and lunged forward, using Thief's Punishment. He used the hook of one blade to redirect the automaton's weapon and expose its wrist. Then, with his other blade, he cut off the thing's wrist, forcing it to drop its blade. The automaton appeared to not even notice as it didn't recoil in the slightest. Instead, it used its partially amputated arm to slap Kiru across the chest. He skipped across the ground like a rock being thrown along the water's edge. The psion quickly rolled back up to his feet.

"I know these things are strong, but getting knocked around by them is becoming way too common of an occurrence," Kiru said as he put on his Mask of Fenrir. The beast mana in the mask flooded his face, morphing his eyes, nose, mouth, and ears. There was noise coming from behind him. The rhythmic sound of metal on stone.

"*Master, I detect another hostile is inbound. We stand to gain nothing since the information has been lost. Think logically. Retreat,*" William urged.

Kiru grimaced, both sad and frustrated. He didn't like it, but he agreed. He could take this one out, but multiple of the adaptable powerhouses at once? He was less sure of that. The psion was about to make a break for it when the automaton who'd hit him picked up its amputated hand and threw it directly at him. Determined to make it go flying this time, Kiru focused on the incoming projectile and gained control of it with Telekinesis. As it neared, he made it slow down so he could catch it with his blades. He spun as his blades contacted the metal and used the momentum to fling the thing right back at the automaton.

The hand crashed into the thing's chest, and it was knocked off its feet and sent back a few meters.

Even though he knew it wasn't dead, Kiru gave a wolfish grin under his mask. He didn't have time to revel in triumph, though, as he could hear the other automaton nearing. William gave him an escape path, and Kiru took off, eventually making it to the section of the city covered in those fleshy roots.

Finally feeling safe and sitting in a dark corner of rubble and overgrown roots, Kiru spoke. "Well, that could've gone better."

"*Indeed,*" William sent.

"It was my fault," the psion admitted. "I got cocky. I assumed that since I beat the first of those things so thoroughly that I should've been able to handle another one, even if they did learn from the experience."

"*The data does correlate with that,*" the imp replied. "*The good news is that now that you know that, it should prove useful for us in engaging with these foes in the future, Master. Maybe you will learn from this and not be so emotional. I mean, I've found that your inability to assess our situations accurately has made things much more dangerous. Your lack of logic is disturbing.*"

That was the last straw for Kiru. He still had a lot of pent-up anger and annoyance from all the hazards he'd faced recently. He'd been in this nightmarish underwater prison for around a month so far with nearly everything wanting to kill him whether it be monster, beast, machine, or even plants. While he'd had momentary reprieves, Kiru realized what he'd been missing: the feeling of friendship; of camaraderie. His friends were still prisoners to that cruel monster and his pirates, and there was nothing he could do about it. All the while, he was stuck in this place alone. While William could be undeniably annoying, the imp was still Kiru's best friend. Kiru missed his friend.

William's evolution had been extremely helpful, but Kiru couldn't help but bemoan the cost. "You know what? I don't care right now, William. We've been in here a month already, and who knows how much longer it will take us to get out? My friends could be dead right now, not as if you care. All you care about is gathering more information so you can become more and more 'useful.'"

William was uncharacteristically silent at Kiru's words.

Kiru only paused for a moment before summoning the imp out of him. As soon as the floating, three-eyed little creature appeared, the psion continued his tirade. "You certainly have been helpful since the tower in the swamp, but the old you had his uses too. When I got mad at you back in the swamp, I wanted you to grow, to be able to mature past thinking just about yourself and your pride all the time. That didn't mean that I wanted you to become a completely different person. You may not have been as 'useful' back then, but you were at least my friend." As Kiru finished, he realized his cheeks had grown damp. He hadn't cried like this since his mother had passed. In a way, he realized he was grieving for the loss of his friend just like he had been for her back then.

William stared at his master, keeping his face neutral, but the more Kiru spoke, the harder it was for the imp to maintain his stoic facade. He was utterly shocked at his master's words. Ever since he had scolded him back in the swamp, William had been angry. First, it was at his master. Then, it was at himself. Then his master again. At Kiru's reproach, the imp realized just how unhelpful he'd been, though he was loath to admit it.

William was embarrassed by his previous antics. He knew how much Kiru was counting on him and his . . . admittedly impish nature got the better of him.

So, when he had touched the Chaos Core relay, William had taken the influx of new power and information to improve both his mind and body, to change himself in personality and form until he was unrecognizable from the worthless creature he once was. He'd been proud of what he had become and proud of how helpful and useful he could now be to his master. William believed his current state to be superior to his previous form in every way. So, when his master had started making slight complaints here and there, it had confused him, but William didn't pay them much mind. After all, his master had told him he'd wanted him to be useful. Now, though, at this unprompted outburst, William started to truly see what Kiru had meant. The psion wanted William to be useful, yes, but he still wanted a friend. Kiru didn't desire a solely data-driven companion nor one who could bring a smile to his face and nothing else, but a combination of the two instead. William understood now.

He couldn't change his appearance, but he could change his mindset. He could help his master. He could help his *friend*. Once Kiru had finished speaking, tears streaming down his face and looking down at his feet, William floated over to the psion's shoulder. Then, doing something that the imp had never done before, he wrapped his arms around Kiru's neck and hugged him. Kiru's body went still in apparent surprise, but William just gripped him tighter.

"You have always been my friend," the imp said in the sincerest display of kindness and maturity he'd ever performed.

Kiru wrapped his arms around the small, strange imp in a tight embrace. More tears streamed down his face—not in grievance now but in joy. It was like his friend had been brought back from the dead. Kiru was struck with sudden relief as he no longer felt alone. It was only at William's groans of discomfort that he realized that he may have been squeezing a little too tightly.

"Oh, sorry," he said as he let go of the floating imp and wiped the tears from his face.

William floated back and started to shake the feeling back into his arms but gave the psion a warm smile, nonetheless. At least, it was as warm of a smile as the mutant imp could muster. It was good enough for Kiru.

"Thank you, William. I didn't know how bad I needed to hear that."

William nodded.

"So, how do we get out of here? I'm ready to leave this level and get closer to hopefully saving our friends," Kiru said.

"I am happy to devise a map for you, Master, but may I make a suggestion . . . as a friend?" William asked.

"Please," Kiru replied.

"We can't leave yet. There is too much here to just abandon it. We may never find a bounty so rich with regards to mental mana ever again. How can we justify *not* getting stronger before we go to try and save our friends? That Vatrenex's cultivation rank was odd, but he was at least a Sapphire. Even with our improvements, I calculate our chances of defeating him as we currently are at less than 2%," the imp explained.

Kiru's heart sunk at that. He didn't like the idea of delaying any further, but the risk of failure was too high. "What do you suggest then?" he asked.

William put his hand to his chin and began floating back and forth in front of Kiru, looking to the psion like he was a professor pondering over a subject he was meant to lecture on. "Hm, the way I see it, the automatons are competing with us in a race, so to speak. It's a race for knowledge. We are racing to take as much information we can get on mental mana while they are racing to both stop us and learn how to better defeat us. Right now, I believe they are winning."

Kiru was about to interject when the imp raised a finger to pause him. "But that's about to change. Why? Because we are going to use guerilla tactics. Then, we'll crush them under your heel," he said with a bloodthirsty grin and a clenched fist.

Kiru smiled too, happy to have his friend back.

CHAPTER TWENTY-FIVE

Memories

For the next month, Kiru and William caused havoc in the abandoned city that was the Database. William had a surprisingly good plan. What had been doing them in was that the automatons were alerted as soon as the obelisks were tasked with guarding within a half-mile radius of where their pedestals were damaged. So, it only gave Kiru a limited amount of time to get in and out. It also only left one way for him to escape, which would increase the chances of him having to fight the adaptable constructs.

So, they decided to change their approach. William still had the obelisks of interest identified on the map of the Database, which Kiru discovered was 115 square miles, emphasizing even more how much larger this level was compared to the others below. So, Kiru skulked about, making sure to stay out of the line of sight to find one of his targets. If there wasn't a damaged piece of wall that exposed the glass hubs that contained the desired information, he would make one. Instead of rushing directly into each obelisk, however, Kiru would then run away to avoid a confrontation with the automatons altogether.

He continued to do that, cutting and smashing the walls of the obelisks. Fortunately, too, since there was no obvious pattern or method to the structures that he was targeting, the automatons couldn't seem to predict where he would strike next. Since they couldn't find him, they couldn't fight him. And since they couldn't fight him, they couldn't learn how to better adapt to defeat him. After performing eight-to-ten hours' worth of property damage, William would guide Kiru to the damaged parts of the Database to recover and cultivate for the evening. With the constant purple light, however, there was no obvious indication of day and night, so, the imp's ability to keep track of time came in handy in helping maintain a regular sleep cycle.

It took Kiru a week to eventually strike every obelisk once. Since they'd all been triggered, there was now no way any automaton would be alerted that he was entering one of the structures. The second stage of the plan was admittedly more difficult. He needed to go back to every obelisk and create a second opening on an opposite wall. With two different exit points, Kiru wouldn't be boxed in by an automaton if it followed him in. Kiru remembered the last bit of information he'd learned about the automatons from William—that they would periodically check the areas that they guarded that had been previously under threat.

That resulted in many of them making formal patrols circling the obelisks he'd damaged already. To make things more difficult, whenever he managed to create a second opening in an obelisk, all of the other obelisks he would target next would be more carefully patrolled by the automatons. William told Kiru that, according to his calculations, it was no accident that this was the case. Though they couldn't see Kiru, the automatons were still learning based on his attack patterns. The psion knew, too, that a good number of the automatons' territories overlapped, so he had to be careful not to alert multiple ones at a time.

Kiru's conversations with William made the sneaking-about much more tolerable. Kiru didn't even mind the imp's occasional expletive-filled declarations of violence, because it meant he had his old friend back. At least the imp was now much more mature and helpful. It was honestly the best of both worlds.

After two more weeks like this, Kiru had finally made two openings in all his desired obelisks. As he neared the end of his task, the psion discovered that some of the automatons were no longer leaving the structures he needed to target, ignoring their typical patrol patterns and instead staying put. When he had just ten remaining, he had to come up with a new plan. He managed to trick the first four constructs by attacking another obelisk and forcing them to investigate. The last six weren't fooled, however. Even when he made another hole in the same "distraction" obelisk, they didn't leave to investigate.

Kiru was tempted to take all the information in that unnecessary obelisk since the automaton refused to leave its post, but he was too wary to try. With how smart the artificial guardians had shown themselves to be so far, even with their restrictions, Kiru didn't want to chance it. So, he opted to fight each of the constructs. Though he knew that they would get progressively harder, after a couple of weeks of running and hiding, both he and William were itching for a fight.

Since they each seemed to grow and change based on how Kiru had encountered them before, the psion and William knew that he needed to beat them using as few new methods as possible. The less data he gave the automatons, the less they would be able to improve. So, he only used the tricks that they'd seen so far: his swords and his Telekinesis. He targeted one's elbow on one, then the back of the knee of another; meanwhile, he took out the third with a sword strike to the neck, and a fourth by slashing its ankles and then stabbing it in the back under its armor cuirass.

The fifth was more difficult as there were no more overt weak points aside from its open face, but Kiru wanted to leave that as a last resort in case of emergency. He finally managed to defeat it via a Telekinesis-empowered punch when he used the sharpened hand guard of his blade to perform a Blade Fist sword form. The sixth automaton didn't even fight Kiru. In place of armor, roots were growing over its body as an uncanny form of protection.

He nearly walked into it as it turned a corner to continue its patrol around the damaged obelisk but managed to stop himself just in time. With its back turned to Kiru, the construct abruptly stopped. Sensing his advantage of surprise might have been lost, Kiru readied himself to charge the automaton when it abruptly turned away from both Kiru and the direction it had originally been going and quickly marched away deeper into the Database.

"Did something else draw its attention?" Kiru asked William via Telepathy.

"That is the only logical reason I can think of, unless those growths have corrupted its functioning," the imp sent back.

Not wanting to question his sudden good fortune, Kiru crept to the obelisk. He was tempted to just take the information and risk having to encounter the automaton but decided not to. With fewer obvious weak points and the data from his recent five fights in its system, Kiru decided not to chance this one. The abnormal behavior of that automaton just gave him a strange feeling. So, he just smashed a second hole into its wall and bolted back into the ruins.

Once he made it back to relative safety, he took time to analyze the five new pieces of data that William had tagged for him. Unfortunately, there was no information regarding how to get to Sapphire. Still, what he had taken was, without a doubt, revelatory. Instead of just acquiring pure information or vague lines of text, this time, two out of the five hubs contained memories. After he had his customary crab for dinner, Kiru sat in lotus position, closed his eyes, and accessed the first memory now stored in his brain.

His psyche was transported, and in a blink, he was in a large metal room, filled with artificial white light. Kiru looked down at his body and saw that it was entirely transparent. He then realized that he wasn't alone in the room. An arboth was standing ten feet away, its eye directly focused on him. Kiru recoiled and jumped, but as his hands reached for his blades, he found that they were not there. He also noticed that the arboth was focused on where he had been standing originally, not where he was now. *Odd,* he thought.

Kiru then walked around the motionless monster. "Is it frozen?" he asked himself.

"Yes, it is, Master," William replied as his form manifested out of thin air.

Kiru let out a gasp but quickly composed himself. *Of course William can appear here. This is an implanted memory—an artificial mental space, not real life,* he chided himself. Kiru cleared his throat before addressing his familiar. "Okay then, how do we unfreeze it?"

"Just stand where you were originally, and it will start," William said. "Then, all you need to do is watch."

Kiru was curious as to exactly *how* William knew all that, but figured it was due to the imp's ability to process information more quickly than he could. So, trusting William, Kiru moved back to stand where he was. Immediately, the arboth began to move again, its tentacles rippling in an unsettling manner. Kiru had to force himself not to grimace at the sight.

"*Listen closely,*" it spoke directly to his mind. Its voice was deep but also a little garbled, as if it had two tongues in its mouth, making its Telepathic speech some-what difficult to understand. "*Telekinesis is one of the two fundamental techniques an arboth must master. Knowing both Telekinesis and Telepathy allows one to not be relegated to being drudges or slaves, but it is not enough to keep one from being assigned to a lower caste. You must show the hivemind that you can grow—that you can take what you've been given and improve upon it,*" the arboth said before moving a few feet back to be in the very center of the room.

"*I will give you a demonstration of how one technique, Telekinesis, can have a surprising amount of uses,*" the monster said before swaying its tentacles back and forth in a pattern that reminded Kiru of how some students back at the academy would move when practicing an ancient pre-Ragnarok martial art called Tai-Chi. Then, it snapped a tentacle to the right, and a bolt of mana shot out faster than a crossbow could fire. It struck the metal wall hard enough to leave a fist-sized indentation. A split second later, it repeated that attack on the other wall.

"*The lesser arboth think that Telekinesis must require an external target to be moved. This is false. If lesser beings such as the wretched nebulor can manifest bolts of darkness mana, we who are superior can certainly replicate that,*" the arboth gloated. "*So, we move mental mana out of our bodies and fire it forward with Telekinesis. We do not need to have a complex array of techniques with only one use. Instead, we just use our superior few techniques flexibly instead.*"

The arboth continued, "*By having the ability to move anything with mental mana, we of the upper caste are above even other arboth. We can move mental mana itself. It isn't just an energy source for our techniques, but it can be molded into a weapon on its own.*"

At that, the memory paused. Kiru just stood there for a long period, trying to process what the arboth had said. It seemed both obvious and not at the same time. William, for his part, didn't say anything. He just let Kiru take his time to understand.

The psion continued to ponder. He even made William replay the memory a few more times, paying careful attention to the arboth instructor's words and his techniques, which Kiru decided to call "Telekinetic Bolts." *Move mental mana itself,* he thought. *It's like moving fire mana with more fire mana so to speak. No, that's a poor comparison. I guess . . . it depends on what a technique truly is.*

The psion's heart raced as his mind seemed to pick up on something important, the beginning thread of a revelation. *A technique is forcing your mana to perform a certain function. When Zhaden creates a duplicate of himself, he forces his dream mana to leave his body and create an illusion. When I use Telekinesis, I force mental mana out of my body to take control and guide something. Why can't I just concentrate a portion of mental mana inside one of my meridians and force it out by Telekinesis?* he thought in growing excitement.

At Kiru's request, William brought the psion out of the memory, and he stood up. He wanted to immediately try out using the Telekinetic Bolt but didn't want to alert any of the automatons. William reminded him that he had one more memory to try out. So, reluctantly, he sat back down and closed his eyes. This time, his psyche was sent into a familiar place. He was in the tower back in the swamp, only this time, it was pristine and sterile. That same arboth he'd seen from his previous memory was there, along with a three-foot tall, ghostly pale rat stuck in a large cage. Kiru quickly identified the rat as a quist from his previous experience in the tower.

The arboth radiated power, the first Pearl that Kiru had witnessed. It then spoke with Telepathy, *"The great hivemind has acquired much knowledge over the eons. One piece of information has been a boon to its most loyal servants. That is, the power to combine techniques. Normally, it would be impossible for a cultivator to perform such a feat, but the superiority of mental mana shows itself in this endeavor once again. As the great hivemind has taught us, all physical bows to the mental."*

Kiru let out an involuntary gasp at that last statement as it was the exact same piece of data that he'd taken from the hub that had the info about reaching Tier-Two Sapphire after Tier One.

"Observe as I combine a bolt of Telekinesis with a Telepathic Screech," the arboth said, then wrapped a pair of tentacles around each other once, twice, three times. The monster then pulled its appendages back as if it were charging.

Kiru had William pause the memory to look at the tips of the tentacles more closely, and indeed, he could see a distortion of mana and air a couple of inches above it. When William un-paused the memory, Kiru watched as the arboth whipped its tentacles back in the direction of the caged quist. A spiraling bolt of mana shot out from the monster in a flash, striking the poor quist straight in the head.

The quist's head whipped back, slamming hard against the metal bars of the cage. Kiru suspected that would've killed anyone below Sapphire from the sheer force alone. The quist managed to stay alive, but it didn't last. As soon as its head bounced back off the metal, it let out a bloodcurdling scream of terror and grabbed its head before it promptly exploded. The memory ended.

"Okay, that was gross," Kiru said.

"But extremely satisfying," William added, a hint of Kiru's old friend shining through. "Shall I repeat this memory once more for you, Master?"

Kiru waved him off, "No need. Oddly enough, I think I understood what that arboth did."

"With just one go, like that?" William asked in obvious astonishment.

Kiru nodded. "Yeah, the way he moved his arms like that, it was clearly intentional. It looked like the arboth had an individual technique flow down each tentacle and then had them overlap around each other three times before releasing them both at the same time." He then smiled. "Oh. William, we have to try this out!"

The warden was furious. With the millennia that Gaal'cothdreek-duun had remained dormant, much of the power and controls from the top floor had waned. Plus, with the chaos mana running rampant, his beloved home had mutated until it was barely recognizable. To make matters worse, there was now some sort of insect—a roach—that was skulking about his fortress, and he could do nothing about it. Mal'throk was only able to even observe the other floors because, fortunately, a few hundred of the fortress's hundred-thousand monitoring eyestalks remained functional.

He did try to use a Telepathic Screech to subdue him on the bottom level through one of the monitoring eyestalks, but like a roach, the intruder proved impressively durable. So, the warden was stuck monitoring him until he could find a way to trap him. The bottom floor had become some sort of subterranean swamp and network of roots. The intruder managed to navigate through there with an ease that angered Mal'throk even more. *He must have stolen our information about the fortress' schematics,* he thought.

The warden lost track of the intruder when he made it to the engine room. He had monitoring eyestalks on that level, but it had become so contaminated with darkness mana that they were useless. So, for a month, he planned and plotted on how to trap the intruder on the fourth floor. Given how persistent the trespasser had been so far, the arboth was confident he would make it to the Database level. Fortunately for Mal'throk, the fourth floor remained mostly unchanged.

The arboth tried to use what power he had available to enact safety measures and counters for the insect when he arrived. He cackled in glee when he saw the automatons. They were the perfect tool. Unfortunately, when he tried to pilot them, he received an error message. "The transmitter is down?! Gaah!" he screamed in fury. "How can this be? Am I doomed to watch this pest just take our precious information that we've harvested over the millennia without consequence. No!" He slammed a tentacle down on his control panel as he shouted, unintentionally sending a pulse of mental mana into it.

Then the warden abruptly stopped, feeling new connections. Those tendrils, those roots that had pervasively grown all over his ship, they were a strange mix of flesh, plant, and fungus. It was alive, and it was full of chaos mana. Only the mind can bend chaos. Mal'throk's tentacles wriggled in sadistic glee.

"All physical bows to the mental." he chuckled.

It would take him time, but he knew that eventually, he would catch this pest.

CHAPTER TWENTY-SIX

The Truth

After William brought him out of the second memory, Kiru moved deeper into the ruined part of the Database with the intention of finding a place to practice combining techniques. As he did so, he and William also went over the other three pieces of important information they acquired. While they weren't in-depth, re-examinable memories like the others had been, they were still nice to have. The first was how to do what the arboth had called a "Telepathic Screech." Contrary to what Kiru had thought, it wasn't *just* screaming into someone's mind, though that could be effective.

The information showed him that he needed to aim it directly into the center of a target's brain. Kiru didn't need to *see* the brain but just visualize it. One of the other two remaining pieces of data taught him about resonances. Kiru realized he'd learned a lifetime's worth of information on the subject. He instantly knew at what decibel level to send a screech in order to cause blood vessels to rupture. He now understood more fully why that quist's head exploded. Coupled with the force of a Telekinetic Bolt, the screech was able to make easy work of the rat man's brain.

The last piece of data he had intentionally acquired was about the krakens. Besides the arboth, they were the only other things Kiru knew of that could use mental mana like him. He was curious to know more, especially about how the one was able to heal his broken legs. They were originally arboth pets that were experimented on, conditioned, and bred to be beasts of burden and war. Over centuries of conditioning and careful breeding, the arboth had created a creature that could use mental mana but was entirely subject and obedient to the monstrous race.

As for *how* the kraken healed Kiru, apparently, they could use their blood to help accelerate the healing of another. Somehow, they could wield their mental mana in such a way that they could force the blood to do what they willed, using a technique called "Psychic Mending." With what Kiru had discovered about morphing mental mana techniques to perform new functions, he was genuinely curious if he could perform Psychic Mending too. Since there was no specific information on how to do that, however, the psion knew that he would have to attempt it via trial and error.

With that, Kiru brought his focus back to his environment. He had traveled to the outskirts of the ruins, as far away from the intact obelisks and their automaton guardians as he could get. They were in a secluded crater, and there were large mounds of rubble placed about—perfect targets for what he was about to attempt. The first thing he did was try to achieve a Telekinetic Bolt. Using what he'd learned from the memory, he used Telekinesis to compress a line of mana inside the meridian of his right arm. Like pressing down on a ball of snow, with a little effort, the mana condensed with a *pop!*

Kiru instantly understood that he had succeeded in forming his bolt. Then, copying the flowing movement he'd seen the arboth instructor perform, he snapped his right arm forward while taking a firm step with his right foot at the same time. Acting on instinct, his hand formed a fist, and a Telekinetic Bolt fired straight out from his knuckles. It struck a rubble pile with a *boom!*, sending up a pillar of dust.

"Well done, Master! That was really cool!" William sent. *"To be fair, I did think of this technique before we even got the arboth technique."*

"No, you didn't," Kiru said, smiling at the imp's words.

"Yes, I did," William snapped back.

"When?" Kiru asked.

"When we were in the swamp on the bottom level. I recall suggesting you create a bolt of Telekinesis to force a path out of the acid fog."

Kiru paused for a moment, thinking about it before his perfect memory helped him conjure up that moment. "You specifically said a 'wave,' not a bolt," he said.

"Pssh, a wave is just a really big bolt when you think about it," the imp retorted.

"Agree to disagree," Kiru said as he chuckled, glad to have his friend back.

He couldn't attempt to use Telepathic Screech, as he had no actual living hostile enemies to use it against. The psion did wonder if the automatons could be affected by the technique or not. *I may have to try it out when I go after the next hub,* he thought. His musings were stopped when he looked back to where his bolt had struck. There, exposed in a hole Kiru had created, was a glowing purple light. It was another hub and incredibly, it was still intact. "William, based off your map of the Database, what information does that hub have?"

"Looking at our location and how there are more pieces of rubble than original structures, I estimate that the rubble is from one of three possible obelisks. With each obelisk containing an average of ten hubs, of which each hold four-to-five pieces of

vital data, I can deduce that it has something from a list of 150 options. So . . . simply put, I don't know, Master," William answered.

Kiru nodded before looking around to see if any potential threat loomed. When he was satisfied that there were no hostiles around, he decided to go and absorb the mystery information, as he saw no benefit in just ignoring it. When he reached in and pressed a hand to the glass, a prompt appeared in his vision once more.

Database Archive 1991
Select Information option(s) to request:
-The Chaos Core
-Harbingers and Automatons: The Successes of Fusing Flesh and Metal
-Breeding Patterns for Producing Ideal Arboth Offspring
-Psychological Warfare: Effective Defensive Strategies

Kiru grew excited at reading the prompts—all except the arboth breeding patterns. That was disgusting. He'd obviously heard about the Chaos Core and how it powered the fortress he was in. It was one of the Chaos Core's relays that William had touched that had changed him so much, after all. Kiru was eager to learn more as that could potentially help him get out of the place quicker. Kiru also had memories of hearing the term "Harbingers" on more than one occasion. Knowing more both about them and the automatons he'd been dealing with should be beneficial as well. Lastly, he couldn't see how learning about defensive strategies to deal with psychological warfare wouldn't be helpful. So, he quickly approved all other than the breeding patterns.

Kiru's body went rigid and his vision white as he took in all the new information. When he was finally done, an hour had passed.

"That was . . . a lot," William sent.

"Yeah," Kiru agreed, feeling like he'd had an entire shelf's worth of thick textbooks shoved into his brain. He was all at once grateful for the information he'd just learned and terrified at the same time. Learning about psychological warfare was uncomfortable. The visual exercises he'd acquired from the hub should help him if he ever found himself facing an opponent that employed some sort of psychological strategy or manipulation, though. That was the most benign of all the information. The rest was . . . unsettling.

Kiru discovered that the Chaos Core was a shard of pure chaos mana that could regenerate itself over time that the arboth had discovered in the void. They'd used it as a fuel source for their ship as well as a subject for an innumerable amount of cruel experiments. The only reason the arboth could wield such an unruly source of energy was that, for unknown reasons, chaos mana easily succumbed to the power of mental mana.

Given what Kiru had experienced during his cultivation inside the prison fortress, it all tracked. The information confirmed once again that the black, wild mana that latched onto his mental mana when cultivating was truly chaos mana. That's why it was so erratic, and that's why he was able to easily separate and remove it. It was somehow subservient to mental mana, so that made it ideal for the arboth to conduct their horrendous acts. That tied into the next subject, the Harbingers and automatons.

Apparently, the arboth could manipulate the Chaos Core to perform an innumerable number of things, from powering the ship to creating gemstones to even mutating a person's body. The limits were one's own mana, the overall mana inside the Chaos Core at any given time, and one's imagination. Even though chaos mana gave into the pressure of mental mana, it was still chaos. So, the results weren't always as intended. Despite that, the arboth reaped many rewards from the core, and it was from their malicious minds that the automatons and Harbingers had come to be.

It pained the psion to discover the truth about the Harbingers. They were experiments performed on the "lesser races" and even the lower caste of the arboth to create living weapons. It was a subject that apparently many of the race were fascinated by. They attempted to mutate their subjects to take on the aspects of weapons so that they could summon them at will, all while still being enslaved to the arboth. They had had many failures but eventually did succeed in making "war-slaves," as they called them.

Those successes were from one of each of the four main races that inhabited the void: the rat-like quist, the whale-like nebulor, the dual-headed V'keth, and even a lower-caste arboth that wasn't proficient at mental mana use, all of which were literally fused with weapons. While it wasn't the intended result, it was extremely powerful and created literal living weapons.

One was a pair of war claws, another a dagger, a scythe, and a blade. The one problem with the weapons were that whoever wielded them would get their minds and bodies taken over by the slaves. If those wielders weren't powerful enough, they would eventually erode away due to the corrosive nature of the chaos mana. The slaves were effective killers and were deemed Harbingers of certain doom to both their wielders and their opponents, thus giving them their moniker. Kiru parsed through the information he'd absorbed, as he couldn't help but feel it was important to know all he could about the Harbingers.

He discovered they were erratic and could only be controlled when someone was directly using the Chaos Core to rein them in, forcing them to obey the will of whoever controls it. It also prevented the Harbingers from getting too far from the core, like a set of invisible leashes. The last things Kiru learned were the Harbingers' names. All were assigned numbers, one through four, but there was an extra name for a certain Harbinger. Number One was Vatrenex.

Kiru ran his hands through his now-shoulder-length black hair and fell to a knee as his mind processed all that information he'd just taken in. "William, does that information mean what I think it means?"

"Based off the data we just acquired, your known behavior patterns and thought processes, your rapid heart rate, and trauma back on The Marauding *Citadel, I can deduce what you are thinking. And the answer is . . . yes. It means what you think it means,"* William sent.

Kiru nodded, but he still couldn't come to terms with it yet. "Why don't you say exactly what you think I'm thinking, just so there's no assumptions."

William sighed inside Kiru's mind before making a noise like he was clearing his throat. "*Er, hem. The data suggests that Vatrenex, the same monstrous pirate captain you encountered, is one of four living weapons that take over whoever wields them, called 'Harbingers.' He and three other slaves were cruelly experimented on by the arboth in order to become what they are today. It is unclear as to exactly how, but your past experiences support that he and likely the other Harbingers escaped this prison ship after it left the void and crashed into the ocean during the events of Ragnarok. They appear to not be entirely free, however, because, although dormant, the Chaos Core's power is still in effect, keeping them tethered to the ship but unable to enter after the prison's defense systems kicked in,*" William explained.

Kiru just blinked. Apparently, his familiar understood *exactly* what he was thinking and put together a lot more pieces of this mystery than he had. Still, the truth of the information was a bit overwhelming for him to digest at the moment. So, he decided to put his focus elsewhere: on the information he'd learned about the automatons.

From the hub, Kiru learned that the arboth had decided that using living subjects was the problem. So they instead merged the thousands of corpses they had from their wars and experiments with piles of acquired metal. With that, they were able to create the automaton constructs. Therefore, the psion figured that what held the automatons together was flesh. Those were the exposed weak points he'd noticed in the joint spaces. What fueled the automatons were the brains of the unfortunate victims that the arboth had warped into makeshift power sources that respond to any commands given through the Chaos Core via signals being relayed through the many chambers of the prison. There was even a small snippet of information about the arboth's plans to create a gigantic version using only a nebulor's corpse, but he found nothing stating it had ever been accomplished. *Glad I've found no living arboth in this place, otherwise the automatons would likely be much more coordinated. Those things are strong enough already, and I'm not eager to try and deal with a whole army of the things,* Kiru thought as he stood back up and recomposed himself.

He shuddered, as the plethora of knowledge he'd acquired in such a short time was both boon and curse. Kiru learned about many of the tortuous things they did to their prisoners, surgically and magically experimenting on them. Some of the worst things were the psychological torture and testing they did. Kiru couldn't even mention them out loud without breaking into tears. He had certainly gained much power and was eager to acquire more, but learning about the atrocities that the arboth so willingly committed was horrifying.

If I'd had any doubts before that they were evil, they're gone now, he thought.

"Master, after seeing such things that the arboth have done, I have a request," William sent.

"Yeah? What is it?" Kiru asked.

"That we grind any remnant of these things to a pulp under your boot. I would offer to do it myself, but . . . I don't have feet anymore," William said, referring to the cloud lower-half he now possessed.

Kiru nodded. "Deal. I agree wholeheartedly. We can't allow any arboth to live, if there are any." He then clenched a fist. "We will use their own power to snuff them out."

William let out a deep, villainous chuckle at that. *"Good. Now, show me how you intend to combine your techniques."*

Kiru smiled, all too happy to. It was their original intent in going deeper into the ruins, after all. The hidden hub they'd found was just an incidental side quest. He then moved back towards the center of the crater in which he'd stood before and summoned William out from his core to give a demonstration.

The floating three-eyed imp just crossed his arms and nodded for Kiru to continue as if he were the psion's teacher, giving him permission to proceed.

Kiru let out a chuckle and managed to keep his eyes from rolling before speaking again. "So, I think it has something to do with how the arboth's tentacles made contact with each other. Obviously, I don't possess tentacles, but I believe I understood the concept. They wrapped around each other three times as the monster was channeling a separate technique down the meridian of each appendage."

The psion then began moving both of his arms in a flowing motion, each limb going in the opposite direction of the other.

William raised an eyebrow, clearly skeptical. "Is this some sort of dance move or mating ritual that elves use or something?"

"Shh," Kiru said to his familiar, as he tried to concentrate. It was taxing, but after a minute or so, he eventually began moving two different techniques down the meridians of each limb at the same time: Brainstorm and Telekinesis. Making sure they were in similar spots along each arm, Kiru the limbs in contact with each other, flowing through the motion. The mana in each meridian intensified just slightly on contact, and Kiru repeated the process, forcing the techniques to continue traveling along his arms. The second time went just like the first. The final time, he pressed both wrists together, cupping each hand. The techniques emerged from each of his palms with a *BOOM*!

Instead of merging into one technique, the two clashed, sending out a cacophonous and wild display of mental mana. Kiru was slammed forcefully onto his back, his arms spread wide apart from the collision. Each palm sizzled slightly. Kiru's ears were ringing and he groaned as he slowly stood up. He glanced down at his palms, noticing they were twitching on their own but fortunately unharmed.

Then, all of a sudden for some reason, William floated down, getting right in his face. He was shouting something at the psion, but Kiru couldn't make out the words. Though he couldn't even hear himself speak, he raised his hands up to try and calm William down saying, "I know. I know. I messed up. It looks like I'm not ready to combine techniques yet." Then, like a switch had been flipped, he was able to make out William's words.

"Master, we have to move!" his familiar exclaimed, panic in his voice.

Kiru was about to ask why, but then he heard why the imp was so worried. The sound of at least a dozen sets of loud metal footsteps were coming his way. They were undoubtedly automatons, and they were coming quickly. His heart began to pound in his chest, and he instantly recalled William into his core before jumping to his feet.

"Running is pointless, thief!" a hollow voice declared.

Kiru snapped his head to the side to see an automaton standing on a piece of nearby rubble at the crater's edge, looking directly down at him. His eyes widened. *It can talk?* he thought, shocked. Unlike almost every other version of the construct he'd witnessed, this one was completely covered in the black roots that had invaded multiple levels of the prison. It was still bipedal but not as uniform or symmetrical as the other ones. There was also one other stark difference: its face. Instead of a void of kaleidoscopic colors, it was black, with a large singular eye with a red pupil in the center.

Imp's Label.

Name: Corrupted Arboth Automaton
Race: Construct
Rank: Error
Mana Type: Chaos
Path: Error
Status: Hostile—Piloted
Pilot Status: Sapphire

An arboth automaton corrupted by chaos mana. Though it typically would've been unusable, an arboth has clearly defied the odds and managed a way to control this once-inert construct.

On top of all that information that William helped Kiru process, there were a few glowing spots: its eye, armpits, groin, and where its waist met its abdomen.

"So it seems that not all of you arboth died after all when this place crashed and fell to ruin. Who are you?" Kiru asked as he drew his blades. While he said that, he telepathically pleaded for William to help find him a way to escape, as being in the middle of a canyon surrounded by opponents was not an ideal place to be.

"What has befallen Gaal'cothdreek-duun is regrettable but manageable. As for what happened to our people, know that as long as one of us lives, the arboth can always come back, thief. I am Mal'throk, the Warden of Gaal'cothdreek-duun, and you," he said as he lowered his great sword to point at Kiru, "have gravely offended my race and the great hivemind. You not only dare to use the hallowed mental mana of which only we arboth have been ordained to wield, but then you have the audacity to steal and destroy the sacred information which we have stored in our Database."

Kiru wanted to point out that, technically, it was the automatons that had destroyed the hubs of information, but he decided to let that go. *William, how's that escape route coming?* he asked via Telepathy.

"Almost done," the imp replied.

Kiru then noticed the footsteps he heard earlier come to a halt as a dozen more corrupted automatons—all a little different but still possessing the same central eye—approached the edge of the crater and surrounded him. Kiru could feel the aura of a Sapphire coming from each of them.

"As I said, running is pointless, thief," Mal'throk said, his voice coming out of each of the corrupted automatons at the same time. "I control all these automatons. You cannot hope to escape me. Now, normally, for your crimes, I would slowly dissect you while still alive, but I do find what you've accomplished to be . . . impressive," the warden admitted, with obvious reluctance. "From what I've observed, your strange companion is the most intriguing creature. Truly one of a kind. He's helped you reach heights you have no business reaching. The fact that you were nearly able to combine techniques even without reaching Sapphire is a rarity, but your efforts are pointless. You cannot master what only an arboth can achieve."

So, I need to be at Sapphire to combine techniques? The memory I absorbed didn't say anything about that. Maybe it's just supposed to be easier at Sapphire? Kiru thought.

Mal'throk continued, "So I will make you an offer. Hand over your familiar to me so I can study him, and I will make your death quick and painless." At the warden's words, all thirteen automatons lowered their blades to point directly at the psion.

Kiru's nostrils flared in annoyance. William was infuriating at times and prone to being both childish and unreasonable—and that said nothing about his cold, numbers-driven mindset over the past months of captivity—but he was Kiru's friend. He was his *best* friend. Through thick and thin, he'd been by him. Sure, they'd had a rocky start, but he'd only just gotten him back, and he would *not* lose him again. Even if the constructs were stronger than him, the psion would fight to the death before he gave up.

Thinking about the difference in rank did give Kiru an idea, though. He just needed to get away first. "*William?*" he sent again.

"*And done,*" the imp replied. "*I have calculated the best route past these hostiles. Just follow my commands, and we should make it to the next level.*"

Kiru nodded before looking up at the first corrupted automaton. "Counteroffer, you let me absorb all the information in this Database without hindering me, and I will make your death quick and painless. I'm coming for you and any other arboth I find, Warden."

CHAPTER TWENTY-SEVEN

Growth & Ascension

*F**ollow the markers I've placed in your vision. Fly up now,"* the imp sent.

"But the turrets—"

"Fly!" William interrupted, shouting in the psion's mind.

Trusting his friend's plan, Kiru used Telekinesis to shoot himself up in the air and out of the crater he'd been in. It was a good thing too, because a split second after he left, five automatons had leapt down and struck right where he'd been with their blades.

Kiru raised his head up to see a semitranslucent wall that William had made. It was only about fifty feet in the air, and right by it, there was an arrow pointing him back toward the intact portion of the Database.

"By my calculations, the turrets won't register you as a threat by staying at this elevation. Also, the automatons shouldn't be able to follow your path as easily," William said, seeming to predict Kiru's questions.

Kiru nodded, grateful for the explanation before he made a sharp turn to follow the arrow. He spared a glance back to see if he was being pursued, then gasped. The five automatons had already jumped back out from the bottom of the crater and were sprinting toward him with impressive speed. Their eyes all completely fixed on the psion as they ran, not daring to lose sight of him. While that was scary, it wasn't nearly as intimidating as what the remaining eight were doing. They were flying.

Somehow, the corrupted automatons had morphed their bodies to sprout a set of wings on their backs, composed of a conglomeration of metal and the black growths.

"They can fly now!?" Kiru shouted in surprise.

"I did not take that into my calculations. That is . . . unexpected. We must adapt our strategy," William sent.

William's words made the psion think about the automatons themselves. Even before they'd encountered these corrupted variants, every single time he defeated one, the rest of the others would morph their bodies to better adapt to fight him. Because of that, Kiru hadn't used every trick he had. Seeing as Mal'throk had somehow used the chaos mana he was controlling the automatons with for new abilities, it was time for the psion to do the same.

He fired a Brainstorm and struck the flying automaton closest to him. Fortunately, as they all had metal bodies and were close to each other, the electrical technique hopped over and connected to all eight of the constructs at once. The airborne automatons' momentum all suddenly stopped as they were hit by the Brainstorm, and they crashed to the ground, sending up plumes of dust and debris. Kiru knew that if they possessed a fraction of the warden's Sapphire-rank power, they definitely wouldn't be out of the fight. Despite that, Kiru had a stroke of good luck because the dust that shot up obscured the psion from the other five corrupted constructs that were on the ground chasing him. Kiru could still hear their footsteps, though, so he knew he wouldn't have this reprieve for long, so he quickly descended to hide by a nearby obelisk.

"*William, we're going to need to change our plan,*" Kiru sent via Telepathy.

"*Agreed. I will create a new route to the nearest exit now for you to travel on foot,*" the imp replied.

Kiru shook his head. "*No, we have to go back to the obelisk that has information about reaching Sapphire first.*"

"*But why?*"

"*If I'm going to stand any actual chance of killing the warden, I'm going to need to reach Sapphire too. I may have to fight those corrupted constructs, but ideally, I would minimize that chance and focus on removing the warden instead. Even when I do reach Sapphire, fighting one opponent is better than thirteen. Second thing is because of what he said about being surprised that I would attempt to combine techniques before Sapphire. So that means it should be much easier to do it if I am a Sapphire. Also,*" Kiru sent before pausing and clenching his fist, "*they threatened you. I won't let any of them do that to my friends and get away with it. I'm going to kick his ass.*"

Kiru couldn't see William as the imp was now back inside his core, but he could somehow sense how he was feeling. He knew he was giving a bloodthirsty grin. "*I like that attitude, Master. Let's make this fool regret ever crossing Kiru the Conqueror and William, the Breaker of Wills!*"

Kiru and William stuck to the shadows as they formulated a new strategy. The thirteen corrupted automatons were still searching for him. Kiru could hear their footsteps echoing throughout the Database and could see a few of them flying around too.

Kiru would occasionally hear the warden's voice bellowing out a taunt, insult, or threat in order to make Kiru reveal himself, but he didn't take the bait. He made sure to not cycle his mana and to suppress his power as much as possible to help prevent Mal'throk from detecting him. Kiru also noticed that there were still plenty of the regular automatons about, standing motionless at their pedestals and ready to act should a threat arise. *So, the warden isn't able to take full control of all the automatons. Good,* Kiru thought as he would stand no chance of fighting hundreds of the things on his own.

Kiru also discovered that while Mal'throk couldn't take direct control of the uncorrupted automatons, they were still linked with the ones he did have control over. They tested that out by having Kiru telekinetically strike it with a piece of rubble from a direction opposite to where he was hiding. As expected, the automaton stepped off its pedestal and went to investigate. Only a few seconds later, a couple of the winged corrupted automatons landed nearby and scanned the area as well. The psion was already moving stealthily, but seeing that connection reinforced his theory.

As Kiru stalked across the Database, he and William came up with a plan. They had three primary goals: Acquire the information to reach Sapphire, escape to the next floor above, and prevent the automatons from being able to follow. As they thought about it, there was only really one viable option. They had to split up. They presumed that as soon as information was being absorbed from a hub, that would alert the warden, and knew for sure that it would alert any other automaton that may have that obelisk in its radius to their location. So, they needed one of them to distract the automatons while the other took the information.

Naturally, Kiru assumed he would be the distraction, but William surprised him. *"Given my scan of the corrupted automatons and how the warden was able to pilot them using unusual means, I believe I can do the same,"* the imp said.

"Really?" Kiru asked.

"Yes. I should be able to meld with its power source and use a modified version of your Subjugation technique. I will only be able to control one, though," William sent.

"Well, that would be awesome, but I still don't like it. I don't want to put you at risk," Kiru protested.

"Your logic is sound, Master, but you forget, I am William, the Breaker of Wills. I know every technique you do. I also have two things that you don't."

Kiru gave a small smile. *"Oh yeah? What's that?"*

"First, I still have the Hot Hand technique you created back when you had your fire mana core intact. Second, I have the element of surprise. The warden will be expecting you to appear. What he won't be expecting is for an automaton to be piloted by someone else. I will distract him, then attack his automatons when they are alerted of your stealing the hub's data," William explained.

The psion nodded. *"That is a clever plan, but how do we prevent his automatons from following us?"*

The imp cackled in Kiru's mind. *"Oh, don't worry about that, Master. I've got another trick up my sleeve."*

Kiru tried to press the imp as to what that was, but William clearly intended to keep it to himself for now. The psion didn't like it, but he trusted William. The imp still delighted in violence, but since his growth and their heart-to-heart, William had notably matured. So, Kiru let him have his fun for now.

The warden continued searching for the psion for hours. After Kiru found a reasonably safe place to hide and sleep, he'd hoped the arboth would lessen the intensity of the hunt. When he woke up and nearly got spotted by a flying automaton, he realized that hope had been unrealistic. So, with an abundance of caution, Kiru spent the next few days moving carefully about the Database to get William into position. They crept through small alleys and sometimes hopped back into obelisks he'd previously made an opening into to find places to hide or rest. They had moved about stealthily for so long because they planned to have William take over an automaton not too far from the exit but towards its right. That would help William draw the attention of the corrupted automatons in the direction opposite of Kiru since the obelisk the psion needed to take information from was on the very left side of the city near the ruined rubble. He could hear at least four automatons moving about near the exit, so they took extra care to move with caution and not get detected.

Eventually, they found a prime candidate for William. The automaton was standing on its pedestal, its back toward them. After checking once again for any signs of Mal'throk's forces and not detecting any, Kiru sent William floating toward the construct. The imp moved across quietly and seemed to meld into the automaton's back. Kiru watched as the construct's form slackened for just a moment before stiffening and standing up straight once more. Then, it gave Kiru a subtle thumbs-up. As they had been moving toward their destination, the two had discussed that, since the warden had some sort of connection with the uncorrupted automatons even though he couldn't directly control them, William shouldn't do any sort of movement that was too obvious with his line of sight. If he did look back and see Kiru, that would alert their foe. They didn't even attempt any Telepathy, to be safe.

Satisfied that the first step of their plan was complete, Kiru began quietly moving toward his desired obelisk. He quickly ran into an issue, though. Without William in his core, he no longer had access to the imp's map. He didn't have his perfect recall, either, so while he had a general idea about which way to go, he wasn't 100% confident. Those things led to him having to move about with even more caution, which decreased his pace significantly. He put on the Mask of Fenrir to enhance his senses in order to help prevent any run-ins with any hostile automatons or stray monsters that made it up to this floor.

Whereas it took him a few days with William's aid, it took Kiru nearly two weeks to reach his destination on his own. He often thought about his familiar, hoping he was okay and that William trusted him enough to wait. Sometimes, he would get lost in thought and almost alerted an automaton to his presence a couple of times because of it.

He was extremely grateful that he required far less sustenance than he had at his previous cultivation ranks; he now only needed a little bit of food and drink every other day or so. When he wore the mask, however, it amplified his hunger and thirst, forcing him to eat and drink at least twice a day or start drooling and growling like a starving wolf. Fortunately, the plethora of crabs in his mother's storage ring along with canteens full of water provided all he needed. Still, eating crab wasn't a silent endeavor. Kiru found a way to rectify that issue, though, by only eating in the obelisks he'd previously busted holes into as temporary bases. It helped to muffle the sounds of shells breaking and his munching.

They were also places where he could rest and cultivate. He didn't need much sleep due to his half-elven lineage, but he still needed at least four hours in a twenty-four-hour cycle. Fortunately, in terms of cultivating in the fortress, it still didn't take him long with how much mental mana was present. There was just the typical strain of forcing the chaos mana out of his body because it still latched onto the mental mana when he drew it in.

Kiru imagined that William was stewing due to having to stay quiet for so long, but knew that he couldn't do anything about it. That is, until now. Kiru and William had devised a signal for when the psion was ready. Using Telekinesis, he sent a burst of wind down one street. It billowed loudly, echoing throughout the entire Database. He knew some of the automatons would come and investigate, which would thin their forces even more. Kiru had his mask on, and his wolfish ears twitched as they heard flapping wings and metal footsteps. That was as good of a confirmation as he was going to get, and he quickly moved into the obelisk.

He began checking the different hubs for the information about how to reach Sapphire and was successful on his fourth try. Surprisingly, that one just had one subject: *Breaking the Barrier Between Ruby & Sapphire*. He assumed it may be due to how complex or detailed the information was but didn't have time to question it. He accepted the prompt to download the information. The psion's vision went white as his brain was flooded with knowledge. At the same time, his mind was transported into a new memory.

He was standing on the center of a gray platform that was only a couple of feet wide, round, and completely smooth. Surrounding him on all sides was utter darkness, yet he had some source of heatless illumination on him that allowed him to distinguish his own body and the platform he stood on. Then, a giant red eye appeared. It was massive, at least a hundred feet tall, looming over Kiru, staring directly at him. He shuddered slightly as he got the feeling that despite this being a memory, the eye was somehow looking at him through it.

Did . . . did it just check my cultivation rank just then? Kiru thought. *Is this really a memory?* Unsure as to what to do and not wanting to draw the ire of whatever possessed such an eye, he continued to look up at the thing. They just stared at each other, Kiru not daring to blink. They continued to do that for what felt like an hour when a voice finally spoke to him.

"You have come to break through the barrier separating Ruby from Sapphire on your path of cultivation. As you are one who uses my mana, I will instruct you on how to ascend," the eye said, its voice deep and scratchy, making Kiru think it was constantly inhaling as it spoke. It radiated such power that it made him tremble.

Its mana? What is this thing? he thought before the being spoke again.

"As you know, to reach the upper tier of Ruby, one must saturate their entire physical body with their mana so that every part of their form is homogenous. This provides a new state of power and balance. While this is a feat that many will never accomplish, it is wholly inadequate for those who wish to conquer, those who wish to impose their will and bend the world to it, those who have taken from my yoke," it said.

Kiru once again did not miss the implication that his mental mana power had been taken from this thing. He had an idea of what it was but didn't want to anger it as this still seemed like more than a memory. The eye then moved back, putting some distance between itself and Kiru. The dark around Kiru began to brighten as pinpoints of light began appearing all over, revealing what looked like stars in the night sky. The psion could see the body of the being with the giant eye, but it was still surrounded in darkness, so all he could see was its silhouette.

It was round but lumpy and irregular. No appendages were visible, either. Based on how big it was even from a distance, Kiru presumed it to be at least a thousand feet tall and just as wide. It spoke again. "To achieve Sapphire, you must create a shroud around your entire form. You must extend your mana out from every direction to become a second layer of flesh around your body. You must visualize this mana as an extension of yourself, because it *is*. It is *your* mana. It is *you*. Now, take this knowledge, take this boon, and grow your power. Use it to show your worth to me and prove you can make all others fall to my power, which is superior above all others."

At those final words, the darkness covering the being lifted, revealing a mountain-sized brain pulsing and writhing in an unsettling manner. Its singular eye never stopped focusing on Kiru, and when its pupil constricted, knowledge and power flooded him and brought his focus back into the outside world.

The psion took in a sharp inhale as his consciousness was brought back to his environment. His hand was still on the hub in front of him, and right when he moved it away, a thick, braided net landed on top of him. He fell flat on his face and groaned, but it wasn't because of the weight. The net seemed to have a secondary effect. Wherever it made contact with on Kiru's body, little suckers emerged and bit down into him and his armor. He could tell he was starting to go numb wherever they touched his skin, and even his mind became a little foggy. He did his best to use Telekinesis to push the net off, but then a pair of loud foot stomps slammed down on both sides of him, forcing the net back onto his body.

He turned his head up to see one of Mal'throk's corrupted automatons standing over him, its eye staring down at him. "I knew you would be tempted to take more, thief. Though I must say I am surprised it took you this long to come here. I had been observing the pattern with which you were looting obelisks, and I thought you would've visited this one weeks ago. That was even before we had our formal introductions," the warden said.

"Despite my current limited abilities, I was able to reactivate these sensory-dulling contact nets," the arboth continued.

Kiru's eyes widened at the description. *So, they only dull me if they are making contact. I just need to break contact, then,* he thought, his mind racing to try and find a way to escape.

"I do appreciate that you so willingly relinquished your companion to me, though. Once I rip him free from the automaton he currently controls, I will enjoy dissecting him," Mal'throk said before the automaton he controlled raised its large blade up above Kiru. "For the crimes against the great hivemind and all the arboth, I sentence you to death."

Kiru snarled. *This asshole!* He could hear the sadistic glee in the warden's voice and he would not let this happen. Before the automaton could strike, all the pieces clicked together in the psion's mind—how to get free of the net and how to make Mal'throk pay. It was just a split second of clarity, but that was all that he needed. All the information he'd acquired from the hub now made complete sense, and he acted on it.

The way to make the major jump to reach Sapphire was to form a stable shroud of one's own mana around their entire body, making it a "second skin." With the understanding he just acquired, he forced mana out of every pore. It rushed out of him and even went over his armor. Before it could leave him completely, however, he telekinetically manipulated the mana to not go more than a centimeter away from him. It was incredibly easy once he realized what needed to be done, especially now that his innate connection to his mana had gotten even stronger with how he'd morphed himself to get to Tier-Two Ruby.

Even though the mana had left his body, it was just as the giant brain had said: it was *his* mana. It was an extension of Kiru, so, it *was* Kiru. Truly realizing and adopting that concept was the final piece he needed to gain full comprehension, and with that comprehension came ascension.

CHAPTER TWENTY-EIGHT

Sapphire

As the corrupted automaton's blade descended, the gem in Kiru's forehead glowed for just a moment before changing from Ruby to Sapphire. Immediately, Kiru's shroud had formed and stabilized, providing a new barrier against the suppressive sensory suckers. His mind sharpened, and he felt a rush of newfound power.

"Fuck off!" Kiru shouted as he pushed the net off of him and knocked the construct back with Telekinesis.

The automaton flew and crashed through multiple of the glowing purple glass hubs before landing hard on its back and nearly cutting off its left leg. It forced its upper body up, the black tendrils of chaos mana spreading down to reconnect and heal its leg.

"Resistance is futile. Even if you are stronger, you cannot hope to take on all my automatons. You are outmatched," the warden scoffed.

Kiru stood there, glaring at the piloted automaton. He felt . . . *more*. More powerful, more intelligent, and more connected. The psion felt his shroud surrounding him like a second skin, but unlike his skin, it could bend and change to his will.

"You said something before, Warden. That me being able to nearly combine techniques even without reaching Sapphire was a rarity. I figure that means it should be pretty easy for me to be able to do it now," Kiru said before starting to move his arms in a mirroring pattern, bringing his mana down the meridian of each limb.

The pupil in the automaton's eye constricted in obvious fear before quickly switching to anger. "Your efforts are pointless. Only arboth can truly combine mental mana techniques," Mal'throk asserted as his construct stood up.

Kiru continued to move, channeling his dual techniques to become one. A spark of electricity shot out from his left arm as he maneuvered Brainstorm down his left arm and it made contact with his Telekinesis technique on his right.

The automaton shook its head. "Cease this charade. You've used your electrical technique on the automatons already. So, this construct has adapted to be impervious to it," Mal'throk said.

Kiru didn't respond at first as he strained to keep his focus on what he was doing, although never taking his eyes off his foe. Finally, he couldn't help quipping, "Oh, you've never seen *this* before."

The construct shook its head once again in disappointment before readying its blade. "If you refuse to realize the truth of your inferiority on your own, then I will make you, vermin." At those words, the corrupted automaton charged at Kiru, its sword already beginning its swing to bisect him. "Die!" he shouted as he quickly stood up and hefted his blade.

While the warden was speaking, Kiru had been continuing his plan. He moved his arms in a specific pattern as he sent mana through them for specific techniques. Once, twice, and on the third time, the mana left each of his palms as he cupped them, and combined. Floating just centimeters away from his hands was a Telekinetic Bolt surrounded in the crackling electricity of a Brainstorm. Feeling the power fuse together and coalesce into a sum greater than its parts made Kiru grin. Then, with a defiant scream, he thrust his hands forward.

There was a loud *whoosh!* as the combined technique fired out from his palms with blinding speed. The electrified bolt sent out waves of force in all directions, shattering the glass hubs nearby, breaking apart the floor, and destabilizing the obelisk as a whole. The bolt went so fast that the warden had no time to guard as it punched a hole straight through the construct's chest and continued on through the obelisk itself. The automaton was knocked off its feet once again as electricity racked its body, and Kiru watched as the metal surrounding the fist-sized opening through its chest instantly caved in due to the force.

The automaton slammed its back into the wall where Kiru had knocked a hole through already, wedging its body into it, and causing the wall of the obelisk to break even further. Kiru dropped his arms and took in a deep breath as the twitching automaton sizzled and smoked, the tendrils of chaos mana literally being burnt away. Mal'throk's voice was unintelligible from the damaged construct, and before Kiru could make out any words, the automaton died.

The hairs on the back of Kiru's neck stood up as he marveled at his new power. He wanted to cheer, wanted to jump up and celebrate, but he couldn't—he had to find William, and the obelisk was crumbling. The damage that Kiru had done to the wall was too great. Cracks climbed up it, and the entire structure began to shake. Kiru could tell that it would collapse right on top of him if he didn't manage to get out in time. So, that's exactly what he did.

In what seemed like a flash, he made it out of the obelisk. Kiru spared just a moment to note how his body now felt with his aura around him. He not only felt stronger, but he somehow also felt both faster and denser at the same time.

He didn't pay too much attention that at the moment, though, as he needed to find William.

He drew both his blades before using Telekinesis to fly upward to get a better vantage point to find the imp, which he managed to after only a few seconds. He could see an automaton off in the distance, running about the winding streets of the Database while dealing with and being harassed by three corrupted variants. The imp was doing a good job of parrying strikes and even burning one with Hot Hand, but he was clearly on the defensive, being forced to move and counter as the hostiles flew around like pestering birds. Kiru assumed the only reason William's automaton hadn't been fully destroyed was that Mal'throk had expressed clear interest in him.

Though Kiru was happy to see his friend alive, his heart still raced as he didn't know how much longer the imp could hold out. So, like a bird of prey, the psion descended in the direction of the automatons. The warden had clearly been waiting for that, as four different corrupted automatons emerged from around the Database with their blades all aiming for him. The freshly minted Sapphire didn't slow down for them, though. *I just need to throw something at them that they haven't seen me do before*, Kiru thought.

The psion didn't have time to fight his incoming foes, however, so he resorted to a defensive measure. On his mental command, the psyslime changed shape to completely surround him in a protective dome as he continued his descent. He knew instinctively that, with the aid of his shroud, he was connected to the slime as if it was a part of him. So, he knew he could "feel" through the slime if he desired.

When the dome formed and he suddenly lost his field of vision, he extended his senses and his eyes immediately widened experiencing new sensations, realizing what it meant for his capabilities. So, as he flew, despite his inability to see, Kiru knew he was now able to both protect himself from the constructs and strike back.

Kiru retaliated right after four different swords struck his psyslime dome all at once. The dome caved in slightly but held due to its inherent malleable nature before four long spikes jutted out right under the sword strikes. Using the connection from his shroud, Kiru could tell that all four constructs were caught unaware. Three of them had been launched away while a fourth was stabbed directly in the head. Its body went limp and fell off the slime as Kiru dismissed the protective dome.

Two down, eleven to go, Kiru thought as the slime opened up and morphed back into its usual sword form. As soon as he was able to see his surroundings once more, he found that he was about to crash face-first into an obelisk—in a burst of adrenaline, he moved himself to the right and narrowly avoided it. His momentum continued, however, and he nearly ran right into the fleeing automaton that William was controlling.

Pulling back hard via Telekinesis, the psion halted himself just in the nick of time. The imp's construct was significantly damaged, with slash marks and holes all over its form. Its right arm appeared to be pulled out of the socket at the elbow, hanging by loose black flesh instead of metal.

"William, you're okay!" Kiru said with joy.

The automaton hobbled and stopped to look up at the psion. Despite not having an eye, it was clear that William was observing him.

"You succeeded, Master?" William asked through the construct, sounding out of breath.

"I have," Kiru answered, pointing to the now-blue gemstone in his forehead.

"Good, because I . . . may need help," William admitted.

To punctuate his point, three corrupted automatons came running around a corner, just a block away from the pair. They each now had only thin, slitted visors instead of open hoods for faces. *They've already adapted based on the one I killed midair. I've got to deal with them quick*, Kiru thought.

"Give us the imp, vermin," Mal'throk growled hatefully through the three constructs at once before they all charged at the psion.

Kiru was confident he could deal with them, but it would take time. Time was a luxury they didn't have. They needed to leave the fourth floor, and fast, as the automatons' learning capabilities would surely give them victory in a war of attrition. Kiru charged a Brainstorm and fired it from his forehead directly at the lead construct. Like before, it spread and connected to the other two.

All three of their bodies stopped and stiffened from the sudden assault, their heads tilted down slightly. Slowly, they all raised their gazes in defiance. "Have you already forgotten? They adapt," the warden said through the lead construct.

"Oh, yeah?" Kiru asked sarcastically. "But they haven't dealt with that attack being powered by a Sapphire," he said before empowering the technique even more with his aura. The technique thickened as it grew more powerful, and it was too much for the lead automaton to take. The construct shook violently before it suddenly went limp and a thick black cloud shot out from the armor in all directions, obscuring the street.

With that distraction in place, Kiru used Telekinesis on William's construct, and the pair began zooming through the zigzagging streets of the Database towards the exit. Having William back to guide them, and focusing on speed instead of stealth, allowed the two to rush across the Database in mere minutes. As they flew, Kiru noticed William averting his gaze so as not to look in the direction they were going. He wondered why and was struck with the memory that the warden could see through all of the automatons—including William's.

"Crap. William what are we going to do when we get to the exit?" the psion asked.

"I have accounted for that, Master," William replied. *"Do you remember what you did to protect yourself from the umbrafangs that attacked you from multiple angles at once?"*

"Yeah, I made a protective dome around myself. I actually just did it again when I was flying over to you," the psion replied.

"Good, then as soon as we get to the edge of the Database, I want you to do the same thing—maybe even make a cool bulwark or something. Then, I'll jump on top of the protective orb you make, and you will zoom forward like an arrow at the tunnel entrance. Once there, fly up as fast as you can. I'll follow," William sent.

"How are you going to prevent them from following us?" Kiru asked.

"During my time piloting the automaton, I've grown familiar with its controls and systems. More importantly, I've figured out how to overload them," the imp said.

Kiru raised an eyebrow. *"You mean . . . ?"*

"Yep. Boom," William explained.

Kiru stopped abruptly at that. *"I'm not going to let you blow yourself up. Neither of us is dying today. You are not leaving me, William,"* the psion said.

"Who said anything about me blowing myself up?" the imp asked. *"No, Master, I will make the construct detonate ten seconds after I leave it. There's no way I'm leaving you alone, Master. This violence and your new level of strength is too much fun,"* William explained.

"Oh." Kiru said. *"Well, good, then. Let's go,"* he sent, and they took off once more.

After another half minute, they got to the edge of the tunnel that looked like the bottom of a slide. Unfortunately, of the ten remaining corrupted automatons, six were guarding the exit, and they all immediately turned their heads to Kiru and William's position.

"Are you ready, William?" Kiru asked as he ordered the psyslime to create a protective sphere around him.

Kiru heard the imp shout *"Let's go!"* as William's automaton jumped on top of the orb right before the dome sealed over Kiru completely.

"Come get it, bitches!" William shouted triumphantly as his damaged construct grabbed on tight to the floating orb that was moving quickly towards the tunnel. He had to drop the large blade as it wasn't very useful with only one good hand, but that did mean less weight for his master to carry.

"You're mine, imp," Mal'throk declared through the half dozen automatons as they all charged at the duo.

William smirked inside his automaton. He tapped the orb his master was in and sent a telepathic message that their enemies were incoming. To William's utter joy, his master had the psyslime orb form a large wedged bulwark on its front. It was just as the imp had hoped.

The corrupted variants were undoubtedly tougher opponents than the other constructs, but that didn't mean they were superior to William.

Sure, perhaps he couldn't handle them all in a fair fight . . . but the imp had no intention of fighting fair. The construct he piloted wasn't a superior model, but his skills were clearly better than Mal'throk's. Because unlike the corrupted automatons, William's could use his techniques. As the corrupted automatons got within ten feet of them, William aimed his own automaton's free arm directly behind him.

Taking a page from his master's book, William fired a surge of Telekinesis from the construct's palm into the air behind them. Like an engine being activated, the orb and William shot forward with a *whoosh!* and an impressive burst of speed. The sudden boost in acceleration clearly caught the warden off-guard as the bulwark slammed into half of the charging automatons and knocked them off to the side. The other half were too slow and missed the swings of their blades entirely as William and Kiru zoomed right past them.

They gained only a little bit of distance, though, before they turned back and followed them. William calculated that they had only four seconds before they'd be within striking distance again. As they neared the tunnel, the imp realized that if they didn't stop, they would crash hard into it. So, he sent another telepathic message to his master to get himself ready and counted down for the psion.

"Three, two, one, now!" the imp sent, and Kiru instantly changed the slime's shape again, back into its usual hook-blade form.

"Go, Master. I'll be behind," William ordered telepathically.

Kiru gave William a look of concern but reluctantly nodded and began flying up the smooth tunnel.

William had his automaton stand right in front of it like a guardian and pointed the construct's one good hand at the charging foes. He could see the remaining four off in the distance flying in their direction too.

"Feel the wrath of a superior mental mana user, Warden," William declared before firing a Brainstorm at the nearby six constructs.

The corrupted automatons all stopped for just a moment before they began moving again. It was a forceful march instead of a sprint, but they were coming nonetheless. Despite the loud noise of the Brainstorm, the warden's voice boomed over the technique. "Superior? Bah! Don't make me laugh, imp. You are just a familiar, a mere assistant, and one who serves a lesser being. Your master may have surprised me earlier with his new power, but you cannot compare," Mal'throk spat out.

William's construct's void of a face glowed brighter as it continued to fire the technique but to no avail. That was intentional as the continuous use of his technique was hiding the true reason the glowing intensified—rerouting his automaton's power. Satisfied, William had the construct back up, doing his best to place more distance between him and Mal'throk's forces until he was at the inside and at the bottom of the slide/tunnel. Knowing he only had six seconds left, William enacted the final step of his plan.

He forced himself out of the back of the construct and began flying upwards. He heard the automaton's hand drop as he was no longer using Brainstorm through it. Before he lost sight of it, he spared a final glance down at the thing. It was standing and leaning over, a group of shadows nearing it. Then, *BOOM.*

Air and sound shot through the tunnel, followed by a wave of heat. The tunnel William was going up began to shake and . . . brighten? William noticed that illumination was coming from behind him. He looked over his shoulder to see a growing orange glow, accompanied by another wave of heat. "Oh, shit!" William said before putting even more effort into his ascent. His ears picked up the noise of the incoming wave of fire and destruction. "Come on, come on, come on! Faster, faster, faster!" he cried as he pushed his half-cloud body to move even faster. As greatly improved as William had become, he was realizing that that his own speed was unfortunately lacking.

Luckily, he wasn't on his own. In a split second, he felt a force tug hard on his body, pulling him upward rapidly. William soared around a winding curve before noticing his master once more. The imp gave a small smile before remembering what was behind them. "Master, we've gotta move."

Kiru's smile turned instantly serious. "Then we better get to the third level, and fast," the psion said before recalling his familiar back into his core. Feeling whole once more, Kiru took off, flying at breakneck speed to the next floor of the prison.

CHAPTER TWENTY-NINE

The Blind Acolyte

Again!" Vatrenex ordered before he swung his curved great sword at the orc once more.

Mutt proceeded to deflect the weapon and perform the pattern of strikes he'd been taught, stabbing and slashing at specific intervals.

Vatrenex grunted in frustration as he deflected a strike and kicked the orc square in his chest, sending Mutt rolling back ten feet along the deck of *The Marauding Citadel*. "You still swing too wide on your right side. Again," he said before leaping at the orc once more with his blade at the ready.

Mutt snarled and let out a growl but quickly moved into position again. He made a set of clicking noises to detect Vatrenex's specific location and parried the captain's strike using the claw weapons he was forced to wear. They were essentially two cutlasses that one of the corsair smiths had forged into metal wristguards as makeshift grips, each claw weapon possessing two blades. The orc was used to fighting like a beast with his clawed technique, but Vatrenex's goal was to make him into a more-refined warrior. Plus, the orc's previous experience fighting with claws was perfect for the captain's plans.

Mutt forced the captain's blade away and proceeded to go through the pattern that had been quite literally beaten into the orc's memory. This time, he made sure to keep his swings with his right claw weapon more controlled and direct.

Vatrenex continued to block and parry, his vertical mouth giving a grin of approval after he deflected the orc's final strike, making Mutt stagger.

"Good," Vatrenex said as he nodded. The captain wasn't tired from the exertions, unlike the orc, but despite that, he saw that Mutt had that same focused visage from when they had first started training. The orc had been reluctant to train with a weapon at first but became more willing once he'd learned it was a set of claw weapons.

The Harbinger could admit that, despite the blind orc having no formal training in fighting with a weapon, his natural aptitude for combat was one of the most impressive he'd ever witnessed in his centuries alive. In the two weeks of intense training and tutelage the captain had provided, Mutt had quickly grasped many of the nuances of fighting with his claw weapons. Normally, Vatrenex would've forced the orc to use a blade like the cutlasses the corsairs all wielded, but he needed to make sure Mutt was able to host one of the Harbingers.

"You have done well, my acolyte," Vatrenex said to Mutt.

Mutt managed to convey a slight eyeroll at the words. "'Acolyte' is a strong word, Captain." He said the last word with some forced strain.

Vatrenex's mouth twitched all the way down his chest as he growled. "Still holding onto the belief that your friend will best me?"

Mutt nodded. "I told you I would follow you, but I still have no doubt that you will be beaten by the boss," he said.

Vatrenex's blade pulsed rapidly like an angry heart, and this time his hideous maw opened up, looking like he was going to eat the orc he was standing over. The fool's trust in the psion was one of the captain's main sources of frustration. Despite Vatrenex's intimidating visage and his clearly overwhelming power, the damn orc still held onto the unwavering belief in this friend of his. The Harbinger flared his aura at the orc, making him fall to his knees.

"There is no way that broken man you call a friend could truly rival my power," he declared.

Mutt had both his hands pressed against the deck, doing his best to keep from falling on his stomach.

"He already be followin' yer orders, ye villain. Now, stop," the left half of his face suddenly came to life and blurted.

"Gaah!" Vatrenex shouted before kicking Mutt away and directing his will to suppress the stubborn dwarf host once more. He pressed his free hand to her face and growled, "Quiet!" While she had been the most stable host he'd had in centuries, the dwarf was both a blessing and a curse as she proved to be more resistant than any he'd ever encountered before.

Once the dwarven half of his face closed her eye and went limp, Vatrenex turned back to the orc. The blind cultivator was standing up and wiping a thick line of drool from his mouth.

"Your ability to grow as a combatant is noteworthy, Mutt," Vatrenex said as he walked towards the orc. "How goes your growth in cultivation? Are you nearing a breakthrough?" He'd been trying to teach the orc for weeks about Sapphire, but it seemed that if it didn't involve fighting, Mutt struggled to grasp it.

Mutt looked like he wasn't ready to switch topics and seemed to physically restrain himself from attacking Vatrenex once more. After a couple of deep breaths, however, he regained his self-control and answered, "It is not as good, *Captain*," with obvious venom in the last word.

Vatrenex growled in frustration. "How can you be so talented yet so inept at the same time, orc? Once you understand that your techniques are subservient to you, and extend your mana's influence around your entire body, you should achieve Sapphire."

"I've told you before, *Captain*, that makes no sense to me. Even after cultivating with the Sapphire beast mana cores around me, all I feel is just more mana in my body. I don't know how to keep the mana around me in a shroud," Mutt retorted. "Also, when are you going to tell me where Stabby is? I know you're keeping him alive even though he wouldn't agree. So, where is he, *Captain?*"

Vatrenex's teeth chittered like an angry insect. He didn't know about beast mana and had refrained from forcibly making the orc ascend through other means as he did with many of his followers. The Harbinger refused to make the three slaves official corsairs. Doing so would require essentially removing all mana from their bodies except his own specific chaos mana, making them "his." In terms of chaos mana, he could help the orc, but that came with a cost. Any cultivator full of Vatrenex's mana could not be a host for one of his brothers. That's why he almost killed the alchemist for his liberal use of Vatrenex's body when experimenting on the gold drakonid. Weevil nearly rendered the rogue useless as a host for Plio.

Fortunately, the takeover was successful, and Plio was now fully in service to Vatrenex, whether the rat liked it or not. Thinking about his fearful brother, Vatrenex resolved himself *not* to let the orc know what his fate would be. *No need to have his mind clouded with doubt. It's better to keep the simpleton ignorant,* he thought and went to change the subject.

Before Vatrenex could say anything, however, the orc began sniffing loudly, his head snapping from side to side. "Do you smell that?" Mutt asked.

Vatrenex closed his eye and took in a big inhale. "That is . . . decay," the captain said, knowing what that meant.

As if sent there to confirm his suspicions, Saltbeard came running up. "Cap'n, we picked up their trail," the dwarf said and gestured for Vatrenex to follow him to the side of the deck.

Both Vatrenex and Mutt did what the first mate asked, and there, they had proof. A smattering of rotten and decayed flesh dotted the water, forming a trail. Numerous aquatic scavengers and predators were eating the remains with reckless abandon, threatening to remove all evidence.

"What is it?" Mutt asked.

"A path to our quarry, orc. A path to the Mourners," Vatrenex answered before turning to Saltbeard. "First Mate?"

"Aye, sir?" the dwarf said as he saluted.

"Get all hands to stations. The *Citadel* has a path, and we will not lose it," Vatrenex said, making his threatening implication clear.

Saltbeard gulped as he nodded and quickly rushed over to his mount. Vatrenex watched as his first mate began bellowing orders to all who could hear him. "All hands to stations! Cap'n's orders! Prepare to make full sail. Hoist the mainsail and unfurl the topsails. All the slaves to their oars. We be needing the *Citadel* at top speed, lads!"

Vatrenex nodded in approval. His first mate was a sadistic drunkard, but he was an effective leader amongst the corsairs. It also helped that he was—like all official corsairs—bound to Vatrenex and utterly terrified of him. Satisfied that things were in order, the captain moved his eye down to the orc beside him. "Come with me," he said before heading down a path below deck.

Vatrenex led Mutt through the winding pathways among the myriad living quarters, shops, storage rooms, and kitchens until, eventually, they made it to the intended destination: the slave pens. There was a fetid stench to the place, but Vatrenex didn't care. He was there to find someone who could help. Eventually, they located who they were looking for. There, scrubbing the floor of the hallway, was Weevil Jutherford. The alchemist still had his goggles on, but he was now covered in rags and wearing manacles around his neck, wrists, and ankles.

When the gnome looked up to see Vatrenex coming his way, he gasped in terror and quickly backed away, pressing his back against a cage door. He put his arms up defensively but didn't dare look the captain in the eye.

"Weevil," Vatrenex said with a sinister expression, his large mouth opening wide and his long tongue sticking out as if he was going to eat the gnome. "Weevil!" he shouted.

"Y-yes, Captain?" the gnome asked nervously. His head was now bald, with numerous healing cuts across his scalp. There was also a nasty vertical wound traveling from the left side of his neck to the top of his head. The worst wound was his nose—or lack thereof. It had been completely cut off, exposing the two holes to his sinuses and making the gnome look more like some sort of undead creature than an alchemist.

"My orc acolyte here needs help breaking through from Ruby to Sapphire. As I cannot cultivate beast mana, and he lacks the proper understanding to ascend even with two Sapphire beast mana cores at his disposal . . ."

Mutt snorted loudly at that remark, but when the Harbinger snapped his head angrily toward him, the orc put his head down in deference and submission.

"As I said," Vatrenex continued, turning back to face Weevil, "due to that, I have resorted to using a different way to help him. The other alchemists have not matched your capabilities so far, so I am forced to rely upon you once more."

Though the gnome's eyes couldn't be seen behind the black-lensed goggles, he was clearly surprised at Vatrenex's words.

"You have served me faithfully after all your years aboard my vessel, so I am willing to *overlook* your previous mistake. Prove yourself loyal and capable of following my orders and I will reinstate you as the head alchemist of *The Marauding Citadel*. Fail me or dare to defy my orders by using my body as any part of an alchemical ingredient for his ascension, and you will receive a fate worse than torture and slavery. Understood?" Vatrenex asked as he leaned down to get to eye level with the terrified gnome.

Weevil's lips quivered, but at the same time, Vatrenex saw a faint hint of hope. "A-Aye sir," the gnome managed to stutter.

The captain gave a menacing grin. "Good." He then shattered the chains and manacles with his impressive strength. "You have one week."

The gnome slowly stood up and rubbed his bruised wrists. "Th-thank you sir. I-I won't let you down."

Vatrenex didn't say anything, just staring at him intensely.

The gnome clearly understood the implication and scurried over to Mutt and tugged on one of his ripped pant legs. "Come with me, orc."

Though he couldn't see, Mutt raised his face to Vatrenex questioningly.

"Do as he says," Vatrenex ordered.

And with that, his blind acolyte left with the gnome.

"Do you think he will be a suitable candidate, Brother?" Plio asked, the Harbinger stealthily emerging from behind a column, scaring a group of slaves from a nearby cage at his sudden appearance. An elderly man let out a cry of terror at seeing the rodent-like Harbinger, which caused Plio to visibly shudder. The Harbinger rogue then turned and glared at the slave before throwing a blade, killing the old man in a blink. "Silence," he hissed.

All the other slaves inside the cage went deathly quiet, doing their best to not provoke the easily spooked Plio once more.

"My apologies, Brother. I am unused to such noise," Plio said, lowering his head in deference to Vatrenex.

Vatrenex just shrugged before addressing his brother's previous question. "I have never found a better candidate to host Zis'Piel. Normally, I believe the orc would need at least a year to be ideal, but with a trail to Zis'Piel and his Mourners now found, it is only a matter of time before a battle occurs. So I must accelerate the orc's growth. Since I cannot force him to ascend with my own power, relying on the alchemist once more will have to do."

"I must say, his abilities speak for themselves," Plio said, gesturing to his own body. "This host you provided me with has been quite excellent."

Before he could say more, the ship seemed to have been hit by a large wave of water, making the wood creak loudly. Plio flinched, as if it had caused him physical pain, then he readied two more blades and scanned the surroundings. After a few seconds of silence, the Harbinger relaxed.

Vatrenex nodded. "Yes. That host's fear nearly rivals yours, Brother. I don't know if the orc's attitude will match Zis'Piel's, but his durability and fighting style should be comparable. Now, keep an eye on them, and report to me what occurs in the gnome's laboratory," he ordered.

Plio nodded before taking off in a flash.

Vatrenex gave a bloodthirsty grin. *Once we are all four united under my banner once more, we will finally break through into that prison, destroy the Chaos Core, and be free of these accursed waters once and for all.* His grin grew even more menacing at the thought. *At last, I will bring war to this realm and let chaos reign.*

CHAPTER THIRTY

Painful Promotion

*D**ata Log for the Trials to Alchemically Elevate Subject A from Tier-2 Ruby to Tier-1 Sapphire.*

Day 1
Experimenter: Weevil Jutherford
Subject A: Male orc, early 20s
Mana Type: Beast Mana

After thoroughly questioning Subject A and analyzing a tissue sample donated by him, I hypothesize that, in order to possess such strength in such a bestial form of mana at his young age, he had to trade his cognitive capabilities. I do not have any other logical explanation for how he constantly refers to me under the nickname of "Goggles," instead of my given name or job description. It would also account for his poor ability to explain the nuances of his mana type aside from his techniques. Thus, it is truly surprising that such a simpleton has been able to reach the upper echelon of Ruby, a rank known for its connection to insight versus raw strength.

Subject A's techniques are powerful and are from five different beasts rather than all from one sacred beast. They are as follows:

-The vocal cords of an unknown creature called a "Bounder."
-The thick fur of a Dweller Bear.
-The teeth and jaws of a Gnoll.
-The taloned feet of a Horned Harpy Eagle.
-The claws of an Alpha Dire Wolf.

After learning about the techniques and their diversity of sources, I questioned Subject A about any special or inherent gifts, training, or rare treasures he may have come across. That is when I learned that he is from noble descent. It further reinforces my hypothesis about his abnormal behaviors and speech patterns. To become a master of beast mana, one would have to become more like a beast in body and mind. So, I believe much of his ability is purely instinctual.

On theorizing about how to make his body reach Sapphire, I unfortunately know only some minor basics as I am just a Gold. It is known as the "Shroud Rank," and one needs to essentially make a stable barrier of mana around one's body. I believe that if I can force Subject A to move it on instinct, success will be achieved.

Day 2
No success.

Day 3
After forty-two attempts, I have still not been able to induce Subject A to create a shroud.

Day 4
After looking back at my data log entries, I was reminded that the captain had said the subject had two Sapphire cores with him. Upon request, Subject A presented two 6.2 x 6.2 inch perfectly symmetrical Sapphire beast cores, each of which had a dark-blue center with a lighter shade around the edges. Subject A said they had once belonged to gnolls before they were used in a cursed staff. After shaving off a small part of one core as well as filing off a small layer of one of Subject A's teeth when using his gnoll beast mana technique and comparing them under a microscope, I was able to confirm the claim that the cores contained gnoll beast mana. The next step is determining how to stimulate this specific type of beast mana.

Day 5
It took twenty-three different attempts, but at long last, I was able to discover what causes the gnoll beast mana to have a chemical reaction and start to move: Pain. After my twenty-second attempt (applying heat to the core) failed, I accidentally burned myself by touching the surface of the core to confirm it had truly elevated in temperature. When I felt pain and recoiled, Subject A reported to being able to "feel" the mana moving inside the core. After a few more corroborative tests, it was established that pain itself was the catalyst needed to stimulate the gnoll beast mana. When Subject A experienced a minor level of pain from the core, he reported being able to feel a connection with the mana inside it. The data supports that inducing pain throughout the entire body at once should be what is required for Subject A to manipulate the mana fully.

Day 6

After discovering that pain was the proper catalyst, I spent the rest of Day 5 concocting a set of potions that would fit the parameters of what was needed according to my theory. The parameters include:

-Inducing a state of pain across the entirety of external tissue on Subject A's body.

-Improving the flow of Subject A's meridians to allow for faster distribution of mana.

-Improving Subject A's overall connection with beast mana to allow for better control.

After some alchemical experimentation and trial runs using Subject A's blood, I have crafted a poison that should accomplish all three of the goals. Details found below.

Potion of the Sapphire Beast Ascendant

Description: A specialized elixir designed for cultivators who harness beast mana. This potion is a viscous, dark green liquid with flecks of gold, symbolizing its potent and primal nature.

Ingredients:

1. **Essence of Golden Lion Shark:** Extracted from the heart of a sacred beast known as a golden lion shark, this essence should enhance the primal connection to beast mana.
2. **Spikeberry Resin:** A rare and potent fruit only found in the Torn Empire that has both a sweet and sour flavor. Its juices solidify with whatever it makes contact with, creating a spiky crystalline layer that induces a sharp, stinging pain.
3. **Nightshrivel Berries:** These berries are poisonous when consumed on their own, more damaging to a liver than any barrel of alcohol. When dehydrated, however, the poisonous effect is heavily suppressed, causing them to instead increase the effect of any substance they're mixed with by forcing the liver to more rapidly absorb it.
4. **Phoenix Feather Ash:** Ground into a fine powder, this ingredient aids in the rapid absorption of the potion into the meridians, where it then spreads to the muscle and external tissues.
5. **Moonlit Dew:** Collected under a full moon, this dew enhances the potion's overall potency and effectiveness.
6. **Shadowroot Pulp:** Aids in providing extreme control of one's own mana. Shadowroot trees have an impressively thick layer of bark that has been theorized to be their own version of a shroud.

7. **Two Sapphire Gnoll Beast Mana Cores:** Provides a source of beast mana directly compatible with the subject and is the most critical ingredient in the entire mixture. The cores were melted into a liquid after making contact with the Phoenix Feather Ash, allowing for a smooth integration of the other ingredients as well.

After all my testing and theories, I have deduced that this is the ideal elixir to achieve the captain's orders. Results to come.

Mutt was both bored and annoyed. At first, he'd felt bad for the gnome with the goggles who Vatrenex had ordered him to follow. The smell of wounds not healing correctly as well as the distinct scent of dried blood was all the orc needed to tell the gnome had been badly hurt. When Mutt used his other senses to "see" the alchemist, he realized how significantly the small guy had been mutilated. Mutt also figured out that the gnome was deaf but had clearly compensated well for his lack of hearing by how quickly he responded to Mutt.

After spending the last week being interrogated by the gnome, poked and prodded by various sampling tools, and having his intelligence insulted on a daily basis, however, that pity had quickly faded. He could now tell why the gnome served under Vatrenex. The alchemist was just as cruel and conceited as his captain. *At least Vatrenex would fight me,* Mutt thought. *And even if she doesn't speak, I still get to sense Brunhilda's face since he finally stopped wearing his mask.*

The orc tapped his foot impatiently as he sat on a chair, waiting to do whatever the gnome bid. It was boring, and what was worse, he couldn't even train or fight in the meantime while he waited for the gnome to finish with whatever he was concocting. Mutt didn't know what he was making, but from the smell, it was somehow both foul and citrusy at the same time.

After what seemed like forever, the gnome left his table full of beakers and ingredients and walked towards Mutt, holding a jar in hand. Despite their size differences, Goggles still managed to give the sense that he was looking down on Mutt. Mutt didn't care, doing his best to suppress another groan of frustration. "I take it that the thing in your hand is your best attempt to help me ascend?" Mutt asked.

"Attempt? How dare you question my abilities, simpleton?" Goggles retorted, his ruined face snarling in anger. "I am the best alchemist on *The Marauding Citadel.* It is thanks to my efforts that the Hushed cult has been eliminated. I do not attempt. I *succeed.* And this," he said, holding up the jar containing whatever it was that smelled both like brimstone and fruit at the same time, "will bring you to Sapphire, simpleton. Of that, I have no doubt."

Yeah, right, buddy, Mutt thought, not believing a word of the alchemist's boasting. Even now, he could hear a quiver of doubt in the gnome's voice as well as feel his body shifting nervously through the vibrations of the floor. Mutt could also smell his fear. The gnome was scared shitless and was doing everything he could to appear calm. Mutt couldn't blame him given what Vatrenex had already done to the alchemist.

Mutt sighed. "Okay then, Goggles. If you are so sure, then give it to me. Let's get me to Sapphire."

Goggles hesitated, evidently not expecting to be called out, but eventually groaned and relented, handing Mutt the jar.

Mutt went to drink it, but the gnome raised a hand. "Wait."

He stopped and quirked an eyebrow at the gnome.

"Go behind my glass wall first. Just in case it works *too* well," Goggles added with a nervous chuckle, not convincing Mutt.

Still, the orc complied, still believing without a doubt that no matter what happened to him and his friends, Kiru would come save them. He knew Stabby no longer believed the boss would help and had even tried to run away, but what the boss had accomplished so far was more impressive than anything Mutt could've done on his own. So, the orc continued to follow the gnome's instructions and went through a doorway past a glass wall. When the alchemist closed the door behind him, he was struck by the abrupt silence.

A soundproof door? he thought. It didn't bother Mutt, though, as he could still sense the gnome via the vibrations on the wood floor underneath his bare feet. He could sense the weird little guy looking at him expectantly, a journal and a quill in his hands. Not seeing any reason to delay, Mutt raised the vial to the alchemist. "To roaring like beasts and drinking at feasts," he toasted before downing the contents of the vial in two gulps. It was thick, almost like honey.

The elixir was remarkably sour, however, and Mutt scrunched his face up tight after consuming it. It even tickled his nostrils somewhat; he sneezed a couple of times. After rubbing his nose with the back of his hand, Mutt started to notice a warmth gathering in his abdomen. It felt familiar to the orc. Despite his blindness, he closed his one remaining eye and turned his senses inward.

Almost immediately he figured out what it was: beast mana, and a kind that he had intimate knowledge of—namely, gnoll. It sloshed around in his stomach, fully integrated, and mixed with the other ingredients of the potion. That movement only lasted a few moments before the liquid went abruptly still. A split second later, Mutt's stomach wriggled, and the potion spread throughout his body in a flash. It was as if he were composed of extremely dry sand and the potion was the first source of moisture it had ever experienced because his bones, muscles, tendons, organs, and even skin were soon covered in lines of the substance.

Mutt let out a gasp in surprise as he scanned his body, but his curiosity was soon overwhelmed by pain. At first, it was just a slight sting, reminiscent of getting lemon juice on a paper cut, but it quickly increased.

"What? What's going on?" Mutt asked, as the stinging quickly elevated to a stabbing before worsening even further into burning.

Mutt let out a desperate roar of anguish, his entire body shaking before he fell to the ground on his side, paralyzed. Truly, *everything* hurt. Every inch of his body, even parts that had no nerves to feel, like his nails. It was as if every cell of his body had been submerged in lava. Mutt didn't know how long he lay there, crying and moaning in pain. Minutes? Days? All sensation of the outside world was gone. There was only his body and the pain.

Eventually, though, a sense of clarity came over him. A primal part of him—the beast inside his mind—forced his body to adapt, to survive, and to overcome. His mind coerced him into adjusting to this new normal. When that happened, Mutt's breathing finally slowed. He still couldn't sense anything outside of himself, but his body truly did begin to calm.

The blind orc couldn't tell where he was or even if he was sitting up straight. No sound came to him. His current position, location, or the presence of anyone else was completely lost to him. Still, one sense started to come back to him—his sense of mana. It was . . . *everywhere* inside him, every part of his body completely saturated with mana, down to the last cell. Curious, Mutt tried to move a little bit of it in his right leg. That was when he experienced a new heightened sense of agony in that limb just for a moment. He winced and stopped right as that happened.

He tried again and experienced the same sensation. It was a few seconds after the second time that an epiphany struck him. *The mana and the pain were one*, he thought. Sensing he needed to act, Mutt embraced the pain and began to cycle his mana in his meridians once more. When that happened, he noticed a distinct pain just an inch outside of his body. *How? How am I feeling pain that's not from my body?* he pondered before he realized that the mana around him was still connected to him. He could still feel it. It wasn't just any mana, either; it was that same beast mana laced with whatever painful gnoll variant Mutt had imbibed.

As soon as he gained that insight, Mutt convulsed, and he let out a large gasp as if he'd been dead and brought back to life. The pain immediately dulled to a much-more-subdued level, and a myriad of sensations struck him all at once. His sense of balance returned as well as his sense of smell and hearing. Most distinct was his sense of touch. He could tell he was still on his side, lying on a few wooden planks in the glass room the gnome had led him into.

A foul odor struck his nose, and he pushed himself up to a sitting position. As he put his hand on the floor, he felt a thick, viscous liquid there, quickly realizing that it was a puddle of impurities that had been forced out of his body—the source of the smell. One thing still hadn't changed, however. There was pain. It may have dulled, but it was still there in his body, and slightly around him, too. His eyebrows raised in comprehension. "The mana and the pain are one," he repeated. "That's my shroud . . . I'm a Sapphire."

CHAPTER THIRTY-ONE

The Mourners I

Vatrenex stood atop his tower and watched Mutt sparring with his first mate, cultivating the spiral of chaos mana inside it through a narrow hole at its pointed tip. The captain spread out his senses in order to determine that the orc had indeed reached Tier One in Sapphire, but there seemed to be something slightly off about the blind acolyte. While he could sense the shroud surrounding him, Mutt also seemed to be in pain—he continuously gritted his teeth and occasionally winced, even when not being struck by one of Saltbeard's blows.

Vatrenex then summoned the alchemist's notes from a nearby storage device. When he had ordered the gnome to explain how he'd accomplished his task, Weevil had just said that everything was in his notes before he collapsed from exhaustion. Apparently, he hadn't eaten or slept for a week straight. Vatrenex was angry at the gnome and wanted to kill him on the spot for his audacity, but given his apparent success, the captain was willing to let it slide . . . for now.

Vatrenex quickly read over the formula that Weevil had used and what he'd found after the orc had imbibed his potion. It was of course, another poison, but he couldn't deny the gnome's genius. After he was done reading, the captain raised his head to look out to the sea. He followed the line of blood and bits of rotten flesh until he finally saw his target in the distance.

"Plio," he said.

Just a moment later, his brother had appeared beside him, kneeling. "What do you command, Vatrenex?" the quist Harbinger asked.

"Wake the alchemist and inform him that he can resume his previous post. He has won his promotion, but he will have to wait to rest. War is coming, and our corsairs will need as much poison for our weapons as we can get. Tell him he has four hours to bring out what he has stored," Vatrenex said.

Plio just gave a subtle grunt of approval before disappearing to do as bid.

Realizing that the time had come, Vatrenex grew a pair of wings and flew down to the main deck right by the sparring cultivators. A large crowd had gathered around to watch the two Sapphires and to place bets. At Vatrenex's sudden landing, all went quiet.

"Corsairs!" Vatrenex shouted.

"Aye, sir?" the pirates replied in unison, all saluting their leader.

"Our target is dead ahead. With the wind in our favor, we should make contact by midday."

"Aye!" all the corsairs shouted in response.

"The Mourners are a tricky sort. They are likely to try and ambush us if we're not careful. Slaves will bring barrels of poison on deck. Coat as many of your weapons in it as possible. All hands, battle stations!" Vatrenex ordered.

"Aye, sir!" the corsairs said in unison once more as they saluted and took off in different directions.

"First Mate?"

"Aye, Cap'n?" Saltbeard replied as he walked up and sheathed his cutlass.

"I leave you in charge for now. I must speak with the acolyte," the one-eyed monster said.

"Aye, sir," Saltbeard said and nodded before walking over to a mast and ringing a bell. Seconds later, more and more bells began to sound out all around the top and throughout the bowels of the *Citadel*. "Close all shops! Cease all merriment! Get yer damn shite together, and get to yer battle stations! Cap'n's orders!" the dwarf shouted and continued giving orders and directions, but Vatrenex walked away and gestured for Mutt to follow.

He led Mutt to the front of the ship. "Can you sense our target ahead?" Vatrenex asked.

Mutt stuck his head out past the deck and clicked his tongue a couple of times. "Not completely. The smell of death is too strong, and the winds obscure too many of the noises and vibrations for me to get a full grip as to what it is. Best guess, it's another ship, but not as tall as yours," the orc answered.

Vatrenex shook his head. "No, it is a giant turtle. The creature has a giant cavity in its shell that is constantly festering. It is both around and inside that wound where the Mourners make their home."

"They make their home in a rotten wound? Gross," Mutt said in disgust. "Why would they do that?"

"Their leader, Zis'Piel, prefers to always be in a state of despair and agony. So do the Mourners. With the turtle constantly healing but also perpetually suffering from its festering wound, it is the perfect source of despair for the despicable fools," Vatrenex answered.

"Okay, well, good to know, I guess," Mutt said. "But why show me all this?"

Vatrenex gave a hideous grin. "Because you and my brother are going to sneak onto the turtle while we fight the Mourners and remove their sacred weapon right from the very center of that crater. Now go, gather your things and prepare yourself for battle. You have thirty minutes until you are to be outside my tower, understood?"

Mutt nodded, "Understood . . . sir," he grunted before quickly running off to a door leading below deck.

Once the orc was gone, Vatrenex flew back to the top of his tower to both cultivate and analyze their foes. His tower was the tallest structure on *The Marauding Citadel*, giving him an unparalleled view of the sea in all directions. There, about a mile out, was the Mourners' home. The turtle was gigantic—even larger than *The Marauding Citadel*. Its limbs and head were pitch-black while its shell sported a sprawling city and a thick jungle surrounding it. The buildings were simple wooden structures, which blended in well with the foliage and canopy. The one stark exception was the festering pink-and-black wound on the left side of its shell, the source of the smell that now permeated the air. Every minute or so, a small stream of pus, blood, and fetid flesh would erupt like a squeezed abscess into the ocean, providing the trail that the corsairs had used.

Now, so close to a full-on battle, Vatrenex thought more about the Harbinger that led them: Zis'Piel. He was a V'keth before the arboth had used the Chaos Core to transmute his body. The V'keth race had two faceless heads that made them look like distorted mannequins rather than a race of sentient beings. They were remarkably durable, possessing metallic skins. *The Chaos Core clearly enhanced Zis'Piel's resistances when it fused him with his weapon,* Vatrenex thought.

The captain then felt a familiar presence appear on top of the tower by him. He turned to see Plio on one knee. "It has been done, Brother," the former quist said. "A contingent of slaves are bringing up barrels of the alchemist's poison now."

"Good," Vatrenex said as he nodded and looked back out at the turtle.

"Brother, if I may be so bold to ask, it is clear you intend the orc to be Zis'Piel's next host. Who do you intend to host Waayoo?"

Vatrenex snarled loudly at the mention of the other Harbinger. He truly disdained his boasting and prideful brother. "Oh, I have something special planned for him," he said through gritted teeth. He planned not only to force Waayoo to serve under him but to humiliate his brother for all time. "I plan to crush his mind and have him serve under someone he will detest for the rest of time."

When Plio didn't say anything after half a minute, Vatrenex turned back to face him and changed the subject. "Brother, back before we had broken out of Gaal'cothdreek-duun, do you remember what Zis'Piel would do when we had to fight?"

"Uh, yes, he would always take the brunt of our foes' attacks, delaying and disabling them while we would deal the finishing blows," Plio answered.

"Indeed. He always had the strongest base aura out of all of us, but it was primarily defensive," Vatrenex added. He knew it was due to this, plus the mobility of the giant turtle home, that the Mourners had such a large number of cultists. Vatrenex hated Waayoo and his Joyful the most, but the Mourners were certainly the bigger pests, as they had attacked *The Marauding Citadel* on numerous occasions.

It is time I dealt with them once and for all, Vatrenex thought as he stood and turned to his brother. "Plio, I have new orders for you," he said.

Plio nodded and grunted, ready to receive them.

Vatrenex pointed his curved great sword down on the street below, toward the orc walking to his tower. "You and the orc will sneak over onto the turtle and into the heart of the Mourners' territory. There you will find Zis'Piel's weapons and remove them," Vatrenex said before slamming a palm onto Plio's shoulder. The captain of the Swordstrike Corsairs then flared his Chaosbind technique— the same technique that all Harbingers had. It was what they used to control their hosts, and what Vatrenex used to instill control and dominance over his brothers.

Plio let out a high-pitched squeak, and his whole body tensed. He felt his mana being fed by Vatrenex's, the other Harbinger's power seeming to fill his body to the brim. Vatrenex's mana overwhelmed Plio's, seeming to consume it and swallow it whole, like a serpent. The meridians of Plio's host body swelled and felt as if they were going to rupture, irreparably damaged. But, before that could happen, the mana instead just painlessly leaked out of his meridians and into his body. The chaos mana continued to ooze out of the gaps in between the host's scales. After a few more seconds, the mana outside his body stabilized in a strange wiggling pattern. Plio gasped as he seemed to realize that, with a donation of mana and a flex of his will, Vatrenex had forced him to ascend into Sapphire.

Vatrenex leaned in and growled. "I already made you mine back at the Whispering Isle, Plio. You can never outrun me or hide from me again. My mana is now laced into yours. So, when you grab Zis'Piel's weapons after they are removed from his host, I will use my Chaosbind through you, and he will be bound to me, too." The cruel Harbinger let go and Plio let out a sigh of relief, shuddering in fear. It was just how Vatrenex liked it.

"I am . . . honored by this gift you've given me, Brother," Plio muttered. "But I am confused. Why are you not coming with the orc and me? Surely, with your power, we can easily access Zis'Piel's weapons."

Vatrenex gave his brother a wicked grin. "In all your centuries of hiding in your swamp, you never encountered Zis'Piel, did you?"

Plio shook his head. "No, just some occasional scouts that sailed too close to my old home."

Vatrenex nodded. "Tell me, why do you think this creature who's had a rotten, open wound in its shell hasn't died for centuries?"

Plio narrowed his eye at the question. He looked at the turtle in the distance, then to Vatrenex, and back to the turtle again before his face took on a look of shock. "You mean to say, that turtle—"

"—*Is* Zis'Piel," Vatrenex finished.

"But how has his host not degraded over time like all others? Is it special, like the one you gave me?" Plio asked.

"No, I believe it is due to its size and his followers. The Mourners are notorious killers and scavengers. From prisoners I've captured and interrogated before, I've learned that they throw most biomatter they collect into the festering wound as sacrifices. I believe it somehow delays the desiccation of Zis'Piel's host. That doesn't matter, though. What matters is that I will fight the turtle directly, keeping our brother distracted while you and the orc sneak into it and rip Zis'Piel's weapons right from his rotten wound."

"You believe his claw weapons are in that wound?" Plio asked.

"Of that I have no doubt," Vatrenex answered. "While my corsairs battle with the Mourners, you and the orc will have the opportunity to sneak onto Zis'Piel's shell undetected. You two will also only have to deal with a minor set of cultists left on the island instead of their entire army."

Plio nodded.

"You will still have to contend with Zis'Piel's aura, however. Which is why I needed to get both you and the orc to Sapphire in order to resist his strength. You will still feel Zis'Piel's influence, but it won't be directed at you. So, you should be able to handle it," Vatrenex said.

"You are . . . most wise, Brother," Plio praised, both reverence and terror evident on his face.

"Indeed," Vatrenex agreed.

Just then, the turtle made an abrupt left turn. The creature's blood-red eyes seemed to be staring directly at Vatrenex before it let out a bellowing roar, a new wave of foulness from its breath rushing over the entire deck of *The Marauding Citadel*. That roar seemed to be a declaration, because right after, a whole fleet of ships disembarked from the beast and sailed directly towards the corsairs. The turtle gave another fetid roar, and the power from its breath was caught by the sails of the Mourners' vessels, instantly accelerating their speed towards the *Citadel*.

Instead of being scared, Vatrenex gave a bloodthirsty grin. "Come now, Brother," he said to Plio. "We have a war to wage."

CHAPTER THIRTY-TWO

The Mourners II

Mutt's ears were beset by a loud roar, and he reflexively covered them as he approached Vatrenex's tower. The deck rumbled below his feet as Saltbeard's cyclopean mount stomped by with him riding atop it.

"Hard to port!" the dwarf shouted and beat a drum on his lap three times. Immediately, the message was sent and spread throughout the deck and even down to the corsairs driving the rowing slaves in the lower levels of the ship. After only a couple of moments, the vessel began turning to the left.

During Mutt's months on the *Citadel*, he'd experienced a dozen different types of storms, as well as monster and beast attacks from both atop the vessel and when he was rowing down below. His sense of touch and hearing allowed him to witness the impressive system the corsairs had for relaying messages, composed of multiple people, drumbeats, and wires. *These guys are cruel, but they are competent sailors, at least,* Mutt thought.

His thoughts were interrupted when both Vatrenex and his brother landed right beside him. Though Mutt could sense their bodies were nothing alike, except for each having only one eye, they both had the same strange smell to them.

"Acolyte, you are to follow Plio and do as he commands. Do you understand?" Vatrenex asked.

"Aye, Captain," Mutt answered with a sarcastic salute. The orc knew that there was a big fight coming up, and while that excited him, he wasn't ignorant of the real danger he was in. He was about to walk away from Vatrenex but wanted to make sure that if the worst were to happen, he ended things on a high note. So, before Vatrenex could fly away, Mutt grabbed his head and kissed the side that was Brunhilda's face. "I love you. Don't worry, the boss will find a way to get us out of this," he said.

Vatrenex screamed in anger and backhanded Mutt, sending him crashing right into Plio, who was cowering and covering his ears. "Idiot! I would kill you for such insolence if you weren't so useful," the Harbinger growled.

"But you won't . . . *Captain*," Mutt said with a smirk as he wiped the blood off his lip and stood up.

Vatrenex snarled as his large mouth began to unfurl, as if he were about to eat Mutt whole, but then—

"I love ye too, Mutt. May Hlin protect ye," the dwarven side of his face awoke and said.

Vatrenex gripped his face and let out an unintelligible snarl as he turned his back to Mutt. "Both of you, begone!" he shouted before he took to the air with a mighty flap of his wings.

Mutt just smiled, feeling victorious. He could sense the rat guy staring at him from behind, dumbfounded. "What?" Mutt asked, turning to him. "Got something on my face?"

"You . . ." The guy trailed off, his lip quivering exaggeratedly. "You are either the bravest or most foolish being I've ever come across."

Mutt scratched the back of his head and said, "Probably both, but let's go with bravest. That sounds much better."

The rat guy looked past Mutt up in the air—at Vatrenex, the orc presumed—and shuddered in fear before gesturing for Mutt to follow. "Come, let us try not to anger our leader any further," the guy said before taking off toward the back of the ship.

Mutt just shrugged and followed him. *This guy is as on-edge as Stabby is,* he thought. Eventually, he was led back down into the lower levels of the ship to a tiny dock in the back he hadn't known about. There, he and the strange guy got aboard a small boat and managed to sneak out through the back of *The Marauding Citadel* to find a bloodbath.

After the orc and his dwarven host had dared to act so audaciously towards him in front of his fellow Harbinger, Vatrenex was furious. It made him look weak and could inspire a lack of confidence from his followers if word got around. Even worse, Vatrenex couldn't really do anything about it. He needed the orc for his plans to work with Zis'Piel and eventually, Waayoo.

There was nothing else he could do about the dwarf, either. Unfortunately, she seemed to be getting stronger and more resistant to Vatrenex's control with his Chaosbind technique. "I have not spent all these centuries preparing, only to lose control to a mere child," he growled to himself as he flew higher. The situation with his host made him feel a sense of urgency that he couldn't remember ever having had before. He *had* to break into the fortress, destroy the Chaos Core, and leave the accursed waters he'd been bound to. There, he could find hosts more powerful in rank but less resistant to his control.

Vatrenex planned to find a way to reach Diamond, to ascend to godhood and become immortal. Then, he would never need a host again. With a mere Ruby occasionally overwriting his control, he felt as if his power was slipping away. That made him angry, and he planned to use that to lash out. Vatrenex was now a few hundred feet above the *Citadel* and stopped his ascent. He locked eyes with the beast that Zis'Piel controlled.

Vatrenex pointed his blade at the creature. He could have offered his brother a chance to surrender, but his bloodlust kept him from giving it true consideration. His blade wanted blood, and it would have its fill. "Brother, today you and the pathetic moaning insects who follow you will fall before my might," Vatrenex declared.

The turtle raised its head, giving another roar that sounded both defiant and sad at the same time.

This seemed to be the signal for the fight to begin, as scores of Mourners launched technique-powered projectiles at the *Citadel* while the port-side cannons and ballistae of the ship fired back in response.

Vatrenex swung his blade with reckless fury, launching a dozen Chaos Rift slashes.

The turtle let out a depressed moan before it redirected the attacks by warping the space around them, making them splash harmlessly into the water away from him.

Vatrenex growled and flew down with his blade at the ready.

The turtle groaned before whipping its head in an impressive display of speed and striking its beak against the edge of Vatrenex's sword. The power of the two beings clashing echoed across the water and sent a shock wave out in all directions.

The winged Harbinger grunted as he tried to chop his opponent in the face, but the power of Zis'Piel's aura blocked the strike. Both Vatrenex and the turtle were forced back, neither managing to hurt the other. Still, while he would have preferred to cut his foe to bits with his blade, Vatrenex knew that wasn't his true goal. He only meant to serve as a distraction, and it worked. Sensing Plio's location via the link they'd formed when he was bound to his service, Vatrenex cackled and gave a grin. *They made it,* he thought as he readied himself to strike again.

"Well . . . that was something," Mutt said as their ship crashed into an area of the giant turtle's shell. The sheer chaos of the aquatic combat surrounding their small vessel nearly killed them more than once. Numerous projectiles from both friend and foe had whizzed past them. Being unable to see, Mutt had to resort to his sense of hearing to judge.

After an arrow cut a line into the side of his shoulder, Mutt resorted to lying down in the boat and rowing from that awkward position so nothing could hit him from anywhere but above. The rat guy had hissed and complained about Mutt's recklessness, but the orc had just shrugged. He didn't know how to sail or use a boat outside of rowing, so he contributed the only way he knew how. His companion was upset that he didn't regulate his speed or slow down to allow them to turn more gracefully, but in the end, it didn't matter. They made it.

The rat man hissed at Mutt before hopping off the boat and onto the—for lack of a better word—shore. As soon as he landed, he instantly stopped and groaned as if he had been frozen in time. He shook for a couple of seconds before letting out a sigh of relief and starting to move regularly again.

"What was that?" Mutt asked as he hopped off the small boat. Right when he landed, he discovered the answer. It was the turtle's aura. It struck Mutt like a sudden windstorm; he staggered and took a step back from the force. It was as if an invisible but physical embodiment of despair had surrounded him from all sides. It probed and pushed at him, trying to find a weak point to seep in.

The orc felt like it was about to envelop him, but then he noticed something protecting him. His own aura was keeping his body and mind safe. Otherwise, he had no doubt that he would either have passed out or been in the fetal position, crying. After ten or so seconds, he adapted and could move once more. His sense of touch also helped him to "see" the dense jungle ahead of them. He realized that many of what had he'd assumed to be trees were actually strangely shaped fungi.

"Oh, man. Why didn't you warn me about that aura?" he asked, putting a hand to his temple.

"Shh!" the rat guy angrily hissed. "Our mission depends on our stealth," he whispered before turning back to scan the forest before them. "We cannot fail Vatrenex. We mustn't," he muttered lowly as if he were about to cry. Before Mutt could ask if he was okay, the strange guy started snapping his head from side to side, scanning their environment so quickly that it didn't seem possible that he would have been able to see anything besides a blur.

Then, breathing rapidly, the rat guy said, "Quickly. We move without a sound," the guy whispered before sprinting forward through the jungle remarkably quietly, even to Mutt's enhanced hearing.

Not wanting to be left behind, Mutt followed. While he couldn't say he moved without a sound, he was pretty proud of just how quietly he did manage to proceed. With the rat guy's speed and Mutt's ability to see so much of their environment thanks to his sense of touch, they were able to avoid the sparse guards and patrols as they rushed toward the Mourners' city proper.

Mutt could sense that it was a crudely built primitive city despite the multistory buildings with uneven, zigzagging streets. As they got closer, the putrid smell grew stronger, too. It was almost too much for Mutt's sensitive nose to bear; he had to force himself not to vomit a couple times. Fortunately, over time, he acclimated to the stench.

Despite how efficiently the two were moving, Mutt had a sinking feeling that it all seemed too easy. The turtle was moving this whole time, due to it being distracted by the corsairs, Mutt assumed, but there hadn't been a single instance of conflict yet. He couldn't say how he knew, but he had a feeling that to achieve their goal, there would be at least one good fight ahead of them. As they neared their destination, that feeling only grew. He equipped his claw weapons and couldn't help but give a grin. *This is going to be a real good fight.*

CHAPTER THIRTY-THREE

The Mourners III

Mutt and the rat guy made it into the foul-smelling city with ease. The strange, roguish fighter had gone off ahead to eliminate any sentries watching out for them. Mutt couldn't hear a thing, only able to tell what was happening through his sense of touch. Once they got in, they were able to navigate the haphazardly designed city mostly due to Mutt's senses. On feeling the vibrations with his bare feet, he essentially had a real-time map of the place that was constantly updating. If he perceived any threat, he'd just warn his ally and the guy would take out the cultist before it became a problem. That had only happened a couple of times so far.

Since they had to move together in close proximity, Mutt noticed that the rat had scales on his arms. It reminded him a lot of Stabby. *His fighting style and anxiety remind me of Stabby a lot too,* he thought. A few minutes later, he noticed that the rat guy had two daggers, one of them being a very familiar stiletto. Mutt let out a sharp inhale as his mind put the pieces together.

"What do you sense? Is there a foe coming?"

Mutt pulled the guy into an empty alley and grabbed him by the chest piece so they were face-to-face. "Stabby, is that you?"

The rat-like face snarled, and he batted Mutt's hand off him. "Don't call me that. Your friend is gone. Only Plio remains."

Mutt just smiled. "Oh, I know you're in there, Stabby. I know you've been mad at the boss, but don't worry. I know he'll come for us. Just hold on."

The rat guy drew a blade and pressed it to Mutt's throat. "I do not know you, orc. Nor do I have any fondness for you. If I weren't ordered to keep you safe, I would kill you here and put an end to your annoyances once and for all."

Mutt just smirked. "Whatever you say," he said, raising his palms in surrender.

The guy snarled but withdrew his blade.

Then, Mutt heard shouting in some unknown language not far from them and could sense a few spear-wielding guards rushing towards them. So, they climbed on top of one of the buildings to get away and quickly made it to their destination. They were hiding behind a tall, thin tower and carefully scanning the area ahead. Using echolocation by clicking his tongue, Mutt was able to get a rough idea of the crater. It was roughly a quarter mile long in all directions while only a couple of hundred feet deep. Sharp, jagged bones surrounded the craterous wound in all directions, making it look like the mouth of a giant sandworm.

A couple of cultists stood on the edge of one large bone, heaving bucketfuls of indiscernible debris from a large sled into the crater. Mutt wondered what exactly it was until one of the cultists pulled a head out from the sled and tossed it in. *Okay, so body parts*, Mutt thought. *And we're going to have to go in there . . . Great.*

He leaned over to the rat guy and whispered, "So why are they throwing dead things in that wound? Wouldn't that just make it worse?"

Plio grimaced but whispered, "The theory is that giving Zis'Piel a constant source of biomatter prevents complete desiccation of his host."

Mutt opened his mouth to find the words but couldn't. "Uh . . . what?" he whispered.

"It doesn't matter," the rat guy replied in an angry whisper. "We just need to go in there, retrieve the weapons, and get out."

Mutt rolled his one remaining eye and nodded. After the crater shook and erupted a small fount of pus and rotten flesh, the two cultists fell to their knees and wailed loudly as if all their efforts had been in vain. It made Mutt even more confused, but he saved his questions for now as his companion clearly wasn't in the mood right now. After a couple of more minutes of moaning and crying, the two cultists dragged themselves and their sled away, heads hanging low in defeat.

Once they were gone, Mutt and the rat guy snuck out, and the rogue tied a rope to one of the bones on the edge. Then they used that to climb down. While Mutt had gone nose-blind due to the stench of the place, the damp humidity was on another level inside the wound. As soon as he registered it and his bare feet sunk into a rotting wound, he retched. He was able to hold back from actually vomiting, but his body went through all the motions a couple of times before he could compose himself.

Mutt's sense of touch helped him see *so* much more than he wanted to. It was as if he'd submerged into a giant cauldron full of flesh, blood, bones, and viscera, all in varying states of decay. The nastiness was so thick that it entirely covered both of Mutt's feet. He could also sense pillars of sharp bones that jutted out in a concentric pattern and were remarkably thick and not at all decayed. The only other thing Mutt noticed was a raised pedestal of flesh about chest height in the very center of the wound. It was adorned with various bones and a skull on each side of the top. In between them, on the very center of the pedestal, were two claw weapons, just like the ones he had on.

Right after Mutt registered what the pedestal was exactly, the rat guy took off towards it in a dead sprint.

Though fast, when he had only made it halfway to the pedestal, the mound of flesh and bone changed. It twisted and morphed, and Mutt could suddenly smell the scents of brimstone and ash, just as he could on the rat guy and Vatrenex. In a heartbeat, the mound of flesh had transformed into a two-headed, bipedal creature. Its body was boxy and had sharp features, the exception being its faces, which were just two smooth round orbs. In each of its hands was a claw weapon, each with two blades just like Mutt's.

The rat guy stopped his charge, and it was just in time too, as the two-headed humanoid swung one of its claws at him. The guy managed to deflect the strike but was sent sliding back amidst the muck of the rotten flesh.

Then it shook its heads from side to side, each a perfect reflection of the other. "Oh, Plio. I have two heads. You must've known I would sense you even if I was distracted. Why did you come?" the being asked sadly, only one voice emerging from both heads, surprising Mutt. He was also thrown by the thing's voice in general. To Mutt, he sounded young but hoarse, like a sniveling, mopey teenager.

The rat guy readied a second blade so that he now had a dagger in each hand. One was a wickedly curved, thick dagger while the other was Stabby's stiletto. "Vatrenex is too strong, Brother," the rat guy replied. "I . . . I have been caught, and he has forced me into his service," he uttered fearfully before spinning his blades, shifting to a more offensive stance. His lower lip still quivered as he said, "Now, I must take your weapons or he will kill me."

The two-headed creature lowered his heads and shook them from side to side once more. "Forcing me to kill both my own brother and so many other innocents like this stranger here," he said, gesturing to Mutt with one hand. "Damn that Vatrenex," he moaned before each of his faceless heads raised up, each one locking onto an opponent. "I will mourn your deaths," he said before letting out a haunting wail and throwing that same Chaos Slash technique Mutt had seen Vatrenex use.

The rat guy that was controlling Stabby was ready and launched a slash from each of his own blades. One managed to deflect the incoming strike while the second continued forth at the two-headed opponent, unimpeded.

Mutt took that opportunity to charge at their foe. As he ran, he changed his feet into Horned Harpy Eagle Talons, giving him much surer footing in the muck. Activating his techniques hurt, but he pushed through it. His newly enhanced Sapphire power helped him close the distance in a few seconds and leap at the two-headed moaning figure. As he jumped, his heart raced in excitement. Despite the pain, he felt strong. He was eager for a good fight. Both his Fenrir's Claws technique and his claw weapons were ready to rend flesh.

The two-headed enemy deflected the rat's second slash technique with his own claw weapon, and his right head managed to notice Mutt when he was just feet away. "Time Halt," he said as he raised his right palm up.

Immediately, Mutt's downward momentum was stopped as he became frozen in time. The orc was terrified, as he couldn't control his body and couldn't rely on his sense of touch to help him sense his surroundings. He could hear blades clashing, indicating the rat guy was busy engaging their enemy. Still, the two-headed being sounded like he was about to cry as he said, "You poor fool. I am sorry you have been made a sacrificial pawn. I will mourn your fate."

Mutt's heart raced as he heard his right arm move towards his gut and thought he was about to die when another noise instantly sounded off to his right.

"Time Step," was all that he heard directly beside him before he was promptly kicked and sent sliding left in the muck.

Mutt coughed but was grateful as the technique that had paused time had been broken as well. With his feet able to feel vibrations once more, Mutt was able to "see" more clearly too; he understood that it was the rat guy who had saved him. The two continued to fight, their blades sparking off each other as they slashed and parried.

"Time Halt," the two-headed guy said as both of his featureless heads leaned forward at once toward the rat.

"Chaos Step," the rat man said a split second later, and he instantly vanished. It was a good thing, too, because right where he'd been, a pulse of mana suddenly manifested, indicating where their foe's technique had been targeted.

To Mutt's surprise, the rat guy appeared a couple of feet above him, landing on a tall bone behind the orc that curled over Mutt's head. "It is clear that you are indeed both brave *and* a fool, orc," the rat guy spat. "Do you have a ranged technique?"

"Uh, yeah," Mutt replied.

"Good. On my order, use it. Do not attack him until I tell you to. Just keep him distracted while I try to find a weakness."

Their foe shook his two heads sadly. "What you are looking for is impossible. You know already that my aura is too strong, Plio. You are merely delaying the inevitable. Your efforts are admirable, but in the end, it's all so . . . futile." He sighed before sending a volley of Chaos Rift Slashes in their direction.

Mutt deflected one of the slash attacks with his left claw weapon. It was successful in knocking it away, but the blades instantly crumbled to ash. "Oh, crap," Mutt uttered and instantly began rolling, jumping, and cartwheeling as best he could to dodge the incoming techniques. *Glad I used my weapon and not my nails. That would've been bad,* he thought.

Mutt eventually found refuge behind another large rib bone fragment. Their opponent was still firing slashes in all directions, and he could sense his rat-man ally moving about even more impressively than he had been previously. "Now!" the rat man shouted.

Mutt rolled out from his hiding spot and let out a Bounder's Howl. Sound laced with beast mana projected out from the orc in a cone directed at the two-headed man.

Their foe instantly stopped attacking with his slashes and flared his aura. It covered his whole body, providing a layer of protection which forced the technique to roll off him harmlessly. "What a pity, to be so strong yet so foolish. I mourn for what you could've been, child," he said before raising a palm in Mutt's direction. "Time—"

His words and technique were interrupted as a blade flew down and embedded itself in his chest. Another second and the stiletto's enchantment kicked in, making the rat guy appear right beside their opponent, with the blade's grip in his hand. "Enough!" he shouted and flared his aura out. The sheer force of it dislodged the dagger in his chest and sent the rat man flying and Mutt sliding back amongst the muck.

Mutt felt the whole turtle shake and vibrate at that declaration, the gigantic being letting out a cry of distress. He also felt the suppressive power of their foe's aura once again, as a heavy sadness pressed down on him from all directions, forcing him down to a knee.

"This is just so pointless. You cannot hope to defeat me. Gah!" the man said suddenly as if struck by an attack that Mutt couldn't detect. The turtle cried out even louder in even more distress and everything shook once more, but this time, the oppressive aura being targeted at them diminished.

"Yes, Brother," the rat guy said as he stood back up. "But while you do have two heads, you cannot truly fight both us *and* Vatrenex with your full power."

"No no no no no," their foe started muttering sadly to himself.

"Hey, Stabby," Mutt whispered.

"Don't call me that," the rat guy snapped back.

"Whatever, just listen. I've found his weakness. He's strong, but his defense falters right when he attacks. That's the reason your dagger actually hit him. He was starting to use his technique. So—" Mutt squeezed a fist in excitement and grinned. "—we just need to keep attacking him as fast as possible at different times until one of us hits him when he's trying to strike back."

"That is a foolish plan. No, wait!" the rat guy called out, but Mutt was already charging forward.

"Nooo!" the two-headed figure screamed. "To have my own brothers do this to me! How horrible. It seems I really must kill my family," he said before his heads turned in Mutt's direction. "Resorting to recklessly charging me again, how sad," he said before raising his hand up. "Time Halt," he said.

Though Mutt was running at him once more, he had learned his lesson. Just as his opponent finished the words, he abruptly jumped to the left, allowing him to narrowly avoid the technique but prevent his own path forward. Fortunately, his ally had gotten over Mutt's surprise charge and capitalized on the opportunity.

"Voidflare Barrage," the scaled rat-man hissed as orbs of chaos mana appeared all around him and zoomed toward their foe.

Mutt could only sense the airborne projectiles due to their strange distinct smell.

The first few orbs struck the two-headed cultivator, and he groaned in obvious pain. Yet before any more could strike, he flicked his hand to the right toward Mutt and said, "Warp." Immediately, the laws of physics were bent as the cultivator somehow bent the space in front of him and forced the orbs of mana to make an acute ninety-degree turn directly at Mutt.

Mutt didn't have time to dodge but presumed the technique would be just as devastating as the slash he parried earlier. So, he did the only thing he could think of: he crossed his arms in front of himself, crouched his body down to make a smaller target, and activated his best defensive technique, Dweller Bear's Fur. Voluminous amounts of thick brown fur grew out from every pore of his body, covering him completely until he was unrecognizable. A heartbeat later, he was beset by the barrage.

The twenty or so orbs of mana crashed hard against him, each feeling like they were fired from a crossbow. Wherever they made contact with his fur, the hair would instantly wither away. The technique was still doing its job in taking the blows, however, protecting Mutt from becoming riddled with holes and dying on the spot. Despite that, the orbs *really* hurt, so Mutt gritted his teeth throughout.

From that pain, however, came a sense of clarity. Mutt was reminded of his torturous ascension to Sapphire. Experiencing this much pain wasn't daunting to him anymore. In fact, he seemed to have an even better connection to his mana when he was in pain. He could tell his mind was onto something—a concept of or connection to his mana that was just barely eluding him.

While he couldn't grasp exactly *what* he was gaining insight about in terms of his own mana, he did gain a clearer understanding of what he and the rat guy were facing. *The two-headed guy isn't really a guy at all. How did I not realize before that that's why he's barely moved this whole fight?* Mutt thought as the final orb finally dissipated. While he was in that strange, heightened state, he had realized that the two-headed, faceless foe had no feet. Instead, the bottom of his legs—covered in the layer of rotten bodily remains—were actually connected to the wound itself.

That meant that what they were fighting was more like an appendage than an actual person, like an uncanny extra finger the giant turtle had equipped his weapons onto. *We just need to disconnect him from the main body*, Mutt thought. He growled as the final orb of mana struck, singeing off more of his fur. The orc then went down on all fours and activated Fenrir's Claws, sprinting directly at their foe at top speed.

"Stabby, use that barrage again!" Mutt shouted.

The rat man hissed but complied and sent another volley of his mana orbs at their two-headed foe.

The man shook his heads. "It didn't work before. So sad that you think it will work now," he said in his typical melodramatic fashion before warping space in front of him again and redirecting it at Mutt.

Mutt was ready this time, though, and submerged his whole body in the muck to avoid the attack. It also helped him maintain his momentum. It was only for a couple of seconds, but the smell was even more pungent to his sensitive nose, and he could barely take it. So, when he was just a foot away from their opponent, he leaped out and began swiping and slashing with both his claw technique and his one remaining claw weapon. The enemy was still putting up a good defense, however. With Mutt so close and attacking so quickly, he could do little else, but he blocked, parried, and countered with impressive skill, preventing Mutt from getting a good hit in. That was until the guy controlling Stabby rejoined the fight.

The rat man was the fastest out of all of them, and his speed started to become too much for their two-headed opponent. Both Mutt and his ally began to occasionally strike their foe. Mutt smiled as his training with Vatrenex was clearly bearing fruit. The two-headed creature's aura was still up, though, so only a couple of their blows had done any damage, and what had been done was minor. Mutt knew he just needed to strike when their opponent attempted to attack him. That was their one opening.

"It's so obvious now. How did I not notice before? The reason you're so good at defense is because you *can't move*," Mutt said as he ducked a counter and went to cut the bottom of their foe to amputate him from the main body. That was when the two-headed being warped his own body.

Before Mutt's claws could hit their mark, the bottom of the guy's body abruptly bent out of the way. Mutt could also sense the top of his body spinning out of the way from the rat guy's attempted stab, as if he had no bones. Mutt couldn't stop his swing and, meeting nothing but air, his swipe made him stumble forward and fall to his knees. His ears picked up the noise of the rat guy being struck and sent crashing into one of the large bones inside the crater. "Oh shit!" he said, and before he was able to get up, his sense of touch warned him that their foe was already stabbing down at him with one of his claws.

Mutt turned to face the guy and made to dodge, but his weapon was already too close. He was about to impale Mutt straight through the head. It was a moment where he couldn't think. Mutt just let his instincts act. In desperation, he activated Gnoll's Bite and intercepted the bladed claws by biting down on them.

"What?" the two-headed enemy asked, in clear shock. That shock then turned to horror as the power of Mutt's teeth dented the metal blades, slightly bending them. "Gah! Noo!" he shouted. To Mutt's surprise, his opponent sounded like he was truly in pain.

Mutt grinned at the sudden turn of events and intended to bite down harder when his opponent's other claw blades came at him. He attempted to block them with his own claws, but he forgot one crucial thing: he needed to keep moving to not be a sitting target.

"Warp!" the guy said, and Mutt's arm immediately bent at an unnatural angle, breaking the bones of his right forearm with a *snap!*

Mutt let out a cry of pain which turned into a full-on roar when his foe's claws stabbed straight into his gut. He slapped away the claws by his face as he howled in agony, managing to not get stabbed through the head, but they did slice through his one remaining eye. The pain only grew worse as the two-headed man began to lift Mutt in the air, the orc feeling the two blades exiting out through his back.

The rat guy was stuck, partially embedded in the bone he'd struck, and therefore unable to help Mutt at the moment.

Mutt's enemy made a shushing noise before shaking his heads sadly and clicking his tongue. "Shh," he said, and Mutt stopped his howling as he began to cough out blood. "You poor fool. We all are doomed to die and suffer. If you would've accepted your fate earlier, this pointless struggle and pain could have been avoided. Take comfort, however, that your suffering will soon end. Now, die," he said right before he began to point his partially bent claws towards Mutt's chest.

Mutt hadn't been listening to his foe's words. He was too lightheaded and racked with pain to notice any noise outside of his own body. He could hear his heartbeat and feel it pump blood slower and slower through his veins. He also felt the wounds on his abdomen and back, his lacerated organs, his broken right arm, and even his eye dripping out blood and ocular fluid down his face. He was reminded once more of his ascension to Sapphire.

The pain he was experiencing right now helped heighten his connection to his entire body and the beast mana that flowed through it. He felt the mana listening to him and his will. Mutt seemed to understand his mana more now and saw new possibilities as insight came to him. *So, that's what Vatrenex meant when he said that I can manifest a technique elsewhere despite its name. I get it. Guess it's too late now, huh?* he thought to himself as his heart began to slow.

Mutt felt death call to him and was about to embrace it, when a loud voice broke through his internal focus and hit his ears: "Mutt, watch out!" Zhaden's voice hissed loudly from the other side of the crater.

Mutt gasped and his heart began to race as he regained awareness of his surroundings. Instinct took over once again and he grabbed his opponent's wrist before the strange being could stab his head. Right after, he grabbed his foe's other wrist—the one that was wielding the weapon still impaling his gut.

The two-headed cultivator began to shake as he tried to force his weapons forward, the only movement being some slight wiggling. "How?" he asked, surprised that Mutt could fight back, especially with a broken arm.

Mutt didn't answer. He only gave him a stern look as blood continued to flow forth from his mouth, and said, "Gnoll's Bite." Immediately, his Fenrir's Claws technique faded and the thick, powerful, sharp teeth of a gnoll formed along Mutt's palms. They sunk deeply into his foe's wrists and tore both his arms off completely.

Mutt dropped, somehow landing on his feet but barely conscious. The two-headed being tried to say something, but Mutt couldn't make it out as he felt his foe's entire body collapsing in on itself as if it had been a sandcastle struck by a raging wave of water. Mutt's arms went numb, and he didn't know what happened to his opponent's weapons. *I guess he's dead now, so it shouldn't matter*, he thought. *I need to find a good place to take a nap.*

Before he could lie down, the ground underneath the orc's feet started to shake and he began to stumble. He couldn't hear Stabby or smell the drakonid anymore, but he did feel a familiar set of scaley arms keeping him from falling. Mutt felt his claw weapon being removed and something else being shoved into his hands.

"Put these on," the rat guy's voice said, now barely a whisper.

"Okay, I guess," he said and proceeded to do as requested. His body continued to shake, but the rat guy that was clearly controlling Stabby continued to keep Mutt upright. "Can you stop all that shaking?" Mutt asked as he put on the second claw before he lost consciousness.

Vatrenex cackled triumphantly as he flew over the battlefield below. The massive turtle that Zis'Piel had conquered had abruptly went limp as Vatrenex was fighting him, allowing the winged Harbinger to behead the mighty beast before the entirety of both the Mourners and Corsairs. Vatrenex's forces shouted in triumph while the Mourners began to wail even louder.

Both the gathered armies had been fighting on the water as well as on *The Marauding Citadel* itself. When the Mourners' leader had apparently perished, they truly became crazed. The pale cultists began attacking anyone they saw with reckless abandon, heedless of their own safety. They even attacked each other.

Saltbeard was a competent first mate, however, and atop his cyclops mount, he ordered the corsairs to regroup and began taking down the lunatic followers of Zis'Piel with deadly efficiency.

Vatrenex didn't need to deal with the cultists fighting in their boats. The dead turtle took care of that for him. Before its massive body could degrade fully, its bulky form began to sink. The force from such a large entity being submerged began to drag the small schooners and other vessels with it. Seeing their miserable lives being ended by their own leader's dead body brought Vatrenex a great deal of joy and made him laugh even more.

"Yes, vermin! Cease your endless whining and be wiped from existence!"

Before the turtle fully sank, however, Vatrenex did detect a familiar set of mana signatures: two fellow Harbingers, each laced with his own mana and bound to him. He flew down and grabbed his brothers' wrists, saving them from the water, and brought them to the top of his tower.

Plio was breathing quickly, looking waterlogged and haggard. He also reeked of rotten flesh. Vatrenex wondered if he shouldn't have left the former quist to swim back on his own in order to get clean. He wouldn't have drowned like the others, so the only thing that would've been an issue would be the time it took for him to come back. When his eye locked onto Zis'Piel, Vatrenex gave a large grin that extended down to his abdomen.

"Brother, so glad that you have joined us," he said.

All the Harbingers resembled their original races to varying degrees, Zis'Piel most of all. He possessed nearly all the features of a V'keth except for his skin tone and his lower half. Typically being a bipedal being, he now just had one long tail, like the serpents of this realm.

"To be doomed to fight under your banner, Vatrenex. Why is fate so cruel?" Zis'Piel shook his heads and looked like he would cry if he had eyes. "I mourn for those I will have to kill and for my followers below. Please, Vatrenex, will you not spare them?"

"Spare them? Those fanatics you called followers are too crazed to even use as slaves, Brother. Death is all they will get from me. Mourn all you want, as long as you both continue to follow my orders." Vatrenex waved off his brother's laments before turning his back on them and looking down at the slaughter below. *One to go,* he thought to himself.

CHAPTER THIRTY-FOUR

Level Three

Kiru and William quickly flew up the tunnel to the third level. They did so to avoid the surge of fire coming from the explosion below that William had set off. They zoomed up and emerged from the floor and out of a cave mouth. The psion immediately moved away to the side and took a deep inhale of fresh air, feeling both relieved and refreshed. He then heard a set of cacophonous booms begin to echo from the cave, and backed away even more to put some distance between him and it. It was a good call, too, because about ten seconds later, a plume of smoke and ash emerged from the cave, and it continued to flow out, not indicating it would stop anytime soon.

"Haha! Yeah! Those bastards won't be able to follow us now!" William cheered.

Kiru agreed and turned back to take in more of the surprisingly fresh, crisp air. As he inhaled, he closed his eyes, enjoying how pure and good it felt. "After being stuck in such artificial, horrific places, you forget how good fresh air can be, you know?" Kiru said before he realized his words. "Wait? Fresh air?" he asked and opened his eyes to truly take in the floor he'd made it to.

What Kiru saw defied his understanding. They were in a giant valley that was so vast, he couldn't even see all of it. Kiru was standing on a group of large rocks at the edge of a small grove of trees. Despite there being not many trees, those that were there were notably thick, with a lush canopy of white and pink leaves. Beyond the small grove was a giant thick grassland, but instead of green grass, it was such a dark blue, it was almost black. The grassland went on for miles in all directions with moss-covered rocks and strange pieces of metal dotting the landscape as well.

Way off to the left in what Kiru decided to identify as west for reference was what looked like a swamp with a dense layer of willow trees with red leaves. The psion even noticed the predatory fleshling trees interspersed throughout the swamp as well. A stream of water came from that direction and seemed to feed a large lake centrally located in the grassland. Even further away to the northeast was an absolutely massive mountain. It was surrounded by rocky fjords in all directions along the ground and was bright purple with a mix of blacks and grays dotting it, made of the same purple metal that the ship was composed of, and was surrounded by rocky fjords in all directions. The mountain was so tall that Kiru could barely see its peak in the sky. It shocked him to see that there *was* an actual sky rather than a ceiling.

In its very center was a giant orb of light serving as an artificial sun. Unlike any sun Kiru had ever heard of, though, it had a series of lines jutting out from it in all directions, making it look like a massive snowflake. The edge of one line extended so far across the sky that it nearly touched the peak of the mountain off in the distance. Seeing so much natural beauty despite the odd, alien nature of the place in addition to the fresh air caused Kiru to doubt what he was seeing.

"William, are we . . . outside?" Kiru asked.

"Negative, Master. The data indicates that we are indeed on the third floor of the prison," the imp answered.

The psion sighed, all of a sudden feeling tired. He was still too curious to rest, though. "How can that be, William? I mean, there's a literal sky with trees, water, and everything. And look, there are some strange-looking boar off in the distance," Kiru said as he pointed towards a small herd of bulbous porcine creatures taking a drink by the lake.

"I do admit that this is . . . abnormal, even given what we've witnessed previously, Master. Despite that, I can confirm that we are in Level Three," William said, promptly touching the gem in the psion's forehead, making the map of the fortress appear in his mind. It zoomed in on the third floor, and it indeed was the largest floor of them all, but the scale still didn't convince Kiru. William seemed to understand the psion's skepticism because he quickly spoke up and explained, "The third floor was where the arboth once ran their wartime drills. They also had their slaves fight for sport on this level, too. Even with it being so large, the monsters wanted even more space. So, they had numerous crystals containing spatial enchantments placed on it. The formula I have approximates the total space that the floor has with the special enchantments still active at around 1500 square miles, give or take a couple hundred miles if any crystals have malfunctioned over the centuries."

"Fifteen hundred?" Kiru asked, clearly shocked by the numbers. The Database had been 115 square miles, and the place was huge, taking the psion weeks to traverse it. Admittedly, he had to move with caution back there due to the automatons, but he presumed this floor had no shortage of its own dangerous beings present.

Needing time to process everything, Kiru walked over to a nearby tree and sat down, leaning his head against it. "It took us around a month to get out of the fourth floor. If this place is over ten times larger . . ."

"Then we can logically conclude that it may take that much time, but we were also moving very cautiously then. So, it very well may not take us ten months," William finished for Kiru. "At the same time, however, with how my map doesn't match any of this floor and the likely danger that both the flora and fauna represent, it wouldn't be unreasonable to assume that our travels will take even longer. I need more data before I can give you an accurate estimation."

Kiru sighed as he closed his eyes.

"I don't think it will be as serious an issue as you worry, Master. Don't forget, we have the time dilation on our side."

"That does make me feel better. I don't want to keep our friends waiting too long," Kiru admitted after releasing a large exhale. He immediately felt his eyelids getting heavy. "Um, William, I think I'm gonna close my eyes for a bit," he said before his consciousness went to black.

Kiru blinked his eyes open and groaned. He shook the bleariness and rubbed his eyes to look around. He quickly discovered that he was not where he had fallen asleep—at least, not exactly. He was still leaning against one of the trees but was now high up in the branches instead of on the ground. The foliage was so thick that, aside from the branch he was on, all he could see were the leaves.

"Oh, thank Surtur, you're finally awake," William groaned as he floated over to the psion.

Kiru quickly picked up on the fact that something was not right based on his location and the nervous energy his familiar was exuding. "How long was I out?" he asked.

"Five days," William answered.

Kiru's eyes bulged. "Five days?! How?"

William sighed, "When I used Imp's Label on you, it said you were 'recovering.' I assume it was a likely repercussion of your ascension, or maybe that extended battle we had, because no matter what I did, you still wouldn't wake. When night fell, I thought it best to use Telekinesis to hide you up here," he said. "Fortunately, your recent ascension was both curse and boon as I determined that your body didn't need any sustenance."

"Wow," Kiru said. "Thank you for looking after me. Wait, there's night here?"

"Yes. As for looking after you, it's what friends are for," William said before a large grin grew on his face. "But you can make it up to me."

Feeling like the other shoe was about to drop, Kiru asked, "What do you want?"

William began rubbing his hands together nervously. "You see, while you've been sleeping, I've been exploring some nearby areas on this floor, updating my map and examining the local flora and fauna, and I found the most delicious-looking creature I've seen since before we left the continent," William said before asking Kiru to recall him.

The psion complied, and his mind was shown a memory from William's time out. The little imp had carefully moved across the tall grass towards the lake Kiru had seen earlier. There, he was able to get a better look at the creatures the psion had noticed from a distance. The things were called "Farigaboars," according to William's Imp's Label, but the psion was pretty sure that name was completely fabricated by his familiar. They looked like someone had fused a boar and a fruit fly together. Their bodies were black and hairy with six legs ending in hooved feet. They had large, red, compound eyes which reinforced their fly-like appearance when they twitched their heads from side to side to look for possible threats. Instead of thin, porcine tails, they were short and ended on a large round bulb with two red dots. Kiru was reminded of how some butterflies had certain patterns on their wings to look like eyes to fool predators into thinking they were being watched. The psion reasoned that the tails provided the same benefit. Still, no matter how impressed he was with their evolutionary adaptations, it still didn't mean they looked appetizing.

"Master, to pay me back for such a great job I did, I require meat," William sent.

"We have food though," Kiru replied. "We have so much crab that we could probably go another six months before needing to restock."

"Master . . . with all due respect, you may like crab, but I am sick and tired of eating the things. Yes, it's fine for sustenance, but the old *William is desperate for some raw, bloody meat. And with your new powers, catching one of these things should provide you little trouble,"* William sent.

Kiru sighed before nodding in agreement. While he did enjoy the void crab meat, surviving on it as the primary source of food for months on end wasn't the most appealing thing. He could use some variety. "Okay, I just hope they taste better than they look," he said.

"What are you talking about, Master? They look delicious—so fat and juicy. Oooh, I bet they're also crunchy like bugs, too. It's the best of both worlds!"

William had always had pretty low standards for food, rodent heads being a favored delicacy of his. So, Kiru guessed the farigaboars were a step up for his friend.

"William, tell me how this place can somehow have a day and night cycle?" Kiru asked as he hopped down, deciding to change the subject.

"It's kind of strange actually, and also really freaky. Night occurs when the tip of the purple mountain rumbles and shifts," William answered.

"The mountain . . . moves?" Kiru asked.

"I know it's weird, but the tip of it will shift abruptly. A bell-like sound will ring out from the mountain across the whole valley, then the entire thing will rumble a little, and the mountain tip bends." William then sent Kiru a memory of what he

described occurring. Just like he said, the mountaintop abruptly bent as if a giant finger had pressed down on its side. When the mountaintop shifted, it touched the edge of the snowflake-like shape that extended from the artificial sun. That apparently turned off the light, so to speak, plunging the valley in darkness.

"I've timed it, and the day and night cycles are twenty-four hours each, making them twice as long as it would be outside. And before you ask, yes, you slept five full days in here. So, you technically slept for ten days," William explained.

That made Kiru's eyes widen. It also made him even more appreciative of William looking out for him that whole time. *I really owe him that pig now. And I guess he rarely asks for much, so it's the least I can do*, he thought before another question came to him. "You called the nighttime freaky. Why?"

"That would be because of the nocturnal monster people," the imp replied before sending the psion images from William's memory. What Kiru saw were only small silhouettes of the beings from a distance, but he could tell they were a nightmarish sort, coming in two forms: four arms with two legs, and two arms with four legs. They all had small bestial heads with needle-like teeth and a large whalelike tail. They mostly wielded spears and shields with a couple holding large, crude-looking swords. Their language was an indiscernible set of deep moans and clicks.

"I didn't get too close to them because they moved fast, and they clearly weren't friendly," William said as the memory showed Kiru one of them holding a small humanoid impaled through the chest by one of their spears, and slung over one of their shoulders.

I'm not shocked that they don't appear friendly. Nothing so far has been, Kiru thought. The psion quietly moved past the small grove where he'd been sleeping and treaded northward into the tall, dark blue grass. He noticed that, thankfully, the column of smoke had stopped coming from the cave he'd emerged from, and the cave mouth itself had collapsed in on itself, now just a pile of stone rubble. To better improve his senses, he put his Mask of Fenrir back on again. Slowly, he stalked forward, using the training Mutt had given him back in Imakandi to help him stealthily close the distance. Due to the mild breeze, he made sure to stay downwind of the boars.

He paused as his enhanced sense of smell picked up on what seemed to be mental mana. He crept closer and saw that the lake of water the boar was drinking from was indeed *liquid* mental mana! Kiru's eyes widened as he realized that this was what his father, Ruken, had sensed and had told him to come find in order to heal his body. Pure liquid mental mana. After finding an alternate way to heal himself by ingesting kraken blood, Kiru had forgotten all about it. With his immediate survival being so pressing, it was also understandable why he'd forgotten about that previous goal.

With so much liquid mental mana so close, Kiru wondered why he could only sense it now. *Maybe because my injury. If that's the case, how could my father have sensed this from so far away when he was alive? How could he have known about this place?* he thought, his mind producing no answers. Kiru resolved to ask the projection of his father when he next acquired another artifact. As he got within about twenty feet, he quietly drew his blade. Before he could strike, however, his now-wolflike ears twitched. There was a rustling to the left, and it was not from another farigaboar. It had a distinct *squeak* to it. Feeling strongly that they weren't alone, Kiru lowered himself even further into the tall grass and backed away slightly.

"*Master, we don't have much time until night falls. Three minutes and twenty-seven seconds, to be exact. So, uh . . . bring me the bacon,*" William sent.

"*William, in all your time scouting the area, have you noticed any predators?*" Kiru asked via Telepathy.

"*I have discovered two different types of umbrafangs: small pack hunters the size of housecats with disproportionately large heads, and large solitary ambush predators as big as lions. Oh, and I observed a few abominations aimlessly floating about. Those things really are everywhere,*" William said.

"*William,*" Kiru urgently sent, as he felt a growing sense of danger. On instinct, he started to back away from the lake and the boars. "*Did any of them ever make a squeaking noise?*"

"*No, how useful would that be for a predator?*" William asked. "*And why are you backing away from the pigs? We're on a time limit, you know.*"

Before Kiru could retort, the boar let out a loud squeal and bolted to the right. Just then, three rodents the size of dwarfs leaped suddenly out from the tall grass and high in the air. They were to the left of the congregated farigaboars, and their gazes were focused intently on the strange beasts. They were all ghostly pale and wore haphazard brown and black rags. The three rats all gave off the power of Silvers, and the trio all threw sharp daggers at one of them.

Despite their speed, however, their surprise attack clearly wasn't enough to catch the insect-like boar off-guard as its compound eyes seemed to be able to detect them before they had leapt out. All three of their small blades missed the boar, landing in the dirt where it had previously been standing. As the creatures were descending, Kiru used Imp's Label on one of them.

Name: Unknown
Race: Quist
Rank: Silver, Tier 3
Mana Type: Unknown

> **Path:** Unknown
> **Status:** Neutral
>
> *One of the four main races of the void. Quist are a rodent-like people with an affinity for darkness, chaos, and time mana. They are not strong in body but are quick-footed and prolific breeders, making them one of the most numerous denizens of the void realm.*

Kiru blinked in surprise. *An actual quist, not some corrupted variant or mutated cousin?* he thought to himself, astonished upon seeing a living, breathing, sentient, and possibly friendly race.

They didn't notice Kiru as they each landed with a roll and picked up their blades in one smooth motion. Then, they began to run in pursuit of the boar.

Kiru wanted to approach the quist, but just because he hoped they would be friendly, didn't guarantee that things would go down that way. So, he opted to just follow them for now. William was all for it because he didn't want the rat people to "take my promised meat." Kiru had also noticed something else that Imp's Label had never shown before—the specific tier of the target's cultivation rank. So, he asked William about it.

"That's simple, Master. With your ascension to Sapphire, Imp's Label has improved as well," William answered.

Kiru nodded in approval as he followed the quist running east. *I definitely don't have a problem with my abilities improving,* he thought. For another five minutes, the quist were still chasing down the boar. *For just Silvers, they do have impressive speed and stamina,* Kiru thought. Eventually, the quist followed the farigaboar into an area of the grassland that had a smorgasbord of random piles of misshapen metal, partially covered with a weird, glowing moss.

One of the quist—the smallest of the three he'd been following—sped up and moved to the boar's right. They drew their blade and stabbed the boar in its side. The creature let out a loud cry of pain before flailing its head to the side and slamming one of its tusks into the small quist. The beast hit them hard enough to dislodge the rat person's blade and send them flying into a metal boulder, knocking them unconscious. After the boar had dealt with that attack, it made a hard left turn.

The other two quist had clearly planned for this—while the smallest one moved to the boar's right, another had moved way off to the left, with the last continuing to chase the insectoid pig from behind. Kiru realized that the quist who had sped ahead must have used a technique, as it seemed to instantly teleport a short distance twice in about ten seconds. The last time they used their technique was when they all of a sudden disappeared by a piece of metal, only to appear atop the spiky, jagged, ten-foot-tall piece of debris when the boar had come running by. They then jumped off and stabbed the beast right in its two large eyes before it could realize what was happening.

There was a loud crunch of bone as blue blood gushed from the boar's eyes. It let out one sad cry before its body went limp, dead. The two quist made a series of light screeches and squeaks of triumph as they cheered their success. The third one looked like they had a concussion as Kiru noticed they were still lying against the boulder it had hit, their head wobbly and eyes moving about unfocused. *At least they're not dead*, Kiru thought. *They also don't appear to be these nocturnal monster men either.*

"Oh, crap! William how much time do we have left?"

As if in response to the quists' celebrations or Kiru's telepathic question, a loud gong sound rang throughout the entire third level.

"Master, that's the bell sound I told you about that heralds the night," William sent.

The two celebrating quists' faces instantly went from joy to terror at the noise. They looked back to their injured companion, seeming to assess what to do about them. Kiru kept low to the grass to not be spotted. The purple mountain then rumbled, and the top somehow bent to the side, making contact with the edge of the sun snowflake, and darkness immediately fell over the entirety of Level Three.

The two quist had originally walked over to go help their comrade, but when the darkness came, they appeared to go instantly into self-preservation mode. One squeezed themselves in a hole under one of the boulders while the other found a distinctly flat stone that seemed polished and out of place amongst the overgrowth-covered stones and metal debris. With ease, the quist lifted the stone, hopped into a hole already dug out under it, and then placed the stone back on top.

So, they've marked out safe places to hide in case they're out when night falls, Kiru thought.

"What imbeciles, leaving a perfectly good pig to waste," William grumbled in the psion's mind. *"Master, put that boar in your mother's storage ring before the nocturnal monster people arrive. Those things are not getting my food!"*

Kiru ran up and pressed the dead boar to his ring, making it disappear into one of the slots before making his way back to the grove where they'd established some sort of base. He also decided to help the concussed quist, as he hoped it would provide some useful information on how to escape.

As he turned around and began moving back to the grove, William spoke up again, *"Master, what are you doing?"*

"I'm going to head back and wait until it's day again. I'm not interested in fighting a bunch of nocturnal monster people if I can avoid it," Kiru said.

"But why?" William pressed. *"You're a Sapphire now, Master. Why not test your capabilities and discover your limitations? That way we can get you even stronger. You're not some helpless Bronze anymore."*

That made Kiru pause. The last sentence hit him especially hard. He wasn't helpless anymore. It was something that he personally promised himself that he never would be again. He wanted to get stronger. No, he *needed* to get stronger, and the only way he was going to accomplish that was by pushing himself. His heart began to race with excitement at seeing what he could do, how high he could ascend. *Instead of carrying the quist away, I can just defend him here, right?* he thought before shaking his head in realization, "Damn. William, I think you're making me more like you."

"*I can only conclude by the large amount of data I have on myself that you mean that I am making you more awesome,*" the imp haughtily replied.

"No," Kiru said as he drew his weapons. "More like a battle maniac."

CHAPTER THIRTY-FIVE

Nocturnal Monster People

As Kiru unsheathed his blades and turned, his enhanced hearing from his mask started twitching as a chorus of hoarse, bestial cries came echoing across the rolling hills of the valley. They grew louder as their source neared. From what the psion could tell, there were a dozen foes incoming. To give himself a better vantage point, Kiru moved up towards the top of a nearby hill and peeked around a hook-shaped piece of metal that was partially embedded into the ground.

His eyes widened as he saw the creatures with his own eyes for the first time. They were just like William had showed him but even more grotesque-looking as they neared and more of their features could be discerned. Their heads were far too small for their bodies, with three large eyes placed randomly on their faces. Their mouths looked similar to the quists', but they had gnarly-looking underbites and numerous amounts of needle-like teeth. The things had pieces of metal fused onto different parts of their bodies in place of armor with thick skin growing over their wounds. They had no fur to speak of and their pure black eyes and drooling maws spoke of their savage hunger.

He used Imp's Label on the lead creature as it got closer.

Name: Unknown
Race: Nocturnal Monster Person
Rank: Gold, Zeta Tier
Mana Type: Unknown
Path: Unknown
Status: Hostile

A hostile tribe of mutants that hunt at night and are known to kill humanoid beings.

"Nocturnal Monster Person is literally the name of their race?" Kiru asked William via Telepathy.

The imp gave the mental equivalent of a shrug. *"The data I've collected from the ship has nothing on these creatures. So, I gave them a useful name that accurately describes them. Don't forget that we used to call umbrafangs "flesh wolves" before we tasted their blood. Once we collect a biological sample for us to ingest, I should be able to provide more data,"* he explained. *"In the meantime,"* William sent, and then numerous areas on the incoming monsters' bodies were highlighted in Kiru's vision, weak points for the psion to exploit, *"let's bathe in the blood of our enemies. Then we can return so I can finally have my meal!"*

Kiru tightened his grip on his blades and rushed out to meet his foes. When the monster people noticed the psion, their heads all locked on him and they moved with renewed vigor and bloodlust, shrieking a battlecry in unison. On quick survey, nine had spears and shields while only three wielded crude great swords. Their eyes, armpits, thighs, and waists were all highlighted in his vision, the waists notably lower on the four-armed variants with two legs versus their quadruped brethren.

Given that their cultivation was multiple ranks below his, Kiru decided to test out his Sapphire body some more and only fight them with his blades. He ran forward and closed the distance in only a couple of seconds, attacking the lead monster first with Demon's Inciting Strike. His blades easily bit into the beast's flesh, easily amputating its right arm. Without even looking back at his opponent, Kiru reached both of his blades back, using his Fu Tao to hook into its open wound and throw the beast at its incoming allies. All three were sent flying and skipped on the ground like a stone on water due to the sheer power of the throw.

The remaining nine all growled and snarled but paused their charge at Kiru's sudden display of strength. They all then lowered their weapons to point at the psion and carefully began spreading out to encircle him.

"No way I'm going to let that happen," Kiru said before taking one of his blades and hooking it onto the hook of the other. He grinned before he used a rarely utilized sword form, Pitchfork the Hay. Kiru began spinning his blade in a circle like a bladed lasso. The handle guards of his weapons were blades as well, so it was just as deadly an attack. The psion quickly got the speed of his spinning up to blinding and then began tearing through the monsters, his weapons easily breaking their spears and blades and slashing through their flesh with even greater ease. In just a couple of seconds, four of the monsters had been killed, their black blood spraying out in violent bursts as they fell. That last part brought William much excitement. Even Kiru couldn't help but give a smile. This was fun!

The five monsters still living all backed away, their faces betraying their fear. The three Kiru had previously knocked on their asses had gotten back up and regrouped with their comrades. Their leader—the one whose left arm Kiru had cut off—stood proudly in front, despite an obvious nervous twitch and the pain it clearly felt from its still bleeding stump of a limb. It bared its needle teeth at the psion and spoke something in its deep and croaking dialect.

Kiru furrowed his brow in confusion but quickly realized that the words hadn't been spoken to him but rather to the monster's allies. Kiru figured out that it was some sort of order because, right after those words, he felt all eight of them release a pulse of chaos mana from within. *A technique, then?* he thought. The psion didn't know which techniques they had just activated or if they were all the same one, but he assumed they were different ones based off of what happened next.

The leader regrew a new arm where the stump had been. The new limb began to sprout some small tentacles as well. Its other arm suddenly sprouted out even longer tentacles. The others behind the leader all had varying reactions. The metal on one's body stuck out like randomly adorned armor, while another swelled up until it doubled in size. Two more grew new limbs in seemingly random areas, while three of them were somehow drawn to one another as if by magnetic force and fused together.

"What the fuck?" Kiru said as he saw what the three monsters had become. They were now a hideous conglomeration of at least fifty eyeballs and a dozen tentacles. Though the psion was loathe to do it, he licked the blood off one of his blades to update the information that William could provide him with, shuddering and suppressing a retch as he did so. "William, could you please tell me what in the abyss I'm seeing here?"

All he got was an emotionless "*Updating Info,*" from William.

The good news, from what Kiru could sense, was that they were all still at the lowest tier of Gold, even with their sudden mutations. So, until he got more concrete data from William about any serious danger, he would push himself to deal with these foes using only his blades, not any techniques—or at least not any techniques directly on them. *It improved itself with mana; it's only fair that I can use some mana on myself to be faster and stronger,* he thought. His strength had increased dramatically with his multiple ascensions, and it was time to continue to familiarize himself more intimately with what a Sapphire could do. These enemies were the perfect practice targets to get used to his new strength and improve his control before he inevitably had to face the warden.

The lead monster person let out a war cry, and the now six others following him all charged at Kiru with feral bloodlust.

Kiru bent his legs and concentrated his mana in them. Using Telekinesis, he jumped forward in a flash, clearly faster than the monster people were expecting. He used Stag's Desperate Charge, impaling the leader straight through their chest with both of his hook blades. The force of the strike was so intense that it literally ripped their torso straight off their waist, bisecting them. Kiru landed on the ground, impaling the monster's torso into the ground.

Another one of the creatures—the one that had doubled in size—wielded their great sword like it was a dagger in a reverse grip and came slamming it down to stab the psion. Kiru easily jumped away to dodge the strike, causing the torso of the leader to get crushed to paste. While in the air, Kiru spun and used Sweep the Barn to cut off the giant's wrist. Two of the others threw their spears at the psion, thinking him to be an easy target while in midair. Kiru proved them wrong, however, when he used a burst of Telekinesis to fling himself forward and decapitate the giant by using Hammer the Boards.

Kiru continued to fly forward for a few seconds, before landing on the ground and turning to face the remaining enemies. All of that only took about five seconds, and Kiru grinned like a madman, feeling the excitement his new strength brought. William's analysis of the blood also finished at that point, too, as information appeared about one of the monster people—the one with pieces of metal jutting out from their body.

> **Name:** Unknown
> **Race:** Zier'Knacht
> **Rank:** Gold, Zeta Tier
> **Mana Type:** Chaos
> **Path:** Chaotic Growth
> **Status:** Hostile
>
> *The Zier'Knacht are a race that have come about from the remnant prisoners and experiments that remained in Gaal'cothdreek-dun after the ship's downfall. Their culture worships the mountain as it protects them from "the Evils Above" while they hunt the beings below, especially the quist. They view the quist as blights—fellow prisoners who survived but chose to stay in the old ways, not embracing the mountain's blessings and thus, allowing the memory of the evil that had once enslaved them to live on.*

Kiru took all that information in an instant. It gave him a better idea as to what the things were but didn't help him better understand what they'd done to morph themselves.

William then spoke up, as if he were reading the psion's mind. *"Their blood told me about their technique too, Master."*

> **Chaotic Growth:** The technique that is the namesake for the path that all Zier'Knacht take. They imbue their bodies with chaos mana, causing randomized and often grotesque temporary mutations.

The information made sense to the psion. They all had mutated in random ways. He used Imp's Label once more to highlight new weak points on his enemies' now-changed bodies.

The remaining five Zier'Knacht all hesitated at the sight of their decapitated ally and Kiru's smiling form, but they quickly regained their courage and charged at Kiru.

He easily handled the others with his blades. He even let one of them try and hit him in the side in order to test his aura. The Zier'Knacht's weapon broke before it even could touch the psion. The only one of the monstrous people who provided even a modicum of true challenge was the opponent that had become a conglomeration of eyes and tentacles. Every single eye was a weak point in Kiru's vision, but it could regenerate them and also fire them like projectiles. It chose to keep its distance, seeming to assume the psion could only do close-range attacks. It was wrong.

Kiru growled in annoyance. "Okay, I'm done with just using my swords. Time to try a technique out *directly*." At his words, Kiru fired a full-powered Brainstorm at the mutant. The mana-charged electricity fried its numerous eyes and limbs at once. The thing shrieked as it sizzled, its form blackening before it collapsed, becoming nothing more than a smoking husk on the ground.

"Now that was awesome!" William cheered. *"See, you didn't need to run at all."*

Kiru nodded in agreement with the imp. "Did you notice that in that description it said the mountain 'protects them from the Evils Above?' It's a hunch, but I bet that means the mountain is the way to the next level," Kiru said.

"Your logic is sound, Master. Based off of my map of the original floor and the information that brought about that deduction, I calculate a 63.8% chance of that being correct. So far from what I've found, there are no other pathways up," William said. His voice turned faux-melancholy as he said, *"I guess we'll just have to keep slaughtering our way through these Zier'Knacht to get to their sacred mountain. Oh, well."*

Kiru shook his head as a wry smile grew. "Yeah, you sound real sad about it." Then he heard some squeaking off in the distance. He turned back to where the disoriented quist had been and now saw that their two companions had returned and were helping them stand once more. "But you know, I think there is a way to get more information about this place and hopefully increase our odds of success . . ."

CHAPTER THIRTY-SIX

Quist

The two rat people watched Kiru warily, trying to get their compatriot to focus while not losing sight of the psion. Despite being cautious, their gazes also contained a mix of awe and gratitude.

Kiru didn't approach them right away. He waited until they'd aroused the third was pulled out of their concussion-like stupor. They initially took a few steps back and made to run when he began to approach them but stopped after he did and putting his hands out in a placating gesture when it seemed like they were about to bolt. He'd already sheathed his weapons and removed his mask to look less intimidating. "I'm not here to hurt you," he said, intentionally making his voice sound lighter and calmer to ease the trio. "My name is Kiru, and I'm . . . lost. Can you help me find the way out of here?" he asked.

The quist all turned their heads in different directions, clearly confused. The one on the left—the tallest and skinniest of the three—began to squeak and chitter at Kiru, making various noises as air whistled through their buck teeth. Though Kiru couldn't understand what they were saying, he noticed that the quist was pointing past him and toward the multiple dead Zier'Knacht, littering the tall grass.

"Oh, them? You won't have to worry about that. If more come, I'll deal with them," Kiru said before drawing a line across his neck and making a clicking noise, indicating he'd killed them. After that statement, some more roars, growls, snarls, and cries of pain could be heard far off in the distance. "At least, I dealt with *this* group of Zier'Knacht. As I said, my name is Kiru, and I'm a friend."

The quist seemed a little more relaxed but still looked at Kiru suspiciously. The smallest of the rat people, the one in the center, then gripped their stomach before an impressively large growl came from their belly.

"Oh, I guess I did take your dinner," Kiru said before activating the grid on his storage ring. He paused as his vision caught on something in there. His mom's secret items . . . he could see them now that he was a Sapphire. There were two rings and a large scroll. His heart raced as he desperately wanted to look at them, but he needed to focus on gaining the trust of the quist first. *If I give them some of the boar they were hunting, that'll hopefully buy me some goodwill,* he thought.

"Master, that pig is mine. Don't you dare—" William spoke up, but Kiru ignored his protests and summoned the dead farigaboar on the ground beside him.

The three quist let out cries of fear and jumped back but quickly stopped as they saw the dead insectoid pig they'd killed seemingly appearing out of thin air.

"Master, I demand you store that boar back in the Flamebringer's ring at once," William said, referring to Kiru's mother by the nickname that she'd gained in her youth.

"I can get you another boar, William," Kiru replied via Telepathy to keep their conversation secret. *"Think of how much more* useful *it will be to have the favor of some natives,"* he sent, intentionally using the word "useful" to drive home a point.

William let out a mental *harumph. "While your logic is wise, Master, I am not a being of pure logic. I am a proud imp and the familiar of a conqueror. I should be able to take what I want, and what I want is to eat this boar now, not some mangy underweight substitute later."*

Kiru sighed. *"How about I cut off a whole leg for you to eat now and let the quist have the rest? I know you like to eat, but you're not going to be able to consume all of this thing in one sitting. You'd get a stomachache."*

William grunted in annoyance but quickly agreed to the deal. The quist began to lean in and inspect the boar Kiru quickly put a finger out for them to wait. He took out his psyslime blade, albeit slowly so as to not scare them, and after he'd fully unsheathed it, changed it into an axe. Then, in one clean swing, he cut off one of the creature's hind legs. Blood sprayed out in an arc, covering his boots.

Fortunately, the quist weren't disturbed by this. They did, however, jump back in surprise when Kiru summoned William out from his core.

The imp just wrinkled his nose at the rat people before he took the proffered leg from Kiru and began munching down on it, not caring about the mess he was making. William was moaning in pleasure with each mouthful, being unnecessarily loud, in Kiru's opinion.

Kiru noticed the rat people's faces turn from fear to confusion at the floating three-eyed imp before looking back at the boar, settling on wide-eyed hunger. Sensing an opportunity, Kiru quickly chopped off three more legs and offered them to the trio of quist. They looked at each other and squeaked before quickly taking the boar meat and scarfing it down like they hadn't eaten in weeks. Kiru idly wondered if that was the case or not. The three ate with such ferocity, it even rivaled William, their two large front teeth breaking the bones of the beast's legs with ease. After only a minute, all three of them had devoured their meals and now looked at the psion expectantly.

Kiru put up another finger, indicating for them to wait, and cut off a large slab of meat off the flank. The gray and white meat was unsettlingly slimy. The psion suppressed a grimace before putting it in his storage ring. He may eat it later, but only after it was thoroughly cooked. Kiru then pushed the rest of the dead boar towards the three clearly hungry quist.

All three pairs of eyes widened in amazement at Kiru's gift. They all then fell to their knees and began bowing to him like he was some sort of deity.

"Oh, now *this* I can get behind." William laughed as he finished off the last of his meal. "Yes, grovel before your superiors, plebs!"

Then he furrowed his brow as the quist looked up and chittered at him. "Excuse me?" he asked, clearly offended.

"Can you understand them, William?" Kiru asked.

"Kind of," the imp answered. "I didn't gain access to a cipher for their language, but I picked up some basic information. I imagine that I can attain complete understanding after a couple days of listening to them speak, though."

"Okay, so what are they saying?" Kiru pressed.

"They are claiming that they are praising *you*, not me," William answered, affronted. "It sounds like they're implying I'm not . . . worthy of praise? The audacity of these rats! If they only knew how much I contribute to your success. I mean, I at least provide a 42.7% increase in our survival!"

The smallest quist then spoke up.

"They are . . . asking if you are a god," William interpreted.

"No!" Kiru answered emphatically as he shook his head. He didn't trust William to be honest if left to answer that particular question for him. Though Kiru didn't speak their strange language, he got the message across.

William rolled his eyes.

The small quist then began speaking again, this time in excitement.

"It says that if you're not a god then you must be a . . . chain-breaker? No, that's not right. Freedom-bringer? That's close, but—ah, that's it! Liberator," William said.

The small quist kept speaking before the other two chittered in the exact same pattern and began bowing to him over and over again.

"Well . . . that's interesting," William said.

"What?" Kiru asked.

"Apparently the quist have a prophecy about some hero that would come down from the heavens to save them from the prison the arboth had put them in. Not a god, but a mortal warrior whom the gods or . . . realm?—I can't tell—had blessed to smite the arboth after the . . . demons they created broke free. Hey, I am a proud demon, you know, and I will not stand for this abyssal propaganda," William protested.

"William!" Kiru interjected.

William sighed and continued interpreting. "Whatever, apparently the arboth created some demons that had escaped this place after it crashed, leaving it in ruins and the prisoners to their fate. These rat people think you are some sort of prophesied 'liberator' who will free them from their prison. They say that they are grateful for your gift and await your orders."

"Oh . . . um, can you ask them where the exit is? Is it by the mountain like I thought?" Kiru asked William.

William did his best to mimic the quists' language. It was a little grating, but after a minute of trying, the imp was able to choppily convey the question.

The three quist all converged, murmuring to themselves as they deciphered William's question and figured out the answer. Eventually, they separated, and the smallest quist spoke up once more.

"They say they don't know for certain, but their ancestral history tells them that metal rained from the sky on the day the demons revolted. Well, that makes sense," William said, nodding to the piles of moss-covered metal and debris around them. "And that the most notable area had a mountain form from a hole in the sky? What a weird history. No wonder they turned out so strangely," William said.

"Well, that does reinforce the idea that the mountain is where we need to go," Kiru said. "What's the probability of it being the right target destination, now?"

"After that supplemental data . . . 80.2%," William replied.

Kiru shrugged. "I've had worse odds," he said before another set of Zier'Knacht snarls echoed out from the valley, though this time much closer. "Okay, I've got new orders for the quist. There's no way I'm going to babysit a bunch of Silvers all night or to play the prophesied hero. So, William, tell them to hide and stay safe, until either I return or a path is opened up for them. I don't want to wait out the night any longer. I'm a damn Sapphire now. If they really are in danger, tell them to head towards the mountain as that's where I'm going."

William complied, though based off of how hard of a time he was having speaking the quists' language and how unpleasant his words sounded to Kiru's ears, the psion didn't have full confidence that the message had been conveyed exactly as intended. Still, despite that, the three rat people all bowed in deference to the psion before shoving the boar's remains under a distinctly moss-free rock and squeezing themselves in small pre-dug holes under different pieces of metal and stone interspersed throughout the area around them.

William just stared at the pig hungrily as they did that.

The quist managed to hide just in time, too, as another half dozen more Zier'Knacht came into view.

CHAPTER THIRTY-SEVEN

Little Flame

After Kiru handled the newest contingent of monstrous raiders—with even more ease than the first group—he pressed forward to find a small hill to press his back to. He settled down and let the thick blue grass cover him. Feeling a bit of relative safety, he activated the grid of his mother's storage ring once more. There, he saw the three slots he'd been prohibited from accessing when he first got the ring.

Eager to see what his mother had left him, he pulled out what was in the first slot. It was a signet ring that contained a flawless ruby in its center. Engraved in the jewel was an image of a bird—a phoenix, perhaps—emerging from an erupting volcano. Kiru instantly realized what it was: a signet ring of the royal family of Anor'Voren. His mother was sister to the queen, making the psion technically a noble of not one but two nations. After Kiru had received his library internship assignment, he had spent much time researching the elven nation to learn more about his mother and her people. So, he knew without a doubt that the ring was meant to prove his identity when he came across any elves of the royal family.

The next slot was another ring, but this one was even more exciting. It had an orange jewel in its center. There was no description for it nor piece of parchment explaining its function. Given he had no reason to not trust his mother, he slipped it on the middle finger of his right hand and . . . nothing happened. He sensed that the ring was giving off some mana; it even felt a little warm against his skin. Because his sense of touch was warped by what he had done to get himself to Tier-Two Ruby, he wondered if it would have actually caused severe pain to anyone else.

Not knowing what else to do, he fed it some mana. Still nothing. *Maybe the third item has something that could help*, he thought before pulling out what was in there: a set of scrolls. One had a wax seal with the elven royal family crest on it. The other two weren't sealed at all. Kiru unfurled the bigger one.

My Little Flame,

If you are reading this, it means that you are a Sapphire, and I am no longer by your side. My heart aches knowing I cannot be there to see the man you have become, but I trust in your strength and the path you must walk. Plus, by the time I'm writing this, you'll have already whipped that impudent little imp into a pretty steadfast little familiar, despite his bloodthirsty nature.

There were times when I thought I was better off bringing you home to Anor'Voren. Times when I thought my family would know better, but I couldn't risk it. First, I didn't want word of your identity to leak. Second, I wanted you to grow strong, to learn the ways of the world without the burden of your lineage weighing you down. You, my little flame, now have something most nobles don't—perspective. You can now understand the wants and desires of both the ruling class and the commoners. Even with that perspective, my little flame, you must never forget who you are. You are more than a prince; you are a cultivator and the son of two mighty warriors. Though your fire mana core may be ruined, I see that fire of ambition inside you. I have no doubt that, despite that, your inner flame will become a beacon of hope, a light in a world that has seen too much darkness.

The items you seek, scattered across the nations, are not just relics of your father's reign. They are pieces of a puzzle that, when assembled, will reveal the truth and restore justice to our land. Each item holds a part of his spirit, and through them, you will come to know him as I did.

Remember Kiru, that true strength lies not in power or titles but in the love and compassion you show to others. Lead with your heart like your father did, and you will find allies in the most unexpected places. Trust in yourself, for you are destined for greatness. Still, remember when you do have to fight, that at the end of the day, what matters is who is left standing. So, don't worry about the "proper" way to be an opponent. Just beat them. Remember rule #1: Always fight dirty.

I have watched over you every day, and though my soul is with the Archfey, I will continue to observe you from beyond, as my love for you is eternal. I have left you a few things that should help you when you journey to my homeland. The first is my signet ring. Though it has the royal crest, it also possesses a drop of my blood crystallized inside the jewel. Show it in addition to the sealed scroll when you come into contact with a royal guard. The next is a summoning ring. Just put a drop of blood on the jewel in its center to claim ownership. Then, send a small amount of mana inside it. What it will summon is a surprise, but I will give you a hint. Though you may not be able to use fire mana directly anymore, that doesn't mean you can't use it at all. The last thing I leave you is my image, so that you know I am always with you.

Go forth, my little flame, and reclaim what is rightfully yours. Restore our family's honor, and stop the dragons from invading once more. May you be the spark that ignites the changes needed in the world. I believe in you, now and always.
With all my love,

Mother

Kiru's eyes began to well up with tears. He always got a little emotional when thinking about his beloved mother, but to receive this message from her after her death was the greatest gift he'd ever received. The tears then began to flow down his cheeks when he grabbed the other unsealed scroll and rolled it open. There he saw a drawing of his mother. The artist had been quite skilled as it captured her visage with amazing attention to detail. Kiru did notice that his mother looked a little younger in the image than he remembered. Her face had a few less wrinkles, and her curly red hair was less frizzy than it was when he was growing up.

Surturia had a warm, confident smile on her face, conveying both her power and capacity for kindness. "Hi, Mom," Kiru whispered before sniffling and wiping the tears from his eyes.

"Wow, the artist was able to capture her likeness so well. I can tell the Flamebringer possessed great power even just by looking at the image. Who drew it?" William asked, showing a surprising sense of tenderness.

Kiru looked at the bottom of the image. He couldn't make out the scribbled signature, but he could see the date. "I don't know for sure, but it looks like this was done in 885 Post-Ragnarok. So, it was before I was born," he said.

"Do you think it was your father?" William asked.

Kiru smiled. "I'm not sure, but it would be around the time they were together. And I do like the idea that he made this," he said before taking in the drawing for a few more moments and then putting it back in his storage ring. "Let's try this summoning ring again." He pricked one of his fingers just slightly and let a couple drops of his blood land on the jewel. The jewel went from an orange to a deep red and physically shook on his finger.

Kiru stood up and, following the instructions his mother gave him, fed a small bit of mana into the ring. Out from the jewel burst a giant snake made entirely of orange flame. It was a cobra as long as a giant constrictor, and its fiery body encircled the psion a couple times. The burning scales around its head flared out as it looked down at Kiru.

Despite its intimidating form and his conflicts with snake cultists back in Imakandi, Kiru felt no hostility from the elemental serpent and felt none in return. Wanting to gain more information about it, he used Imp's Label. Fortunately, it seemed that his ownership of the ring allowed the psion to garner more information.

Name: Little Flame
Race: Fire Elemental, Serpent
Rank: Sapphire
Mana Type: Fire
Path: Gem Beast
Status: Loyal

An elemental being created by skilled fire mana cultivators of the royal house of Anor'Voren. The creature was enhanced by treasures and powerful items to reach Sapphire and bound to a jewel enchanted by master elven rune-smiths. This being once belonged to Surturia Barat'nel, sister to the queen of Anor'Voren, before her passing; she named it in honor of her only son. Due to the artificial nature of this creature, being formed by cultivators instead of being birthed naturally, it doesn't contain much intelligence or sentience. The serpent can be summoned for thirty minutes a day as it's bound to the jewel and needs to recharge before being able to interact with the outside world again. Its true being is attached to the gemstone so even if it is defeated in battle, it will never truly die as long as the gem remains.

Tears started to flow down Kiru's face as he looked at the serpent. "Little Flame, huh?"

The serpent nodded, seeming to understand.

Goosebumps traveled down Kiru's skin in shock at the creature's response. "Can . . . Can you talk?" he asked.

It just hissed, showing its teeth and extending its forked tongue. No words came out, but Kiru could somehow understand its meaning. It was asking for orders.

"Master, this is possibly the most amazing gift I've ever seen," William said. *"I calculate we are now 212% more intimidating with this by our side. Or, to put it in laymen's terms, we're really fucking scary. Can I ride it?"*

"You can fly now. Why would you want to ride it?" Kiru asked via Telepathy.

"Why wouldn't you want to ride it?" William sent back.

Shrugging, Kiru summoned William and ordered the serpent to allow the imp to sit atop it. Apparently, the flames didn't hurt the imp at all. The elemental was clearly lacking in intelligence, as it still just stood there, silently waiting for Kiru's next command.

William shouted a declaration of how great he was, which was immediately met with a chorus of roars and howls from all directions. Then, roughly thirty Zier'Knacht appeared from within the tall grass. Kiru could tell that all of them were still at Gold, just like the others, so they were no significant threat.

Little Flame let out a hiss of anger at the incoming foes. Sensing an opportunity, Kiru thought that the monstrous people would not only make a good set of practice dummies for himself but also for his new elemental companion.

"Attack," he said.

Little Flame let out a cry that was equal parts glee and fury and surged forward towards the Zier'Knacht with impressive speed. In a matter of seconds, it had bitten two opponents in half and set half of them ablaze with a fire-breath attack. The rest of the Zier'Knacht started to activate their Chaotic Growth technique but were still no match for Little Flame. The serpent just rolled over a handful of them with its fiery body, burning them on contact while William cackled maniacally on top of it. The imp aided in firing a couple of Brainstorms at the monstrous people, burning them with electricity instead of flame. In less than a minute, they had all been killed.

Small fires burned all around them, setting the remains of their opponents ablaze. "Well done, both of you," Kiru said.

William gave a wide grin while Little Flame just looked at the psion expectantly.

"I'll take it from here," Kiru said and raised his ring to bring the serpent back in.

"Wait, Master, but why? With me and my mount here, we can wipe out all of our foes in one night, leaving only ashes," William said.

Kiru shook his head. "It can only be out for thirty minutes a day. With how big this place is, even with your powers, I don't think we can eliminate them all in that time," Kiru said before bringing the elemental back into his ring and recalling William back into his core at the same time. "Besides, I can't let you two have all the fun."

CHAPTER THIRTY-EIGHT

Onwards & Upwards

Kiru spent the next ten weeks on Level Three fighting his way towards the mountain. Now, it wouldn't have taken the psion near as long if he could have aimed there directly, but there were a few mitigating factors. First, he was making sure to kill all Zier'Knacht he came across. Their settlements were scattered all around the mountain they worshipped, and the psion didn't want to leave any enemies behind to follow him. Next, there was the space mana that was very prevalent on this floor. It made it even larger than William's previous numbers had calculated. Kiru concluded that the entire floor could be larger than even the entire Kingdom of Blades.

Third was the geography. As he got closer to the mountain, the rolling plains became more and more barren and rocky until it resembled a warped version of the Wastelands back in Imakandi—barren of all but the most dangerous of creatures that were savage enough to survive in such lands. Of course, that included multiple populations of abominations. They seemed immune to physical damage, which was frustrating, but Kiru fortunately had many ways to attack with mana at range. So, he kept his distance from them as much as possible. He found that Telekinetic Bolt was particularly effective at eliminating them.

The landscape became a winding maze of stones and more than a few traps that the Zier'Knacht had as defensive measures, as Kiru continued to push deeper in and closer to the purple-and-black mountain. There were plants as well, but mostly the terrifying fleshing trees, doing their best to eat anything and anyone who got too close. He encountered no more quist on his trek. The rat people seemed to stay as far away from the mountain and the direction he was going as possible.

Lastly, he wanted to push himself, to gain a better grasp on his skills and better control of his increased powers, too. The Zier'Knacht didn't seem nearly as dangerous or battle-hungry during the twenty-four-hour day cycles, so Kiru would sometimes wait and take on multiple villages during the night to push himself.

William didn't mind, as long as Kiru truly took the time to get his daily "fix" of violence.

Little Flame was especially effective in helping Kiru with his extermination jobs. The elemental serpent didn't have much of a personality, but it did seem to enjoy doing one activity above all else: burning things. When it came to the Zier'Knacht, Kiru happily obliged. He viewed the serpent as a pet of sorts, its desire to burn things similar to William's thirst for violence. Because of that trait and the fact that it was a gift from his mother, Little Flame soon became very precious to the psion.

Little Flame was also given a special job when fighting the Zier'Knacht: killing younglings. During his initial times fighting the Zier'Knacht, Kiru had hesitated at the thought of fighting their children, but when he saw one of the monstrous people he was fighting literally explode and die to give birth, spawning a dozen spider-like babies who began to eat her still-warm body before charging at him, he lost any sense of mercy for the brutal mutants. Little Flame was fortunately *very* thorough in making sure none remained alive nor tried to hide in Kiru's armor.

One day, when he was sitting down to take a short break, Kiru asked William if he could use Imp's Label on himself to create a personal status page. That way, the psion could keep better track of his own strengths and progress. It took the imp the better part of that day to figure out how to do it, but William was successful in configuring Imp's Label to show Kiru's information when called on by the psion. William even added extra information that he proudly declared would be useful to his master.

Name: Kiru Chromebane
Race: Half-Elf, Half-Human (Psion)
Rank: Sapphire, Tier 1
Mana Type: Mental (Sapphire Tier 1), Fire (Inert)
Path: Path of the Puppet Master (Mental), None (Fire)
Techniques: Telekinesis, Telepathy, Subjugation, Brainstorm
Evolved Techniques: Telekinetic Bolt, Telepathic Screech, Telekinetic Shield, Telekinetic Air Shield, Flight, Telekinetic Air Beam
Combined Techniques: Telekinetic Storm Bolt, Telekinetic Domination Bolt
Weapons: Fu Tao, Psyslime
Sword Forms: Monarch's Razors, Cruel Mantis
Artifacts Acquired: 3/7 (Psion Circlet, Psyslime, Mask of Fenrir)
Companions: William the Breaker of Wills, Little Flame
Special Skills: Imp's Label, Summon Flame Elemental Serpent

During his time fighting and training himself against the Zier'Knacht, Kiru had improved on his ability to adapt or, as William labeled it, "evolve" his techniques. Fighting actual living beings rather than artificial constructs, he was able to practice and truly get a handle on Telepathic Screech. He also improved his control of Telekinesis to an even greater extent to create a number of stable evolved techniques from it. The psion was able to hone his skills with Telekinetic Bolt on the abominations. Using the protective domes he could create around him to mentally guide the air, Kiru was also able to create a powerful beam of spiraling air to fire out from his fist. It dissipated out only a few feet away from his body at first, but when he exerted enough control on the air to keep it contained and spiral, it shot out for fifty feet to deadly effect.

Using that same logic to control and compress the air, Kiru was able to form a temporary shield by condensing an area with his mental mana during his fifth week of traveling. In truth, he was elated by his discoveries. Before coming down into this nightmarish prison, Kiru had had no idea he could use his techniques in such varying, creative ways. He had known it was a risk to limit himself to only four techniques when he ascended himself to Ruby back in Imakandi, but he knew that it made his techniques more powerful too. Now he realized that the number of techniques wasn't the limiting factor at all; it was his own imagination. From his four initial techniques, he discovered eight new ways to use and improve on them when he counted flight too.

Kiru even discovered on the third week how to combine Telekinetic Bolt and Subjugation so that he could control the mind of an opponent from a distance. It took him about a week of practice and meditating on the particulars of both techniques before he was able to combine them adequately. He presumed it was because, while Bolt was a purely damaging attack, Subjugation was more nuanced, focusing on subtler and more covert means of achieving the technique's intended goal. Eventually, though, the psion was able to meld the pure power of the bolt with the brain-targeting aspect of Subjugation. The biggest success in that arena was forcing back the speed of the bolt, as when it went too fast, it just punched a hole through the Zier'Knachts' small heads.

The one thing that had kept eluding him was combining Telekinetic Bolt and Telepathic Screech. He'd seen it done so easily in William's replayed memory, but he found himself unable to repeat the result. He moved about in the same manner to combine techniques, working to move even more fluidly than usual, but he kept failing to produce the desired effect. Often, the bolt would fade, causing an ear-piercing screech to echo out or the screech would seem to be more of a mutter, as the worst any Zier'Knacht he attempted to try it out on only seemed to recoil and raise an eyebrow in confusion as Kiru could sense only the hint of any telepathic noise. He figured it was proving to be such a challenge because the two techniques he was attempting to fuse were both evolved versions. *With the challenges required to create these evolved techniques, they must require even more fine control to combine them into something more powerful*, Kiru thought as he meditated on it one morning.

Kiru began to adopt a nocturnal cycle too, to be fully energized to fight the monstrous cultivators. In the day, he'd spend some time hunting the beasts that called the third floor home, even trying some farigaboar after he'd thoroughly cooked its flesh. While the meat was very rough and chewy, he couldn't tell much difference between that and overcooked steak once he'd essentially burnt it. Kiru did admit to William that the imp was right. After eating so much crab, having something else—even unseasoned insect-pork—was *very* satisfying.

He chewed on a piece of bacon that both he and William discovered was quite literally the best they'd ever had as he looked up at the mountain he now stood at the base of. He could feel the chaos mana exuding from the structure. *No wonder they worship this thing*, Kiru thought when pondering the Zier'Knacht's religion. He could sense more powerful members of the monstrous race scattered in a few villages on the mountain itself. *Likely their elites.*

Kiru knew that, while he considered the Zier'Knacht monstrous, they likely thought the same of him. He'd been exterminating the hostile, murderous people by the dozens, not even feeling bad about it, especially seeing how savage and murderous they were, right from born. Part of him thought he should stop, but he knew he couldn't trust them to not hurt him when he had his back turned. He also had no doubt they would continue their nightly raids attempting to massacre the quist.

Kiru didn't know everything about the quist but, based off the information that William had acquired and passed on, they were a peaceful people who tended to keep to themselves. A tribe who wanted to commit genocide on their entire race and any other peoples they came into contact with was not a tribe worth keeping around, in Kiru's opinion. *They want a genocide, they'll get one*, Kiru thought, resolving himself to wipe the Zier'Knacht clean from the realm along with the arboth.

He idly wondered if William's bloodthirsty nature was rubbing off on him too much but quickly dismissed his concern. Kiru's goals and the path he intended to take to achieve them had been littered with corpses, and he knew that there would be much more violence to come. He had enemies who would not just step down, so he resolved to become strong enough to make them. Many cultivators spent their lives fighting. Kiru just had bigger goals than most, which required even more violence.

He looked up at the mountain's peak once again. "One more mountain for me to conquer," he said. "You ready, William?"

"Abyss, yeah! Of course I am. I'm with Kiru the Conqueror," he said.

Kiru put on his mask, gave a wolfish grin and began his ascent.

The warden slammed a tentacle down on his panel in fury. Many of the monitoring eyestalks weren't functional on the third level—which had somehow morphed into its own unique biosphere with an artificial light source providing ultraviolet radiation, but he was able to discern small snippets of what was going on from a distance. Mal'throk noticed that the insect was making his way towards the mountain of rubble. The damn mental mana thief was exterminating all sorts of creatures and descendants of slaves that had made the floor their home. This pest was becoming more of a plague.

"He's already reached Sapphire. I must eliminate him before he ascends any higher," the arboth growled. When that damn familiar of the boy had blown up an automaton and destroyed the path up, he had been shocked. The imp had even damaged some of Mal'throk's forces beyond repair. The warden snarled when he thought about it. To be utterly humiliated by some whelp of a lesser race and his pet demon was an insult he couldn't bear. It was a memory he could never share with the hivemind once he'd repopulated his race and found their lost god.

He had only had four functioning corrupted automatons left, and they were his only tools left to stop the damn intruder. He needed to kill him, but he also needed the evolved demon. Mal'throk's body had been severely damaged during the Harbingers' revolt, and the connection the imp now had with the Chaos Core after directly contacting one of its relays made the creature's body perfect for the arboth's needs to fix himself. The Chaos Core was what stabilized the warden and kept him alive. So the imp was just the solution he needed. "I need that demon's biomatter," he said to himself.

Since the original ways up and out of the fourth level were no longer usable now that the imp had blown up the tunnel, Mal'throk had ordered his construct minions to search the area for any flaw in the walls of the chamber. Finally, after months, one of the automatons had found an area in one corner from which the vines of chaos mana had burst out, exposing the inner workings of Gaal'cothdreek-dun. Mal'throk gave a harsh laugh when he saw the flaw. He had access to a map of the entirety of the fortress, including the bowels around and in between the levels. Sure, things had clearly changed, but with this, he had a way to find that blasted vermin.

After a few more days of sending one of his minions crawling through narrow spaces, Mal'throk found an opening. It had now been ten weeks since he'd been able to hunt the psion, and he had finally found a way to reach the same level to resume the chase once again. There was a massive pipe that had been clearly warped by chaos mana some time ago due to its strange configuration that was now shooting a constant burst of water out through a wall, which led to the next floor.

Mal'throk sent his four automatons through the hole to find that they were standing atop a waterfall that fed a massive swamp. The warden's monitoring eyestalks had spied a swamp earlier, so he now knew where he was in relation to his target.

What surprised Mal'throk was that there was a village in the swamp. "Quist?" he asked. "Of course the rats of the void would find a way to persist!" he spat out.

Upon noticing the warden's automatons above them, the quist instantly bolted, scattering in all directions to find cover. Mal'throk recalled how it had looked like the psion had helped some sort of beings back in the dark, but the arboth couldn't tell at the time, as his monitoring eye was too far away. Now, seeing the quist before him, the warden realized who the thief had been helping.

"Of course, vermin like to stick together," he said as his constructs raised their blades in unison. He was about to begin the systematic elimination of the quist once and for all, but then he stopped as a cunning idea came to him.

Mal'throk ordered his automatons to attack, only not as targeted. They jumped down and swung their blades wildly. Scores of the rats died with every swing, but nowhere near as many as if Mal'throk had them focus their strikes in a concise, systematic effort. They fled, which had been his goal. "Yes, fools. Lead me to him!" he said, laughing maliciously all the while.

CHAPTER THIRTY-NINE

Battle for the Mountain

Kiru spent the next week going up the mountain. There, he found and fought the more-elite Zier'Knacht. They reminded him of termites and the mountain their mound as they came out of numerous holes that dotted the structure. To his surprise, most of them didn't have any new techniques, still only using Chaotic Growth when needed. It made sense as to why so many of them were at the lowest level of Gold, as the highest rank required at least three according to his knowledge. Still, just because most didn't have more than one technique, that didn't mean that was the case for *all*. Kiru fought a few that could release a pulse of chaos mana from their body as a defensive measure while others had a berserk state they went into, heedless of both friend and foe.

The Zier'Knacht at Ruby were notably tougher as they were naturally stronger than their lower-ranked brethren. They also possessed two of three chaos mana techniques Kiru had observed their people having. He reasoned that they must have their own unique way to reach Ruby because they would have to skip the top tier of Gold entirely to do so with so few techniques. *Maybe something like the Ippo Ogre Method that I used?* he thought. All of the Zier'Knacht had Chaotic Growth. As for if it was their "Chaotic Berserk" or "Chaos Pulse" techniques, as he called them, it seemed to be random. Their leader was by far the strongest, somehow reaching Tier-One Sapphire like the psion.

The Alpha possessed all three techniques, making him strong, fast, and durable. The Alpha's Growth technique gave him eight arms, three of which ended in new heads, which drooled and attempted to bite a piece off of the psion whenever they could. That coupled with the speed and strength of the berserk state added up to the monster really putting up a challenge for Kiru. Where it had strength, though, it had no technique. Monarch's Razors helped, but Cruel Mantis style especially aided the psion as the latter's forms were semi-defensive and allowed him to dismantle and deflect the Alpha's blows repeatedly.

While Kiru's defense was good, it wasn't perfect. He couldn't match the raw strength and speed of the Alpha, either. So that was why the Zier'Knacht managed to land a surprise attack by punching him straight in his stomach with one of their arms that ended in an additional head. The bite force of the extra mouth, coupled with the speed and strength of the Alpha's strike caused the lower part of Kiru's bone armor cuirass to break as he was sent skipping across the stone and metal mountain, nearly falling off the edge.

"Get up, Master!" William shouted. "Use your techniques and show this fool who's the conqueror here."

Kiru stood up quickly and pressed a hand to his side. There was a semicircular wedge missing from his cuirass, with more of it cracking by the second from the bite attack. *That thing's bite strength has to really be something to go through dragon bone*, Kiru thought as he removed his hand and saw blood. He quickly glanced down and exhaled in relief that his wounds were only superficial.

His relief was short-lived as the berserk Zier'Knacht let out a series of roars from its multiple heads and charged him. It jumped up to slam its weapons into Kiru, and he managed to roll out of the way just in time.

"Tch, guess you're right, William," Kiru said as he used Telekinesis on a nearby boulder to slam the Alpha on its side. It turned and roared in the direction the boulder came from, thinking that someone other than Kiru was there. That gave the psion just enough time to form a Telekinetic Storm Bolt at the Alpha.

The monster's body went stiff, and it went sliding back a couple of inches, the combined technique wreaking havoc on it. The Alpha then flared its Chaos Pulse defensive technique to stop the Bolt's effects, and it let out a roar of anger. Before it could do anything else though, Kiru was on it. While it had been fighting against the bolt's power, the psion closed the distance. Kiru reversed the grip of his Fu Tao and punched the Alpha with his bladed guard. That wasn't all, however—he channeled a Telekinetic Air Beam at the same time. The combined force of Kiru's physical strike and technique was more than the Alpha could take, and the monster was sent flying off the mountain.

The bulky, berserk monster crashed hard to the bottom of the mountain and wasn't moving. Kiru wasn't done, though. He then flung two nearby boulders with Telekinesis at the downed monster. He didn't know if it was dead or not, but he was going to make sure. *Lesson number one, always fight dirty*, Kiru thought to himself. When the Alpha's body burst and its blood splashed out in all directions after the boulders struck, Kiru finally heaved a sigh of relief.

He looked out over the valley from his vantage point, and it really was breathtakingly beautiful, even with its dangers. Kiru then noticed movement down below. It looked like a large group of insects from this distance, all of them moving as one cohesive unit. He then noticed their pale forms.

"The quist? What are they doing here?" William asked.

"I don't know," Kiru answered. "It's night right now, so I figured they'd be hiding under some rock somewhere. Let's go find out." He then floated down to meet the rat-like people. There were roughly a hundred of the quist, and they looked both exhausted and terrified. Most seemed like they were about to flee when they saw the psion, but a few loudly cried out over the others which seemed to make them pause, at least momentarily. As Kiru neared, William pointed out that the ones who had cried out were the trio of hunters he'd saved almost three months ago, and took off his mask once more.

The three quist immediately bowed their heads and kneeled. The others behind them looked nervously to each other before the smallest of the three tugged on the rags of the nearest quist behind them to take to their knees. Once that one did, the rest rapidly did as well. The tallest of the three lead quist then began speaking in their chittering, squeaky dialect.

Kiru summoned William. "Translate, please," he said.

"Oh great Liberator, we . . . beseech thee to wall off—No, protect us from the metal protectors? What? Protect you from the protectors? That doesn't make sense," William said.

"What do these 'protectors' look like? Ask them," Kiru said to William.

The floating imp took in a deep inhale through his nostrils and did his best to ask Kiru's question in the quist language.

The rat people cocked their heads in confusion at first, but eventually the middle quist responded.

William listened intently before his face took on a grimace. "Yeah . . . they said that they were hooded purple and black giants with wings and giant blades."

"Shit," Kiru spat. "I can't believe that warden found a way to follow us. Ask them how many of the automatons are there and where they're located."

William communicated the message and they replied, "Four and . . ." William didn't need to finish as Kiru saw all three quist pointing towards the distance. There—a couple miles out but unmistakably there—were the four winged corrupted automatons flying directly towards Kiru.

His heart raced. "William, tell them to hide. Lead them to the caves up top here," he ordered before running up the mountain and waving for the quist to follow. The hundred or so quist quickly stormed towards the psion and began filing into the various caves scattered up top. There was one large cave mouth in the very back. That was where Kiru had found the Alpha previously meditating when he first came up there. Kiru made sure that none of the quist hid in there, as it radiated chaos mana like no other place he'd experienced so far since being stuck in this prison. He wasn't sure if the mana would affect them, but he didn't want to take a chance with the rodent-like peoples' lives. It gave him a sense of unease that he couldn't shake. There was also a massive, crooked bell made from what looked like scrap metal. The psion presumed it was the source of the ringing that made everything go from day to night. *Does that mean the Zier'Knacht ring the bell once night hits, or have they been making it day and night on purpose somehow?* he thought.

Though Kiru had good darkvision, he knew he wanted every advantage he could get, and it would no doubt be easier for him to observe his surroundings and opponents in "daylight" than the dark. So, going off that hunch, he made his psyslime blade change to a mallet and struck the bell. Kiru winced and pressed his hands to his ears as the loud sound reverberated in his head and spread out through the floor. The mountain then shook under his feet and the peak that had been bent forcibly straightened, bringing with it the daylight.

This close to the floor's source of light, Kiru closed his eyes and turned away reflexively, his hands still pressed against his ears. This was not what he intended, to hamper himself in not one but two ways right before a big fight. *Come on shroud, protect me*, Kiru thought in frustration. Strangely, right after that, the ringing subsided and his eyes seemed to adjust quickly to the extremely bright light source.

To his relief, the light also seemed to catch the automatons off-guard, as they all nearly fell out of the sky from the sudden brightness. They were doing their best to recompose themselves, and Kiru let out a wolfish grin even before he put his mask back on, enhancing his senses.

"I've got plenty of new stuff to deal with you, Warden, and this looks like great target practice," Kiru said as he prepared a Telekinetic Domination Bolt at one of the flying constructs. Kiru started channeling his mana through his meridian and after a couple of seconds, the mountain started to shake again. His body then went stiff as he was struck by an aura from behind him, radiating the power of a Tier-Two Sapphire aura.

Kiru fought off the urge to run as he slowly turned back. He then saw that the cave mouth exuding strong chaos aura was actually just a *mouth*. It snapped closed and emerged with the rest of the body attached to it, revealing a bone-chilling creature. A giant centipede made from the stuff of nightmares crawled out from the hole and gazed down at Kiru. It had twenty glowing eyes that looked like orange stars arranged randomly across the entirety of its face. No mouth was discernible on the creature until its face split in half, revealing a crooked maw that separated its eyes both above and below it. The thing was at least thirty feet tall and half as wide, and was made of a conglomeration of purple metal and black flesh. Wrapping around its body in different places as if they were bandages or thick stripes, were the ever-present tendrils of chaos mana that invaded every floor.

It had hundreds of limbs that spiraled around its body in a double helix instead of the expected parallel lines. Kiru let out a gasp as he got a better look at the limbs. They weren't insect legs at all but rather humanoid arms and legs. Noticing the familiar purple hue of the limbs, Kiru looked back to the hideous face of the monster before him and realized he'd seen those strange eyes before.

They were the same eyes present on the automatons down below. The psion could now tell that this thing was somehow composed of hundreds of the automatons compressed, compacted, and fused together. Fighting back the fear, Kiru used Imp's Label.

Name: Chaos Amalgam
Race: Ascended Construct
Rank: Sapphire, Tier 2
Mana Type: Chaos
Path: Chaotic Growth
Status: Hostile

A hideous being brought about from the remains of ruined automatons, biological creatures, and chaos mana, their bodies warped together into one cohesive being. Given the random and wild possibilities that chaos mana can bring about and the sheer abnormality and strength it possesses, the amalgam appears to have gained true sapience unlike any other automatons previously encountered so far. Though a biological sample hasn't been analyzed, it can be inferred that, given its location, the Zier'Knacht worshipped it instead of the mountain, as previously hypothesized, and that it shares both a path and techniques with its followers.

Kiru took in all that information, and his vision highlighted weak points for him to target. There were various joints and junctions along its body, but its numerous eyes were most prominent. "*William, I need your help to fight against this thing's aura,*" he sent through Telepathy.

"*On it, Master,*" the imp replied and flared his own power to boost Kiru's own.

The psion felt his body come fully under his control once more and he reflexively took in a breath. His regaining control was just in time, too, as the amalgam seemed to sense Kiru's scan of it and was *not* happy. It let out a terrifying roar that was equal parts bestial and mechanical before it surged down to bite the psion in half. Kiru formed a Telekinetic Air Shield and commanded his psyslime to change into a large bulky shield under it. The Air Shield took the initial brunt of the strike, but it only lasted a little over a second until the amalgam broke through and struck Kiru's slime shield.

Kiru gritted his teeth as he fought against the force of the construct's attack. While he was holding, the ground underneath him couldn't. The metal and stone under his feet cracked from the immense weight and pressure from the attack. Kiru screamed in surprise as both he and the amalgam were sent plummeting down the mountain. Despite their rapid descent, Kiru still had to keep focus on the monster above him as it was still trying to eat him, its eyes keeping intense focus on him and seeming not to care about what would happen when it hit the ground.

He glanced down to see the ground coming up fast and grinned as an idea came about. Just a second before he would've hit it, Kiru used Telekinesis on himself to abruptly send his body to the side. He had to leave his psyslime stuck in the creature's mouth, but that was fine. He no longer needed to physically touch the item to control it. As Kiru flew off to the side, he mentally ordered his slime shield to change shape, turning into a large lance.

The amalgam crashed to the ground with a *boom* that shook the whole valley and sent a large plume of dust up.

Kiru guided his legs to the ground and slid back, crossing his arms to block the debris from getting in his eyes.

"We got him! Take that, you ugly worm!" William cheered.

While Kiru was hopeful, he had a healthy degree of skepticism that the thing was actually dead. So, he snapped his Mask of Fenrir back on, enhancing his senses once more. Though dust surrounded him on all sides, obscuring his sight and smell, his wolfish hearing was able to pick up something coming from his left . . . and fast.

Kiru leaped back and narrowly missed a sword slash from a corrupted automaton that had approached, before barely deflecting another with his steel blade. The power of the construct couldn't be ignored, and Kiru saw its sword take off a chunk of his blade from the strike. "You cannot escape me, vermin," Mal'throk's voice spoke through the construct.

Kiru's ears twitched, and he ducked a horizontal slash from behind that would've bisected him, before spinning and firing a Telekinetic Air Beam at the construct behind him. The automaton was forced back but not truly damaged. To the psion's surprise, the automaton actually had a small shield composed of raw chaos mana strapped onto its forearm. The shield wriggled as it took Kiru's attack but didn't break. He grunted in frustration and a little concern at having to face them both at once.

"Your tricks have clearly run out. My automatons have adapted to deal with anything you can come up with," Mal'throk spoke through the second automaton.

"Oh, yeah?" Kiru asked, his enhanced senses coupled with William's constant analyses easily picking up on what was happening. The two were about to strike him at once with their blades while a third was flying down toward him and another was hovering farther back, the noise made by the flapping of their wings obvious to him. He came up with an idea to deal with them on the spot, reminded of another one of his mother's lessons: *Strike first. Strike fast. Strike last.* "Then let's see you deal with this trick. Little Flame!" Kiru shouted as he raised his fist up and summoned his elemental from his ring.

Little Flame shot upward and attacked the descending construct, biting down on its head and coiling around its body repeatedly, binding both its arms and legs. The construct shrieked as the flesh and chaos mana burned and bubbled, and the automaton crashed down to the ground in a burning heap, ruined.

Despite Kiru's surprise attack, Mal'throk was still on the offensive as the psion's ears picked up the sounds of the metal beings surging forward towards him. Kiru turned to face the one on his left and mentally ordered Little Flame to deal with the one behind him. Kiru stuck out his hand as he ran towards his opponent. The construct had already closed half the distance and was already beginning its sword swing. With an effort of will, Kiru pulled on the connection he had with the psyslime. There was a loud groan, sounded like it had been ripped through the amalgam's face behind the dust cloud before the slime came flying towards the psion.

Kiru knew he couldn't likely deal with the brute force of the construct directly, but he should still be able to parry if he was creative. He asked William to donate some mental mana to empower his swing, and his steel hook blade managed to knock the great sword down with a use of Clean the Cracks" from his Cruel Mantis style. Kiru heard a loud *pop!* noise from the blade when it struck that he knew wasn't good, but it fortunately held. Even with the empowered swing, the only reason Kiru was able to stop the blade was because he forced it to hit the rocky ground, further halting its momentum. His damaged blade felt wobbly, now only barely holding up. *It won't last another strike,* Kiru thought.

The warden had the construct quickly reach out its free hand to choke the psion, but Kiru was faster. His psyslime came flying in from behind. It was still in the shape of a lance and punched through the back of the automaton's chest. The corrupted construct went stiff, before the light faded from its armored form.

Two down, two to go, Kiru thought before ducking an attack from his left. A projectile flew over him with a *whoosh*, crashing hard into the mountain behind him. The sheer speed of the thing formed a clear path out of the dust cloud he was in, and the psion saw the still-flying automaton readying javelins of pure chaos mana to throw at him. He blocked the next javelin with an Air Shield before reforming his psyslime into a hook blade and running to help Little Flame.

The elemental serpent was keeping the corrupted automaton preoccupied, but the metal foe had already clearly adapted to the power of its flames from the fall of its counterpart. Little Flame spat fireballs at the construct and mixed in strikes from its tail, but the automaton remained unharmed. On the contrary, it was swinging its blade with impressive power and speed, managing to cut Little Flame again and again, truly dealing damage to him. Seeing as the element of surprise was now gone, Kiru commanded the serpent to return to his ring.

The dust had finally settled and the psion jumped back so that both of the automatons were in front of him. They were slightly to his right while the still form of the amalgam was to his left.

"Why won't you die?" Mal'throk growled.

"You're going to need something a lot stronger than these suits of armor to stop me," Kiru retorted, pointing one of his blades in the constructs' direction. "If you're so superior, then come fight me face-to-face."

Just then, the amalgam's head surged upwards and let out a terrible roar of defiance. Many of its eyes were ruined or gone, the damage wrought by Kiru's psyslime apparent. The amalgam first turned towards the automatons, who looked like children compared to the sheer immensity of this creature. It cocked its head to the side before its eyes locked back onto Kiru, the hate clear in its glare.

Kiru's entire body tensed as the amalgam focused its aura directly on him again, only it didn't convey a primal sensation like before. This time, Kiru felt pure wrath.

The warden began to laugh. "What good fortune! It appears this strange construct is also bound by chaos mana," he said before looking at the psion. "You said I would need something bigger to deal with you, vermin. Well, it looks like I now have it," he said, and then the free arms of the two remaining constructs reached out to the amalgam, palms out. The warden's voice then came out of both automatons in unison: "Give me control."

Immediately, Kiru felt the amalgam's aura turn away from him. He watched as the hideous, part-biological/part-technological insectoid monster began to shake its damaged head back and forth and screech.

The automatons pushed their arms out further. "Give . . . me . . . control," Mal'throk repeated, saying each word with evident strain.

Is he using Subjugation? Kiru thought. Before he could ponder it further, though, the amalgam released another defiant roar, sending its powerful aura out in all directions and forcing the psion to cross his arms defensively and take a knee. As the aura washed over him, Kiru could somehow understand that the amalgam wasn't just conveying its emotions but reaching out with its will. Pure and undiluted, it was empowering its aura, giving it both the direction and energy to achieve what the amalgam desired: *Freedom.*

Though the amalgam didn't use its Chaotic Pulse technique, a wave of chaos mana cascaded out of the monster, cracking loudly as if it were lightning. The monster raised its head and released a defiant roar into the sky, its desire to not be controlled too strong for Mal'throk, who Kiru presumed was in the top floor, deigning to try to tame it.

"Gaah!" Mal'throk cried out as his two automatons staggered back as if physically struck. "What? How? How can you defy me? How can you sense my true body?" he asked the monster in a mixture of anger and awe.

The creature snapped its gaze to look down on the two in reply, its ire focused now solely on the pair of winged constructs.

"No!" Mal'throk shouted and the automaton that was still on the ground shoved its arm out. "Give me co—"

The warden's words were interrupted when the amalgam descended on the humanoid construct with vengeful fury, biting down on the automaton and crunching it to pieces.

Kiru saw the one remaining corrupted automaton, still airborne, recoiling back with an audible gasp. It looked to the amalgam, then to Kiru, back to the monster, and then to Kiru once more. He growled, but he could not hide the fear in his voice. "This is not over yet, vermin," he said before launching the automaton straight up in the air with a powerful flap of its wings.

Kiru watched it go and fly up to the very top of the mountain and continue upward, disappearing into the sky right above it. "Huh?" he said in surprise before looking back at the amalgam biting down and tearing the corrupted automaton to shreds. He would've been more excited and astonished by how the warden's last automaton had escaped, but his primary focus was elsewhere. His eyes were focused on the monstrous amalgam as his mind began to comprehend what he just witnessed. There was something there—something he just saw that was beyond him. It was as if there was an important crucial concept that was on the other side of a door in his mind, and the door had just been cracked open slightly. Kiru just needed to force it open.

"William, did you just see what that monster did?" Kiru asked, goosebumps traveling all along his body.

"Y-Yes," the imp replied, clearly in amazement. "It appears that the amalgam has the same makeup as the corrupted automatons—which makes sense. So, it was susceptible to Mal'throk's control, but it defied him with its aura. I know auras are extended shrouds that convey emotions, but . . ."

"It was more than emotion," Kiru finished for him. "It was its will," he said as he pushed the door open in his mind. "We knew that those who flare out their auras typically convey an emotion. Still, that tells us nothing about *how* to flare our auras. When people flare out their auras, they are imbuing their mana with their will and sending it out. Emotions are deeply intertwined with someone's will, but they aren't actually what empowers an aura. It's the user's will alone. I get it. Our minds—which hold our will and command the power of our bodies—affect the outside world. As the arboth say, all physical bows to the mental," he said as his mind reached a higher state of enlightenment and understanding about mana and the mysteries of cultivating.

Kiru's body became tingly, and somehow, he just *knew* that the Sapphire color of the gem in his forehead had grown bolder. "I am Kiru the Conqueror, accompanied by my companion William the Breaker of Wills, and you . . . !"

he shouted, imbuing his shroud with his will and flaring it out to the monster.

Instantly, the amalgam stopped its hateful destruction and snapped its head to Kiru, many of the limbs on its body flaring up like an angry cat being challenged by a fellow predator. It growled as black blood trailed down its mouth in twin streams.

". . . You will submit to me, or die!" Kiru said through gritted teeth before sending his aura at the monster full force. The psion imbued the mana of his shroud with his will once more. He made sure the monster felt his anger and his confidence, but most of all, he made sure the amalgam experienced his will. He was a conqueror, and he would not be stopped by anything. The monster may have been huge, but if it stood in his way, it would just be another corpse he would leave along his path.

The amalgam recoiled slightly upon feeling Kiru's aura before flaring out its own aura in response. Both monster and psion stared at each other with sheer and utter resolve, neither backing down as their auras struck one another. Flashes of lightning sparked from the friction of the auras pushing against each other, the monster's aura uneven and wild, Kiru's smooth and bright white. The amalgam conveyed its desire to kill the challenger while Kiru's aura gave off the impression of an unyielding force, of pure desire and utter surety that he would push through the monster and anything else that dared to obstruct his path.

Both the air and ground shook as the two pressed against each other's auras constantly for minutes. Despite the strength of his will, Kiru felt his body weakening and his power diminishing as he fed more and more mana into his aura to force back the monster's. Blood started leaking from one side of his nose from the effort. He couldn't win a battle of auras. He had only just reached this tier of Sapphire and was too inexperienced to handle this foe on his own. Luckily, he wasn't on his own.

"William, this thing isn't going to submit. We need a plan. Show me how to kill it," he sent via Telepathy.

"Showing weak points," William sent to the psion.

In Kiru's sight, the creature's remaining eyes all glowed as spots to exploit. Multiple joints further down its body were illuminated as well. One area in particular stood out to him. In the large wound on its face, there was one small pinpoint dot in the midst of all the darkness around it. Despite its size and its solidarity, it shone brightest of all.

"William, I always assumed this was the case but never confirmed it. Does the intensity of the glow indicate how significant a weak point is?" Kiru asked, feeling frustrated for not bringing that up earlier.

"Indeed, Master," the imp replied.

Kiru grunted as a plan formed in his mind, *"William, can you feed my aura? You know, empower it?"*

"Analyzing," the imp said, and after a couple of seconds of silence, he had an answer. *"Your aura is an extension of your shroud imbued with your will. Since your shroud is made of mana I calculate a 64% chance of success. If I align my will with yours, though, I predict a 96.5% success rate."*

"Good, then do it!" Kiru hurriedly sent back, his body shaking and blood dripping out of both nostrils. He then instantly felt a flood of mana flow out of his body, moving with a will of its own, flowing into and boosting Kiru's aura. The psion's aura suddenly pushed out against the amalgam's. The suddenness and surprise nature of the boost caused the monster to stagger back, slightly disrupting its focus and will, making its own aura temporarily lose cohesion.

With a split-second opening, Kiru seized the opportunity. He turned the psyslime into a lance and surged forward with a burst of blinding speed at the amalgam. With a primal cry, Kiru closed the distance in a blink and thrust the spear into the open wound on the monster's head and directly into the weak point. There was a series of loud cracks and pops as the lance pierced the target and continued forward, bringing irreparable damage to the terrifying hybrid monster and pinning its head to the mountainside. The amalgam twitched just slightly before its entire form went slack, dead.

"Now that, was some useful data!" William cheered.

Kiru dislodged his weapon and stood atop the dead amalgam as its freed body collapsed limply to the ground. He didn't want to admit it, but William had been right about the psion "forcing enemies to fall under his boot." Despite the incredulity of his life and circumstances though, he was standing on top of a nightmarish monster that he had slain personally. With William's aid, he'd done it. A predatory grin grew on Kiru's face under his mask, as his success empowered his will even more, which he knew would make his aura even stronger in the future.

He then looked up to the sky right above the mountain where the final automaton had fled. "You're next, Warden."

CHAPTER FORTY

The Final Harbinger

Vatrenex stood atop a large hill overlooking the capital of the Joyful Cult. While much of the island was covered in smoking ruins, the headquarters of their organization, the home of Waayoo, the last Harbinger, was remarkably intact. Vatrenex growled at the sight of the large stone city. While the Hushed had terrain and the Mourners possessed mobility as well as a large quantity of members, the Joyful had three distinct advantages over the other two cults Vatrenex had fought.

First was the sheer size of their island nation. It was enormous, at least one hundred times larger than the *Citadel*. Second was the cult's training. The quality of their cultivators wasn't more impressive than the corsairs, but in terms of warfare, they were much more cunning, excelling in guerilla tactics. Third was their followers. The Swordstrike Corsairs boasted many warriors from numerous races, but the Joyful only had two: humans and a remarkably high number of drakonids, whose breath attacks made them ideal warriors.

Due to these factors, Vatrenex and his forces had been forced into a month-long campaign against the Joyful, which was truly more of a war of attrition. The Harbinger had lost many of his corsairs and war slaves to Waayoo's machinations. Quicksand pits, poison darts, pitfalls filled with either spikes or flames, and even a giant block of stone that flattened two lower-ranked fighters were just some of the myriad traps that the Joyful had laid out.

Worst of all, Waayoo had somehow made the island an area that prevented flight. It was some sort of gravitational effect that drew Vatrenex downward as soon as he crossed the island's borders. Vatrenex suspected it was an array of some sort that had been spread all around the perimeter, restricting his ability to use his wings. He didn't have time to search and remove it during his campaign, though, as he had to maintain his focus on pushing in further. Despite all the traps and setbacks, however, with Plio and Zis'Piel at Vatrenex's side, the corsairs were steadily making progress, albeit at a much slower pace than he desired. So, finally, after cutting and burning their way across the thick jungle foliage and through the cultists, the corsairs had finally broken through to the capital.

Waayoo's city was made entirely of stone with a tall perimeter in place all the way around. Vatrenex could see five main pyramid structures, the one at the end taller and more resplendent than the others. Oddly enough, the capital was eerily quiet and devoid of life. Vatrenex suspected another trap; he could sense his brother's mana inside. He motioned for his corsairs to stay back and use the dense jungle foliage for cover while he motioned for both Plio and Zis'Piel to follow.

"We strike the front gates as one," Vatrenex sent to the others through Telepathy.

Zis'Piel slowly nodded both of his heads while Plio snapped back in sudden surprise despite Vatrenex having telepathically communicated with them in the past. Still, they complied without any dissent. All three Harbingers raised their weapons, coating them with chaos mana before slashing down and sending a trio of Chaos Rift Slashes forward. The techniques struck the thick stone doors with ease, obliterating the rock everywhere they touched. The chaos mana ate away and destroyed where it struck and continued surging forward, causing the doors to crumble and collapse.

Vatrenex watched as the techniques flew forward into the city before crashing into the ground and dissipating. Zis'Piel's stopped about five feet in, Plio's went about double that, while Vatrenex's technique reached even farther. The Harbinger, narcissistic as ever, grinned at his superiority to his brothers. He looked deeper into the capital, planning to demonstrate his superiority to his third brother as well.

The entire city was abandoned, except for Waayoo. The Harbinger had been a nebulor in his previous life, and the natural hatred between the arboth and them had leaked into Vatrenex's relationship with his brother even before they had crashed into the Torn Empire. It was due to that relationship that Vatrenex let out a growl of annoyance upon seeing Waayoo's giant grin. Waayoo looked like a giant black bipedal whale, with the exception of his four red eyes and the two dorsal fins on his head that looked more like horns. He sat on top of a throne at the peak of the central stone pyramid, looking down at Vatrenex and the others with utter confidence and joy. His smile displayed rows upon rows of sharp teeth, more like a shark's than a whale's, and he was adorned in some sort of tribal dress. In his right hand, was his weapon, a scythe as large as he was, which he held with a firm grip.

"Brothers, it brings me so much joy to see you all together once again," Waayoo said, seemingly unbothered by their incursion into his domain. It made Vatrenex uneasy. Then again, everything about Waayoo made Vatrenex either angry or uncomfortable. "I can only presume that after all these centuries of fear, misery, and wrath," he said, gesturing to Plio, Zis'Piel, and Vatrenex in that order, "that you've finally come to your senses and realized that we can only achieve true joy together as a family, with me at the head."

"Cease your prattle, Waayoo," Vatrenex spat out. "You will kneel before me, submit your weapon, and join us under my banner."

Waayoo continued to grin, but his two right eyes seemed to twitch slightly. He then turned to the other two. "Plio, Zis'Piel, is this true? Have you sworn fealty to our brother here?"

Plio's lip quivered, looking over to Vatrenex in clear worry, before giving Waayoo a hasty nod.

"It's true. We have been bound to Vatrenex. Oh, the violence. What a sad fate we have," Zis'Piel lamented.

"Worry not, Brothers," Waayoo said, his smile never leaving. "For I believe fate has smiled upon us all this day," he said, then stood up and began walking down the pyramid. His form was massive, at least as tall as Saltbeard's cyclops. "For your bondage to Vatrenex here will not last. Because you and our misguided brother will now serve me."

"Enough!" Vatrenex shouted as he flared out his aura, the force of it shattering more nearby stone. "If you will not kneel before me, then I will cut your legs off until you are forced to crawl."

Waayoo chuckled, stopping about midway down the pyramid. "Oh Vatrenex, though you are the same petulant brother as ever, I thank you. I thank you because I will have such great joy in crushing your spirit," he said, his ever-present smile widening until his face was nearly split in two.

Vatrenex snarled, his anger rising to a boiling point. He lowered the point of his blade and fired a Voidflare Barrage. The orbs of chaos mana shot forward, all in the other Harbingers' direction. Many of them were spread out in a wide arc.

Waayoo took a casual horizontal swing of his giant scythe, firing a barrage of his own. He easily intercepted the orbs coming for him, not even bothering with the ones that had spread out and wouldn't hit him, and sent a few more toward Vatrenex and the others.

Vatrenex and his brethren managed to either dodge or deflect Waayoo's attacks. After Vatrenex knocked the last of Waayoo's orbs away, he let out a low growl and flicked his long tongue. He knew that Waayoo likely had more schemes and traps up his sleeve, but to his annoyance, accepted he couldn't proactively remove all of them. Still, his wariness did bear fruit as, where many of the orbs of his barrage technique struck the environment, hidden spikes, gouts of flame, and giant swinging blades emerged. Feeling more confident that they had removed at least some of the traps, Vatrenex said just one word: "Attack."

Vatrenex leapt forward with Plio and Zis'Piel close on his heels. Waayoo just stood there and released a series of Chaos Rift Slashes at Vatrenex at close distance, which forced the corsair leader to block one of the strikes and get knocked off-course. He landed on one of the stone bricks near the base of the pyramid. It cracked, and he heard a distinct *click*. Sensing danger, he immediately rolled to the side, narrowly managing to avoid a ballista bolt that shot up from under the false stone.

Vatrenex looked up to see Plio instantly closing the distance with the use of his Time Step and lunging at Waayoo's face.

Waayoo's four eyes widened slightly but showed no fear as he knocked Plio's dagger out of the way with a two-handed swing of his scythe before gracefully knocking the rat back with the butt of his weapon.

Zis'Piel had hung farther back from the other two in the trio, but that seemed to be on purpose as his two heads were leaning in Waayoo's direction with both palms facing outward as well.

Waayoo let out a small chuckle before taking a casual step to his left, avoiding the Time Halt technique that Zis'Piel had fired the moment before.

Vatrenex seized the opportunity and swung his great sword with all his might.

Waayoo's four eyes widened a little more, showing true surprise. Vatrenex's blade pulsed in glee as the edge cut into Waayoo's cheek, tasting his blood. Before the swing could cause more damage, the whale-man's body turned into a cloud of inky darkness. Waayoo's form faded, causing the continuation of Vatrenex's swing to miss, and his side received a nasty gash from Waayoo's counterstrike.

Vatrenex groaned and put a hand to his side as he spun to reorient his focus on his foe. He saw Waayoo's body reforming from the Pure Darkness technique he and Plio shared and coalescing about ten feet away from Vatrenex.

Waayoo pressed a finger to the cut on his nose, then looked at the blood that was there. "I commend you three for actually injuring this host body of mine. I admit that, on an even playing field, I would not win against you," he said before a malicious chuckle came from his lips. "Unfortunately for you, this battle-field belongs to me." Then he raised his scythe in the air like a staff and sent a pulse of out above them all. All five of the pyramids vibrated with power, and the gravity of the entire city increased threefold.

Vatrenex and his allies all grimaced as they dealt with the sudden force, but they adjusted. They all resisted, slowly standing up as Waayoo rambled on about his own greatness. Vatrenex growled, his anger growing. He grimaced and forced his body to heal the gash on his side.

Waayoo just shook his head. "It brings me joy to see such fire in your eye, Brother. I look forward to using that against my enemies after I break you like the beast you are. I've planned for every possibility because for centuries, I've known what you can do. You've already lost. So surrender. It will bring me such joy to finally be united once again."

Vatrenex's entire maw split wide from face to navel, his teeth bared and tongue lashing out like a snake. He wanted to rush at his brother once again, but what

Waayoo had said made him pause. Vatrenex knew that Waayoo's statement was false because they *did* have some hidden aces. A plan formed in his mind, and he sent a quick set of orders to Zis'Piel and Plio through Telepathy.

The four Harbingers continued to fight. Orbs and slashes of chaos mana crashed about them as the very laws of time and space were bent. Piles of rocks and clouds of dust and flames spewed forth. The entire island seemed to shake from their fighting as the city was being further damaged every second. Waayoo slowly gained the advantage against the others as he was unaffected by his own gravity trap, and he still used a myriad of other deceptions. Eventually, though, they were able to get Waayoo cornered and enact Vatrenex's plan. Plio threw a dagger—not the weapon that contained his consciousness but the favored weapon of his host body, the Bloodstep Stiletto. Since Waayoo couldn't move to dodge as he was engaged in fighting the others, he went to block it, but on Vatrenex's timed mental command, Zis'Piel used Warp on the projectile. The stiletto's path instantly bent at an unnatural angle and stabbed Waayoo right in the thigh.

The blade's enchantment kicked in, teleporting Plio right to its location. The former quist took his other dagger and quickly began repeatedly stabbing Waayoo in the side. Vatrenex fought against the increased gravity and jumped in the air, his massive blade held up to bisect his foe.

"Enough!" Waayoo shouted as he slammed the bottom of his scythe on the ground and sent a pulse of mana from his body out in all directions. Vatrenex and Plio were forced back, and the four Harbingers watched as from the top of each pyramid shot out a beam of black light. The five beams all aimed at a central location above the central pyramid. The light rapidly coalesced into a miniature black hole, which—before Vatrenex could take another swing at Waayoo—began pulling on everything around it, sucking whatever it could into its dark vortex. This included detritus, dust, and debris, followed by pieces of stone and rubble from the fighting in the city. It pulled on the Harbingers as well, trying to sweep them off the ground to their doom.

Damn him, Vatrenex thought, anger mixing with surprise at his brother's newest trap.

Zis'Piel groaned and lamented his "terrible fate" as he gripped onto a nearby pyramid while Plio's feet began to rise. He did manage to wedge his bonded dagger into a crevice between a couple of stones and held on tight. Vatrenex was the only one who was fighting against the forces against them with his own power alone, having to deal with the increased gravity pulling him down to the ground with one hand and the force of the black hole with the other. For whatever reason, the two didn't seem to cancel each other out.

Vatrenex took a couple of slow steps forward, his anger growing as he watched Waayoo's smirking visage growing increasingly more prideful. Desperate, Vatrenex was forced to use his trump card, a technique called Mind Crush. Unlike the

Chaosbind technique that all Harbingers possess to control their hosts' bodies, this technique targeted the mind with the intent to bring ruin, not take over. It wasn't without cost. It required both Vatrenex's willpower and the mana from his shroud to fuel it, leaving himself susceptible.

I have no other choice, he thought before firing the technique at Waayoo. "Mind Crush!" he shouted, conveying all the hate he had in him.

Waayoo's four eyes went wide in surprise; the leader of the corsairs' technique struck the former nebulor's shroud but managed to punch through and directly hit his mind. Waayoo visibly recoiled, and Vatrenex clenched a fist tight as he sent his mental attack to do its work. Vatrenex felt his attack do its opening salvo, but then it was suddenly destroyed.

Waayoo snapped his head back to Vatrenex, streams of blood coming down from his four eyes, which somehow seemed to also be full of manic glee. "Oh, what joy it will be to pay you back for that one, Brother!" he said before letting out a crazed giggle.

Vatrenex fell to his knees, his energy nearly all spent. He slammed his great sword into the ground and held on with his severely depleted energy to avoid being sucked into the black hole above. He saw Waayoo leap forward in an impressive burst of speed, his scythe pulled back to the right and ready to cleave him in two.

Brunhilda's face then suddenly snapped to life, and Vatrenex's right hand shot up without him intending to do so. He felt the dwarf's mana—only . . . different than before—surging through the host's body and then through his own channels. Out of options, he just let it happen. He couldn't stop her, anyway.

"Divine Shield," the dwarf shouted, and a column of holy fire surrounded Vatrenex's body, its light a mixture of white with black flakes appearing here and there.

Waayoo's weapon struck the technique, and it retaliated by setting him ablaze. The black hole trap suddenly vanished.

Vatrenex gasped as he helplessly watched his brother burn—a prisoner somehow in his own body, the roles between him and his host reversed.

"I don't have me shields. So, ye need to finish him off, ye cruel bastard," Brunhilda said to the Harbinger before relinquishing control to Vatrenex once more.

In the next moment, as Waayoo began to roll in a desperate attempt to extinguish the flames, Vatrenex felt the gravity let up, too. Full of fury at both his brother's pride and the audacious dwarf's resistance, Vatrenex ran up to the still-burning Waayoo and swung his great sword in a wide horizontal position, slamming his blade into the side of his brother's abdomen. Waayoo's blood sprayed out as if a dam had burst, and Vatrenex repeated his swing. Over and over, he hacked at Waayoo like an angry lumberjack until his brother's host's form gave out, and he faded to ash, leaving only the husk of the large drakonid he controlled and the scythe behind.

Breathing angrily, he gripped Waayoo's weapon and used Chaosbind, imbuing it with his dominating power, binding the last and final Harbinger to his service and getting all of them under his banner once and for all. He shouted in triumph and raised the weapon in the air in victory.

Plio and Zis'Piel slowly approached their leader and bowed in deference. Zis'Piel began to mutter under his breath about how terrible things would be for the innocents they would slaughter, sounding like he would cry if he physically could. Plio was looking all around, constantly keeping surveillance, his lip quivering in clear and constant fear.

Vatrenex didn't care how his brothers felt. They served under him, and even the prideful Waayoo had been broken. They were his tools to use. He gave a bloodthirsty grin, then said, "Next, we strike Gaal'cothdreek-duun."

"Brother," Plio said meekly, "now that you have defeated Waayoo, will you tell us who his host will be?"

Vatrenex laughed. "I never said he would have another host, Plio. Just that he would be wielded. For the rest of time, and by someone he detests: *Me*."

CHAPTER FORTY-ONE

Heaven's Gate

Kiru flew to the top of the mountain, looking around and up at the ceiling where the warden's final automaton had gone through. To his great frustration, he couldn't find any exit. "William, can you detect anything?" he asked.

"The chaos mana is so dense up here that it obscures any ability I have to find a hidden passage," William answered.

Kiru landed on the ground and growled in frustration. He attempted to sheath both of his blades, but the steel hook sword had had enough and abruptly broke into three pieces. That stoked his anger even more and he let out a shout.

"We were so damn close, William!" Kiru said. "We had his final automaton, and then he has it run away like a coward instead of fighting. And now, we can't follow him!" At that, he sat down on a stone, now truly feeling the fatigue from the fight. With his ascension to Tier Two in Sapphire in just two-and-a-half months, he felt great, stronger than ever. Oddly enough, though, the fatigue felt even stronger in that moment. His eyes grew heavy as if he'd just spent a night drinking Strongjaw back at the academy with his friends. Remembering his passing out after his previous ascension, Kiru grimaced in frustration. He did not want that to happen again, but he couldn't stop it. His vision was getting blurrier as his head began to lull.

"Master? Master, your focus is fading! Summon me!" William urgently sent.

Barely able to nod, Kiru used the last of his strength to summon his friend before collapsing flat on the stone, unconscious.

Kiru awoke to darkness, feeling both sore but also refreshed in both mind and body. He slowly sat up, causing a blanket made of strange cloth and leather to fall off him. He was still in his armor and gear, and though his mask was now off, he could smell the dried sweat on his body. There was also some strange chemical smell mixed in with it. Though it was dark, there was some sort of light source outside as he quickly discovered he was in a thin tent of some sort and could see the orange glow of a fire, as well as hear its crackling outside.

"William?" Kiru asked in a low voice, not sure what was going on. Immediately a quist standing nearby the tent's entrance that Kiru hadn't noticed at first let out a surprised squeak and quickly scurried off. *A quist? Well, that's probably a good sign*, he thought as he began to stand up. Then, he noticed his body felt extremely full, as if he'd been feasting for a week straight. Kiru also noticed a wet feeling on his neck, and a dried thin layer of . . . something around his mouth. He touched his neck and noticed a thick, viscous substance as well as chunks of . . . *flesh?* Kiru couldn't tell. His gut sank as he took a better look and realized what they were—pieces of brain matter.

"William!" Kiru shouted this time and stormed out of the tent to find the imp relaxing by a fire with his eyes closed, getting his shoulders and cloudy bottom half massaged by four different quist. A fifth one—the one Kiru suspected had been standing by his tent—was speaking into William's ear.

Despite Kiru's volume and tone, the imp just casually opened his third eye on his visible brain and looked over to him. "Oh, great! My idea worked," he said with clear joy.

"What did you do?" the psion asked.

Upon seeing Kiru, all the quist immediately fell to their knees in deference to him.

William opened his other two eyes and rolled them all at once. "Well, there goes the best massage I've ever had," he said. "And as for your question, me and my exceedingly clever mind full of useful ideas saved your ass from wasting a lot of time. You're welcome."

Kiru raised an eyebrow, silently gesturing for William to elaborate.

The imp sighed. "You passed out again, just like you did when you reached Tier-One Sapphire. Now that you have reached Tier Two, I was afraid it would take even longer. We can't afford to wait. So, I had a thought based on the data about the arboth I got here. They cultivated mental mana and replenished their energy from a chemical compound their alchemists called 'phenethylamine,'" he said in quotations.

"It is found primarily in brain matter. So, given that you experienced a five-day coma last time, I calculated a 92.1% chance of an even longer recovery from your rapid, energy-demanding ascensions. Since we had a large supply of brains from all the Zier'Knacht you slaughtered, I believed that we couldn't afford *not* to try feeding them to you, and—wouldn't you know—you've now awoken after only ten hours! I do believe it would've been faster had the brains been fresher, though. Those Zier'Knacht had tiny brains that began to decay *really* fast. We had to feed you *a lot* of brains. By the end, you'd eaten thirty-two of them in total," William explained.

Kiru had to forcibly suppress the urge to vomit. A line of bile and drool did come out, though, which he wiped away with his forearm. "That was . . . unsettling to learn, but I can't argue with your results, William. Thank you," he said.

"Oh, anytime, Master. Whenever you need me to make you eat our enemies, I'm happy to help," he said with sadistic joy.

It was Kiru's turn to roll his eyes. He then fully processed what had happened to him—not the brain-eating part but his ascension. He was now a Tier-Two Sapphire! He now not only had a shroud but could extend it out as his aura, affecting the world with the literal weight of his will. It was a level of cultivation that only elites ever reached. Kiru looked down at his palms in wonder before looking around to see at least a hundred quist kneeling on the stone around them. Kiru turned back to look out into the distance to discover that he was still on top of the mountain. "We really did it? I'm a Tier-Two Sapphire now?"

"Of course. If you planned on beating an Onyx one day, you were going to have to reach this rank eventually," William replied confidently, like it was no big deal.

Kiru chuckled. "I guess you're right. Hey, why is it night?" he asked.

"Well, that is a bit more complicated, but the good news is that the quist here actually found the way up, with my help of course," William said. He then went on to explain that after Kiru's shout of anger and subsequent collapse into unconsciousness, the quist all came out of their hiding places. Under William's "precise and perfect instructions," they made camp around Kiru. When they asked William what Kiru was mad about, the imp went on to explain about their escaped enemy, who he dubbed "the fallen angel," and his strange escape from Kiru's retribution. Apparently, William's ability to speak the squeaky language had increased.

After the imp's explanation, the quist took it upon themselves to help "the Liberator" to find what William called "Heaven's Gate" and surprisingly did succeed in discovering a strange defect or crack in the ceiling by the artificial light source. William told Kiru that they only did so because of his "genius intuition" by ringing the bell once more. As with the crystals down on the second-from-the-bottom level, the vibrations from its sounds caused an effect. Rather than making an artificial light source, however, it affected the mana around the mountain's tip, causing it to abruptly bend back and forth.

It was during this abrupt distortion of space that the way up had been revealed. Then, William's face took on a sheepish expression.

"What aren't you telling me?" Kiru asked.

"So, remember how I told you that the quist had taken it upon themselves to help you? Well, that small one from the hunting party you saved decided to rush into that distortion on her own. And . . ."

"She hasn't come back since?" Kiru asked, suspecting he knew what the imp would say.

"Yeah . . ." William answered. "But I'm not terribly concerned. "If these quist have been able to survive for almost one-and-a-half millennia in this place on their own, that one should be able to make it. I've calculated a 62.5% chance of success."

Kiru suppressed a grimace. That percent was far too low for his liking. These quist, though he found them fearful and a bit odd for considering him to some great Liberator, had been the one species that hadn't been hostile to him or William. Even the spowts—the lizards back in the acidic fog swamp—had been antagonistic towards the imp. One had even put itself at risk to try and pay him back for eliminating the Zier'Knacht. He didn't want to be responsible for these people, but he wouldn't let them die needlessly, either.

"William, we gotta go. Show me where this 'Heaven's Gate' is. I've still got my psyslime, so I should be able to cut the warden down," Kiru said, his tone serious.

"Of course, of course, Master. But first, on that note, the tribe here has a gift of thanks for your 'great purge' of the monsters," William said, before turning back and speaking an order to the quist in their language. Quickly, two quist brought the psion an item wrapped in ruddy brown cloth.

Curious, Kiru bent down and accepted the proffered gift and nodded to the pair of rodent people. He quickly undid the cloth to reveal a dagger, larger than any he'd ever seen, more akin to a hybrid of a short sword and a long knife. The blade was made of the same bright purple metal the fortress was composed of. It was a forward-curving weapon with a distinctive, single-edged blade that seemed to be designed to be more effective chopping and slashing versus stabbing. The closest thing Kiru's mind could equate to it was a kopis, an uncommon blade that the psion had read about during his time back at the academy's library.

The kopis certainly wasn't a Fu Tao, but the purple metal it was composed of had to be durable if it was the same type that the fortress was built of. Gaal'cothdreek-duun has lasted being underwater for centuries and was still holding up. The purple blade was also curved, reminding the psion of the hook of his Fu Tao. The kopis wasn't his ideal choice, but it was the best he was going to get. After all, *any* weapon is better than no weapon.

"Tell them I am deeply grateful, and I will use it after I ascend through Heaven's Gate," Kiru said.

William grinned widely before turning back, arms wide, and giving a booming declaration to the quist, who all raised their heads and cheered in unison. "Great, now I'll just get one more massage before g—"

"No, you don't," Kiru said as he recalled his familiar back into his core.

"*One more rack of boar?*" William asked inside the psion's mind, trying once more to get some relaxation time.

"No," Kiru replied, not brokering any argument.

William grumbled before saying, *"Fine. Now that I have seen the distortion in space where the exit is, I'm able to spot it easily. Showing target now."*

In Kiru's vision, a blue circle appeared in the sky on the ceiling directly above the mountain's tip. He equipped the kopis' sheath to his belt and then drew both of his blades before making his way to the mountain's tip. He walked up and heard the quist chittering excitedly behind him, following him like he was some sort of divine being. Kiru didn't have time to dissuade them from their illusions at the moment, however. So, without a word, once he'd made it to the tip, he used Telekinesis and flew through the hole that William had highlighted. It seemed like a solid wall, but he still floated right through it only to find a gigantic tangle of wires and metal all around him.

As soon as Kiru passed through the passage, the light from below faded and it sealed, leaving him in complete darkness. Kiru put his feet on the ground beneath him because he literally had nowhere else to go. His darkvision helped him see that he literally only had inches of space to move in any direction.

"William, what the fuck is this?" Kiru asked in a growing panic.

He wasn't necessarily a claustrophobic guy, but the suddenness plus the sheer restriction from every direction made him seriously concerned.

"Scanning," William said emotionlessly.

Kiru slowly moved around to allow his familiar to better assess their surroundings.

"Scan complete," William finished before making a clicking noise that Kiru would often make when someone was telling him rough news.

"Just tell me, how bad is it?" Kiru asked.

"Well, it looks like the entirety of the second floor, or a significant portion of it, has collapsed in on itself. So, it's pretty bad, Master. I know the previous data from the pillar on the bottom floor had stated that there was damage, but I didn't think it would be to this level. I cannot determine its exact cause, but due to how smooth some of the broken fragments appear to be, I suspect that it was due to a recent assault on the structural integrity of this level," William explained, highlighting a few pieces of rubble in the psion's vision.

"Vatrenex," Kiru growled.

"Probability puts it at a 95% likelihood that he caused this, yes," William confirmed. *"Given his intimate familiarity with Gaal'cothdreek-duun, he likely knew how to damage the second level enough in order to hinder our ascension without causing the entirety of the floor to fall in. I guess he can't afford to let it collapse it entirely."*

"That's good. That means we can still find a way to get up there and crush the life out of him," Kiru said.

"I like that intensity, Master! I knew we had to kill him, but crushing the life out of him? I think I'm finally rubbing off on you," William said excitedly. "As for finding a way to get up to the warden, I have two options. First, you extend

your aura out in all directions while also using Telekinesis to send all the debris surrounding us back. It has only a 31% chance of success but should hopefully allow us to get to the top level within a couple minutes. The second—" William said, and a small, angled hole above Kiru and to the right glowed in his sight. Small claw marks could be seen on one side. "—is we follow the quist."

CHAPTER FORTY-TWO

Crawling & Confrontation

The quist having gone ahead of them turned out to be a blessing in disguise for Kiru. It gave the psion a path to the first floor with a much higher chance of success, according to William. It would take longer, but it also meant he would hopefully find the small quist and bring her safely back to her people.

So, Kiru put away his weapons, reequipped his Mask of Fenrir, and began crawling. The journey became very difficult within the first ten minutes. The tunnel he went through was narrow. The quist was a great deal smaller than he was, and his dragon bone armor was not built for getting him through tight spaces. After being stuck for a good twenty minutes, he decided to summon William once more. With the imp's comparatively small size and the fact that he now floated instead of walked, he was able to assess areas of the tunnel the psion otherwise couldn't reach.

Kiru had been afraid to expand the tunnels because he didn't want to cause the structural integrity to collapse on him. With William now outside, however, the imp was able to delicately use Telekinesis to expand the tunnel just slightly and help the psion continue on. William floated ahead of Kiru and scouted for any issues. By this method, they were able to make slow-but-steady progress over the next few hours. "At least this floor is supposed to be a lot smaller than all the others we've been in," Kiru said as he waddled his way forward.

"You are correct, Master. The second floor is approximately fifty-thousand square feet, not even one square mile, and the only floor smaller than it is the top one," William explained.

"Good, I don't want to be here any longer than necessary," Kiru said. "I am concerned, though. The quist . . ." he said as he shoved himself through a particularly narrow segment of tunnel. "There's been no sign of her besides these tracks."

"Her survival percentage decreases the more time passes and we haven't found her, but the fact that the tunnels she's made still exist is a positive indicator,"

William said. They continued for another fifteen minutes, when the imp turned a corner that contained the first bit of light that the pair had experienced since they started their spelunking.

"*Wait! Master, I sense something,*" the imp sent via Telepathy, his tone immediately serious.

"*What is it?*" Kiru asked before his ears picked up the noise of the quist. It was squeaking in a manner that conveyed clear distress.

"*The quist appears to be in trouble. I'm going to scout ahead,*" William sent.

"*William, wait,*" Kiru sent back as he desperately tried to crawl as fast as he could but also do his best to stay as quiet as possible. William did not heed his warning. Kiru crawled around a corner and saw a straight tunnel that then went abruptly up.

"*Master, I've found the quist and the warden,*" William telepathically whispered. "*He's got her in a tra—oh, crap! Master, he has me! Save me!*" he sent before the communication was abruptly cut off.

"*William!*" Kiru cried out via Telepathy. He then crawled with all his might, not worrying about being either safe or quiet. His armor caught on some of the rubble, but he pushed through, causing some dirt and debris to fall on him. Kiru still pushed on. He flared his aura out just slightly to form a protective ring around himself as he moved closer and closer towards the light which was coming from the upward section of the tunnel. The wires cut, the stone cracked, and the metal bent as he quickly crawled forward and then up. As he ascended, the light source coming from the top floor got closer and closer into view.

When he finally reached that area, putting his arms and head out, he was greeted by a terrifying sight. There, standing in the purple-and-black armor of a corrupted automaton, was an arboth, its single red eye gazing with malice directly at him. It was, without a doubt, the warden. Unlike the arboth Kiru had seen in the memories he'd taken, the warden's form was now bipedal. That was because he was fully ensconced within the purple armor that the automatons were made of.

Guess that answers where the final automaton went to. How did he manage to take the construct's armor? Kiru thought.

The psion also noticed that the warden's back had a bunch of thick black tubes connected to it, all of which led to two black boxes flanked by a third one made of glass from which shone a strong light that illuminated the top floor. Even more so, it exuded a wild, palpable power which made Kiru's heart race and beat erratically. *The Chaos Core,* Kiru thought to himself before refocusing on his foe.

Mal'throk held the quist by the neck with a set of tentacles that formed his right arm, and held William by his head with the left.

The imp's eyes were distant, staring blankly at the psion, his mind in some kind of stupor.

Before Kiru could attack the arboth, a surge of mana struck him and the rubble around him like an ogre's fist.

Kiru barely managed to hang on and not get knocked back into the tunnel, but the rubble all around him wasn't as sturdy. Immediately, it all collapsed on him; he cried out in pain as his body was pinned by the extreme weight of all the debris. He tried to pull himself up, but even with his Sapphire strength, he was stuck.

"You managed to stick around. Good." Mal'throk laughed. "You are like these damn quist—vermin that will not die. Since you refuse to accept yourself as inferior, I will make you suffer for your audacity," he said before severing the quist's neck. There was a loud crunch of bone before her head literally fell off her body.

Kiru's eyes widened in horror and his heart raced. "Bastard!" he cried and fired a Telekinetic Bolt directly at the warden's face.

The purple hood around the arboth's eye morphed into a slitted visor and easily took the blow. "Fool, the data gathered from the automatons does not get lost," he said as he tapped his armored helmet with a tentacle. "While I admit that you have been creative with your variety of techniques, you've clearly hit your limit. You've no more techniques or combinations that can harm me. Even your flame serpent won't help you," Mal'throk said, gesturing to the ring on Kiru's finger.

Kiru grimaced as he struggled to figure out what to do. He tried to use Telekinesis to move the rubble off of him, but it caused the sharp pain in his chest to increase; he coughed up blood. The psion immediately stopped the technique. *Something must've pierced one of my lungs*, he thought.

Mal'throk chuckled at Kiru's plight before he continued, "The power of the Chaos Core has kept me alive, but only *just*. I need it to survive, forcing Gaal'cothdreek-duun to rely on auxiliary power and fall to the pitiful state you've found it in. I only needed to feed the Core the flesh of another being to heal me, but I refuse to corrupt myself with these vermin," the warden said as he kicked the quist's body away from him.

He then raised the dazed William up to his face and cackled evilly. "Your familiar, however, is an exceptional specimen. I will not only use his biomatter but take the power his mind has acquired and use it to crush you . . . slowly," he said and then began walking to the Chaos Core.

"No! William! No!" Kiru screamed.

"Ah, your cries of anguish bring me such pleasure," Mal'throk said as he strode to the Core about a hundred feet away from him.

Kiru's heart sank, and despair gripped him. There was nothing the psion could do. Not even his techniques would work against the automaton armor. It was as the warden had said: he was helpless. Kiru was reminded of his gruesome injury back in his hometown, at his sheer vulnerability and weakness, and how this par-alleled that.

"No," Kiru growled, the fires of his resolve burning strong inside him. He was reminded of his promise to himself. *No matter how weak or pathetic I am, I promised to never be helpless again, and I won't break that promise!! I still have my arms and my mana. Come on,* think! *I just need to use something he's never dealt with before. What combination can I do?* Kiru thought before inspiration struck.

The warden's back was to the psion, thick tubes evident, and he had made it half the distance to the core. Kiru began moving his arms in a specific rhythmic pattern—a pattern that he'd practiced time and time again as he moved the mana for a technique along each appendage. With his ascension to Tier Two in Sapphire and now with greater control of his shroud, he mastered the powerful techniques with much more ease. Once, twice, then three times his limbs contacted each other, both Telepathic Screech and Telekinetic Bolt merging. It tried to break free from his palms and run about wildly, but Kiru forced them to stay together with his will.

The arboth tapped the glass cube, which opened up to reveal an ever-changing source of light underneath. It was dizzying and mind-boggling to take in, as the colors and shape of the Core were perpetually shifting in ways that the mind couldn't fully grasp.

Kiru's primary focus wasn't the font of power that had been revealed, however, but on his foe. "Hey, asshat!"

The warden scowled as he turned his head to the psion.

"Got a new one for you!" Kiru shouted before firing a Telepathic Screech Bolt at the arboth. The psion had so effectively contained the technique up to that point that the pressure had built up before he fired, causing it to zoom directly at Mal'throk with blinding speed. Before the warden could react further, the bolt struck with such force that it caved in his helmet, piercing his eye. Mal'throk screamed in pain and terror, and he flung William up in the air as he gripped his ruined head.

Kiru gave a bloody grin and watched in satisfaction as Mal'throk's screams turned into shrieks. At the same time, the warden's entire body shook until his head finally exploded. Flesh and metal flew out in all directions, smoke exuded from the stump where the warden's neck had been moments before, and his body fell limp. Kiru then gasped as he remembered that William was airborne, but let out a sigh of relief when the imp landed on one of the black boxes next to the Chaos Core and not on the core itself.

That relief was short-lived however as the erratic way the core behaved caused it to stretch at an unnatural angle and touch William's hand. The imp suddenly arose from his stupor and cried out in fear.

"Master, what is happening?!" he asked, his body refusing to disconnect from the core, and his color changing to mirror that of the item's. It began pulling William in, and despite the imp pulling back against it, clawing and reaching around desperately for any way to free himself, its force couldn't be denied. William then turned to look directly into Kiru's eyes. "Master, I'm sorry. I guess you'll have to hear the lamentations of our enemies without me."

Kiru blanched. Even after eliminating the warden, he was still going to lose his friend. William had barely survived earlier when he'd simply touched something that had relayed the core's power. Touching the Chaos Core directly had to be immeasurably worse.

"No. Fight it, William!" Kiru said as he used Telekinesis once more. First, he tried to pull William away from the core. When that didn't work, he tried to move the rubble pinning himself down again. He coughed out more blood and wheezed, but he didn't break his concentration.

"It's okay, Master. Don't kill yourself. You can't free yourself in time. Focus on getting yourself out safely so you don't die. You killed that bastard," William said, nodding to Mal'throk's corpse. "And you also popped his head like with the quist. A perfect retribution. I can't think of a better end," he said as most of his body was drawn into the core, only his shoulders and head now remaining.

Tears streamed down Kiru's eyes. He had been separated from all of his friends, not sure if they were alive or dead. Only William remained—a part of him, the fire inside of him. He refused to let him go. It was reckless, but to make sure his familiar didn't die, Kiru took a gamble. He didn't want to live without his friend.

"NO!" he shouted, flaring his aura out in all directions with his will. The rubble was pushed back along with the wall he'd been pinned against, freeing him. Blood came down in twin streams from his mouth as well as from the section of his armor that had been previously bitten off by the Zier'Knacht Alpha.

It hurt to breathe, but he ignored the pain, and flew forward with a burst of speed, touching William's exposed brain. Kiru's arm shook and bent erratically as he made contact with William. To his surprise, the connection didn't hurt. It was as if his arm were made of gelatin. "This is not your end, my friend. We have too much blood left to spill for us to stop here. We'll get through this together," he said before William could be completely absorbed, and Kiru's arm made contact with the core proper.

CHAPTER FORTY-THREE

Convergence

Kiru's eyes rolled to the back of his head as his consciousness was somehow flung into the powerful source of chaos mana. The psion's sense of time and space as well as sense of himself was lost as the chaos mana's influence spread further and further. His mind spun amidst a kaleidoscopic storm of colors and feelings, as he experienced a complex variety of sensations all at once, by turns pleasureful and tortuous, encouraging and disheartening, joyful and infuriating. It was so much that he nearly lost himself in the psychedelic conglomeration of emotions.

Oddly enough, it was the feeling of anger that brought Kiru clarity. When his fire mana core had been intact, his temper had been much more difficult to manage. With all the terrible injustices that had been done to him since then, he was accustomed to the feeling. Still, the pure uncontrollable fury he felt in his core and wanted to unleash was indescribable. It brought about a sensation that only other fire mana cultivators could understand. That anger he felt from the Chaos Core struck resonance with the disparate broken pieces of his fire mana core, snapping his focus back to himself for a moment.

Though his consciousness was connected to the Chaos Core, he could also still feel both it and his body. The psion couldn't comprehend *how*, but he could perceive what was going on both in and outside his body at the same time, as if he were an omniscient outside observer. The chaos mana was so strong—as overwhelming as a tidal wave—that Kiru could barely do anything to resist it. He felt the chaos mana worm its way through his body, the areas that somehow resonated with anger drawn to his fire mana core fragments and piercing them like blades.

Kiru screamed and laughed at the same time as he felt five different fiery sensations all at once. Most burned him, one renewed him, but all gave him the sensation of power. He watched as the broken pieces of his Chaos Core grouped into five pierced fragments, each ablaze with its own unique type of flame. One burned with a white flame that was cold instead of hot. The next was black and orange, looking like molten rock. The third burned the hottest and was pure red with a fire that Kiru was familiar with, fueled by rage and inspired from Muspelheim. The fourth was a sickly green flame that seemed to desiccate all that it touched. That one hurt the most.

The fifth and final fragment glowed a radiant orange that both soothed and healed. *What is this?* he thought in wonder as he observed the five burning fire mana fragments, each with their own unique flames and properties. Kiru then mentally probed the red infernal fragment. *"William is that you?"* he sent out with a Telepathic message. The flame didn't respond with words, but it did seem to react. Kiru could tell that it wasn't his friend but was surprised that it had seemed to comply to his words. *No, not my words*, Kiru realized. *It was to my mental mana.* Then the motto of the arboth came back to him: *All physical bows to the mental.*

Then, reinvigorated, he sent out a pulse of mental mana in all directions, giving him an even better sense as to what was happening to him and his friend, and more importantly, *where* his friend was inside the Chaos Core. Deep inside the mind-boggling, space-warping depths of the core was William. All of his body had been rendered down into pure matter for use by the core. Like Kiru, he had possessed two cores, but both were now significantly eaten away, just a fraction of what they once were. Kiru knew that his friend's consciousness lay in his mental mana core, and gauging by its poor state, was barely just hanging on.

Kiru's own mental mana core was still untouched for now, but the Chaos Core's tendrils were slowly reaching up until it had just touched his jaw. Most of the psion's body was drawn in too, now only having his torso still visible to anything outside, except for his right arm, which was remarkably still intact for the moment. Kiru knew on an instinctive level that the core demanded a price and would forever change anything it came into contact with. He also realized that neither he nor William would ever be whole again or even possibly sane, but they wouldn't be helpless or alone, and that was good enough for the psion.

Emboldened by his realization that he had some control over what was going on, Kiru began to enact his plan to save his friend. He merged the two fragments of William's core together and pulled it towards him. He intended to fuse it with the infernal fire mana core, but while he had some control of the chaos running about, it was still shaky. While he'd been putting all his focus on bringing what remained of his friend back to him, the tendrils of chaos that pierced the fire mana fragments surged forward out in random directions as if they had a will of their own and were scared of the psion's influence.

Most went up, and the icy flame fragment merged with the circlet embedded in Kiru's head. The infernal fire core struck the top of his skull directly while the molten fragment burst out through his throat and struck his mask. Kiru groaned in frustration at the infernal core because he intended to use that to merge with William. The sickly green flame snaked around his arm, causing a portion of it to blacken before leaving his body and fusing with the gem on his summoning ring. The finger that wore the ring blackened into a dry husk.

The renewing flame went straight down into his gut. There, it made contact with his intestinal meridian and merged with it. It sent soothing orange flames out, renewing and healing his body. It even wrapped around his torso like a cuirass. Kiru could sense the black streak that the green flame created healing and leaving a smooth scar, as if months had passed in only a few heartbeats. His finger was still black and withered, however, the power of the ring pushing back against the flames.

While everything that was happening to him was amazing to behold, he couldn't just watch. Otherwise, the changes would act of their own accord. He needed to work fast.

"Crap!" he said, thinking of the best place to put William. In the end, he forcefully merged the imp with the cold fire fragment in his circlet. The circlet made contact with his brain and core, and even though it didn't have infernal fire mana, Kiru believed it would be the best way to somehow reach his friend once more.

After that was done, Kiru focused on separating himself from the core. He saw a deposited amount of biomatter just floating about, which the core was slowly devouring to feed its own power. It was what remained of both Kiru and William's bodies. With his will, he used his mental mana to guide the matter to his body while also ordering the Chaos Core to let both of them go. Kiru made sure to do that so the core wouldn't begin asserting its own influence again.

Kiru ordered the core to separate from his form and give him a body of the same size with two hands and feet. The core complied and spat out the psion intact but changed. Kiru took a deep inhale as both his mind and heart fought to calm themselves after the utter torrent of sensations and change he'd just undergone. He felt if he didn't force himself to get a grip, he would fall into unconsciousness again.

"No," he growled, his voice sounding much more bestial than he remembered. "I will not get stuck in another situation where I lose an ally," he said as he looked to the headless quist, forcing his mind to still but stay focused.

He took a few deep breaths, and once he had gained a measure of calm, fully assessed what had happened to him. His right arm was mostly unchanged; there was just a white smooth scar that traveled from his chest to hand. The Sapphire Summoning Ring's gem had changed. Its orange was now full of green flakes. The finger wearing the ring looked like it belonged to a corpse, all black and shriveled, but to Kiru's surprise, it moved with ease and no pain. His left arm only had two notable changes. The first was that he only had four fingers; the middle one was just . . . gone. The second was that the fingers he did have were notably thicker than before.

To Kiru's surprise, he found that the warden had a mirror as tall as the psion against one of the walls; he walked over to take in the rest of his new form. Kiru gasped in a mix of horror and curiosity at what he saw. He looked utterly monstrous, like a demon summoned from Muspelheim. His mouth was made of molten rock, and he had a maw of curved and sharp teeth. His eyes and ears were still wolfish but even more so somehow. What was even more disturbing was his head, which was on fire.

Kiru let out a cry of alarm and tried to pat the flames out, but they didn't diminish. He also realized that it didn't hurt either. He then looked at his reflection carefully once more and saw that the flowing red fire was actually his hair. The circlet embedded in his skull bulged out like a giant white vein all around his head, making him look like a demon prince, a true son of the fire giant and archdemon Surtur. Kiru chuckled at the irony since his mother's name was Surturia.

His dragon bone armor hadn't gone unaffected, either. The Chaos Core changed the thick armor into an off-white sleeveless gi the same color as bone that left most of Kiru's now-well-muscled torso exposed. It extended down and covered his upper thighs but left the rest of his legs bare. He looked more like a true cultivator, a member of an official sect, than he ever had before. His bare legs were exposed, their form muscular, their length a little shorter than he was used to. He only had four toes and each of them ended in a sharp point; his skin was as pale as ever.

Then he thought of William and hoped that he had done enough to save his friend. It made him flex his tail happily.

"Wait, a *tail?!*" Sure enough, he turned back to find that he had a long, thin, bright-red tail that ended in a thick, sharp point like an arrowhead. Kiru shook his head and chuckled. "I guess it just adds more to the demonic look I apparently am going for. I bet William will love this."

As if in reply, Kiru heard William's emotionless voice in his head: "*Convergence complete. Battleform acquired.*"

"*William?*" Kiru probed excitedly via Telepathy. "*What's a battleform?*"

CHAPTER FORTY-FOUR

Reclamation & Reunion

Vatrenex stood on top of his tower on the deck of *The Marauding Citadel*, his corsairs arrayed below at their battle stations. Many were hiding below deck or in buildings holding Joyful drakonid war slaves on collars, ready to unleash them. Vatrenex growled in satisfaction, proud of his foresight for having been so merciful towards many of Waayoo's former followers. The Joyfuls' island home was the furthest south in the Torn Empire and was rumored to have dealings with drakonids and their draconic masters. Now that Waayoo was bound to him, though, Vatrenex discovered that it was more their proximity that had led to any interaction, and rarely was it peaceful on either front. At best, there was an exchange of their young so each group would have new healthy slaves. Vatrenex didn't care except for the fact that his forces were now bolstered.

The *Citadel* was fast approaching Gaal'cothdreek-duun, the prison and its protective ring growing from a dot in the distance. It had taken them longer than intended to reach it due to two different storms hitting them back to back. "Raining sharks," Vatrenex muttered to himself, shaking his head and thinking about the preposterous weather they'd dealt with. They had at least stocked up on food and oil to supply the ship for a month. Vatrenex could hear his first mate barking orders atop his monstrous mount, his fear evident in his voice. The captain had originally thought to make Saltbeard the host for Waayoo, but upon remembering that he was influenced by Vatrenex's own mana, realized it wouldn't work. Plio's host had barely any trace of Vatrenex's influence and had become almost useless. Saltbeard had been Vatrenex's first mate for decades. There was no way he could wield Waayoo. Vatrenex then thought of a much more satisfying use for his scheming brother.

With Vatrenex's improved Chaosbind technique, he considered himself impressive to say the least, which made the dwarf host's resistance all the more infuriating. Despite that, Vatrenex had evolved the Harbingers' signature technique to do even more than he had told Plio about originally. He could now wield one of his own brothers as well as his weapon at the same time.

So, that's what Vatrenex did with Waayoo. He couldn't think of a more fitting punishment for his prideful brother. "Thinking he was so much wiser and cleverer than me, ha!" Vatrenex said to himself as he squeezed the scythe tight. After the battle, he used Mind Crush two more times on the scythe, fully breaking Waayoo's psyche until all vestiges of the Harbinger's personality were gone. *Now, he's just a weapon and will do my bidding for all time, a fitting fate for that damn nebulor,* he thought.

Both Zis'Piel and Plio leapt to the top of the tower and kneeled before him. "We approach the prison, Brother. Oh, the horrible memories the place brings!" Zis'Piel moaned.

Plio looked around worriedly. "Are . . . are you sure we need to do this, Brother? I mean, you have all of us under your command and the krakens are so—"

"Silence!" Vatrenex interrupted Plio's concerns, prompting his brother to wince and cover his ears. "We are here. We are finally united under me and have the means to be free of this accursed ocean. We will attack with all we have until the barrier is broken. I have waited too long to get here, and I will not flee in cowardice."

Both of his brothers nodded in submission.

The ship had closed the distance until the protective barrier was roughly half a mile away. Vatrenex could hear the water rumble angrily. After another minute, a set of tentacles arose angrily beside the ship. Vatrenex looked down to his first mate, who was looking at him expectantly, and nodded his silent command.

"The krakens be waiting for their toll, lads! Let's give it to 'em!" Saltbeard shouted. The corsairs shouted back in response and fired their techniques and ballistae at the creature ahead of them. The tentacles were slashed and pierced, and the kraken let out a bellow of outrage as its appendages recoiled. The corsairs all gave cheers of triumph and even Saltbeard had a wry grin on his face, but it was short-lived because only seconds later, dozens upon dozens of tentacles emerged from the water and surrounded the ship. "This be it, lads! Open fire!"

A barrage of chaos rift slashes, arrows, and even some mana-based cannon prototypes the corsairs had raided from a Merchant Federation ship surged out in all directions. Many tentacles were damaged, but only a few sustained serious-enough injuries that they retracted. The krakens, enraged, whipped and lashed their appendages out in blind fury. Masts were broken, buildings crushed, and the deck splintered from the damage. The corsairs—weak compared to the monstrous being—who were unable to get out of the way, were crushed or sent flying from the sheer force of the strikes. Vatrenex watched one human jump to the side to avoid a tentacle only to be snatched up by another one midair. The man let out a cry of pain as the tentacle wrapped around his body and squeezed, blood pouring out from all his orifices before his cries were summarily cut off by Saltbeard's cyclops.

The monster stepped his foot down on the doomed corsair, crushing him to paste but also smashing the tentacle that was around him. The section of the tentacle popped along with the man's body, sending both human and kraken blood splattering out in all directions on the deck.

"Release the new war slaves, ye damn idgits!" Saltbeard shouted over the chaos of battle.

A set of horns and drums echoed his commands across the entire *Citadel*. His order was fortunately heard, and then hundreds of corsairs dragging collared drakonids came surging out from numerous buildings and below deck.

The drakonids were all former Joyful cultists, and they instantly went to work, firing various breath attacks against the krakens. Thanks to the hundreds of slaves rowing below deck, *The Marauding Citadel* was still moving, albeit much slower than before, and so the momentary hesitation provided Vatrenex and his brothers the opportunity they needed.

"Now, Brothers, together," he ordered and raised both of his weapons in the air. Both Plio and Zis'Piel did the same, gathering chaos mana around their blades. Vatrenex brought all of their mana together to coalesce into a gargantuan blade of chaos mana, tall enough to cleave *The Marauding Citadel* in two. When Vatrenex felt the mana buildup reach its maximum, he cried out, "Now!" and the Harbinger weapons all slashed down, firing the massive Chaos Rift Slash forward.

Some krakens tried to stop it with their tentacles, but they stood no chance. One of the monsters even leapt up in the air to take the strike with its whole body, but it succeeded in nothing besides getting turned into mush. After only a couple of seconds, the technique struck the second barrier. The barrier resisted, seeming to push back against it, but the technique was still pushing. A kraken's tentacle came up at Vatrenex, obstructing his view, but he cut it down with his great sword.

His eye widened and his large mouth twitched like an insect's mandibles in excitement. Cracks started forming around the barrier. And then, *crash!* The second barrier was down. Vatrenex bellowed a cry of triumph with such force that it shook the entirety of the *Citadel*. "Now, Brothers, we end it!"

"What's a battleform?" Kiru asked.

In response to his question, a screen appeared in his vision.

After fusing yourself with your familiar while being exposed to the corrupting tide of chaos mana, your body has undergone some alterations. Due to your mental mana and the process of binding with your familiar, who possesses both mental mana and fire mana elements, you are now able to control both of those elements that are present inside your body.

Then, a silhouette of Kiru's changed body appeared in his vision. Different parts were highlighted. Kiru focused on them one at a time, and new information appeared.

> **Hair:** Your hair contains a fire mana core fragment that has been saturated with fire mana from Muspelheim. As such, you now have ever-burning hair while in battleform.

> **Head:** The circlet on your head has been fused with not only the fragments of your familiar's core, but also a fire mana core fragment saturated with the icy fire mana from Helheim. As such, you become one with your familiar and gained a ghostly crown befitting your royal heritage.

> **Mouth:** You were wearing the Mask of Fenrir when you underwent your transformation, and it has fused to your mouth, which now contains a core fragment that has been saturated with fire mana from the molten depths of Svartelheim and morphed into that of a true Oni, a demon from that realm. The mask still provides a supply of beast mana, enhancing the senses and instincts while in battleform.

> **Hand:** Your ring has now fused with a fire mana fragment that has been saturated with the decaying flames of Jotunheim. This particular type of flame is a pestilence to all in that realm, as it desires to forever consume all life and bring decay. The flame serpent inside has now become a necrotic flame serpent. Due to its blood-bond and affinity to you, it has resisted consuming your body and only settled for draining some of the life from the finger that wears the ring.

> **Gut:** Your intestinal main meridian has been fused and saturated with the renewing phoenix flames of Alfheim. The intestines are the biggest immune system organ in the body and helps to fight disease and aids in recovery. As such, in your battleform, it will passively heal you much more quickly than would normally be possible.

Kiru's mind swam in disbelief. His broken core fragments, the shattered pieces of his fire mana core that had been inert since all those years ago were now . . . active again? "I don't understand. How can the fragments empower my body to such a degree? Plus they were fragments of a Silver core—how can they be this . . . powerful? Also, I know for a fact that every core is influenced by one mana type from one realm, and that mine was distinctly like my mother's: infernal fire mana from Muspelheim. How in the abyss do I have five different fire mana types? And where is William? I heard his voice. . . . William, you still in there? These boxes are great, but where are you?"

Fortunately, the screen answered and provided clarification.

<table>
<tr><td>

Query 1: How do I possess different fire mana types at once?
Answer: The chaos mana from the core caused abrupt changes to the very nature of the fire mana core fragments, making them change the very type of flames they burned.

</td></tr>
<tr><td>

Query 2: Where is my familiar?
Answer: Familiar can be accessed if battleform is dismissed.

</td></tr>
<tr><td>

Dismiss battleform?

</td></tr>
</table>

Kiru didn't hesitate for a moment. "Yes." Immediately, his body changed. He watched in the mirror as his hair turned from burning red flames to a long black mane with red tips that hit his shoulders. The ghostly crown faded, only leaving the Sapphire gem still visible in his forehead. His wolfish eyes and ears reverted back to normal, and his molten demon mouth shrunk back and cooled, leaving his regular mouth visible, his stubbly beard still present. There were some things that didn't change back, however. His ring finger was still boney and black, he still only had four fingers on his left hand, his four-toed feet were still clawlike, and he still had the long, demonic tail.

Kiru shrugged, glad he was still mostly intact. His heart seemed to stop for a long second as all he heard around him was silence. He started to wonder if the box had lied about William, but then he heard the imp let out a deep, excited chuckle in his mind.

"*Ohohoho, you bet your ass I love the tail, Master, and I love the new look even more!*"

Tears ran down Kiru's cheeks. "William, thank goodness you're back," he cried in relief.

William was quiet for a few moments before responding. "'*Back' is . . . not the right word for it exactly, Master. I'm alive but not as I used to be.*"

"What's it matter?" Kiru asked, rubbing his eyes. "You're here. As long as I have my friend to talk to and summon, I'm good."

William gave a mental sigh. "*I am William, and I am you.*"

"What?" Kiru asked.

"*I can no longer manifest myself as I used to, Master. I am one with you now. My body is your body. With mental mana we can possibly one day make a hologram representation of me to interact with others, but I don't have a true body, not anymore,*" the imp explained.

Kiru's heart dropped. "Well, the Chaos Core . . . Maybe we can go back and find a way to give you a new bo—"

"*No!*" Willaim interrupted. "*No, Master. We cannot. While in the core, I learned about it. It needs resources to work, and it constantly demands fuel. That's why we didn't come out "normal," so to speak. It's also constantly changing. That's the reason it's so hard to look at. For whatever reason, it responds to mental mana, but it needs a sufficient amount to do so. That's why we only barely survived. That . . . and you killed its last user, making it somehow belong to you now. I don't know how the arboth managed to control the core, but they obviously must've had a large number of cultivators— and some very high-ranked ones too—as well as some extremely clever crafters. If we try to remove it from the box it's in, we could end up endangering all of the realm."*

Kiru looked back at the core, which was now somehow back in its container. He didn't know what the core now "belonging" to him meant, but he couldn't imagine there wouldn't be consequences. He let out an involuntary shiver when he realized just how fortunate he and William were.

"Well, either way, I will work to give you back your body again," he said.

"There's no need, Master," William said, his tone calm and collected.

"Why not?" Kiru asked.

"Because, I am one with you now . . . Together we *are Kiru the Conqueror, and we will paint battlefields red with our enemy's blood!"*

Despite the gruesome hope, Kiru couldn't help but smile at having his friend with him once again. "I'm so glad you're here in any form, William." Right after he said that, there was a loud *crack!* and *boom!* that could be heard above the top floor. "William, what was that?" Kiru asked.

"Nothing good. You should get back to your battleform. You won't be able to speak with me, but I will be with you, Master. Let's bring some carnage!" the imp declared, his typical zeal for battle back in full force.

Kiru nodded. "Great, how do I do that?"

William gave the mental equivalent of an eyeroll before saying, *"Just think it, just like with Imp's Label."*

"Thanks," Kiru said and, with a thought, his body morphed into its previously nightmarish visage. He drew his psyslime blade and his kopis, and readied himself. Just seconds later, a large set of diagonal slashes appeared on the wall to the far side of the psion, letting in the first rays of true sunlight he had seen in months. Then, what looked like a set of two claws half as long as his forearm popped through from the top of the slash and raked straight down, making a giant triangle. Once the claws reached the ground, the metal triangle—now separated from the rest of the wall—abruptly fell to the ground with a *whoosh!*

Kiru's eyes winced just slightly as the sudden sunlight mixed with a rush of wind and sand from outside became overwhelming for a moment before he quickly adjusted. There he saw three figures that all at once made his blood run cold and simultaneously stoked the fires of his fury. Standing at the lead of the trio was a being Kiru couldn't forget—the monster who'd captured him and his friends and sentenced him to death.

"Vatrenex," he growled.

CHAPTER FORTY-FIVE

Conquerors

Vatrenex took a confident step forward, ready to destroy the core and the damned warden if he was still alive, only to stop in his tracks at the sight before him. There were a couple of headless corpses, one of which seemed to have been a small child, the other someone in purple armor. Black blood that twinkled and shimmered like stars oozed from the stump where their head once had been. One of the decapitated armored form's arms was a mass of tentacles. It was unmistakably the arm of an arboth, and there, standing only a few feet away was a fiery demon. His head was a flame, a ghostly white crown with a single Sapphire jewel in its center. Vatrenex could sense the Chaos Core's signature on the demon, meaning the infernal creature was its new owner and protector.

I was going to kill the warden anyway, so I'll just cut down this fiend instead so I can access the core myself, he thought.

The demon's maw looked like it was made of molten rock, and it wore nothing but a set of battle robes like he was some kind of monk. In his hands were two blades, one a crude and curved short sword made of the same metal as the prison, the other a hooked blade that looked almost made of liquid or like it was at least covered in a strange oil. The demon's yellow, bestial eyes glared at him with venom.

"Vatrenex," it growled.

Vatrenex let out an involuntary gasp as his eye widened in recognition. He remembered that blade, that voice, and that jewel. The jewel wasn't part of the ghostly crown atop the fiend's head—it was embedded *in* the thing's forehead! *This . . . this is that accursed thief of mental mana who the krakens praised. The so-called "psion,"* he thought. Vatrenex was in shock. *Sapphire? Already?*

The psion then flared his aura out until it washed over them. He felt the psion's emotions, his anger, his resolve, and his desire to kill him. Dread struck him for the first time in centuries. It was as if he were a mere drudge once more, chained up by the other arboth and experimented upon. The tortures, the cruelty—it was almost too much, but Vatrenex fought back, flaring out his own aura.

He then suppressed his fear with an even greater emotion: wrath. He would show the arboth—show this wretch—what a real conqueror was. They made him into a weapon, thinking him lesser than and only a tool to be used; now he could use their powers and more. Vatrenex expanded his aura to encompass his brothers. Zis'Piel had been dealing with the psion's assault moderately well, but Plio's entire body had been shaking as he took steps back in evident fear. When Vatrenex's aura washed over Plio, the small Harbinger stopped backing up but continued to shake.

Damn coward, Vatrenex thought. Plio was the only Tier-One Sapphire among them, so he couldn't push his aura out for more protection against the heavy-handed assaults. That plus his overwhelming fear of nearly everything, made him truly weak-willed. His ability to fight was his only redeeming feature.

Fortunately, Vatrenex didn't need Plio to be fearless. He just needed him to be more afraid of Vatrenex than he was of the psion. Vatrenex flared his control over his brother.

"Plio, if you do not fight, I will melt your weapon until there is nothing left," he threatened via Telepathy.

Plio let out a choked noise before quickly nodding and readying his two blades—his true Harbinger dagger and the bloodstep stiletto.

Vatrenex then turned back to face Kiru. "You think yourself a true conqueror. I will show you what it means to conquer."

Kiru took in his three foes as he exuded his aura. He knew that these were indeed the Harbingers he'd learned about, but he also knew that there were supposed to be four of them. *Given how wicked that black scythe is, it can't be a coincidence. Vatrenex found a way to wield two Harbinger weapons,* Kiru thought. He snarled at Vatrenex. What sparked his anger even more, though, was seeing Brunhilda's face; her seemingly dead visage took up half of Vatrenex's face. Kiru wondered if Vatrenex had done that to taunt him. If so, it had worked. He spread his intent out with his aura—his fury, his desire for their deaths, and his utter resolve to conquer them.

Next to Vatrenex was the form of a quist, undeniably rodent-like, but, like Vatrenex, with only one red and black eye. On the other side was what could only be a V'keth, their faceless two-headed body unmistakable, and with a serpentine lower half. They were all caught off-guard by his aura, the quist worst of all, and Kiru took that moment to use Imp's Label on all three.

Name: Plio/Zhaden
Race: Harbinger Quist
Host: Drakonid
Rank: Sapphire, Tier 1
Mana Type: Chaotic Darktime
Path: Harbinger
Status: Hostile
Known Techniques: Chaos Rift Slash, Unknown Body Takeover Technique

Name: Zis'Piel/M'Baku M'Toon
Race: Harbinger V'keth
Host: Orc
Rank: Sapphire, Tier 2
Mana Type: Chaotic Spacetime
Path: Harbinger
Status: Hostile
Known Techniques: Chaos Rift Slash, Unknown Body Takeover Technique

Name: Vatrenex/Brunhilda Lightsworn
Race: Harbinger Arboth
Host: Dwarf
Rank: Sapphire, Tier 2
Mana Type: Chaotic Mind & Chaotic Space
Path: Harbinger
Status: Hostile
Known Techniques: Chaos Rift Slash, Unknown Body Takeover Technique

The anger he felt at seeing Brunhilda's face only grew stronger at the information he'd just acquired. His friends—all three of them—had been taken over. *I will free them,* he thought. He wanted to charge them, his fury stoked by the infernal flames atop his head, but he applied the visualization technique that Zhaden taught him. He slowly fed the flames into himself to fuel him, not burn him out to the point that he couldn't control himself. Kiru looked over to the dagger-wielding Harbinger, noticing Zhaden's stiletto. *They've helped me, now I will help them.*

Kiru's mind, boosted by William's enhanced capabilities, downloaded all the information in an instant. He also knew that his previous experiences, information acquired, and his the contact his aura was making improved the ability of his Label this time. Spots on their bodies were illuminated in his sight, weak points for Kiru to exploit. He was surprised to see that they had variations of chaos mana rather than just chaos mana they had cultivated. He knew that Vatrenex possessing two types must be due to his two unique weapons. *It doesn't matter what mana types they have,* he thought. *It's still chaos mana, and I will crush them either way.* The outrage that both he and William felt coalesced into united righteous fury.

Kiru's reclamation of his focus was apparently all Vatrenex needed as he and the V'keth then pushed their auras against his own. Kiru felt utter despair and resignation from the V'keth while Vatrenex gave off unbridled hate mixed with fear.

He's afraid, good, Kiru thought. He had a momentary hesitation about fighting the three because they held his friends captive but knew he couldn't hold anything back. He would subdue them, kill the parasites leeching off his loved ones, and free his team. Kiru didn't want to hurt his friends and hoped he wouldn't, but injured and free would be better than whole and enslaved.

Kiru somehow sensed Vatrenex sending a flicker of mana to the scared-looking Plio, and the Harbinger quist stiffened before giving a fearful nod to Vatrenex and readying his weapons, a dark dagger and Zhaden's enchanted Bloodstep Stiletto. Zis'Piel readied a two-bladed claw weapon in each hand while Vatrenex turned back to face Kiru.

"You think yourself a true conqueror. I will show you what it means to be a conqueror."

Kiru's molten maw gave a sly grin. "Really? It looks like you can't even conquer your face."

Vatrenex let out a roar as he pointed both of his weapons at the psion. At the same time, forty orbs of swirling black mana appeared all around the Harbinger. "Voidflare Barrage!" Vatrenex shouted, and the orbs shot forward, all aiming at the psion.

Kiru's mind seemed to be able to predict and calculate their paths in an instant, no doubt thanks to William, and he was able to jump, dodge, and roll out of the way. He then heard a strange *whoosh*, and this time, the enhanced instincts seemingly brought on by his Mask of Fenrir came into play. He turned to find that the trajectory of the orbs had abruptly shifted, as if space itself had bent, and were coming right at him.

Kiru fired a Brainstorm and struck the incoming orbs full-force. They all shattered with a concussive set of violent *pops*. Kiru's wolfish ears twitched as they heard the phrase, "Time Step" intoned behind him in the subtlest of whispers. Knowing he didn't have time to parry, Kiru created a Telekinetic Air Shield. He heard the *ting* of metal striking a surface and turned with his blades at the ready. He saw Plio staggering back from the deflected strike, the quist's eye wide in horror. Kiru dismissed his shield and began swinging at Plio with Hammer the Boards but struck only air as he heard Vatrenex use a technique called "Gravitational Pull" to yank the other Harbinger out of the way as if connected by a string.

As Plio was pulled back, he took a backhand swipe at Kiru's neck, but the psion raised a forearm just in time to protect himself. The black dagger cut across his flesh with ease. Kiru winced and then turned back to face his foes. Plio landed on the ground right in front of Vatrenex's scythe.

"You may be stronger, thief, but you cannot hope to beat us alone," Vatrenex said.

Kiru's arm healed before his very eyes, and he gave a monstrous grin with his magma oni mouth. "Who said I was alone?" he asked before sending a pulse of mana into his ring and summoning Little Flame. The fiery serpent now burned green with a sickly flame. Whereas the serpent looked like a cobra before, it now more resembled a viper. Its head was bigger and more menacing, and its teeth were larger and looked wickedly long. Little Flame hissed at the three before surging forward.

Zis'Piel moved in front of the other Harbingers to meet the fire serpent.

As Little Flame moved, Kiru charged a pair of Telekinetic Bolts. As soon as the elemental snake jumped, Kiru fired, once in the direction of Vatrenex and the other towards Zis'Piel. Vatrenex deflected the bolt with ease, but the two-headed Harbinger was completely focused on Little Flame, so he was struck in the gut by Kiru's technique, forcing the Harbinger to stagger off-balance and fall to his back under Little Flame's force.

Some flesh melted off the Harbinger's hands as he held onto each of Little Flame's upper fangs. "Ah! It burns!" he cried out.

"*Plio, deal with him while I eliminate this serpent.*" Vatrenex's voice came to Kiru's mind, which shocked him.

I can hear their Telepathy? he thought, excited. *The sensation of mana I sensed earlier, that was Telepathy. I can hear what he's saying with my aura now!*

Kiru charged towards Plio, who was similarly sprinting directly at him.

"Chaos Rift Slash," the Harbinger said as he sent a quick volley of slashes directly at the psion.

Kiru was forced to abandon his charge and roll to the right to avoid the attack.

"Time Step," Plio said as he jumped and appeared twenty feet above the psion. Ten orbs of mana manifested all around him as he seemed to almost float there for a moment. "Voidflare Barrage," he said as he fired his technique at the psion, his body descending right behind them.

Kiru calculated their speed and trajectory and knew he couldn't dodge them all, but he came up with an idea that could prove advantageous if correct. Kiru knew this Plio was only a Tier-One Sapphire, meaning he hadn't figured out how to turn his shroud into an aura. So, his influence on his ranged techniques shouldn't have been as strong, either. The psion flared out his aura before firing a wave of Telekinesis. Instantly, the orbs' descent halted before going right back up and striking Plio. The quist Harbinger let out squeaks of pain as he was struck by his own power and fell to the ground.

Kiru heard the crackling of flames abruptly die out and turned to see that Little Flame had been dealt with by Vatrenex's greatsword, the elemental's form fading and the V'keth Harbinger's arms black and burnt. The two-headed Harbinger curled up in a ball after that, seeming to be out of the fight. Kiru remembered from the description of the serpent that it would never truly die as long as the gem in the psion's ring remained intact. *He did his job,* Kiru thought as he made to move away from Vatrenex and Zis'Piel toward Plio.

"Gravitational Pull!" Vatrenex shouted as he slammed the butt of his scythe to the ground.

Instantly, Kiru winced and he nearly fell to his knees as the gravitational force on him increased threefold. He turned his head slowly to Vatrenex, who was giving him an evil smile.

The Harbinger leader then leapt at him, both his weapons swung back and ready to bisect Kiru.

Kiru's heart raced at the incoming strikes and recalled his aura to just cover his body as a shroud. He pushed it out only about a foot away from him, and the concentrated effort helped him fight against the increased constraints. He knew he couldn't block the strike directly, so he leapt forward with a burst of speed to get in close and take away the advantage of Vatrenex's ridiculously sized weapons. He used Clean the Hoof, cutting a vertical wound across the Harbinger's side and then went to do an improvised version of Caught Fish but then his body instantly froze in place.

"Time Halt," he heard Zis'Piel say.

If Kiru's eyes could've widened at that moment, they would have, right before Vatrenex kneed him in the abdomen and hit him with a half swing of his two weapons. Since Kiru was so close, he was only struck with the scythe's staff portion instead of the blade.

Still, Kiru took a nasty wound as he was sent flying, ultimately crashing into a wall. He coughed and grimaced as he stood back up, the effect of the Time Halt technique gone. He pressed his hand to his side, his gi shredded and blood flowing readily. Still, Kiru could feel the phoenix flames already doing their job.

"A time-stopping technique." He coughed. "Good to know." *That data will help me improve my chances of winning,* he thought. *So I need to take the V'keth out first.*

Since Kiru retracted his aura, he couldn't hear Vatrenex's telepathic words anymore, but he did hear the Harbinger leader growl and Plio snap back up to his feet and scan for foes.

I can't let them know I'm going for the V'keth either, he thought. Ironically, an idea came to him inspired by the Harbinger himself. Kiru began running toward Vatrenex and Plio, firing Telekinetic Bolts, one after the other. He didn't have time to do a combined technique currently nor could he afford to stay still with the Time Halt. Because he was moving, he had to dodge Chaos Rift Slashes from Zis'Piel instead, making Kiru's charge much more difficult. Fortunately, his enhanced brain was up to the task.

Plio dodged while Vatrenex deflected, the latter doing so with contemptuous ease. "It'll take more than that to harm me," he said.

"Good thing I wasn't going for you," Kiru said, and then used Telekinesis to abruptly turn two different bolts to the side and redirect them toward Zis'Piel.

The two-headed Harbinger said, "What a cruel thing," before he was struck by both the bolts and knocked on his back once more.

Now, without the risk of being hit by a Time Halt at least for a few moments, Kiru went to cut off the head of the snake. With Plio right beside the lead Harbinger, however, Kiru knew that would likely be too difficult. His opponents were strong, but he knew he could handle them one-on-one. To achieve that ratio, he let loose a Telepathic Screech in all directions, hitting both foes at once.

Vatrenex staggered and growled, mostly able to resist it, but the weak-minded Plio clutched his head and began to shriek in terror as he rolled about. "Loud! Too loud!" he screamed.

Kiru gave a bloodthirsty grin. *It's just him and me now.*

CHAPTER FORTY-SIX

Mental Warfare

Vatrenex swung his weapons at Kiru.

He ducked under the scythe's wide swing and then jumped to the right to avoid the massive great sword's downward chop. With Vatrenex's flank exposed, Kiru used Trimming the Grass. He surged forward, making sure to shove the hook of his psyslime Fu Tao in the monster's vertical maw, and heaved with all his might. The Harbinger let out a cry of pain and clutched his wound as he fell to his knees. Sensing an opening, Kiru spun and raised his blades to cut off Vatrenex's right hand when he noticed a faint trace of mental mana exuding off of him.

Kiru had pulled back his aura so he couldn't sense his opponent's Telepathy from much of a distance, but they were very close now.

To confirm his suspicions, Plio suddenly appeared right under him and thrust his blades to stab the psion. Kiru jumped and redirected the strikes. He went to counter when the quist Harbinger then said, "True Darkness." Plio's form vanished as a cloud of darkness surged out in all directions where the quist once was. Kiru—despite having darkvision and improved sight now that he was in his battleform—couldn't pierce through. It reminded him of that month he had spent in that terrible fifth floor of the prison.

He still had his other senses, though. He could hear the rat man running about in all directions. The Harbinger zoomed around him, repeatedly cutting him. Kiru's body quickly became riddled with superficial wounds, but he did manage to deflect some strikes. Oddly enough, Plio made no sound for him to hear, but Kiru started to pick up a pattern in his foe's attacks. After another half-minute of data collection, he *knew* with 100% accuracy where Plio would be.

Kiru took a step back just in time to dodge a thrust to his right. He caught Plio by his hands, intending to rip the weapons free from him. Since his foes were indeed the Harbingers, he also knew how to deal with them. When his left hand made contact with the blade's handle, however, he felt the mind that the weapon possessed. The dagger was, in fact, the true Harbinger. It was full of chaos mana and possessed a mind of its own. Kiru grinned. Both chaos mana and minds were prime targets for his mental mana.

With a flex of his will, he used Subjugation on the dagger. The Harbinger's body stiffened, and his large singular eye fixed on Kiru as the psion's technique took hold almost instantly. Kiru had never met a more susceptible target in his life. "Sleep," Kiru ordered, and his foe's eye closed as he fell into unconsciousness.

With that, the Harbinger's True Darkness faded as well, allowing Kiru to see where he was once more. He was not far from where he'd started, deep in the heart of the first floor, while Vatrenex was back by the entrance with Zis'Piel; both were injured but looked like they were recovering. Their flesh that had been burned and lacerated slowly regenerated before Kiru's very eyes.

I need to end them now, he thought before his body went still again. He had moved quickly enough to get out of the way of the Time Halt.

Kiru pushed against it with all his might but couldn't get through.

"Oh, Brother, I lament that my power isn't enough to keep him contained for long. What a shame. Please end him," Zis'Piel pleaded in a sad, melodramatic manner.

"Gladly," Vatrenex said as he slammed his scythe's blade on the ground and stuck out his free palm in Kiru's direction. "Mind Crush."

In that moment, Kiru's consciousness was sent inward, flooded with pain.

Kiru awoke on an icy tundra, with sparse, leafless trees and bushes dotting the landscape. Snowflakes of cold ghostly flames fell, slightly burning to the touch like when you hold ice for too long. He was no longer in his battleform and instead was in his mother's armor and red academy jacket. "These were ruined. What? How? Where am I?" Kiru asked.

"Your mind," a voice answered.

Kiru turned to see a giant hideous form emerging from behind one of the trees. It moved about in an unsettling manner with its sudden undulations. Kiru took a few steps back as he took the thing in. It stood as tall as an ogre—a mass of black tentacles with one red eye at its center. The psion instantly knew what and who this was. It was an arboth, but twisted and warped to be even larger and more monstrous. The true form of Vatrenex.

Kiru went to reach for his blades, but they weren't there.

"Odd choice for a mental landscape, but I don't care," Vatrenex said before his mass of tentacles surged forward. Kiru prepared to run, but the monster was too quick. Vatrenex caught him, wrapping tentacles around his arms, legs, and face before lifting him up in the air like a doll. "Because I am going to break it and you as slowly and painfully as possible." At his words, tentacles started to burrow in his ears, nostrils, mouth, and eye sockets. Kiru let out a scream of pain unlike any he'd ever experienced as his psyche had been directly targeted. He felt his mind about to give, about to break, when he and Vatrenex were suddenly struck by a burst of burning snow.

Vatrenex's tentacles froze on the spot before an equally gigantic creature came in and chopped into them with its hand, shattering the frozen appendages to pieces and freeing Kiru.

Vatrenex let out a cry of agony and fear.

The remaining tentacles sloughed off and Kiru let out a set of coughs as he took in a fresh breath of the frigid air inside his mind again. He pounded his fist against his chest a couple of times before his breathing calmed.

"Are you okay, Master?" a voice that sounded quite like William asked.

"Yeah, I'm okay, William. William?!" Kiru asked as he looked up. There floating before him, was his familiar, only with some very stark differences. First off, he was *huge*! If he weren't floating five feet off the ground, he would be at least ten feet high. Second, his red skin was now a ghostly white. Lastly, the cloud that made up his lower half was now a ball of the icy white fire from Helheim.

He had his same old shit-eating grin though. "Indeed, Master. The mind is where I live now, where I'm at my best. As I said, we are one now. If this bastard attacks you," he said as he turned to face the Harbinger, hitting a palm to his fist causing a small concussive boom of flames, "he attacks *us*."

Vatrenex shifted his head back and forth nervously.

Kiru just grinned. "William, show him what it means to conquer."

The gigantic floating imp began to tear Vatrenex apart piece by piece. Each time William touched the monster, pieces of Vatrenex froze and broke off. Vatrenex was helpless against the imp, reminding Kiru of a toddler trying to fight an adult. The monster even attempted to run away, but William was too fast and began pummeling him with his fists so hard that a crater formed. After only a couple of minutes, William had thoroughly trounced Vatrenex so badly that only his eye remained.

Kiru walked up, ordering William to stop the killing blow. He leaned down to look at the eye.

"M . . . Mercy," Vatrenex stuttered out, somehow speaking even without a mouth.

Kiru grimaced. "You were dealt a bad hand, but it's clear that your people were cruel and corrupt even before you were made to be what you are. So, I have no doubt you were just like that when you were still just a slave. You are my enemy, Vatrenex, but I do pity you, as it seems that pride and cruelty are all you're capable of knowing. So, I won't prolong your fate despite it being what you deserve." Kiru then put a hand on the eye and used Subjugation. With that, his consciousness was sent out once again.

Kiru let out a gasp as if he'd been held underwater. He looked up to see Vatrenex on the ground, asleep, and only the V'keth remaining.

Zis'Piel's body slumped. "Oh, how cruel fate is! I mourn what could have been. To come so close to freedom, only to be forced to flee!" The two-headed Harbinger shouted the last words as he turned and ran in a desperate attempt to get away from the psion.

Kiru scowled at the fleeing Harbinger who held his friend. He could run him down, but he didn't need to. He dropped his weapons and channeled a Telekinetic Bolt in one hand and Subjugation in the other. With a set of smooth and graceful motions, he combined them and fired. It struck the fleeing Zis'Piel who'd made it about a hundred feet away, and he went completely still, standing on the sandy beach. "*Sleep,*" Kiru telepathically ordered, and the V'keth Harbinger's mind fell into darkness.

Epilogue

Kiru removed the claws from Mutt's hands, the last of the Harbinger weapons. He watched in morbid fascination as the black weapons pulsed like they were hearts and drew the mana away from their former hosts, making their bodies shift and contort to their normal forms. It was both amazing and unsettling to witness.

"It's a good thing that they're all asleep for this, because that transformation would be downright traumatizing for someone to experience," William sent.

Kiru nodded in agreement. His friends all moaned as their bodies shifted to their own again. They would be fine. They'd just need time.

"I am glad we were able to get hold of that awesome ship, though! I calculate we will be 212% more awesome with it," William said.

"Is that right?" Kiru asked, good-naturedly. After he subdued the Harbingers, Kiru discovered he had access to the entirety of the prison as a whole, including its defensive measures, from a set of glass screens he found on the first level. They appeared remarkably similar to the screens that William provided in his vision. One of those defensive measures included the krakens, and that gave Kiru an idea. There was a large battle between *The Marauding Citadel* and the aquatic monsters, and though Kiru was much stronger, he couldn't fly or swim across the Torn Empire in its entirety. So, instead of rendering the pirate ship to scraps, he was able to give the monsters an order to disable the vessel and not demolish it.

With that taken care of, the last thing to do was dispose of the Harbinger weapons. Kiru had used Telekinesis to float the first three sets of weapons to the Chaos Core. William had said the core always needed fuel, and Kiru presumed it received some steady source from the machine it was hooked up to. Still, he thought it couldn't hurt to feed it something extra. It was only when he went to deal with the scythe that Kiru paused. He had extended his shroud to get a sense of it and noticed there was something . . . off about it, unlike the others.

Imp's Label.

Name: Waayoo
Race: Harbinger Nebulor
Host: N/A
Rank: N/A
Mana Type: Chaotic Space
Path: Harbinger
Status: Defunct
Known Techniques: Chaos Rift Slash, Gravitational Pull, Voidflare Barrage

Kiru couldn't help but smile at the status, reminded of his own "Defunct" status back at the Royal Academy. He was a prime example of how dangerous something defunct can be, so he didn't trust that the weapon wasn't dangerous. Still, there was something about that status that made him curious.

"William, can you elaborate as to what the Defunct status means?" he asked.

"*Certainly, Master,*" William replied before clearing his nonexistent throat. "*Based on the resonance of a mind being present, the weapon is indeed functional, but the mind itself has been broken—damaged in such a way that all the real personality of the weapon is now gone. It is simply a living tool awaiting to do what it's told to.*"

Kiru was going to ask how, but when he focused on the scythe, he could detect Vatrenex's mana somehow tied into it, and Kiru instantly understood. "He used that Mind Crush technique on the scythe," he uttered before speaking up. "It looks like Vatrenex did what he tried to do to us, to his fellow Harbinger here." Kiru then focused on sensing the weapon's mental awareness and noticed significant flaws and cracks, confirming the imp's explanation. "It also looks like he did it more than once."

All at once, an idea that was crazy but also possibly brilliant came to mind. He would go over both the success probabilities and threat risks with William first, but he may yet find a use for the Harbingers.

"*What's the problem, Master?*" William sent.

Kiru smiled. "You know, I've been thinking about your title, 'Breaker of Wills.' I think it's about time we help you actually earn that moniker, my friend."

William let out a deep laugh in Kiru's mind, utterly gleeful at the psion's insinuation. "*Ooh, tell me more.*"

"Later," Kiru said, waving off the request. He had heard his friends stirring and needed to make sure they were alright first. He walked over to find them all lying on the beach, groaning and slowly forcing themselves to stand. All three exuded a newfound strength; they had ascended in their cultivation since the last time he'd seen them. They'd also took on some . . . external changes.

Zhaden's eyes were now two orbs of solid black, and the lines in between his scales on his left arm were noticeably thicker and darker. Brunhilda's purple hair had some black streaks in it, and her lips were the same ebony color. The most different in appearance was Mutt. The orc's green skin was now much lighter than Kiru had ever noticed on an orc. That in addition to him now having two empty sockets where his milky eyes once were made him look like a bleached-out living corpse.

As Kiru neared, Mutt gave a loud sniff and a giant grin. "Boss!" he shouted before running to Kiru and wrapping him in a giant embrace. "I knew it! I just knew you would beat that pirate bastard!"

Kiru laughed as his friend picked him up and spun him joyously. "I appreciate the vote of confidence, Mutt."

Mutt sat him down and cocked his head. "Whoa, it looks like you went through some changes like us," he said, seeming to take in Kiru's newly changed body.

"If he thinks that's surprising, wait till he sees our battleform," William said.

Mutt then waved off his previous comment and returned to the original topic. "Well, never mind that. What I was getting at was that I've learned to never doubt you, no matter how crazy the odds are. Even when our plans go sideways, you seem to come up with some miraculous plan to save our asses." Mutt then set Kiru down and turned his head in Zhaden's direction. "You see, Stabby? I told you the boss would pull through. He's always had our backs."

Zhaden visibly stiffened before lowering his head and looking away guiltily. Before the team had been kidnapped by the corsairs, he and Kiru had been working to rebuild their friendship. Kiru felt like they had slowly been regaining progress and trust, but it looked to the psion that imprisonment and likely torture had caused the gold drakonid to have a change of heart. "Come on, Stabby. You should apologize to Kiru for doubting him," Mutt said.

"No, Mutt, he has no reason to apologize. I mean, a giant sea monster literally dragged me underwater while I had trollstone shackles on. You'd be crazy to not doubt me," Kiru said.

"But—"

"No, Mutt. I'm not perfect. I've made plenty of mistakes, and mistakes can get someone hurt or killed," Kiru said, looking back to the gold drakonid, whose black eyes were gazing intently at the psion, his tail moving about erratically, conveying mixed emotions. "But I promise that I will do absolutely everything in my power to keep you safe and lift you up higher with me. I can't guarantee your safety; in the life of a cultivator, that is impossible, but I swear on my core that you three are some of the most important people in my life. My friends. And I will do all I can to help us grow together."

Brunhilda sniffled and wiped away a tear. "Aye, I can get behind that."

Mutt gave Kiru a rough pat on the back. "You know I'm already with you, Boss."

Zhaden scratched his neck and averted his eyes from Kiru's. "I . . . uh . . . doubted your capabilities and intentions, Kiru. You had done amazing things, but I thought them more due to luck and timing. I admit too, that ever since Ebysso . . ." He trailed off.

Kiru didn't press, letting the drakonid take his time despite William's mental protests for him to "get on with it."

Zhaden closed his eyes and slowly controlled his breathing, making Kiru realize that he was doing the same visualization technique he'd taught the psion all those years ago.

Eventually, Zhaden spoke again. "Ever since Ebysso's death, I've had mixed feelings. I've wanted to believe in your intentions, in what you could and would be willing to do, but I also kept my distance, looking for the slightest excuse or failing to vindicate my doubt and leave. When we were taken, that was all the reason I needed. I realize I was wrong. Ebysso's death was not your fault. I'm sorry, my friend," he said, his hissing voice lowering at the end.

Kiru reached out and put a hand on Zhaden's shoulder. "I'm sorry too. My identity as a psion put someone you cared about at risk and ultimately led to their death. I'm also sorry that it took me so long to help you. I can do better. I *will* do better."

Zhaden did his best to give a grin despite his reptilian visage. He then put his own hand on Kiru's shoulder. "As will I, my friend." His tail wagged.

Kiru nodded, his own tail wagging a little. "Good." Kiru then heard some loud smacking noises behind him, and he and Zhaden turned to see Mutt and Brunhilda passionately embracing each other. After a minute of solid kissing, Kiru loudly cleared his throat to get their attention.

Both of them turned to see their friends observing them, shaking their heads and chuckling.

"Glad to see some things are still the same," Kiru said. "So much change has happened."

Brunhilda was blushing, but she managed to compose herself. "Ye got that right, Kiru. Now, I hafta know, how in the world did ye get a blasted tail?"

Kiru blushed and scratched the back of his head. "It's a long story, but it's good you bring it up. All of you need to know," he said, then thought about his true goal now that he was outside once again: to prevent another Draconic Campaign. "Once we discuss what happened to each of us, we then need to figure out our plans to deal with the ship and get back to the continent." He nodded to the *Citadel* that was smoking up top and stuck below, bound by the krakens on Kiru's orders. "How about I tell it over a meal? How does crab and farigaboar sound?"

"What be a farigaboar?"

"It may be the most ugly creature I've ever seen, but trust me, it's *delicious*."

About the Author

Maxwell Farmer is the author of the Ashen Plane, Dr. Druid, and Last Psion series. He spent his youth in Metropolis Illinois, the home of Superman. There, the seeds of his love for fantasy and science fiction blossomed. Like the man of steel, Farmer dons an alter ego: During the day, he's known as *Dr.* Farmer and treats the ailments of all the local cats and dogs. At night, however, he works hard to write captivating stories full of action and adventure with the goal of transporting readers to new and magical worlds. Farmer lives in the Great White North of Wisconsin with his wife, son, and two dogs. To learn more, visit his website at www.maxwellfarmer.com.

JOIN THE FELLOWSHIP

follow us on our socials

 podiumentertainment.com

 @podiumentertainment

 /podiumentertainment

 @podium_ent

 @podiumentertainment